ards of

Power

King's Bard Chronicles, Book Two

Will McDonald

Dedication

To Maid Marie, she led me to the Wardrobe
Tucked away in an otherwise
Empty room.

Preface

The other day my wife Gayla gave me one of the finest compliments I've ever been given; she said in ancient Ireland, I would have been one of the bards, the poetic storytellers. This was a much nicer description of my "gift" than when she tells me "You're full of it." Wisely I've never asked her exactly what the "it" is that I'm full of. My family might say baloney, an Americanization of blarney. My Youth Group "kids" described my "it" by giving their fearless leader nicknames; He-Who-Tells-Tall-Tales was my Indian name. Sir Lies-A-Lot my noble knight's name. I prefer gifted for the term, and bard for the title.

In Ireland, bards often were more powerful than kings, because they owned the hearts of the people; while, except for the High King (Ard Righ) a king's influence was limited to one region or county. Wearing many crowns these ancient storytellers wove Ireland's historical events into beautiful epic ballads and poems. History people waited eagerly to hear, imagine that.

Considered such a difficult literary form, the poets formed colleges for students who were fortunate enough to possess the gift. These schools of learning were not block prison walls with pupils chained to steel desks, instead class was held in the moors, glens, forests, and hillsides. There a heart for beauty was allowed to develop under a roof of sky. Their first curriculum lovingly assembled and inspired by moon and star.

The Riordan series was not birthed in a vacuum. It is the summary of stories, emotions, and experiences handed down by at least two great story-telling cultures; stories that have rolled down through the streams of time, to rest in the pools of my heart. I have not attempted to re-tell these stories the way they happened historically (you can read the source documents for that). Rather these stories are recreations of ancient sources, placed in an entirely different genre, while preserving and making more accessible their ancient worldview.

Praise for Riordan: The Anak of Dagon

Reader's Reviews

"I loved it. If attending the epic film version (hope there is one) movie patrons would be yelling, 'Hey you, down in front!' because I'm standing and cheering for Riordan!"

– John Prescott Athens GA

The characters developed steadily with a good diverse mix of personalities who grew on me evoking strong emotions of all sorts as relationships within the story's context developed. I am drawn in with each and they are real people and places now and I feel a strong connection, my heart is engaged with each. I would say I fiercely love some and am passionately opposed to others...not indifferent to any...not one. There is a beauty and a depth present like a strong thread pattern whose design gets more intricate and intriguing as this moves along until...at the end...I am a riotous tapestry of emotions not knowing what to do with them all while connecting on so many levels. I just needed to run around the block or climb a tree or something but being down with bronchitis, I could only pace around and cough a lot. I don't want to compare Riordan to other works or writers as the author has a voice, story, and style all his own; but Riordan engaged the same deep wonderful areas in me as Lewis or Tolkien. In another ways Riordan is somehow a combination of both, yet uniquely something all its own. The author's own touch. Then...toward the climax...when I had just become so intrigued and engaged by the people, it ended. I hope there is a sequel soon. Like with Downton Abbey, I cannot wait.

-Andie A. Traverse City Mi.

What category or Genre would a person place Riordan? The author weaves historical archeology, and biblical poetry with ancient myth; throws in some personal history, stirs it all up and ends up writing a book in a category all by itself. You can call it Christian historical Celtic American devotional fantasy. I'll call it good, a good book, a good read.

–Michael O'Conner New York

"Riordan is an amazing young man who survives abuse and remains humble in his ultimate success. The story shows the power of God to guide our lives and triumph over evil. Will's humor infuses his talented writing style. Persons of all ages will be blessed by this book. I am looking forward to the sequel!"

Becky Sturdevant, Kalispell MT

"So good my tail came unfurled!"   – Mr. Tumnus

"My Billy has been telling good stories all his life. Like the time he took the car for a spin when he was only four. Or how about the one explaining setting the neighbor's garage on fire, ha ha, those were all good. Wait-a-minute . . . is he telling stories again? Alright, what'd he do this time??

–Billy's Mom

Glossary of Names

Adonai - Master, or Lord

Aella - Whirlwind. Korah's horse.

Anak - Shaman magic user of the Anakim.

Anakim - Offspring of a union between fallen messengers (the Watchers) and the peoples of Domhain (earth).

Anbhás - Violent death, Anakim shaman, or sorcerer.

Atara - Crown. High King from the first age.

Brannan – Riordan's Uncle/stepfather.

Brónach - Sorrow. Grandfather of Riordan.

Capall - People of the horse.

Carraig – Stone or rock. Commander of the Dun.

Cnámh - bone. Battle plain south of Jeshurun's Key.

Domhain - earth/world.

Drochshaol - The bad times, that brought Domhain's destruction ending the first age.

El / Elohim – name of Deity, combines mighty power with sworn oath or covenant.

Esh – (Zaquen Esh) – Aged Flame, large red charger gifted to Riordan.

Jeshurun – One of the names given to a tribal confederacy.

Jireh - He sees. The last Shophetim of Jeshurun.

Joktan - Small. Village birthplace of Riordan.

Korah - Cavalry captain of the Capall.

Mereah - friend. Jeshurun's Crown Prince.

Meribah - Quarrel/contention.

Moriah - Nation of Covenant Law, prophetic vision.

Quillan - Irial lieutenant.

Ragnhildr – Commander of the Irial.

Riail dlí - Rule of Law. Mythical blade forged by Yahweh.

Riordan - King's bard, poet, or song.

Rohi - Shepherd.

Ruwach - Spirit, wind of heaven.

Tanniyn - Dragon, monster, or serpent.

Torin - Chief. Riordan's oldest brother.

Watchers - Fallen messengers that acted as evil guides to the fallen races during the first age.

Yahweh – Another name for Jeshurun's God.

Yara – Active verb form for law, the living gem stone from which Riail dlí was forged.

Chapter one

It is for us to pray not for tasks equal to our powers, but for powers equal to our tasks, to go forward with a great desire forever beating at the door of our hearts as we travel toward our distant goal.

Helen Keller

iordan looked up from a place flat on his back. Korah's head was framed by swirling stars as the captain anxiously examined his young charge for signs of injury.

Another face entered the picture and grinned, "Doing great kid!" Caraig, the Dun Commander laughed sarcastically. "Why I think yuh managed to stay on for at least five seconds that time. Five seconds, don't cha think Mereah?"

Suddenly the sky disappeared completely as the lad's vision was filled by the hulking frame and big beaming face of Mereah the Rapha` Prince. "Much more than five Caraig, don't sell our young friend short, I'd say at least six seconds, maybe seven."

It took a few more moments for Riordan to get his wind back after getting it knocked out of him for the tenth time that day. Finally, he managed to ask, "Where's Sorcha?"

Korah answered, "Well lad, after you were thrown that last time, he kicked up his heels and lit out. He's likely halfway to the mountains of Irijah by now. Want me to go on Aella and fetch him back?"

"No, I want somebody to take up a bow and shoot 'im."

Caraig laughed, "Now we know he's alright, he's as surely as ever."

Korah held out his hand and helped Riordan up out of the dirt. "Sorry lad, I'd shoot '*im*, but you're the armor-bearer of a cavalry captain, and you'll be needing a horse."

"No, I don't, I can run, *real* fast."

Korah started dusting Riordan off, and picking bits of bramble off his back, "Sorcha's not like Esh lad, he's never been gentled for riding before. Trust and motive are the keys to forming the bond between a horse and rider. Esh trusted you because Brónach trusted you. Before Sorcha can trust you, he needs to know your motive. When I give orders do you think they're only to restrict your freedom?"

"No, I think you don't want me to have any fun - ever."

Korah laughed, "That's the way it feels sometimes, I'm sure. We both know all the orders and training are for your benefit, and you trust that I'm doing my best to keep you alive. Sorcha possesses a lot of spirit, and he doesn't yet understand or trust your motive or intent."

Caraig scoffed, "Is the boy needing a horse or a wife?"

Riordan then jumped in, "Well if this is a partnership based on trust and motive, I can tell you I don't trust *that horse* because he's *motivated* to kill me!"

Stifling a chuckle, Korah spoke to Caraig, "I think the lads had enough riding for today. While I fetch Sorcha, do you mind working him a bit with a sword?"

"Not at all, take yer time." As they all watched Korah ride off, Caraig growled, "Alright kid, get that fancy blade of yours, and let's see what you can do."

Hearing this, Mereah offered a suggestion of his own, "Um Caraig, wouldn't it be best starting the young man out with practice swords?"

"Well maybe if he fights somebody using a wooden stick, but since that tain't likely I'll use my iron blade. Don't worry, I won't hurt the boy, I've been training recruits for better'n a hundred years."

Mereah held up both hands palm outward as a gesture of submission, "Alright, I meant it only as a suggestion." And then as he backed away muttered, "The *kid* isn't the one I'm worried about."

Riordan walked forward with both hands gripping the Riail dlí. Mereah marveled at the sword's beauty, the blade shown like aquamarine crystal, nothing else like it existed, he would bet his life on it.

Caraig watched Riordan's tentative approach and smirked "All right lad, let's see what yuh got, attack me." Seeing the hesitation, the stout warrior sneered, "Never show fear boy, now attack!"

His face glowing red from the rebuke, Riordan swung the Riail dlí in a high arc that descended towards Caraig's skull. Lifting his iron blade to easily block the attack, the Dun Weapons Master had already planned his next move to disarm Riordan; except that when their swords clashed, the Riail dlí passed through his best iron blade as easily as cutting air. Riordan managed to stop the Riail dlí just before parting Caraig's hair. Looking up at the Yara Blade resting on his forehead right between his eyes, Caraig slowly reached up, grasped the sword flat between his thumb and index finger and lifted it gently away. "On second thought why take chances? I think Mereah might be right, practice swords would be best."

The young giant laughed, "I tried to warn you, the lad's blade is more than a decorative wall ornament, *that* sword has serious bite."

In the short time it took Caraig to fetch wooden practice swords, Korah rode up on his mare Aella, leading an unrepentant Sorcha.

The Irial Captain Ragnhildr rode beside him with another warrior whose identity seemed something of a mystery. The facial features made the rider appear quite young. And yet the warrior's armor and clothing spoke of someone possessing considerable rank. The face almost seemed the image of Ragnhildr's, but the features were more delicate. To Riordan, this meant a pre-adolescent boy, maybe a few years younger than himself. He just couldn't understand why such fine bronze armor, silk tunic, and beautiful weaponry would be bestowed on an armor bearer or page.

Caraig tossed Riordan a wood practice blade, with a growl, "That was my best sword yuh cut in half boy, so I'm feeling a bit grumpy. And I bet yer thinking as long as I have a sword like that, I don't need to know how to fight cause I'll always have the advantage. But what will yuh do on the day when another warrior comes along with a blade to match yer own? Or El forbid, you are forced to fight with a different weapon? We'll start with the basics. Sheath your sword and we'll begin."

Riordan looked down and fumbled with fitting the thicker wooden sword into the sheath that an artisan had crafted for the Riail dlí. Halfway into the process, Caraig shouted, "On guard!" and charged. Desperately trying to withdraw the glorified stick, in his panic-stricken state the sword got tangled in the sheath. After getting smacked several times very hard by the Dun Captain he lost his footing and balance. Falling on his back, he found himself looking up into the blue sky once again.

Listening to everyone's laughter hurt almost as much as the several smacks taken from the Dun's wooden blade. Despite some padding from gambeson armor, he felt every savage strike. Still, more than anything, he felt embarrassed for being made to look like a fool. Caraig's face now blotted out the blue sky and he offered his hand, "What did you learn from that encounter boy, can yuh tell me what yuh did wrong?"

"Yep."

"Well out with it then."

"What I did *wrong* was trusting *you* and doing as you instructed. What *I learned* is to *NOT* do what you ask or to give up my advantage. You keep the sticks, I want the Riail dlí back."

The booming laughter he heard could only be coming from Mereah, while the softer chuckle would belong to Korah. Knowing the comments scored at least a small point it eased some of his pain, so he took the Weapons Master's hand and allowed himself to be pulled to his feet.

Caraig however did not laugh. He replied as gruff as always, "Don't get smart with me boy, I did that on purpose. When it comes to swordplay, the difference between a second and a half-second is enough to get you dead. Never forget, if it looks like it's to be combat, it takes longer to draw your weapon than it does to strike with it. So, rule number one: a sheathed weapon will only get yuh killed. If there is any possibility of danger, get your weapons at the ready. Now, do you know the second thing yuh did wrong?"

"I didn't duck?"

A sharp whack and the resulting "OOWWW!" taught Riordan the penalty for not taking the lessons seriously.

"I didn't survive untold number of battles in my hunnert and fifty years by being a clown boy. I'm going to teach yuh what you need to survive, even if it kills yuh. Second thing yuh did wrong is panic. You fumbled getting your sword out because you panicked. Reaction time of a fighter that is tense is tight, clumsy, slow. Just a fraction of a second slow will get you dead. So, rule number two-relax. Fear kills as surely as a sword. Know the third thing yuh did wrong?"

Knowing a smart answer would earn another smack, he thought carefully before responding, "I fell because I didn't pay attention to my footing."

Caraig looked hard at the former rohi and told him to bend down. Riordan hesitated but did as instructed. The Weapon's Master reached up and knocked on his head with his knuckles, "Now that's using yer head for somethin' besides providing me a target. Always remember the third rule, a sword fight is won with yer feet. Never let 'em get too close together. Keep em on the ground. Lift yer heals or rock back on 'em and you're likely to lose yer balance or your strikes will lack power."

Ragnhildr spoke up from the back of his horse, "As entertaining as this has proven to be and I hate to interrupt-but a matter of great importance has come to the king's attention. He requests the presence of all his captains and their available officers. We meet in an hour in the king's council chamber. Take a break from training gentleman and get cleaned up."

An hour later, Riordan accompanied Korah to the king's Palace. Built by the Rapha` to accommodate the Rapha`, all the doors were fourteen feet tall, while the ceilings were at least twenty. This feature gave the structure a lofty, spacious feel. It also seemed intimidating because visitors soon realized the building's dimensions weren't simply a choice of décor, they were a physical necessity for the imposing occupants.

Riordan went to the meeting reluctantly. Having little experience or wisdom to offer, he usually stood around feeling positively useless. Fortunately, Ruarc didn't have the personality that had much use for organized conferences either. When something needed to be done, the monarch just wanted to do it, not sit around and jaw about it. The Rapha` are the shortest-lived of all races, rarely reaching the age of fifty. When people understand life is short, it tends to make them a bit hasty.

Korah and Riordan entered the throne room where the king sat, with Mereah at his right hand. Caraig along with his second-in-command Nahor was already there, seated at a table with bench seating.

Then Ragnhildr came in, along with Quillan and the young page that had accompanied him earlier. Only now, without armor or bronze cap to conceal the feminine features, only a blind man would confuse her with a boy. The young rohi felt his neck and face turning red, simply from watching her walk into the room.

"Gentlemen," Ragnhildr began, "forgive me for not making introductions earlier. When I travel with my daughter, I prefer her identity be known only to a few. Permit me to introduce my daughter, Aislin."

With a gesture that can only be described as a cross between a bow and a curtsey, the Irial shield-maiden greeted everyone present with dignity and queenly grace. With her helmet and chain mail removed, Aislin could only be described as a vision. Light blue eyes, and cream-white skin was framed by raven black hair that cascaded down her back. The silken fabric of her dress, while modest and elegant, was unable to conceal her soft curves. Riordan hoped no one noticed his staring. However hard he tried he couldn't take his eyes off her. Mereah did in fact notice but hid his smile and said nothing.

Conspicuously absent from the gathering, were the sons of Irijah, especially Jeshurun's Shophetim. In a sense, Jireh transformed from centaur to the elephant *not* in the room, and the one whose absence everyone pretended not to notice.

Ruarc stood up to address the small assembly, "My friends, I hate to jaw just to hear myself talk. I know it's been but a few months since the defeat of the Dagon and their Anak, but there is a recent development that demands immediate action. I have appointed Ragnhildr Chief Military Adviser and asked him to explain this emergency in greater detail."

With a nod for acknowledgment, Ragnhildr began, "As captains of our respective peoples, I believe we all understand how close we came to losing our nation and our freedom. Just a few short months ago, were it not for a miracle, the eventual outcome would have been the death or enslavement of all our peoples. The Anak may be dead, but not I think the forces that empowered him. Those powers I believe are as we speak preparing for another strike at our hearts. We dare not be idle. We must prepare for what is coming or perish."

Already weary of waiting for the Irial captain to get to the point Caraig interrupted by asking, "Can we get on with it, Ragnhildr, we all know we barely escaped with our lives. What's the big new development?"

In response, with a throwing motion so fast most at the table didn't even see it, a twelve-inch dagger flew and stuck in the oak table right in front of Caraig. "*That* is the development. You know a bit about metals and weapons, what do you see my friend?"

Frowning at the Irial Captain's audacity, Caraig extracted the dagger from the table. He quickly forgot about his annoyance as he looked at the craftsmanship of the blade. Wonderfully made, a ruby gemstone set in a silver circlet on the pommel finished the pearl handle. However, it was the metalwork that astonished Caraig, "It's forged from an ore or alloy I am not familiar with. It feels lighter than iron, even lighter than bronze. Question is, how strong is it?"

Ragnhildr responded, "Stronger and lighter than both. I believe it is an alloy of iron perhaps, with another, lighter, yet unidentified ore. Now tell me, my friend, would an army equipped with such weapons have a technical advantage?"

"You knew the answer before yuh asked," Caraig scoffed, "But the fact that we came within a hairsbreadth of losing the war didn't have anything to do with our army having inferior weapons. Attacks of sorcery from the Anak is what almost destroyed us, better swords would not have helped!"

Ragnhildr responded, "Granted my friend, and we must find a way to better counter those attacks. That will be a topic to be dealt with momentarily. However, let me phrase the question another way: what if the Dagon had swords, axes and armor made with this alloy?"

Caraig hesitated for a moment, then grimly pronounced, "They would have swept us aside and passed through the Keys with, or without the Anak's help."

The enormity of that admission produced a chilling effect on the whole room leaving everyone to sit in stunned silence. After a moment Korah asked the obvious question, "Where did this blade come from, who forged it, and how do we obtain more?"

Ragnhildr smiled and said, "Those are all key questions. As to who forged the weapon, Bearach, son of Atara, commissioned this dagger along with many other fine blades. As far as how they were forged, no one alive today understands the process or the composition of the ore by which this blade is made. That is knowledge lost four thousand years ago, in the worldwide devastation that brought the First Age to an end."

Caraig started laughing, "You can't be serious? Are you going to waste time chasing after a bunch of old legends and myths? Do you have any idea how many stories of lost cities and treasures there are? Let me guess, whoever is telling the story has never seen the place himself! They heard about it from a relative or worse a drunken sailor. The one piece of evidence always offered is a map–a map for sale of course–at a very reasonable price."

Ragnhildr responded a little sharply, "I too have heard the stories and old wife's tales, don't take me for a fool my friend. In *this* case, we have more than a map. The blade you have seen for yourself, *it's* quite real. I can assure you no forge on earth today could have produced this alloy. You know this better than I. Also, if you will look, in the silver circlet around the gemstone, you will find something inscribed in an archaic Irial text. Working from ancient scrolls preserved in Bethel, the text translates Bearach Adonai, or Bearach is lord."

Still skeptical Caraig asked, "And this is important... because why?"

"Perhaps the Dun have forgotten, but the Irial have not, as it is the source of our greatest shame. Atara was the Irial First Born and High King. Not content to be Ard Righ he led the rebellion against El and so brought death into our world. Bearach is the name of Atara's First Born son and heir. The stories preserved by my people say he eventually killed Atara his father by his own hand and waged war against all other peoples to subjugate them. The inscription means the son of Atara declared his crown and authority to be above all others, including that of Yahweh Elohim."

At that point, Ruarc interrupted and voiced his own objections, "I'm afraid I grow impatient as well Ragnhildr, so I have to ask, is this history lesson going to eventually go anywhere?"

"Please indulge me just a moment longer your majesty. This is important because Caraig is right, better swords may have helped against the Dagon, but would have been of little use against powers such as were used by the Anak. Our greatest hope for victory against attacks of sorcery will be powers to counter their dark arts.'

"Legends and some of the earliest scrolls tell us that Bearach foresaw the coming destruction that ended the First Age. In response, he prepared wards to preserve knowledge and technologies for his continued existence and future reign. He not only intended to survive the holocaust that ended as the Drochshaol, the Age of Sorrow; he planned to reign over the earth for eternity.'

"Bearach did not survive the devastation. However, we have reason to believe at least some of his Wards, did. We also have reason to believe this dagger came from one of those Wards."

Mereah spoke up to urge caution, "I know I am not the scholar that you are Ragnhildr, but didn't Bearach prove to be more corrupt than Atara his father? If much of his knowledge come from Nathair, the fallen Watcher, how could we hope to use these Wards? Could not whatever they contain become a deadly snare for the whole nation?"

"I'm afraid I have to agree with Mereah," Korah interjected, "We cannot embrace the weapons of the enemy, without embracing the enemy's will. How could this capitulation be viewed as victory?"

"I understand your concerns Korah, and believe me, I share them. But no one is suggesting anything of the kind. I hoped you would have a little more faith in me than this my friends. I am not suggesting we learn the secrets of sorcery. We seek power yes, but the right kind. It is my hope that Bearach's Wards will reveal information concerning powers of dominion from the First Age. It is my belief that the attacks used by the Anak were simply counterfeits of the original gifts of dominion placed within the children of Elohim on the day of creation."

"But," Korah objected, "Those gifts were lost from the moment Atara chose rebellion."

"Yes of course you are right, and perhaps it is a false hope," Ragnhildr agreed. "But if the attacks of the enemy are spells imitating creation gifts, then it seems to me that the best counter to a fake, is a dose of the real thing. I can only hope that somewhere in these Wards, perhaps, we can find a clue as to how the gifts of dominion may be restored."

The king remained silent through much of the discourse, so it seemed a little jarring when he spoke, "Go on Ragnhildr, tell them the rest. I believe *that* is where we have our greatest hope for success."

The king's adviser acknowledged his sovereign's impatience with a nod and continued, "We also seek a talisman of such great power, that its misuse by Bearach, led to the world's decimation and the ending of the First

Age. This device, many believe to be a symbol only; but Atara's son after killing his father, began to experiment with what we believe proved to be the Scepter of Adon."

Caraig scoffed, "More legends and bed-time stories."

"This bed-time story," Ragnhildr responded, "Was a device with the power to alter and change Natural Law."

Ragnhildr allowed the implications to sink in. "Presented by Yahweh Elohim as a gift, the scepter's intended purposes were that when the Children of Elohim were ready, they would be able to use it to exercise dominion over all of creation. Or so it is believed by the Irial."

"But," Korah responded, "When Bearach attempted to use the scepter, he set off a chain of events that almost destroyed the world. Even if we somehow recovered this talisman, who's to say we would know how to use it any more than Bearach? We'd be children playing with fire. Since nobody alive has a clue as to how to use the bloody thing, what we're talking about is a repeat of our world's devastation!"

"Korah," The king replied, "If the Dagon unleash Anakim sorceries once again, we must be prepared to fight back with powers of our own. We can't be dissuaded by ancient myths told to frighten children. If this scepter offers us such power, we must prepare to use it."

After a moment of silence with the king's words hanging heavy in the room, Ragnhildr attempted to bring calm by making some assurances. "First of all, we don't have any other choice. We must recover these technologies if for no other reason than preventing the Dagon from finding them first *and* using them against us. In our possession, the Scepter may be studied, thoroughly understood, and hopefully never used–except only in the direst of circumstances. But if the scepter fell into the hands of the Anakim... who knows what evil the demon spawn might attempt to achieve with it?"

"There, you see Korah, you worry needlessly." Ruarc's words were meant to be comforting but were so glibly spoken they fell short of their intent. "Regardless, I am asking that you provide pack animals and mounts for Ragnhildr and for however many of the Irial and Capall he deems necessary to recover the contents of Bearach's Ward. Do you have any questions?"

"Only one sire, will we have maps or something to give direction to our search?" Korah asked.

The king replied, "Better. You shall have a guide, the same who recovered the dagger and brought it to us." The king then bawled out to attendants in the entryway, "Show in the Dun Explorer."

One of the entrance doors for the hall swung open and their new guide strode in. Wearing a weather-stained cloak over several braces of weapons and chain mail he proceeded to the end of the table to stand before the king.

Ragnhildr made a simple introduction, "Captains of Jeshurun, I present Ged, our quest's guide."

Ged stepped forward and threw back his hood. Riordan softly gasped. Memories flashed through his mind of the Dun Adventurer who bound and gagged him in the mountains of Irijah, before taking the feral horses.

Hearing Riordan's sharp intake of breath, the horse thief looked closely at his face, recognized him and flashed a big grin, "Hello boy, you've grown some."

Korah turned and looked at his young armor-bearer, "You know this man?"

Shock still registered on Riordan's face and in his voice as he answered, "We met, earlier this year, he visited my father's camp in the Irijah mountains."

Ged jumped right into the conversation to cut Riordan off from what he feared the lad might say next, "And the young feller here served up a lonely, hungry traveler some tasty Coney Stew. A right courteous lad he is, and ah pretty fair cook."

Korah interrupted with a question, "I have been given the task of supplying horses and pack animals for this expedition. What information can you give that will aide in my preparations?"

Ged smiled easily at Korah and replied, "Well I can't exactly tell yuh where yer goin' cap'n, cause then yuh won't rightly need me along... and well, to be plain, I intend to profit from the trip. What I can tell yuh is you'll need horses that can withstand a good four to five weeks of hard riding, much of it through rough mountain terrain, just to get there. Also, it's getting late in the year, we might see some cold weather where we're going.

'Lastly, I'll be needin' a pony. I don't trust horse critters. Why just a short while ago I paid good coin for pack horses, up in the mountains of Irijah they were; only got em half-way home when this big black stallion crashes my..."

This time Ragnhildr became impatient and interrupted once more, "It's *clear* why we need your guidance to find this ward of Bearach's, but it is not clear to me why you would have need of us. Am I right in assuming you have been there once already? Why not go yourself and enjoy a greater profit?"

"Well now, yer sharp as a knife and no mistake, and yuh have got right to the heart of the matter cap'n that yuh have. Well... it's like this yuh see, whether left by yer Irial ancestors, or e' just showed up on 'is own, tain't exactly sure; but that-there treasure is guarded, see?"

Mereah looked the adventurer in the eye in an effort to discern whether or not the man spoke true, "A guardian? What sort of guardian?"

Ged's sun-browned face blanched white, and his fear became palpable, "Can't say, I rightly know. I never really seen 'em *clearly*... and there may be more than one. The lads that were with me though are all dead. They be tough men too, every one of 'em. I think the guardian may be a demon, an 'e feeds on blood. All during the night, my lads and I tried to pack up treasure while realizing we weren't alone. One by one the lads got picked off. I found one of em, his heart ripped out but not a drop of blood- anywhere. Like it was something too precious to be spilt or left in the body. Finally, I told the boys to just drop everything... we're getting out of here. I'm the only one as made it through. That fancy knife the only thing I got out."

"I already knew some of the story," Ragnhildr interjected, "But everyone here needs to know why you would dare to return to such a place."

"Because they were good lads that died back there. Now I don't deny there be more treasure than I could hope to scrounge in a hunnert lifetimes... but all the treasure in the world is worthless if yer not alive to spend it. What I'm proposing is an arrangement of mutual benefit. There is a treasure room sure, more importantly, an armory. Most important, I also found a forge, a forge where we can make weapons and armor of our own. Weapons the Dagon can't match. I need help dealing with whatever is guarding the place. In return you get new weapons, and powers to use against the Dagon, a win-win don't cha see."

Caraig snorted, "If we survive that is!"

Having reached his endurance limits for committee "jaw" Ruarc stood up, clapped his hands together once loudly and made his pronouncement, "So, it's settled, Ragnhildr, Korah, I expect your expedition to be ready to leave no later than three days from now. Have a list of the warriors selected for the journey and have them here for a feast in their honor in this very hall tomorrow night. Now, if you will all excuse me, I have other matters to attend to."

As the king rose to leave, Aislin rose and spoke for the first time. Riordan immediately found himself captivated by the melody of her voice, "Father, I want to go!"

Ragnhildr immediately replied with an emphatic, "No."

"But father. . ."

"Did you hear a word that Ged just said? We have no idea of what we are going up against. It could be very dangerous. Daughter, not another word."

Aislin looked directly at Riordan and fired another challenge, "Well, is this one going?"

"Riordan is Korah's page and armor-bearer," Ragnhildr replied. "His presence on this expedition will be Korah's decision, not mine. You on the other hand are my daughter. The decision is mine alone and I am telling you, *no*."

Refusing to back down Aislin retorted, "I have been named as your shield maiden. Is this an honorary title only? I will be shamed publicly if left behind. Besides," here she flashed Riordan an apologetic glance, "I am twice this one's age, and you saw his training this morning; I am far more proficient with blade or bow, *and* unlike him, *I* can control a horse!"

Riordan felt his face turning red and heat suddenly rising from his body. Ragnhildr however, responded before the armor-bearer could make his own defense, "Riordan is young, and he has much to learn it's true; but he has already demonstrated the courage to face one of the Anakim. Whatever creature wards Bearach's armory it is not likely to be as dangerous as an enemy *he* has already faced. Can you say the same?"

"No," she cried, "Especially not if I am left behind at the whispers of danger likely inspired by too much wine or imagination. Long has our people allowed women to take their place in the Fianna."

Riordan leaned over and whispered in Korah's ear, "How can she be twice my age, she looks no older than thirteen or fourteen."

Korah whispered back, "the Irial live almost as long as centaurs, at thirty she isn't even considered an adult."

After a long moment's thought, Ragnhildr at last partially yielded, "Women have taken their place among the Fianna it is true, but you are not a woman, *yet*. This far I will yield, and if you speak another word, I vow I will leave you behind bound, gagged, and locked up for your own protection. You may accompany us as far as the gates to Bearach's Ward. Once there, you will remain behind with Quillan as your guardian, and Riordan as well if Korah is agreed. You will remain behind at least until we encounter whatever defender this ward claims and so have a better understanding of what we face."

Realizing the extent of her victory and the folly of pressing her cause further, Aislin excitedly lost her composure for just a moment and hugged her father's neck. His dignity thus endangered, she released her embrace swiftly, and bowed elegantly, "Thank you father."

Everyone watched her leave, and then Ragnhildr turned to address his officers for the last time that morning, "I apologize my friends. I regret my daughter's impetuousness should be displayed so publicly. But one thing coming from our morning's conversation is that I hope everyone understands this undertaking is one fraught with peril. I don't believe attendance is an option for Korah and I. For anyone else, only volunteers who fully understand the dangers faced should be selected. Caraig, I'm not sure you should attend, but I believe one or two Dun engineers would be helpful to perhaps discern the use and purpose of some of the warcraft technologies."

"Oh no you don't," Caraig growled, "Yer not leaving me behind, I ain't 'fraid of no booger-man in the dark. Besides, no one understands forges or weaponry better than me, I'll be taggin' along. And I suspect, so will the Rapha` Nightingale here. *Somebody* will be needed to look after 'im."

Mereah flashed a big grin, "Well I planned on stayin' home, sounded much too dangerous for me. Now that I know I have Caraig along as babysitter and protector, how could I *possibly* stay behind?"

Ragnhildr looked everyone over gravely, "Don't speak of the dangers so lightly my friends, I fear the realities will render your glib words foolish. Ged, you didn't tell them its name."

The explorer sat with his chin resting on his chest as he contemplated the impact and weight of his answer. Looking up he spoke softly, "It is called Magor-Missabib, the terror on every side."

Chapter Two

aoine barely made it back to her simple home before moon set. The other residents of Joktan went to bed hours ago. Void of even simple street illumination, the tiny community enjoyed an unhindered (but rarely appreciated) view of a brilliant star canopy. Aesthetic beauty is rarely noted by the malnourished of body, heart, or soul.

In her hands she held a small portion of grain in a sack, the fruits of an entire evening of gleaning from the fall harvest. A long-standing law in Moriah prohibited landowners from harvesting to the edges and corners of their fields. This provision for the poor, widows and orphans did not apply to a woman of Caoine's reputation, however. So rather than fight ridicule for scraps from richer tables, she waited until other gleaners went home. By the time she got started, only the leftovers from leftovers remained.

At one time or another, she'd been chased from every field and farm in Joktan. Her mind returned to a memory of a few years ago-a time when she enjoyed a short reprieve from hate. Alone, desperate, starving, she walked to the one place she swore she wouldn't ever set her feet, the farm belonging to Brannan, her son Riordan's father.

On that day, she climbed to a low knoll that overlooked his fields. Scanning the faces of workers, she did not see Brannon or Riordan, so she headed down the hill and approached the field.

Immediately greeted by jeers and insult, she quickly shut out the words by shutting down her heart, a common survival stratagem of the community outcast. She told herself several times during the long walk to Brannan's remote farm, this was a mistake. Too late did she realize she should have heeded her own advice and turned back.

As she gleaned from a corner of the field, the few meager kernels of grain she'd gathered were knocked from her hands. Then a hard shove threw her to the ground. As Caoine struggled to get up, her tunic was grasped, and a vise grip pulled her up and around. The rough back of a man's hand slammed across her face spinning her around and back into the dirt. She worked her jaw to ensure it wasn't broken, while blinking several times to clear her blurred vision. Unfortunately, Caoine's ears worked just fine, and she could hear everyone's jeers mingled with laughter. The red on her face from the savage slap turned deep crimson, the color of her shame.

Encouraged by the response the harvester walked forward so he could hit her again, when a commanding voice called out, "That's enough!"

When her eyes cleared, Caoine looked up to see a man upon a tall red horse sternly scolding one of the workers, "Cavan, a warrior who would strike a woman is displaying cowardice, not strength. Now help her up."

"I hit her grandfather because she has no right to glean, she isn't anybody but ..."

"I said help her up. I am not aware that you possessed the authority to make judgments about who is worthy of El's grace. However, to strike someone smaller and weaker, speaks only of cruelty needed to inflate one's own importance. There will be a private discussion about this at the end of the day. In the meantime, she is going to rest here at the side of the field while you stop your work and fill her sack with grain."

Thoroughly chastised, Cavan avoided eye contact as he took Caoine's hand and raised her to her feet. Without a word he took her sack and started the task of separating the grain from the stalks and straw. Looking down from the tall red horse, the man asked courteously, "Are you hurt dear lady?"

Lessons of self-doubt taught by crippling shame always forced the hanging of her head. But she looked up for a moment only, to say she wasn't injured, then immediately realized her mistake. A light of recognition flashed in the man's eyes. Fear gripped her stomach; she had been recognized–how she couldn't begin to guess.

Turning away quickly, she responded softly, "No my lord."

Troubled by his thoughts, the man hesitated a moment, then gently urged his horse forward and asked, "Lady I would count it a courtesy if you would lighten the load of my old friend Esh here, and take this skin of water. I didn't consider my old friend's age when I loaded his packs today." The big red horse twitched his ears and looked insulted by the assertion but made no other protest.

Caoine however, spoke so quietly that the rider could barely hear, "I cannot accept your gift my lord,"

"It is not a gift dear lady, it is an easing of old Esh's burden. And M'lady, you may return tomorrow to glean from anywhere in the field and take as much as you need. I will ensure no one molests you."

"Why do you do this my lord?" she asked of the man she now recognized as Riordan's grandfather.

He hesitated a moment before answering, "Because I extended the same courtesy to a woman of similar circumstances many years ago. She proved to be a lady of worth and my kindness yielded a return far greater than my small gift." His words caused his eyes to mist as though he savored a distant memory.

She went home that night with more grain than she'd possessed in a long time. Enough that if she was careful, could last her a few months. In addition, in the dead of night or wee morning hours, little packages mysteriously started appearing on her doorstep. She no longer needed to fear the specter of hunger that for so long haunted her existence. One dark night years ago, on a lonely hillside, Caoine remembered the bargain she made with the El of her people. She would never again sell herself. Now it seemed that the Power of her people had both heard and had kept His end of the agreement making it easier for her to keep hers.

She learned of Brónach's death only a few days ago, he'd been found dead in his small cottage. The cause of death seemed clear enough, his spine had snapped, as though struck a horrific blow. The manner of his death however remained shrouded in mystery. The spine was severed but there weren't any other marks or bruises on his body. Brónach remained a strong man, even into his old age, and he would not easily be overcome. The cause of death spoke of a violent life's ending, but there wasn't evidence of a struggle. How could this be accomplished without Brónach's resistance? Speculation kept the whole village whispering about an attack by a supernatural or mystical creature.

Even more baffling were the stories told by the warrior sons of Capall upon their return from the war with the Dagon. Their stories only added to the mystery; Brónach's old red charger, Zaquen Esh had been ridden into combat and the horse was killed... and then, people lowered their voice to a whisper, "A tanniyn severed the ol' horse's spine they say." These events would inspire hushed whispers in dark tavern corners for years to come.

Rumors were also flying that the boy everyone called Mamzer was riding the very same red horse and that he avenged the animal's death by killing the Anak dragon rider with only a sling and stone. The boy was then declared to be a National Hero by the king himself.

Caoine's immediate reaction? Her words of long ago proved true! Surely now Brannan must wish he could name Riordan his son! And her prayers were answered. El, the Power of their people watched over her son!

Then another realization stabbed at the newfound joy in her heart. Riordan wouldn't be coming home–*ever*. There wouldn't be a need to return to Joktan now that he was in the king's service. Excited about Riordan's improved fortunes, she realized it was likely she'd never see her son again. Nor would he ever come looking for her. Why would he? If he had any memories of her at all, it would be of her abandonment. Suddenly she had the all-too-familiar flashbacks of a small boy being pulled away from her. His cries accusing her–faithless, Loveless, Cruel, Abandoner... Mama!

Few defense mechanisms suffice when the prosecutor's voice in your head is *your own*, able to access your own memories to present their case. How could she *not* be loveless? After all, she gave the boy up. Cruel? Did she not turn a deaf ear to his cries? Abandoner? Yes. She was an abandoner. She left her child in the care of a hard man to endure whispers, shameful naming, the cruelty of an entire house where he was the object of scorn. The pleas that she did what she had to, to save the lad's life, seemed empty next to the vitriolic accusations of the prosecution. Oh yes, she was all the spirit-crushing voices said she was. Worse.

Thoughts swirled like a dervish torturing Caoine's soul as she reached her small one-room home. It was so late in the night that without years of habit to guide her, she might not have found the fabric-covered entrance. Her father built the place, using the cheapest and most available of materials, blocks of sod cut from the Capall plain.

Exhausted, she collapsed against the wall. Ironically, after all these years, the place still smelled of smoke and ash. A bitter metaphor of her own life going up in flames.

Bitter tears spilled salt and acid on her cheek. Yes, she abandoned her son. But, her own parents, didn't they abandon her? Holding the hands of the dying, they followed the sick into death, leaving her alone. Alone to ignite the cleansing flame. Alone to ignite the fires that reduced her life to ash.

She hugged herself as the memories of their last day crowded into her dark thoughts. "My pulse, listen to me, as soon as I pass... I want... don't delay... even to mourn... fill the house with dry thatch... burn everything... including mama and I."

She remembered attempting to hug her father, as much for her own comfort as his. He used his last bit of strength left to resist, "NO! Mustn't... touch... unclean."

Caoine's father died a few seconds later, and she sat in the ashes of her life and wept. All night long. She could not bear to obey her father's instructions, and so left her parents where they lay for another day and mourned. But as the scent of decay started to grow, finally, like a zombie, she lit the cleansing flame and her whole life went up in smoke.

Her parents died, and soon so did all that was left of her soul. The first offers of payment for portions of her heart she flatly refused. With few other options, however, moral virtue can be an expensive luxury when weighed against an empty stomach. Even so, the compromising of the heart carries a price; her soul became dead to pain or joy, leprous, *unclean*. She joined the ranks of the living dead, doing what she must to survive.

Standing at her home's threshold, she reached up and touched the small box that contained the sacred scroll. Placed there by her father, it was all that remained of her parent's possessions, the only thing not touched by cleansing flame after her parent's deaths. For the first time in many years, she withdrew the small parchment from its box. She didn't need light to know the words written there, for they were engraved on her heart years before, "I know the plan's I have for you…"

Her thoughts exploded in protest, "Plans? What plans? If there is a plan for my life … it's a cruel one. Next time El, leave me out of any more such plans!"

Years ago, she had all but made up her mind to give in to despair, and silence the last proof of her existence, her own beating heart. Then she discovered that by taking her life, she would also be killing a second, an innocent life growing in her womb.

In a sense, Riordan proved to be her salvation. He gave her a reason to live. Even after giving her son up to his father, she felt the need to maintain a silent vigil just in case the boy's father Brannan decided not to keep his promise.

Now her son was beyond her reach, likely forever. In her malnourished, depressed state, it became increasingly hard to come up with more reasons why she should continue living. One of her few simple utensils, a crude flint knife, beckoned. It would suffice to satisfy the needs of Caoine's despair.

That dark night, after an eternity spent whispering desperate prayers–with no answers forthcoming from the ever-elusive dawn, she mourned, she wept, no joy came in the morning. Her small hand reached slowly for her final solution.

Chapter Three

"There is nothing like looking, if you want to find something. You certainly usually find something, if you look, but it is not always quite the something you were after."

J.R.R. Tolkien

A wee bit humiliating; Riordan, couldn't tame Sorcha before departure and so was forced to ride an aged broodmare named Cailin. While lacking only a few of Esh's years, and most of his fiery disposition, the aged mare did possess a patient, gentle spirit. This was a temporary compromise, however. As a son of Capall, strong expectations existed that he would be able to train and ride a warhorse.

Each evening while the others set up camp, Riordan was ordered, in the words of Caraig, to "Woo" his 'orse. So tonight, he brought the white stallion a carrot to munch while he gave him a rub down. He absentmindedly scratched his mount's chin and stroked the warm, velvety nose. Unable to ride the spirited horse, at least they were able to settle into an uneasy truce. Sorcha took the treats from his hand, tolerated, and sometimes even seemed to welcome his touch. At least the fear of being bitten, kicked or stomped, was largely a thing of the past. In fact, several days of drenching rain, had left everyone in camp wet, miserable, and grumpy; so, at this point, the Rohi preferred the horse's company to humans.

The party left Flann, the Rapha` capitol fourteen tedious days ago, traveling east over a flat unchanging sea of grass. Riordan recognized the rising rolling hills they recently crossed however and knew their guide Ged was bringing him home. Judging by the presence of the mountains of Irijah laying low on the horizon, the farm where he grew up would be only a few miles away to the south.

Gazing across the terrain, ominous clouds cast dark shadows streaking over the plain. The brewing storm would hit with a vengeance any minute. While they could see the threat rushing to overtake them, unfortunately, they couldn't do much about it; the open grasslands offered no shelter. After a frantic search, they settled on the leeward side of a ravine hoping for protection from the driving wind. They now faced the difficult task of making camp on a steep slope. Pitching tents in the flat at the bottom was out of the question, rainwater was already flowing through. More rain would surely raise a trickle to a torrent, and no one seemed inclined to be washed to the sea by a flood.

Also, complicating matters was the sheer size of one member of their party. As Riordan walked the short distance along the slope to camp, he heard the bellowing voice of Caraig, "Out! Get out Mereah, yer ripping the stakes up again! There's just not room for all of us and you!"

The raindrops were already splattering on the skin shelter as Riordan approached. The center of the tent was pushed up by a big lump underneath, stretching the fabric and lines almost to the breaking point. The normally cheerful Mereah growled, "Friends, I have slept in the rain and mud ever since this monsoon started days ago. It's high time somebody else tried their hand at sleeping in cold winter rain."

"If yuh stay in here any longer *somebody else* will become *everybody else* yuh great oaf!" Caraig countered. "The tent's tearing, lines are snappin' and the stakes pullin', get OUT!"

"I've been miserable for days my diminutive friend, and all I can say is that misery loves nothing more than company!" Mereah roared back.

Standing outside in a rapidly increasing downpour, Riordan recognized the soft chuckle and voice of his captain, "I'm truly sorry my friend. When I purchased supplies and these tents, I did fail to mention one of our party was a son of Rapha`. I take full responsibility *and* since I am to blame, let me fetch my cloak and I will join your misery outside in the deluge. Are you content?"

The Rapha` prince flashed his trademark grin, "Indeed yes, especially if Caraig agrees to join our merry company."

In response, despite the cold and the damp, the Dun Commander gave such a smoldering glare that the temperatures in the tent rose several degrees.

Having received his answer, a giant grin filled Mereah's face with mirth as the light of a brilliant idea popped into the prince's head. Rather than crawling out of the shelter, Mereah stood straight up. Ropes snapped. Stakes and curses flew. Above the raging storm inside and outside the tent, came the slightly muffled sounds of roaring laughter. From under the tarp the prince transformed into a great howling with laughter ghost.

~

"Give it up Caraig," Korah recommended, "Your materials are wetter than we are. Dry dung will burn, wet dung only stinks."

The Dun captain didn't even look up from his soggy embers, when he growled in reply, "I've been soakin' wet for nearly a week, and I want something hot in my belly at least. I'm a soldier of Dun, and I know how to make a fire. I've dry kindling plus a hot coal saved from my firebox."

Ragnhildr peeked over the Dun Commander's shoulder and quipped, "Don't quite know how to tell you this my friend, but your hot coal has transformed into a soggy dark briquette."

"Course it has, why with all this free advice, an' flapping gums it's cooled off! Now let me alone, I'm making a fire tonight if it kills me." Bending down with his face almost touching his fire starter, Caraig made his best attempt to breathe life into a lump of dead coal.

From several feet away, Mereah offered assistance, "You'll never get a fire going that way, let *me* show you how it's done." Filling his great lungs, the Rapha` Prince did his best bellows impersonation, with two unintended results. First black ash blew in the Dun Captain's face; and second, the soggy lump of coal erupted into flames, almost igniting the surprised Dun Captain's beard.

~

"Again Mereah," Caraig pleaded, his face a study in eager expectation despite its being covered with gray ash, "Do it again!"

The Rapha` Prince rolled his eyes and blew half-heartedly for the umpteenth time out of the corner of his mouth. Almost instantly the dying embers of a soggy fire roared back to life. As the flames climbed higher so did the volume of Caraig's amusement, "I don't believe it, took long enough but we have finally found a use for the great oaf - besides ripping up tents and eatin' most of our food that is. I think I'll give yuh a new name, a noble name, Sir Bellows Breath."

"Sir Dragon's Breath is closer to the truth." Korah chimed in, "I'd have bet a hundred in gold coin no one could ignite soggy manure. How *are* ya doing that trick Mereah?"

Warming his hands in front of the fire, Caraig interjected, "T-aint no trick Horse Master, just confirmation of what I've always known, our prince is full ah hot air."

"Well, that theory sounds credible until a man realizes it came out of a head full of rocks."

The booming sarcasm came from the shadows catching everyone by surprise. Riordan recognized the voice immediately, so before the others could react, he was already running and yelling his greeting, "Jireh!"

After a bone-crushing hug, Riordan escorted the Shophetim back to the light of the fire. Everyone came to their feet and surrounded the big centaur, greeting him enthusiastically. As the captains returned to their places by the fire, Korah broke through the excited chatter to ask, "Jireh, to what do we owe this unexpected pleasure? Considering the last few days downpour, I can't imagine you're out for an evening stroll."

"Well, I could ask the same question, mighty nasty weather for a campout. But like many of my people, I have the gift of far-sight. From the mountains I observed your journey and grew curious as to the purpose of your expedition."

Ragnhildr interjected quickly, "There is plenty of time for swapping stories, yours, and ours. First come warm yourself by the fire. We are all extremely puzzled by having a fire at all. Prince Mereah has suddenly displayed an astonishing gift of getting wet dung and sticks to burst into flame. I believe you heard Caraig share his hot air theory, I'm sure we'd all love to hear yours."

Jireh looked at the Irial Commander carefully, as though trying to discern the intent behind the captain's inquiry, "I do have some thoughts on the matter," The Shophetim answered softly, "Likely no better than the previous theory from Caraig's thick cranium, so I'd like to keep them to myself for the time being. But I don't recognize everyone at this merry gathering."

"Forgive me," Ragnhildr replied, "I believe you know all the King's Captains, but allow me to introduce my daughter Aislin. Also, this is Ged, the guide for our quest."

Despite, male riding clothes, and hair hanging like damp strings, Aislin still radiated a quiet beauty and strength. So much so that no one questioned the centaur's sincerity when he said, "I'm surprised the Irial would allow you to hazard the greatest treasure of your people Ragnhildr, on any quest, dangerous or otherwise."

The frown that found its way to Ragnhildr's face made Jireh realize, the presence of the Irial lady did not entirely meet with the father's approval so he quickly changed the subject.

Turning to the Dun Adventurer, "As for Mr. Ged, I am glad to finally make your acquaintance. I have never met you personally, but many of the Irijah has spoken of you. You and your companions have trafficked a considerable amount in and through our mountains. Since you are the leader of this expedition, forgive me I misspoke–its *guide*– might I inquire as to where you are leading my friends?"

All the laughter and jesting around the fire suddenly ceased. The thunderous sounds of silence communicated volumes. Only the singing crickets missed the discomfort the question caused the Captains of Jeshurun.

Ged started to stammer a response when Ragnhildr quickly cut him off, "I am leading this company on the king's business. Before we can divulge any information concerning *our* business, I'm afraid I must ask *you* yours– *why are you here* Jireh?"

The eyes of the commander and Jeshurun's Shophetim locked in a stern contest of wills, while the camp silently watched and anticipated the likely outcome.

"I have already stated my business; I'm gently inquiring if it is this company's intent to enter the mountains of Irijah. I'm certain the Captains of Moriah understand, the eastern mountains fall under the dominion of the Irijah, of whom I remain chief."

All the heads focused on Jireh, turned to hear Ragnhildr's response, "As far as our destination, our good guide has not divulged that much information. I can only speculate that is our intent simply because that is the direction our noses have been pointing each morning. If the courtesy of consent to enter the Irijah's is what you require, I gladly ask. However, I will wager it is not permission you seek, but information. It is also well known that at your last parting, words were exchanged between you and our king. Since we are on the king's business, I must ask are you still a king's man?"

Jireh carefully weighed his response, "A far more important question would be am I El's man? I anointed Ruarc king as you well remember. That means he is El's anointed. To oppose the king would be therefore tantamount to opposing the King of heaven and all His mighty host. No one lives as long as I Ragnhildr by acting like such a fool. I am not Ruarc's enemy. The worst enemy he faces is himself."

Riordan looked over at Mereah, to see how he reacted to the frank discussion of his father. Always enthusiastic and upbeat, even amid the last few days monsoon, the Rapha` Prince simply crouched on his heels and gazed mournfully into a dying fire.

Trying to break the tension, Caraig stretched, and faked a yawn, "Well, don't know about anyone else, but I'm exhausted. Thanks to Prince Bellows-Breath I may be dry enough to actually sleep, we should all turn-in."

"The Scepter of Adon," Ragnhildr replied, completely missing the Dun Commander's attempt at changing the subject, "We are searching for just such talismans to counter the coming of the next Dagon invasion. Also, Ged brought to us a dagger bearing an inscription from Bearach, son of Atara. We hope this weapon may have originated from a source that will lead to the scepter's recovery."

Riordan had never seen Jireh surprised before. So, while the big centaur remained calm, the way his eyes shot open in astonishment spoke volumes, "You're seeking Bearach's Wards of Power?"

"The blade Ged brought to us is of an extraordinary alloy. Lighter than bronze, stronger than iron. At the very least we seek to discover the metals and forging process that produced it. As you know the Drochshaol produced many wonders and technologies we no longer understand. If this blade did indeed come from one of Bearach's wards, and if the Scepter of Adon is among its treasures, we must recover it. If for no other reason than to keep it from the Dagon."

Jireh in a measured voice replied, "I am certain that if the king didn't understand the possible unintended consequences of this course of action, you do Ragnhildr. The Irial should understand as well as any what can go wrong with the misuse of powers they don't fully comprehend. Also, the Wards could quite possibly be guarded by powers greater than the Anakim. All things considered; I think I'd better go with you. Any objections?"

Several around the fire were encouraged greatly by the suggestion, especially Riordan. Then he heard Ragnhildr's reaction, "That is not my king's instructions," The Irial Captain noted quietly.

"Did the king forbid it?"

"Well no... your name didn't come up."

Mereah spoke up for the first time, "Jireh has lived long, and has a great deal of knowledge and wisdom that would increase greatly our chances for success. I will dare speak for the king; I for one, however would be glad of our Shophetim's company."

Ragnhildr considered his words carefully, "It is settled then, with a mission so consequential, it is appropriate for the Irijah to be so powerfully represented."

Riordan watched the Irial Commander thinking the spoken words said welcome; but the expression in Ragnhildr's eyes, were guarded and said, "I will be watching you." Regardless, the young shepherd was thrilled his old mentor would be joining the quest.

Relieved things turned out better than he hoped Korah chimed in, "Well unless Mereah plans on regaling us with further displays of pyrotechnics, we should follow Caraig's example and retire.

Everyone dispersed to their various quarters. Riordan started to return to the tent, when Korah beckoned to him, "Lean in a bit closer lad, what I've got to say is just for your ears. I wouldn't say anything to Ragnhildr about the Riail dlí, especially not that Jireh gave you the blade. I know your teacher doesn't have any evil intent towards the king, but still, that's something best kept between the two of you. We wouldn't want the sword to cause any misunderstanding."

Riordan nodded and looked in the direction of the Irial Commander as he and Aislin moved past the flaps of the tent they shared. A deep sigh revealed the emotions he felt whenever he saw the Irial maiden. Korah noticed the pent-up feelings and smiled, "She's a high lady boy-o, I won't say too high, but high enough that a failed attempt might break your heart. Go get some sleep lad, maybe she'll come to you in your dreams. Dreams are something no one can forbid."

Riordan took his leave and started towards the reassembled, but still in tatters tent. Moving through the opening he kicked himself for not getting to sleep before Caraig. The Dun Weapons Master was already roaring in blissful slumber. The tent flaps were being alternatingly sucked in and blown out again demonstrating that the Rapha` Prince wasn't the only one to possess bellows for lungs. So *that's* why Korah volunteered to stay outside. For a moment he struggled against the temptation of dropping an offering in the snore-cano's open maw. Savoring the idea for a moment, good sense prevailed when he realized a heavy price would be extracted from his hide. Dejectedly he rolled up his blankets and slipped out to join Korah and Mereah outside.

Chapter Four

iordan's feet were firmly planted in the muddy earth. Both hands grasped a large wooden stake as he struggled to budge it more than a fraction before giving up. He slowly straightened his back, wiped his brow, turned, and was mildly surprised to see his captain, standing there watching him. "I appreciate your hard work lad, but I've a more important job than pulling tent stakes."

"Just as well," the young man replied. "I'm not nearly as good as Mereah at yanking these things up anyway."

However, after seeing that Korah was leading Sorcha, a knot quickly formed in his stomach. Anticipating more sudden flights through the air followed by painful sudden stops, the young page quipped, "On second thought, maybe it'd be better if I just kept wrestling with these durn stakes."

The Calvary officer persisted "Walk with me lad, I'll tell you what I have in mind. The rain has flooded the stream at the bottom of the ravine, leaving several deep pools. If you walk Sorcha out to about his chest in the creek, it will make it a lot harder to throw ya off lad. Even if he does it only means gettin' wet, not a lumped noggin."

Reaching the first of a series of pools, Korah looked at his charge and queried, "What do ya say lad, care to give it a try?"

Gazing down at the dark swirling water, Riordan thought to himself he'd much rather take his chances on dry land. His response however was to reach for the stallion's lead and walk to the edge of the pool. Looking back at the captain, he quipped, "Isn't this where you tell me, go on in, the waters fine?"

"Son," Korah stated flatly, "That water's so cold, I wouldn't go in to save me own mother."

~

Thirty minutes later, the Rapha` Prince came to join Korah just in time to watch Riordan ride Sorcha to the shallows and up onto the stream bank. Waiting a moment to ensure the page would remain on the stallion's back, a grinning Cavalry Captain turned to the Rapha` Prince and asked, "Can you give us another display of your fire magic Mereah? I've a couple half-drowned rats needin' to dry out."

As the Prince observed Riordan and Sorcha, a massive smile broke across his face that betrayed his immense pleasure that the page had crossed a major hurdle. The pair certainly did look like drowned rats, however. Sorcha's normally gleaming white coat and mane was deeply stained from the murky waters; the proud head bowed from the shame of the dark smear. While Riordan gave the picture of misery a face. More than the water dripping from his hair, nose, and chin, or the mud-stained clothing; it was the violent shivering, ice blue complexion and chattering teeth that made it clear, the young armor-bearer felt far worse than he looked. "I'm afraid I must be a giant bearer of bad news my friends, I was sent to fetch you both. All is made ready, and the company will soon move. No time for a fire... perhaps a warm, dry blanket?"

Korah removed his cloak and wrapped it around Riordan, "There ya are lad, sorry we didn't try that trick sooner, and at a warmer time of year." Looking up and back at Mereah the captain asked, "Has our guide indicated where we're headed yet?"

"Only that we'd camp just outside the village of Joktan tonight." Mereah observed Riordan look up suddenly, "Ged did say it'd be the last town we'd see for a while, so at least a few folks will ride in for supplies."

Taking Sorcha's lead so his young page could put all his effort into pulling the wool cloak tighter, Korah murmured, "Does seem clear our guide intends on taking us into or through the Irijah Mountains."

"I was thinking the same," Mereah replied. "I'm also certain that if one of Bearach's Wards were in those mountains, the Irijah would have discovered it long ago."

"Agreed, and that may be the reason Jireh has joined our quest. Would you mind keeping Ragnhildr occupied at the front of the expedition while I try to pry a little more information out of our tight-lipped Shophetim?"

Instead of a reply, Mereah flashed a grin and trotted to the head of the column where Ragnhildr waited impatiently.

A few in the company started to chuckle when they watched Riordan ride up, but a sharp glance from Korah killed all laughter in their throats. "I invited Jireh to join us at the rear, where we'll drop further back to avoid inquisitive ears. I want to ask you a few questions as well lad, so stay close."

A few weeks of steady rain had turned the Capall plane into a soggy mess. Staying back meant navigating mud tracks plowed deep by the other riders. Despite this, Korah remained content bringing up the rear, "Lad, when we first were introduced to Ged, he knew you, greeted you, how do you know him?"

Korah noted the young armor-bearer flinch when he asked the question, "My father's family and I made a trip into the Irijah Mountains to capture feral horses. I was left in camp to guard the ones we caught. Ged and a small band of the Dun took them from me."

"He stole them?"

"Not exactly"

"Well, what exactly, did he do?"

"I offered Ged food. While we ate, he threw it in my face, overpowered me, tied me up. Then he and those who were with him took the horses."

At that point Jireh trotted up and joined the captain and his charge, saying nothing, not wishing to interrupt the conversation. "So, how exactly was it *not* theft?" Korah asked

"He left money to pay for the horses," Riordan explained quietly. "My uncle wouldn't sell to the Dun. None of the Capall will, Ged said. So, they have to take 'em any way they can. He also said his people don't mistreat their animals."

Korah considered this carefully and asked, "I'd wager that didn't set well with your *uncle*? Did he give chase?"

"My family gave pursuit, but the Dun didn't have to go very far, they fled into some caves a few miles away from camp."

After a moments silence, Korah turned his attention to the newly arrived Shophetim, "Ah, Jireh, thank you for joining us. I had some questions I wanted to ask but feared their answers might cause... shall we say some anxiety in the larger group. Also, it seems clear we are headed in the direction of the Irijah's, but if there are items of great antiquity in those mountains, I can't believe you wouldn't know of them."

"Friend Korah, are you gently asking me if I know of the where-bouts of the Scepter of Adon?"

Laughing Korah quipped, "More than that, I hoped you have it stored in your baggage!"

Ignoring the jest, Jireh replied, "I haven't carried baggage for five hundred years as you know full well. This much I can tell you, the Scepter is not to be found in the mountains of Irijah."

Slightly chastised by the centaur's stern tone, Korah inquired further, "Riordan was just explaining that he knew of our friend Ged, who used some caves to avoid angry um, shall we say re-negotiations? Are these caverns a possible destination?"

Jireh paused in thought a moment before responding, "The eastern mountains are largely formed by long-extinct volcanos. Eruptions ages ago created a confusing labyrinth of caverns, shafts, and tubes, with many entrances, on both sides of the divide. It is also possible if indeed that is our current destination, he hopes we will emerge clueless as to our true location. I don't know an awful lot about our guide, but the things I have heard leads me to believe, he's not exactly the trusting type."

Korah broke into a grin, "So far, my experience would confirm much of what you have heard. But I must confess, the real reason I desired to speak with you is well... to ask if you feel any of the same reservations that I have concerning an attempt to recover the Scepter of Adon?"

"That friend Korah is precisely why I am here. I understand Ragnhildr's need to make the attempt, and I gather Ruarc is at least partly behind the idea; I am also fairly certain you are aware that misuse of the Scepter by the Irial triggered the destruction of the first age. Almost all traces of that period were eradicated so that it's hard to discern history from myth. But to answer, yes... yes, I am concerned that a mighty captain of the Irial leads an expedition for the Scepter's recovery. Even if the Irial Captain is as trustworthy as Ragnhildr."

For the first time in days, Riordan was enjoying the ride. The clouds were mostly scattered allowing the young page to soak in the sun's warmth and dry off. Not wishing to be completely left out of the conversation, the rohi asked, "Are the legends about the Scepter true? Does it really exist?"

"Lad," Jireh interjected, "A scant hundred years from now, your story will pass into legend, and people everywhere will ask if it's true; did a mere boy kill the Anak of Dagon with a sling and stone? Stories are often the best record we have. In the case of the Scepter of Adon the legend flows from facts. When the Irial King Atara took it to himself, it was discovered the Scepter empowered the bearer to exercise authority over natural law. Atara at least had the wisdom not to attempt to wield such might without understanding the ramifications. Bearach his son, however, did not. I agree with Ragnhildr, the Scepter must not fall into the wrong hands. My fear, however, is that Ruarc must be included among those who should not possess the Scepter's power."

With that ominous pronouncement, they continued their journey nursing their own thoughts.

Chapter Five

"Frost kills the flowers that bloom out of season..."
— Henry Wadsworth Longfellow

linging to the flint knife Caoine slowly moved the blade over her wrist, applying sufficient pressure for no more than a scratch. With no one left to mourn, no one to note her passing, how long would it be before her lifeless body would be found? Would anyone care enough to see to her burial? As for the deepest wound of her heart... how could she rest in peace if her son believed she'd abandoned him?

Caoine remained quiet, still, hoping for a sign that El had heard her prayers. Deafening silence screamed her worst fear, she already had her answer. Because of what she'd done, who she was, her prayers would go unanswered. Rejected, despised, and forsaken, even by El, (or so she believed) she added still more accusations to her story.

Once before, more than fifteen years ago, she'd decided to take her life. A violent kick inside her womb stopped her. Confirming she had another heart beating inside her.

She made a bargain long ago, on a moonlit hillside, the night she gave him up. She struck a deal with the El of her people-never again; never again would she sell herself. She kept her end of the deal, and El kept His. Elohim answered her prayer, acting as father for her son. Against all odds, Riordan was elevated to be a prince and hero.

Her son's new status, however, meant restraints on her final solution no longer existed. Why linger? Tormenting voices of accusation reminded her that the ending of her life would be an act of justified retribution. Spurred on by a confusing cacophony of dark voices, she placed the knife on her wrist once more. Then she felt a sensation as though a gentle hand held hers back...just a whisper, a touch of reluctance, allowed a gentle quiet voice to cut through. The voice spoke to a faint, dying ember of hope, buried in her heart. Forgiveness, redemption, she needed both desperately. Ending her life made receiving these impossible. A still quiet voice cautioned her, suicide is just another form of abandonment.

So, for the second time, she struck a bargain with the power whose name means covenant, "El, my life means nothing, but it is all I have left for an offering. All I am, all I ever hoped I could be, I give it to you. I will not... I will not take what is not mine. I cannot choose the moment of my last breath. I only ask that when the time comes, my son will not accuse, and he will be the one to close my eyes. Then at last, I may know peace."

She relaxed the pressure applied to the blade on her wrist and withdrew the knife.

Then she heard voices. Not cold voices of guilt and accusation. Real voices. Voices filled with blood and warm breath. A small troop of men walked and rode right past her curtain door. One booming voice seemed to rain down laughter from high above. Caoine liked the big voice immediately; he seemed to share a jest with another whose voice was just as deep but spoke from a place much lower to the ground. One of the Dun, perhaps?

Then she heard a voice she instantly recognized, a voice she had buried like a treasure in her heart. Shamed and frightened by a choice she almost made, she threw the knife across the small hut and scrambled to her feet.

As Caoine reached the door and parted the curtain, she froze in fear. The courage of new hope barely lived as a dying ember. Her fear, however, remained as a consuming fire. Did she dare risk her son's rejection? The traveler's voices she'd heard moved away slowly, growing faint. Still, she remained frozen, wrestling with her personal demons. In a panic, she pleaded with fear, I must follow my son or remain forever estranged, never healed. Fear brought countersuit, she dare not hope! Hope disappoints - costs too much! Finally, the small troupe of voices and the voice of her son could no longer be heard. Restraint snapped under the pressure of desperation and panic. Caoine pushed through the veil, saw her son with a party of travelers in the distance moving through Joktan towards the small market. Relieved, she started to run.

One of the ladies from the village stepped in front of her, blocking her path. Caoine recognized her as the spouse of the local priest. "There you are! We've been wanting to talk with you my dear, but you seem to only venture out at night."

Caoine hastily replied "Not today. Please!" Then tried to go around the woman.

Another lady blocked her path, and spoke with a smirk on her face, "But we must insist. One can only wonder at a person's deeds that require such secrecy and the cover of darkness." Ignoring the thinly veiled accusation, Caoine jumped up trying to see over the growing human blockade. despairingly she watched her son and companions move further down the street.

As the crowd grew, the insinuations became more direct, "It's about your hair dear. Local tradition insists that ladies of your um, *profession*, wear their hair cropped short. You wouldn't want people to confuse you with a *lady*, would you?"

A hard shove threw her into a man standing ready behind her. Strong hands pulled her limbs back hard, leaving bruises on her forearms. Someone produced a dull flint knife and offered it to a dignified individual in robes, "Teacher, would you care to do the honors?"

Grabbing a great fist full of hair, the knife was sawn back and forth rapidly by the village priest, attempting to cut through Caoine's long tresses. Far more hair was pulled from her scalp than cut. In time, she couldn't even scream her pain any longer. The strain pushed her to the breaking point of her malnourished physical limits, so she started to pass out. Suddenly the hands of hate that bound her let go, and she collapsed into the mud of the street.

A great booming voice demanded, "What's the meaning of this? What has this lady done?"

Suddenly, the tight circle of feet surrounding her, retreated to a much larger half-circle. Caoine did not look up, but heard the shocked whispers, "Our Shophetim," and "Jireh, Jireh is here."

The temple priest stammered, "We're so glad you're here to witness our zeal for righteousness lord Jireh. This woman has shamed her family, by entertaining um, the men of our village, for many years now."

Jireh glared at the men and women in the judgment circle, every mother's son felt the centaur's eyes bore a hole in their breast as he examined their hearts. After a few very tense moments he demanded, "Tell me, the healers, who treated persons suffering from plague years ago. Is this woman their adult daughter?"

A few different voices murmured, "Yes, yes she is. Now she disgraces their very names."

"Strange that a righteous family would have their daughter go so far astray. I can only assume when her parents died after faithfully serving your village, you followed the law of our people concerning the just treatment of widows and orphans? Before you answer, I must warn you, after several hundred years as Shophetim of our people, I will discern the truth of your words."

Hanging heads, chirping crickets, and silence, was the only response. The dull knife used as a hair-cutting device dropped to the muddy street. Accusation had nothing more to say.

"Just as I thought." he murmured. "All right, you are fortunate to have the high judge of your people here today. We will hold court right here, right now. I have heard the charges, now I require witnesses. Who will step forward? Keep in mind, they must be eyewitnesses. Surely there is a man here who paid for her services?"

Jireh glared at all the men standing in judgment. So did the narrowed eyes of their suspicious wives. No one breathed. Not a muscle moved.

"I see," Jireh growled, "Well then, lacking witnesses, all charges against this woman must be dropped. Riordan, would you be so kind as to help the good woman out of the clinging street filth? I think she had better come with us."

Riordan swung his leg over Sorcha's tail and slid off the stallion's back. Frozen in place by shame, her face staring into the dirt, Caoine didn't hear the Shophetim's request. She couldn't look up, move, or think until a hand reached gently under her arm, and helped her to her feet. She looked up, and immediately choked on regret's bile rising in her throat as she found herself looking in the face of her son, "Come mother, let us leave this place."

Her crippling shame was followed by terror. At last, she would have to answer for her crime of abandonment, the crime that consumed her heart. For more than a decade she longed for the day when she would be reunited with her son. Now that the day was here, she was terrified she might have to answer the question she feared above all others–why? Why did she throw him away like unwanted baggage? Why didn't she love him enough to keep him? Why did she condemn him to a home where he would become an object of derision and scorn?

Then it dawned on her that Riordan had just called her *mother*. Caoine momentarily replaced fear with panic, "How? How could he possibly know who she was?" In horror she realized, nobody must know! My son has been given a great gift, in answer to many prayers, but… if people knew her identity, her reputation? Finally, after the initial paralysis of anxiety passed, she realized, the light of recognition was not in her son's eyes. He had called her mother but used the word as a token of compassion and respect only.

The rest of the party watched the drama unfold. They recognized a moment of joy, then shock, followed by fear that registered on the woman's face. A close relative, at the very least, was the thought that went through Mereah's mind.

Korah remembered going to a farm not far from here recruiting young men for the cavalry. Fury was on full display by Riordan's "aunt" when he referred to Brannan as the boy's father. Mystery solved. The reason for Mara's anger now had a face. The betrayal of solemn vows can certainly serve as catalyst for hate. Whispers in a small community such as Joktan would ensure resentments would fester and boil over into something far uglier.

Caraig, clueless to most social clues found himself wondering, "Who's the Dame?" Then muttering, "Are we planning to adopt the lady like a stray puppy?"

Riordan supported Caoine by placing her arm over his shoulder. Korah met the pair and suggested, "Place the lady on Aella lad, and I'll take her lead. The captain spoke something softly to her as she weakly settled onto the gentle mare's back. Her head lifted slightly, and everyone saw her lips move, speaking too soft for anyone but Korah to hear.

Without a word, the Captain of Capall took the lead rope of his mount and walked towards the edge of town.

It took mere minutes to come to a stop before a simple soddy on the village's east side. Without a word of explanation, Korah went through the fabric entrance and emerged a few moments later with a small bundle rolled in a wool blanket.

"This good lady is known as Caoine," Korah spoke gently, "The village of Joktan is not worthy of her presence any longer, so she shall be our guest, for a time. I encourage all of you to shake the clinging filth from your boots as we leave this *fair* village."

Ragnhildr was there to meet the supply party as they rode into camp. If he was surprised to see a woman riding Korah's mare while the officer walked, it did not register on his face. Addressing his officers, he asked, "Success?"

Mereah merrily chimed in, "The men will be pleased. We've fresh meat for tonight and likely for the next few!"

"Aye," Caraig growled, "It'll be salt pork and hard biscuit after that, unless we can find game in the mountains."

Ragnhildr acknowledged the Dunn commander's remarks then turned his gaze to Caoine. Few details of importance escaped his shrewd scrutiny. Noting the threadbare garments, her jagged, short-cropped hair, skeletal body, and how shame bowed her head; the commander nodded respectfully to Caoine then instructed, "Mr. Quillan, be sure to inform the men I expect their best behavior, we'll be having a second lady among us as a guest when we dine tonight."

For the first time since departing Joktan, Caoine raised her head, struggling to find the courage to speak. With her features revealed, Ragnhildr's eyes moved quickly from the lady's face to Riordan's, then back again. She spoke for the first time, barely loud enough for all to hear, "My lord, say not a guest. Allow me the honor of repaying your kindness, by preparing your evening meal."

A grinning Mereah piped in cheerfully, "It seems your reputation as our chef proceeds you Caraig. Apparently, this good woman is prepared to go to great lengths to avoid your cooking."

Caraig slapped the flat of his hammer down on Mereah's toes, then watched with a grim look of satisfaction as the prince jumped around howling and laughing, "I ain't heard yuh volunteer ta take over cookin' yuh great oaf!" the Dun Captain growled.

Ragnhildr spoke loud enough to be heard over all the ruckus, "Lady, your presence here is an honor, and there are a great many large appetites to feed. In addition to my officers, there is also a small company of men that serves as our guard. Putting you to work in such a way would be a great disservice and a most poor welcome."

Her head hanging once more, Caoine replied softly. Mereah bit his lip to stop his yowling so she might be heard, "My lord shows me great - but unmerited courtesy, knowing full well I'm not a lady, but a humble servant only. Allowing me to serve this great company would be an honor."

Ragnhildr observed Caoine for a moment, then looked back for his daughter, "This is my daughter Aislin," the Irial maid stepped forward out of the shadows, "I've contemplated allowing her to relieve friend Caraig from culinary duties ... except I am afraid if she assumed cooking reasonability's our men would mutiny. It would indeed be a great service to us all if you would tutor my daughter, as she assists you in the meal's preparation."

Ragnhildr could feel his daughter's icy glare boring holes in his back as Caoine softly replied, "Your kind offer of an opportunity to be of assistance honors me."

Ragnhildr bowed respectfully, "Aislin will show you to our larder and supply. And Caraig, would you please bring the fresh provisions and assist our guest, also?"

That night as Aislin ladled more stew on Mereah's trencher and he helped himself to a whole loaf of fresh-baked bread, the Rapha` remarked "Caraig, your services as cook are no longer required. This kind lady has indeed made a feast to shame any king's finest chef."

Korah quipped, "Aye, now that we're all no longer being slowly poisoned by our culinary tormenter-in-chief, a few of our company may have reasonable hope of actually surviving this quest." Speaking to Caoine, he cajoled, "Provided, we can convince this brave lady to join our poor company."

Caoine spoke with a perpetual downcast face, making it difficult to hear as she quietly declined Korah's offer, "Such mighty lords would surely be hindered by my presence."

Ragnhildr interjected, "As this jester troop's captain I can foresee your culinary excellence preventing our warriors deserting due to Caraig's cooking. This alone would make your addition worth more than your weight in gold."

Anticipating a stinging retort, that never came, Ragnhildr cast a glance in Caraig's direction and observed the Dun Commander's mouth too stuffed with bread and stew to make a response. "Also, lady," he continued, "I will be surrendering my place in the tent I share with my daughter. If you could somehow be a feminine influence on Aislin... I would be grateful."

At this comment, Aislin objected loudly, "Father!"

"My daughter, you know this is true." Then offering further explanation to Caoine, he continued, "She has had far too little of the influence of a woman since her mother passed away. I am afraid she has spent a good portion of her life in the company of this old warrior. Perhaps I proved suitable as a father, but I am a very poor mother."

Aislin forcefully objected, "I would have never chosen a life different than the one you have given me. I could not have asked for a better father."

Caoine's mind filled with flashbacks, of a child, protesting his abandonment while being carried away across the Capall plain. She opened her mouth to protest these gestures were not deserved, but the words froze in her wounded heart.

Korah observed every nuance in the woman's response. He also watched Riordan continue to be oblivious to everything except Aislin, relived that his infatuation with the maiden blinded him to the truth of his blood relationship with the woman in their midst. He said nothing about Caoine's familial resemblance because she clearly desired to keep this hidden. Unsure of the woman's intent, and not wishing to cause further hurt to the lad's fragile heart, he honored her silent wishes.

Korah also observed the warfare in Caoine's face. Among the many battles she faced, a burning desire to embrace Riordan. She also seemed to fear his possible anger or rejection. He watched carefully as she opened her mouth to reply to Ragnhildr, but pain choked the words in her throat.

Then Aislin stood and offered her hand to Caoine, so that she might lead the lady to their shared quarters. This act of perfect timing relieved the woman of the need to say anything in response to Ragnhildr's request.

Caraig stretched and yawned, "A good meal after a hard day always makes me nod off, think I'll turn in." He got up and walked away from the cooking fire, followed by Mereah. Suddenly a light came on in the Dun Weapon Master's head and he blurted out, "Hey, I just realized, has anyone else noticed how much our new cook lady looks like Rio ..."

WHAP! Mereah slapped the back of the Dun captain's thick head, "OOWW!!, what'd yuh do that for yuh great oaf?"

Korah strained to listen as the Rapha` Prince made his best attempt to explain why no one else was calling attention to similarities of their guest's appearance to Riordan. Quickly casting a glance Riordan's way, he was relieved his young page kept his attention focused on Aislin's back as she slipped into her tent.

Early the next morning, two hours before sunrise, Caoine backed out through the flaps of the tent she'd shared with Aislin. Relieved the camp was all still sound asleep, she stealthily crept between snoring bodies sleeping by the fire. After getting a short way past the faint light of the glowing coals, she paused to look up at the quarter moon shining through broken clouds. "Sickle moon," She murmured.

She was abandoning her son. Once more for his protection... but this time almost hurt worse than the first.

The conflict of her emotions forced her to look back, then to her shock, she saw the dark outline of a man standing a few feet away, watching her.

Korah's voice spoke softly, but with a force that would not allow refusal, "Why do you hide your identity from the boy?"

Korah felt the torment of emotion as Caoine struggled to respond, "Years ago, faced with the prospect of my son starving to death, I delivered him to his father's care. He extracted a vow that I would never reveal myself as his mother or have contact with him. Beyond that, El has placed my son in company of the great lords of our people. If the truth were known about who I am... some would try to use this knowledge against him. For his sake, once more I break my own heart."

The answer seemed to satisfy the captain, and his response indicated her answer was close to what he anticipated, "Lady, I have given this matter a great deal of thought. You cannot return to Joktan, only whispers and voices of torment await you there. I also fear to hazard your safety by bringing you on this quest. So, I hoped I could impose on you to aid me in another matter. This is Cailin." Korah led an older horse into view. "At the start of our quest, this mare was needed by your son, but her services are no longer required. I fear the journey ahead may be too arduous and it is my wish she be returned to my home rather than suffer the hardships of the coming journey. I hoped you might be persuaded to return her to my farm a few days ride to the west. I took the liberty to pack ample provisions for the journey."

"My lord, I know not the way, and I have never..."

Korah quickly answered her objections as though somehow, he had rehearsed this conversation in his head, "You will not need to know how to control her, she has never lost a rider. As to knowing the way, she knows it well. Simply allow her to follow her nose. Once you arrive in a few days, give this note to my steward. I employ a few maidens to provide meals and shelter for my household, but I have long needed a lady to manage them in their tasks. I hoped you would help oversee my home until our return?"

"My lord, the only house I have ever managed is now desolate."

"Lady, I risk much in this request, but only from the men in camp who have already sampled of your culinary expertise. The thought of going back to Caraig's cooking may spark a revolt. I also know that any person, male or female that has chosen so selflessly for most of her life, is the most qualified person I know to aid the steward in my absence. I have delayed you already long, and soon the whole camp will begin to stir; lady, will you grant my urgent request?"

Caoine, simply nodded, and accepted Korah's help mounting the mare, "When should I look for my lord's return?"

"It is my hope to be home in a few weeks, and Riordan with me. I have chosen to be his redeemer, and adoptive father, out of the respect I owe the lad's grandfather – and for the love I already feel for the boy. And m' lady, when we return, perhaps together we can find a way, to reveal your identity. It would bring healing to your son's heart."

Tears started welling in the woman's eyes, so Korah said no more. Instead, he smiled gently, before giving a lite slap to the rump of the old mare, sending them both on their way. So much more needed to be said, that would need wait for another day.

iordan recognized all too well the next stage of the journey. The expedition's path would soon merge with the route used by his father and grandfather leading to the mountains of Irijah. Searching for wild horses, they'd made the same trip late last spring. He watched the mountains slowly draw closer with mixed emotions. Brónach, filled most of the memories of the place. Granite peaks stood there as grave markers of loss; grim reminders that he still mourned for his grandfather, and that he couldn't even return to confirm his passing.

Riordan and Korah rode beside Jireh, bringing up the rear-yet again, "I'm having some strange experiences as of late," Korah said softly. "If I focus on Aella, I can visualize the world through her eyes. We have rode together for almost eighteen years, yet for the first time I can truly say a bond is formed - and it grows."

Jireh tugged on his beard thoughtfully for a moment before responding, "So Mereah's fireworks are not the only evidence of the restoration of dominion gifts? By the way lad, have you experienced anything unusual in your travels with Sorcha?"

"Well yes, now that you mention it, he hasn't kicked, bit, or thrown me in the mud, *lately*."

Korah laughed, "I don't think that's quite what Jireh meant son."

Jireh continued, "What I meant is that creation gifts are being restored, at least to your companions. Mereah didn't suddenly become a fire-breather. The Rapha's creation gift give them dominion over heat and flame. Korah is experiencing a special bond with his horse. We suspect that your bearing the Riail dlí may have triggered this effect."

"Riordan..." Korah hesitated as if the next topic made him uncomfortable. "It's still not safe to mention any of this to Ragnhildr, or to reveal you possess the Riail dlí. As chief adviser for the King's defense, he must not perceive you as a threat."

"But I'm not a threat!" the young page protested.

"Of course, you're not!" Jireh responded, "But until the Irial Captain comes to know you as we do, he might perceive you to be. You must understand lad, if a person believes something to be true, they will *act* on what they believe, whether it be true or not. If a warrior like Ragnhildr believes you're a threat to his chosen sovereign, his honor will require him to take action. The commander is wiser than most, but rare is the man who takes time to truly examine what he believes."

Riordan hesitated, as though what he was about to ask made him slightly uncomfortable, "Jireh, not to change the subject, but I've wanted to ask; in my combat with the

Anak, he managed to wrest the Riail dlí from me – he used the blade against me. He sought to take off my limbs at first, to torture me. Failing this, he sought to remove my head."

"What?" Korah asked. "I've yet to hear this tale. You mean to say, the Yara blade struck you multiple times, to no effect?" Korah asked incredulously.

"Oh, it had an effect, one of the effects however the Anak couldn't comprehend," Jireh replied. "The Riail dlí is a two-edged sword. That anyone would forge a weapon that heals even as it wounds would never occur to his dark mind."

"But that's what has me confused Jireh. You told me the blade heals, but only if the person struck is innocent."

"And you feel far from innocent, is that what troubles you?" Jireh asked. When Riordan nodded, Jireh went silent for a time to give the matter further thought. "It may be lad, that the suffering you have endured in life, has purified your heart, as though you have been passed through flame."

After a moment's thought the young Rohi responded, "But surely there are many who have suffered in life. Are they then also judged innocent?"

Korah looked over at Jeshurun's Shophetim and grinned, while Jireh laughed softly, "The Riail dlí is a two-edged sword lad, but so is your wit. Likewise, your discernment; wisely have you been chosen. Forgive me, if my speculations seemed to somehow imply I had a factual answer, for I do not. I only know this, the Riail dlí means Rule of Law, and Yahweh the blade's Creator is Himself ruled by the laws He established. Since the blade's nature is to judge and heal the innocent, the only thing that I know to be true is that the Riail dlí has judged you to be innocent.

"It is *not* speculation on my part, however, to say that suffering can indeed have a purifying effect on the heart and soul. But *only* if the pain is given to El for healing. Unyielded pain and suffering can also become bitterness - turn a heart dark with spite. The One whose name is truth is also named Redeemer. That which was intended for your hurt, and destruction, has been redeemed. Even now it works for your perfection. Never forget lad, redemption is salvation working backward, changing not the history of events, but their impact on the heart."

Searching for a place to make camp, they passed the box canyon Riordan's family used as a corral for captured horses. The rohi paused to look longingly past the horse gate and toyed with the idea of riding as far as the waterfall and pool. Ged, riding a pony came along side and followed his gaze up the canyon, "Got to hand it to yuh boy, Ah sure got snookered in our little trade up there. Did I tell yuh I got nothing for all those horses I bought from yer family?"

"Don't you mean stole?"

"Well now, mighty harsh words son. I admit me methods were a bit rough, but ye got good coin for those critters, and in the end, I didn't get a penny. It was that brute of ah stallion it was. Do you know he managed ta find us after we exited from the caves-miles south from here? We were headed for the plain. One night, that black devil charged through our camp, knocked down the picket line, and ran off all those mares and young stuff. Once loose, no sense in our chasing 'em, we knew weren't nary ah chance of catching 'em on foot."

"Serves you right, I got a beating because you took them horses."

Ged looked at Riordan thoughtfully, "Well, we got paid back so to speak? After we lost the horses, pride wouldn't let me go back empty-handed, so we went back in and through those caves. That's when I found the dagger. It's also when I lost all the lads. I surely do miss those boys."

"I'm sorry about your loss, but I sure hope you haven't just led me back into another pack of trouble."

"I won't lie to yuh son, I never figured ta make it back alive... I was sceer'd, that's a fact. The pack yer running with now though, I've ah feelin' there isn't much they can't handle."

At that moment the stallion screamed a challenge from across the broad meadow. The big black was there, shaking his mane and tearing up fragile earth with sharp hooves. Sorcha reared in response and issued a challenge of his own. Caught off guard, Riordan tumbled over the white stallion's rump and dumped unceremoniously into the turf. If not for Korah who managed to intercept Sorcha, the two horses would likely have engaged in combat on a small rise nearby. Riordan, red-faced from shame clambered to his feet, while the cavalrymen worked frantically to secure their own mounts and pack animals.

Korah had to drag Sorcha back, because he still insisted on meeting the black's challenge, "Hardest thing about riding a stallion son, is they will want to fight over breeding rights. Sorcha has never been gelded; sorry lad, that makes him harder to control at times."

Ged, from his pony's back, quietly stated matter-of-factly, "Told yuh, that 'orse is a black-hearted devil."

Korah looked appraisingly in the black's direction, "I have no idea about the color of his heart, he's a stallion doing what stallion's do, seeking to further his bloodline. I'll say this for him; may be the most magnificent horse I've ever seen, with the possible exception of your Esh lad, in his younger days."

In another two hours they were pitching camp on the far side of the valley. Caraig, having resumed kitchen duties, was once again catching an ear-full about his cooking, "Look yuh dumb louts, I didn't send the lady away, that would be Korah's doings, so if yuh don't like it, grouse all yer want to him!"

All eyes were suddenly on the Calvary Captain, who stammered a moment as he composed a response to the camp's fury, "Lads, you saw the poor lady, she was so fragile, a gentle breeze could break her. Except we're not headed into a gentle breeze, more like an ill-wind or a black storm. None of us could live with ourselves if anything should happen to her. Besides, Caraig isn't such a bad cook." Korah then gazed down into his bowl, "Well, what do you know? He managed to put some fresh meat in my soup."

Mereah peeked over the Horse Master's shoulder, "Well lookey there, there *is* fresh meat in his bowl. So fresh, peers to me it's still alive. What's that critter doing in there?"

"I'm not much of a swimmer mind you," Korah replied. "but looks like a back-stroke to me."

Caraig shook his stir-spoon at everyone who laughed at the oft-told jest, "Now don't be blamin' me fer that. It's yer jokes, not me cooking that's drawing flies."

"Quiet down, everyone!" Mereah commanded, "Caraig does us all a great service by his cooking!"

"There, yuh see?" the Dun Commander barked. "Listen to yer prince. Can't believe I'm saying this, but he's finally makin' sense."

"Aye," Mereah quipped, "A great service indeed, I just witnessed three flies completely vaporized by fumes over the cooking pot."

A stern Ragnhildr stormed into the circle gathered around the fire, glaring disapprovingly at all the men howling with laughter. "Must I remind you that we are now at the outer limits of Moriah's borders, and if any of our people's enemies are to be found within a hundred leagues, they are all alerted to our presence by this cacophony of stupidity!"

All the men were falling over themselves while wiping smiles and laughter tears from their faces, while suddenly remembering things they needed to be doing - someplace else. One of those slinking away in the confusion was the Dun Adventurer, "Not you Mr. Ged, if you please. Time to come clean." Ragnhildr pronounced bluntly, "Aislin and I were just exploring to the end of this valley. In a few miles we must either backtrack, go over a high mountain pass - likely filled with snow, or go underground into a cave system. Would you be so kind as to tell us what option we should expect?"

Ged stopped in his tracks, and his back went stiff, "Well Cap'n, I know'd we'd get to it sooner or later, we'll be going in the caves."

Mereah gave a low whistle. All the officers sat down and glared at Ged as he slowly turned around. Ragnhildr murmured, "Did you give thought to having one of the Rapha` in our party, or a centaur?"

"Oh, they'll fit... least I *think* they will, the entrance is the tight spot. But yuh have to admit cap'n, twasn't my doing to bring such large folks along. The king said the 'orse lads, Irial, and some of me own folk. I already knew 'orses would fit, seeing's how I'd done it once before."

"Are Bearach's Wards in those caverns?" Korah asked pointedly.

"Well, I expect no harm will come from my sayin', no... no they're not. The caves are a short-cut yuh might say. Without 'em we'd have to travel a couple hundred leagues around mountains and such. There be dangers from the Dagon going south, maybe worse dangers to the north... trying to pass the Mothar Crann an all."

"What now? Booger men haunted forest legends?" Caraig scoffed.

"No, it's not just legend, "Jireh warned, "those woods are warded. No one is welcome, and the penalty for trespass is death."

"Jireh," Ragnhildr inquired, "Could you guide Mereah through a pass over the mountains?"

"In another five months yes, we could make it, but this is late fall. All that rain drenching everyone on the Capall plain, in the high places fell as several feet of new snow. We'd never..."

A now familiar scream interrupted the Shophetim, and brought everyone to their feet, "The black... he's after the mares!" Korah shouted. He grabbed Riordan's arm and pulled him along as he ran to where the stock was all picketed. Heedless of the low light, they ran stumbling several times over unseen roots or rocks. They arrived too late. The mares were already scattered. Cavalrymen were running everywhere, trying to salvage whatever they could from the situation. Korah pulled Riordan around to where he could establish eye contact, "Look after Sorcha lad, I'll help with the mares."

Sorcha was picketed apart from the others. Riordan found him yanking so hard on his line that he was in danger of breaking his own neck. His first attempt to reach the white stallion's halter resulted in his getting knocked flying. As he picked himself up, he heard a challenge scream from behind. He turned just in time to see the big black rear to full height and send its deadly hooves flying. Sorcha responded in kind and the young armor-bearer found himself caught between two warriors, set on deadly combat. Riordan dived, narrowly escaping getting caught in a furious crossfire. In this life and death contest Riordan fought against his own overwhelming sense of panic and replaced it with concern for Sorcha. For one thing the black was larger and heavier, plus the white stallion was still bound by a tether. As many times as

Riordan had joked about hating the horse, at a moment of possible loss he understood just how much the stallion meant to him. He also realized if he didn't do something–*fast*, Sorcha could be seriously hurt. Heedless of the danger, without time to think of anything else, he ran back between the combatants and screamed, "Stop!!"

The two stallions almost fell over from shock. Riordan felt something, some power, flow out with his command. Despite this, the young armor-bearer felt almost as shocked as the horses. They obeyed! Walking closer to the black waving his arms he shouted, "Get out of here." Biggest surprise yet, the stallion fled. The mares freed from their pickets, followed obediently in his wake. The whole camp was left in chaos. The one bright spot; Aella pulled up short, turned and trotted back looking for her master.

Riordan heard footsteps approaching from behind. Turning, he recognized Korah, despite the failing light. "That was foolish lad, you could have easily been killed. I admit to being a mite puzzled though, no way would I have thought that black could be turned. Definitely not by simply shouting at him. I know it would have been a shame to kill such a magnificent stallion, but if I had to choose between him or you… I think we'd all rather keep you around. Why didn't you draw your sword? When stallions set their mind to fighting, they're blinded by rage, not much short of killing one of them will stop it. Even Sorcha might have killed ya lad."

Riordan looked at his mentor rather sheepishly, "Well, I didn't really think about it at all, I just reacted. But if I had thought about it, I'm not sure I would have done anything different. Nothing could bring me to harm the black. But I... " Riordan started to tell Korah about the power he felt flow from him when he commanded the stallions but thought better of it.

"I know in a crisis if a man stops to think it may be too late to act. Acting without thinking can also get a man in trouble, and it's difficult to discern the difference sometimes. With experience, you'll learn to keep cool under pressure, and so react quickly while still thinking clearly. Meanwhile we need to decide what we're going to do, the stallion drove away all the mares, except Aella." The mare trotted up and nuzzled Korah as he said this. The captain rewarded her with a bite of carrot and a kiss to her soft nose. "We have a few geldings left, and Ged's pony to use as pack animals."

"It's already dark," Riordan replied, stating the obvious, "Are we going after them tonight?"

"No lad, we may not go after them at all. Winter's coming on and that will mean snow in this high valley. If we take the time to attempt recapture, we risk becoming stranded here for the winter."

Ged and the captains were waiting at the fire as they approached, by the heat of the conversation it was easy to ascertain a meeting had already started.

"I've had dealings with the black devil before, I already told yuh!" Ged snarled. "Me and my lads were driving some mares from these mountains in the spring. He found us before reachin' the Dun hills. Drove off every 'orse we had; I'd paid good coin for em too."

Ragnhildr watched Korah and Riordan approach the fire and asked mildly, "Korah, do we have any mounts or pack animals left at all? Aislin and I lost our mares. A huge loss, both were fine animals."

Korah responded, "We've only Riordan's stallion, my mare Aella, a pony and a couple geldings. The geldings were pack horses, we can't use to retrieve the mares without first breaking them for riding. That'd take a couple days we don't have. It might be as long as a week or more to get even a few of our mares back."

"I understand," Ragnhildr turned to address Caraig. "How difficult will it be to carry our provisions with only a few pack animals?"

The evening's events put the Dun Commander in a dark mood, "The Dun among us can carry more than their weight, can't speak for the Irial or Capall. The 'orse lads have had animals doin' their work so long, likely we'll end up havin' to carry 'em on *our* backs as well as their gear." Then, with a glint in his eye, he turned to give Mereah a little dig, "Course, our young prince here, if he's not singing moonshine for the Dagon... I'd dare say he might make a decent beast of burden."

The young Rapha` looked up and grinned, "Aye, pullin' Caraig's fat out of the fire so many times has made me pretty strong."

"What fat?" Caraig growled while thumping his protruding stomach, "This is all bulging muscle!"

"I think he meant the fat in your head." Korah quipped quietly.

Ragnhildr cut off quickly any opportunity for Caraig to respond, "Well that settles it then. We don't have time to spend recapturing our horses, perhaps on a return trip next spring. Leave the heaviest equipment such as the tents behind. Divide the remaining gear among all the soldiers, officers as well; we leave at first light."

As the meeting broke up Mereah suggested while walking away, "We could always leave cooking gear behind, Caraig wasn't putting it to good use anyway."

"Good point Mereah," Korah replied, "Don't need a heavy iron pot just to burn or destroy what is otherwise perfectly good food."

Riordan wasn't sure if it was instinct, or just years of experience dealing with the Dun Chieftain, but Korah ducked just as an iron pan flew over the crouched captain's head.

Chapter Seven

"A certain amount of opposition is a great help to a man. Kites rise against, not with, the wind. Even a head wind is better than none. No man ever worked his passage anywhere in a dead calm."

John Neal

Korah and Riordan led Sorcha and Aella into the entrance of the passage that promised to be a long road in the dark, "See there?" Ged chimed in, "The horses can make it simply by lowering their heads."

Jireh, unable to contain his skepticism growled, "My horse parts are the size of a heavy war horse, not a light cavalry mount. I'll be scraping my torso half the journey, even with my human half completely bent over. *And*, I might add, under no circumstances does a centaur crawl."

"I am physically capable of getting on my knees and crawling," Mereah added, "However as the crown-prince of Moriah I should never have to stoop so low, no pun intended."

"I know yer not that proud yuh great oaf, and taint really any other choice, unless yuh want to sludge through deep snow and freezing cold, by going over the mountain, rather than under it."

"I'm a son of Rapha` my friend, I am not daunted by cold, neither I suspect is Jireh, who calls these mountains home."

"Yuh heard what Ged said, the passage is larger a quarter-mile in. Besides, going over the top will take several days longer; days we don't have." Then Caraig decided to try and use shame where reason didn't seem to be working, "What's the real problem? A great lout like yerself afraid of the dark?"

"He's afraid of becoming a cork." Jireh responded shortly.

"A cork? What's that supposed to mean?"

"What our Shophetim is trying to tell you my diminutive friend," Mereah replied, "Is that neither of us desires to become corks stuck in bottlenecks made of stone"

"Aye," Jireh added, "Whichever one of us brings up the rear of this expedition, should they get stuck, and it proves impossible to move forward, no one will be behind to pull us back out."

Caraig rolled his eyes and made a casual gesture with his hand, "Nothin' to fret about, if that be all that worries yuh, I'll bring up the rear, carryin' rope. Taint seen a bottle yet I can't uncork. Now let's get going."

True to his word after a brief pinch in the entrance, the tunnel opened into a larger, more spacious cavern. Ged sat in the middle of the room, rummaging through a large rucksack, pulling out three curious-looking boxes. "I've only three of these lamps, and not nearly as much oil as I'd like, treat it as valuable as gold. Lots of things can kill a man in here. Losing light the surest."

Ged handed the company's lone torch to Riordan and bent over and attached one of the box's to a bracket that went around his boot just above the ankle. Igniting a small twig from the torch the Dun adventurer lit a short wick in the lamp. It cleverly focused a small beam of light a few inches in front of his boot. Handing the other two boot lamps to Ragnhildr, Ged briefly instructed, "You'll want these lamps in the middle of the line and with the last man. Spect only the Dun will have the necessary brackets for em."

Then addressing the whole company Ged called out, "Not a lot of light, so keep close, eyes open, mouths shut. Sound has a way a being amplified in these tunnels. Tain't any need for announcin' our being here."

Now looking at Riordan, their guide spoke softly, "Douse the torch lad, it'll burn out quicker'n lamps, an we might be wantin' it later."

Having delivered his instructions Ged started for the opening on the other side of the cavern. Receiving an affirming nod, the young page took Sorcha's lead and fell in line right behind Ged. Korah then Ragnhildr and Aislin came next with the Capall soldiers leading the geldings used as pack animals. Mereah, and Jireh followed the Dun soldiers, while Caraig, as promised acted as rear guard.

Riordan pulling Sorcha's lead stayed right on Ged's heals, focusing on the small amount of light shining at the Dun's feet. The almost complete darkness was the least of his worries, however. Adolescent hormones were working up all manner of anxiety over an entirely different problem. Since the expedition got started, he'd felt as though if he didn't talk with Aislin soon, he would die. Adding to the frustration was his absolute certainty the Irial shieldmaiden didn't even know he was alive. That fear convinced the lad, if he *did* talk to her, he likely would die from embarrassment or the pain of rejection. Ignorance of his existence seemed the best the young rohi could hope for. His fear of speaking with Aislin stemmed from a grim certainty that she regarded him with the utmost contempt.

In moments the passage grew smaller again so that the small amount of lamplight brought the cavern ceiling and walls into shadowed view. While Riordan never actually needed to duck his head, he knew Sorcha was forced to hang his. Rumblings from the back and Caraig's feigned anger told him Mereah was not liking the cramped conditions.

"Does the passage ceiling get any lower further on Ged?" Korah whispered anxiously.

"No, it's as I told yuh cap'n, a bit cramped but the centaur and giant shouldn't have much trouble. Actually, this isn't the part I'm worried about at all."

"I'm not finding that answer reassuring," Ragnhildr warned. "Is there something you haven't told us about yet? Something worse?"

A low chuckle made it clear the Dun adventurer found all the misgivings of the party amusing, "Now, what'cha say we cross the bridges as we get to em, eh?"

Ragnhildr objected once more, "You do realize if something happens to *you* in these caverns it seems likely the rest of us will never find our way out again?"

"Aye Commander," Ged grinned in the dark. "Sort-ah like insurance fer me yuh might say. Probably shouldn't allow anythin' to happen tah me."

They walked on in silence for a spell when Riordan suddenly stumbled and reached out to the passage sidewall to regain his balance. Amazed, he realized that rather than being rough, the walls were smooth as glass, "What manner of rock is this?"

It was Korah who responded, "Obsidian lad, my guess is that this passage is actually a volcanic lava tube."

"Aye cap'n," Ged interjected. "But no sign of an eruption for at least a thousand years. Still, should the mountain get angry we'd be in a real tight spot to be sure."

Riordan grew more and more puzzled as he walked along in the dark, despite fear of revealing his ignorance he finally asked, "What's a volcano?"

Ged's guffaw was muffled somewhat by the tight passage, "What? Yuh mean to tell me you don't have volcanos on daddy's farm?"

Korah checked Ged's mirth with a more soothing response, "No shame in not knowing that lad, I've never seen one myself, only heard the tale. It's said to be a portal into the bowels of the earth. Eruptions spew fire and melted rock for miles, destroying everything in its path."

"Is this the reason for all the secrecy Ged?" Ragnhildr asked, "Because you knew we'd never agree to a journey through such a place?"

Ged stopped and turned to face the angry eyes burning holes in his back, his smirk barely visible in the shadows, "It's like I said, if yuh knew where we were headed, I ain't rightly needed am I? I'll admit yer might be more hesitant if'n yuh knew everything that's waitin' for us up ahead. Not ta worry though, nothing worse than a walk in the dark - for a day or so anyway."

Ragnhildr's reply sounded grim, "I realize you meant to be reassuring, what I *heard* however sounded like a dire warning."

After about an hour the passage opened up again allowing Mereah and Jireh to walk upright. After several more hours, the flame in Ged's boot lamp flickered and went out. It took just a moment for him to feel around in his pack and refuel. He then passed the oil flask back to the Dun warrior who had the second lamp so it could be filled. They then walked in the dim lamplight, measuring time by the increasing ache in their muscles. They marched until Riordan thought his feet were wore down to stubs before their guide called for a halt. Everyone managed to fit into a small cavern where Ged growled, "Get some rest."

Looking around in the dim light all the young page could see on the cave floor was gravel, shale, and broken rock, so he asked, "Where?"

"Why for everyone else right here. But for *you* lad, there's a feather bed in the palace bedroom down the hall." Ged mocked. "Would yer highness like a bath before he retires?"

"Very funny." Riordan mumbled as he searched for any place that wasn't sharp rock to unroll his bedroll.

"And put those lamps out," the surely Dun growled, "We'll be lucky the oil lasts past these caves. Don't need light ta sleep."

When the last lamp was extinguished, Riordan experienced true darkness for the first time. Holding his hand an inch from his face, he couldn't see it. This wasn't the dark of night, when clouds hide moon or stars, this was the complete absence of light. He imagined being lost and alone in the pitch black. The thought was terrifying.

Sorcha nickered softly, and so he crawled close and slept leaning against the stallion's flank, drawing comfort from the horse's warmth.

In what seemed to be only five minutes Riordan was jostled roughly and pulled to his feet. As Sorcha scrambled to get to his feet also, Korah tossed the young page a piece of salt pork and a hard tac biscuit, "Not much of a breakfast I know son, and you'll need to eat as we move along. But I agree with Ged on this point. Without a lot of oil for the lamps, we need to get through these caves as quick as we can."

The whole company was ready to move in minutes and followed Ged out of the chamber down another passage. The darkness seemed to cast a spell of depression on the whole company. Even the normally gladsome Mereah moved without comment or playful barbs aimed at Caraig. After about an hour Riordan noted a red glow, a light at the end of the tunnel. Soon the light grew stronger and the passage warmer.

Korah with a slight note of concern asked Ged, "What's the light ahead?"

Ragnhildr was more direct, "If you brought us inside an active..."

"Relax Commander, I've no death-wish." Hissed Ged. "There's a river of fire, up ahead, and soon we'll be able to douse the lamps, for a short while. The river is the least of our worries."

"What's that mean?" Korah interjected.

"Yuh'll see soon enough cap'n."

As the glow got brighter, their eyes were forced to adjust. The corridor temperatures also rose significantly. In another five minutes they reached the end, with the passage floor falling shear away and the ceiling raising a hundred feet or more. A thick wooden beam was suspended in a timber framework and reached over the edge supporting a pully and thick rope.

Riordan started to walk to the edge to look over when Ged's arm shot out to block his way, "Careful boy, take a tumble here an' you'll never fix me another coney stew."

Korah gently pulled the armor-bearer back, then he and Ragnhildr took his place looking over the ledge. The passage ended near the top of an immense cavern wall. Past the opening there was a fifty to sixty feet drop before reaching a narrow stone shelf about three feet wide. Past this narrow shelf the rock face fell away again another fifty feet before turning into an angled scree and ash incline. This slope ran steeply down to a long crack at the very bottom of the massive cavern. A red glow filled the chamber with garish light. The sharp fume of sulfur and brimstone spoke of legends and nightmares.

Ragnhildr spoke softly but his tone hinted of veiled menace, "Ged, this had better not be a trap."

"No trap cap'n. We gotta lower down by the rope an' pully here to the narrow ledge there. By following the ledge along the wall, a hundred feet or so you'll come tah another passage out of the chamber."

After a few seconds looking over the situation, Korah gave Ged an angry glance, "Shimmying down a rope will be fine for men and gear, how in El's name do you intend to lower our horses?"

"Now cap'n, I admit it's never been tried, but I expect a harness under an 'orse's belly an' the Rapha` holdin' the other end of the rope, and the critters will be fine. That's not what I'm worried about see..."

"Jireh," Ragnhildr spoke coolly, "He's not sure the timber structure will hold Jireh."

"Sure, and for good reason, he's as big as a small giant and a heavy war 'orse combined." Ged complained.

Korah grabbed the Dun's cloak at the throat, "You might have mentioned this little snag before now!"

"It's as I said, 'e wasn't with us when we set out!"

Korah threw Ged back against the passage wall. Caraig worked his way forward and groused, "What's the hold up?" Korah used a bent index finger to indicate the sheer drop. Looking over the rim, Caraig became furious and growled, "Why you treacherous little..." Ragnhildr grabbed the Dun Weapons Master's cloak to hold him back as he sought to throw Ged over the edge.

"That won't help!" Ragnhildr hissed.

"Aye, it won't," Ged snarled, "And it's more dangerous than yuh know. On my way-out last time, thought I heard somthin', down in the crack where the fire flows. Somthin' lives in there, an' I'm thinkin we don't want it tah know we're here see? Yuh have got tah tell yer boys we gotta get down to the ledge extra quiet. Now cap'n, I know it'll be nip an' tuck, but my lads an I made it, and it's too late in the year for the high passes. Only other way around is up the river and that takes us right along the Mothar Crann. This is 'bout the only way."

"I'm guessing this mechanism is used for lowering and raising gear?" Ragnhildr asked. "Is it strong enough to lower horses, or one of the Irijah?"

"My people build far stronger than needs be commander, it should hold... but on the safe side the giant an' centaur need ta go last," the adventurer whispered a bit sheepishly.

Korah grabbed Ged by the throat of his cloak and pressed him once again back against the obsidian wall, "We're not talking about some luggage accidently going over the edge. Mereah and Jireh are the Crown Prince and the Shophetim of Jeshurun, you'll need to do a lot better than *it should*. Caraig, what's your opinion? Will this beam hold Jireh's weight?"

Caraig walked over to examine the rope, pully, and support mechanism, started to respond, but didn't. Instead, he slowly drew a long knife from his belt.

Riordan was puzzled as to why Caraig drew his blade, then his eyes moved to where his mentor stood gripping Ged's throat. Somehow in the exchange of threats, their guide managed to pull a dagger and had the point against the captain's ribs. Slowly his hand moved to the hilt of the Riail dlí.

"That won't be necessary lad," Korah spoke calmly. "Ged here wants to live as badly as I do, and I think he knows if he sticks me, I'd still manage to throw him over the ledge. Caraig, your expert opinion please, will the mechanism hold the weight of Mereah and Jireh?"

"It'll hold I tell yuh," Ged squeaked. "But if'n it doesn't I'm not tah blame, I didn't ask yuh to bring a giant or centaur along, that was yer own doing, not mine see?"

Ragnhildr walked over and stood next to Korah, speaking softly into Ged's ear, "When we get out of these caves Ged, we're having a long talk. No more secrets. We need to know what *other* surprises lay ahead. *All* of them. You can let him go now Korah. Caraig, again, what's your opinion on the strength of that beam?"

After a few moments of yanking on ropes and testing the crossbeam, Caraig growled, "Pretty certain it'll hold Mereah's weight. Jireh's? Maybe, maybe not. If not, Korah will have to be quick throwin' Ged over the edge, because I intend to roast our friend here real slow over the lava flow. Simply throwing him over the ledge would be far too quick."

"Amusing as that may be," Ragnhildr murmured, "We dare not hazard Jireh's safety, we must turn back and find another way."

"Well now commander," drawled Ged, "Feared yuh might say that, but it's too late *now* don't cha see?"

Korah savagely turned on their guide once more, "Too late for what?"

Ged flashed a toothy food-stained smile, "Tah go back. Yuh see cap'n, we've only got enough oil tah go forward. We're more'n halfway through, with only nuff oil to make it through tah the other side."

"Looks like we've all been taken Ragnhildr," the deep voice of Jireh chimed in. "Give him credit though, he laid his plans well. Without light, going back is certain death, forward is only *maybe* death, likely mine. If we survive all this commander, make this Dun explorer a general, he's a brilliant strategist."

"It's too much risk, we'll find another way around the mountains." Ragnhildr insisted.

"Even *if* we somehow got out, we still risk being trapped in heavy snows," Jireh argued. "Without enough light to get us out of the caverns however, there isn't any hope in finding another way. He's got us like fish in a bucket so we're wasting time arguing. Mereah and I will go last after the horses and gear."

Caraig snarled, "I'll go last, if somethin' goes wrong somebody will need to be up here holding a rope to keep yuh from falling."

"I don't doubt your strength my friend, but there's nothing up here to brace against except smooth rock. It's just as likely I'd pull you over with me. But," and here Jireh took one end of the thick hemp rope and tied it around Ged just under his arms, "I intend to have the satisfaction of holding the other end of the rope while our friend here makes *his* descent. Korah it's time for you to keep your promise."

Before their scheming guide could utter a word of protest the Calvary Captain threw a screaming Ged off the ledge. Jireh let him free fall for close to fifty feet before stopping the Dun's descent with a hard jerk. The sudden stop sent their guide swinging so that he bounced once or twice off the cavern wall. After slowly lowering the rope through the pully for the last few feet, a trembling Ged crumpled into a heap.

"Oh well done Jireh!" Exclaimed Korah, "But, how on earth did you know when to start tightening your hold on the rope, without looking?"

"Simple my friend, I judged the length of his fall – by the sound of his screams – to be about fifty feet. Did I judge rightly?"

"As only the Shophetim of Jeshurun could," Ragnhildr replied. "I'm afraid our friend isn't in any shape however to untie his end of the rope. I believe he is conscious but recovering from a near heart attack. I'll go check. When I give the line a tug, its ready to retrieve."

Without another word the Irial Captain jumped over the edge grabbing the rope under the pully and sliding rapidly down. Aislin shrieked, "Father!" And rushed to follow.

Korah grabbed the shieldmaiden by her waist preventing her from plunging over the rim, "He's fine lass, see, he's already down. Don't you worry, I'm sending Riordan next to help your father if he needs it, you'll go right after that. After we attach a line and lower you down."

Aislin's glare proved that looks really *can* kill. It was her words however, that caused the worst wounds, "You'll not be sending a mere *boy* before me. I am a shieldmaiden of the Irial." With that she likewise jumped, secured the rope and slid down to join her father.

Moments later a tug on the rope signaled for the return of the hemp line. Jireh started pulling the other end back through the pully. Korah, meanwhile, looked back to see the crushed look on Riordan's face. Even in the dim light, it was evident that his hopes (along with his heart) had just been dashed on the rocks.

Before the captain could respond, Mereah's big hand fell on the young page's shoulder to offer his encouragement. "She wasn't there, the day you slew the Anak of Dagon. Not a warrior in Jeshurun who watched you face that demon-spawn would doubt your courage, or *ever* call you a boy. One day, she will know you as we, our Ariel, the lion of Elohim."

Riordan lifted his eyes, seemed to come to a decision, then ran out of Mereah's grasp and dived for the rope. Korah, Caraig and Mereah watched his rapid descent. "He has set his sights high," Mereah murmured.

"Aye," Korah replied, "But he has the heart for it."

Caraig looked down the length of the rope. "What are yuh talking about? Who has the heart for what?"

Korah just looked at the Dun warrior and shook his head.

❧

Everything went off without a snag, for the next several minutes. All the Dun, Capall, and the Irial archers easily negotiated the journey down the rope, as well as what remained of their supplies. A shuttle relay began moving goods along the ledge to the exit passage. The first tense moment however came when attempting to lower the pack horses. Korah wrapped cloth blinders over one of the gelding's eyes, and they placed a makeshift harness on its' underside. But because the pully was attached to a beam reaching three feet out past the edge it wasn't possible to lift the horse off its' feet directly by pulling on the line. As they pulled on the rope it did move the animal close to the ledge but when placing a front hoof out and finding nothing but air the gelding screamed in protest. A mighty heave on the rope by Mereah and a big push from Caraig at the tail (rewarded by a painful kick) and the dark bay was propelled to swing out into the abyss. Screaming with legs flaying the whole way down, the packhorse couldn't find the narrow ledge below to regain its' footing. Anticipating the landing would be an issue, Korah proceeded down before the horses. With the animal so frantic however, he couldn't reach the rope attached to the lift harness and pull the animal back over to the ledge. Finally, the captain took a great risk and jumped to grab the rope just above the makeshift harness and swung a leg over the gelding's back. Something about Korah's presence seemed to calm the bay almost immediately. A couple of Cavalrymen reached out and took his hand and they pulled the calmed but still trembling gelding to safety.

Feeling the familiar signal tug Caraig, Mereah and Jireh once more pulled on the thick hemp rope and harness back up the pully. Recognizing some weight at the end of the rope, it came as no surprise when Korah appeared riding the harness structure as it neared the pully and crossbeam.

"I thought at first it best to wait below and try to calm the horses as they neared the ledge. After witnessing Caraig pushing that poor animal off the cliff I decided things might go easier if I gentled the animals *before* their descent. If it's any comfort to Mereah and Jireh however, I have just proved the rope and beam will hold at least the combined weight of a horse and rider."

"I never claimed to be a horse master, horse master. Nor do I appreciate your coaxing the beast to kick me on the way down!" Caraig growled rubbing his noggin.

"It's alright Korah," Mereah grinned, "Caraig couldn't have been seriously hurt, the kick hit him in the head. However, I am concerned about the poor animal's foot injury?"

"That'd be terrible," Korah replied grinning, "Can't afford to lose a good pack animal."

"Very funny yuh big oaf," Caraig retorted, "But, if the hoof *is* injured, we could always load the creature's packs on yer's and the horse master's backsides. Being beasts of burden is 'bout all the two of yer be good fer anywho."

Having Korah at the start of the animal's descent did indeed prove to be a better solution. He kept the skittish creatures calm while Caraig, Mereah and Jireh gently lifted the animals easing them out under the beam without allowing them to sway or swing too badly.

"Well, friends it's time to face it," Korah mused. "Way I see it, Caraig and I will need to head down next followed by Mereah. If the beam does break, it will be from Jireh's weight, so I'm afraid he needs to make the trip last. We can use the pully and rope to lower our Shophetim from the ledge below."

"Caraig and I will remain and lower Jireh," Mereah murmured, "We have the strength to lower Jireh in harness. If the beam breaks, we will be holding the rope and t'will be up to us to prevent Jireh's fall."

"It's likely if he falls, he'll take the two of you with him," Korah objected, "The floor of this passage is as smooth as glass, you'll have nothing with which to brace yourselves."

"Korah is correct," Jireh stated matter-of-factly, "And I cannot allow the two of you to risk your lives in this manner."

"And we refuse to hazard the life of the Shophetim of Jeshurun." Caraig responded, "It's impossible to prevent Jireh's fall from below should the beam break. From here, there's at least a chance. You're wasting time Horse Master, you need to get down there. I'd also be obliged if we do fall, that you'd throw our treacherous guide down the fire crack."

"Gladly," Korah replied. "But swear to me nothing will be allowed to harm Jireh. There is only so much, I can teach Riordan, he needs the knowledge only the Shophetim of our people can offer."

The Crown Prince replied with a smile, while Caraig almost glared his response, "What'd ya expect?"

While Jireh was being strapped into the leather harness, Korah slid down the length of the rope to the small shelf ledge below. A quick tug on the rope signaled Mereah to pull it back up. As the Calvary Captain watched the hemp rope retreat through the pully Ragnhildr approached to ask, "What's the plan?"

"Mereah and Caraig will lower Jireh in the harness using the pully and beam."

"Is that prudent?" The commander inquired, "Jireh is the heaviest by far, should the beam break..."

"In which case, Caraig and Mereah are the only two persons in all Moriah I'd give even a remote chance of slowing his descent. Excuse me, I need to speak to Riordan."

Walking over to where the young page stood holding Aella and Sorcha's lines, the captain gave his instructions, "Take the horses to the exit passage lad."

Riordan's eyes grew huge with concern, "But if Jireh falls?"

"We have two of the strongest and most determined warriors in all Moriah holding the rope just in case. They will do all they can. Praying for Jireh's safety would be a good thing, however, I know I will be."

Riordan walked Aella along the narrow ledge, as he passed under the pully he paused to look up. Jireh, looking over the edge, spotted the Rohi and waved. The young page refused to even acknowledge the thought his mentor was saying goodbye.

The fire crack, from still further below, cast a red glow through-out the immense cavern. Rising heat caused beads and rivulets of sweat to trickle down the men's faces. More than the heat made the rohi uncomfortable, however. He also discerned a brooding presence of malice rising from the lava shaft. He turned and tensely watched as Jireh prepared to step out into empty air. Ged shuffled with his back plastered to the rock wall and pulled up along-side Riordan to watch the proceedings. "You realize that if anything happens to Jireh," the young man murmured, "There's gunna be a long line of folks looking to throw you into the fire crack."

Then, Jireh stepped off the ledge. The rope stretched tight. The crossbeam immediately started to bend. Then all light fled the chamber, and everything went pitch black.

Chapter Eight

The dwarves of yore made mighty spells,
While hammers fell like ringing bells
In places deep, where dark things sleep,
In hollow halls beneath the fells.

J.R.R. Tolkien

t first Riordan thought the lamps had burned out. With a start, he remembered all the lamps were extinguished to save oil! The light came from the fire-crack, how could that go out?

Then, everything that could go wrong, did. First, a loud snapping sound, which Riordan assumed meant the crossbeam gave way. Next, Jireh's cry of alarm echoed through the chamber as apparently, he went into free fall. Then, they heard sounds of struggle as Mereah and Caraig shouted encouragement to one another as they tried to keep their footing. A moment later Mereah's panicked outburst announced to all, he also had hurtled over the ledge. Then, Riordan heard the screams of a soldier - falling to his death?

Finally, the dark shadows slowly turned to deep blood red. Everyone held their collective breath anxiously awaiting what would be revealed by the gradual return of light. What they saw was astonishing. Jireh dangled on a rope twenty feet above the narrow ledge where the expedition watched, spellbound. Mereah was holding on also, dangling ten feet above Jireh; all eyes followed the rope up where to everyone's dismay – toes over the edge – stood Caraig. The Weapon Master stood holding on, the veins in his neck ready to pop as he refused to let his friends fall.

"Kingdom of Heaven," Ragnhildr uttered softly.

Korah recovered quickly, urging several Capall Calvary to follow as he shouted up to the Dun Weapon Master, "Caraig, let the rope slide down, quick as you dare, we've got to get Jireh clear before Mereah can come off the rope."

Using his hands as best he could to keep from rubbing on the wall as he descended, Jireh was lowered down quickly. As soon as his hooves touched rock, he moved forward to make a landing place for Mereah. Both heroes had their feet on solid rock after a few tense seconds. Fifty feet above, Caraig abruptly sat down and flopped back, almost fainting while releasing a huge sigh of relief.

Also relieved he wouldn't be facing the party's wrath stemming from harm to the Shophetim or Crown Prince, Ged trotted forward and exclaimed, "Never seen nothing like that in all me born days. But who fell? I heard somebody scream that's for sure."

Ragnhildr responded, "I didn't hear a call of fear, as someone falling, but a cry of pain. And the sound came not from above, but from somewhere on the ledge behind us."

Korah looked back towards the warriors that were with him. One of the Dun was missing. A small step brought him closer to the edge, allowing him to look down. A body lay still, a hundred feet below, broken on the rocks. Also there, glaring back at him, a tanniyn, far bigger than any they'd seen in the recent war with the Dagon. Instantly it captured him in a trance. Jireh, still not free from the harness put an arm around the captain and pulled him back. "You should never meet the gaze of a dragon Korah, especially an incredibly old one. We need to get Caraig down with us quickly... it's no longer safe here."

Korah Snapped out of it and sprang into action, "Caraig, you can nap later, we've got to go, NOW! Everyone follow the ledge to the exit passage. Get moving, go, go, while we still can."

Caraig promptly sat up and crawled over to the ledge for a look-see. What he saw startled even him. Further down to the bottom of the chasm, a massive head and the front legs of a tanniyn emerged from the fire crack below. The jaws alone were roughly fifteen feet in length with twelve-to-eighteen-inch spike teeth protruding in an alternating pattern from the closed maw. Horns and spikes covered the scaly monster down to the hand-like appendages tipped by razor-sharp claws. Quickly tying off the rope to what remained of the crossbeam, Caraig slid down to rejoin the others.

"Riordan," Ragnhildr called, "Please get Aislin and the remaining horses to the safety of the tunnel please."

The Shieldmaiden protested loudly, "Father, I am the one that should be protecting him!" Before Riordan could react, the lady burning with resentment, led the pack horses down the narrow path forcing the young armor-bearer to follow her lead. With every step he could feel her anger grow. Soon as the pack animals were in the passage, she whirled around and as an act of defiance hurried back towards her father. Riordan begged one of the cavalrymen to watch the horses as he chased after her.

Moving along a three-foot ledge was complicated by men carrying gear in the opposite direction. The soldiers were in a hurry also, frantically trying to get away from the very place he was trying to get to. Riordan had to admire the way Aislin gracefully weaved her way through while he struggled to keep from being knocked over the edge or smashed against the wall. As a result, he found himself watching in frustration as the shieldmaiden got ever further ahead. A growing sense of panic over the situation was fed by genuine concern for the girl's safety. Plus, he feared Ragnhildr's wrath for failing to keep Aislin out of harm's way. The maiden arrived moments before Riordan, and much to the armor-bearer's relief, no one seemed to notice. This was because of a heated debate between Ged and the company's captains.

"Yuh don't understand, we gotta get that pack!" Ged sounded well beyond panic.

"It's too late, the Tanniyn has already dragged the body along with the pack into the fire crack," Korah yelled back, "And I don't give a rip what's in the pack, it'll do none of us any good if we're dead. But that's what we'd all be if we go down there."

Riordan caught up to Aislin just in time to witness Ragnhildr's icy glare at his daughter, stopping her in her tracks. Too angry to speak, the Irial Captain pointed his arm back toward the cave passage and succeeded in driving the lady back, but only a few steps. Then an angry defiant glare of her own was directed back at her father. Now Ragnhildr's wrathful stare was directed at Riordan instead, proving true the young Rohi's fear that Ragnhildr would blame him for his daughter's stubbornness.

Slipping around the maiden, Riordan drew close to where the captains were standing and watched the creature's movements below. Seeing the dragon for the first time, he realized this one dwarfed the serpent that the Anak of Dagon rode into battle.

The creature's ugly head turned upward as if it studied them even while they peered down at it from above. Stones clattered as it moved suddenly and began to climb the steep slope toward the ledge. The captains all drew

their weapons. So, Riordan also drew forth the Riail dli'
and waited.

Through hooded eyes the Fire Drake watched Elohim's
children with casual interest, satisfied the trap it set had
worked perfectly. The great serpent was old, and beyond
cunning. So old, he was already a great worm in the days
before the First Age ending. So cunning, he was one of the
few creatures to survive the Ages devastation and the
world's breaking. So powerful, his might rivaled the
Watchers who exercised dominion over much of the
planet.

His network of spies actively tracked the party after
their presence was detected the second day of their
journey through the old volcano. He reasoned while they
struggled bringing animals and luggage down from the
upper passage would be the opportune time to strike. His
timing could not have been more perfect. Withdrawing
light at the worst possible moment was only the beginning
of his mischief. Dark arts ensured the crossbeam would
snap, but the fools were only now learning the extent of
their dilemma. Their demise was accomplished by a
simple shove in the dark.

Testing their metal and resolve, he started moving out
of a passage that emerged just above the lava flow. It
pleased him that some of the fools appeared to be
preparing to give battle. He'd not found any willing to
challenge his might for several millennia. Starting up the

slope he prepared to give a quick lesson as to why warriors of far greater might (and wisdom) fled in terror from his approach. Then the drake's dark musings were interrupted when the smallest, and weakest of his foes revealed an ancient power; a blade that might penetrate even his scale armor and spell protections.

Well and good, his prey proved to be more than what first met the eye. He could wait. No need to risk combat against a Yara Blade. That they possessed such a potent talisman was troubling and problematic. His huge, lithe body undulated backward and then slithered into the shelter of its lava tube. The fire worm smiled in his black heart; he'd already taken steps to assure that none of these pathetic children would ever leave his mountain alive.

Ragnhildr was astonished the massive drake retreated without a fight. Why? What caused the ancient worm to flee back down its hole? Chewing on his thoughts about this new development he glanced around at the captains. Then his eyes fell on the beautiful translucent blue blade wielded by the young armor-bearer.

The commander noted that when Korah saw the blade catch his eye, the lad was quietly ordered to sheath the weapon. This only gave Ragnhildr further cause for suspicion. Why attempt to prevent his getting a closer look at the lad's blade? It was past time to have an open discussion about several concerns. Long past time.

Jireh also observed the fire drakes retreat and commented casually, "I'd almost rather the tanniyn had stayed and fought, I'm almost certain we'll see him again, at a time of his choosing and our greatest inconvenience. However, we'd best get moving, I for one do not wish to wait around to see if the worm changes its' mind."

Once all were safely in the exit passage, Ragnhildr challenged Korah, "It's time I had some answers. First, how is it that a Capall Armor-bearer possesses a talisman as powerful as the Riail dlí? Second question; are any of the captains present involved in acts of treason against their king?"

Because of the darkness of the passage, Ragnhildr couldn't see the shock on the faces of this gathering of mighty heroes, but he knew it was there. He could feel it in the depths of emotion emanating from the sounds of their silence. Finally, Jireh's soft deep voice penetrated the shadow, "The answer to the second question is all and none. We all were aware the boy carried the Yara Blade. None of us however are committed to acts of treason against the king. Not unless you're willing to believe the king's son is conspiring to betray his own father.

The answer to the first question is that I presented the blade to the boy. However, the Riail dlí is living, active, *aware*. The *blade* chooses the bearer. In the hands of any but one so chosen, it is a beautiful, but quite ordinary sword. The Riail dlí was presented first to Ruarc, upon his coronation, but it did not reveal its' power to him. The king therefore, chose weapons he thought to be of greater potency. There is no conspiracy in this, a millennium has passed since the Riail dlí chose anyone, including myself."

Ragnhildr spat out his terse response, "I would assume the Shophetim of Jeshurun would understand that by placing the Yara Blade in the hands of a rohi, and a boy at that, he might as well have placed the crown, on his head. These actions would certainly be viewed as treason by the king and so cost the young man his life. Is he aware of his danger?"

Riordan started to answer but a vise-like grip on his arm from Korah warned him to stay quiet, and allow Jireh to respond, "I followed the guidance of Adonai to find the boy. As Shophetim I am not in the habit of questioning directions from my Master. But yes, the implications and possible cost were explained to the Lad. If Adonai is now the boy's Master, it is also Adonai's responsibility to be a shield of protection for him. We saw the evidence of this in his victory over the Anak. Knowing his weakness and poverty, the lad is not too proud to rely on a greater power. It is for this reason the lad is the mightiest warrior in all of Moriah no matter how unlikely that may seem.'

"Ruarc, however, is still Yahweh Elohim's anointed. None here will ever raise a hand against him. If the king repents of his pride, then I believe the lad will replace me as the Shophetim of our people. Then his role will be to support Ruarc, and in time Mereah as the new ruler in Jeshurun."

The Irial Commander allowed a few moments for these new revelations to digest before responding, "Is it safe to assume that the Rapha' Prince's sudden mastery of flame has something to do with the restoration of the Riail dlí into the hands of one anointed to bear the blade?"

Jireh was not at all surprised by Ragnhildr's depth of lore concerning the Yara Blade, so he responded accordingly, "As you guessed, the gifts of Dominion are being restored. It is the reason why when the great stallion, drove off our mares, Korah could call back his own Aella. I believe we all just had another demonstration of this restoration on display from Caraig. Our friend is strong, but strong enough to stop the fall of both Mereah and I? Our combined weight must be at least seven times greater than his. Plus, he was standing on a rock surface as smooth as glass."

"Caraig?" Ragnhildr invited the Dun's response.

"Aye. As Mereah and I were pulled across the stone surface and the great oaf went over the edge, I knowed we were goners for sure, and then, well, somehow out of desperation I drew power and strength from the stone beneath my feet. I went from sliding to becoming cemented in place, a pillar of rock. I just hadn't time to talk to Jireh about what had happened because of all the excitement. But now, here's a question for you – who blew out the lights?"

"That wasn't an ill wind extinguishing lamps, there is abundant natural light emanating from the fissure at the bottom of the cavern." Ragnhildr commented.

"As to that," Jireh replied, "It was an ill wind, that came from the bowels of the great worm itself. A powerful spell of darkness, was used for the concealment of an accomplice."

"Aye," Korah broke into the discourse, "More than just a cast darkness, the wooden beam had help in the breaking. I suspect the Dun warrior didn't stumble in the dark either. He was pushed."

"For what purpose?" Mereah asked, "Why attack just one warrior, when so concealed, an attacker could engage several targets?"

"Because by attacking one he killed us all! That's what I've been trying to tell yuh." Ged shouted.

Caraig growled menacingly, "What in Domhain are yuh talking about? An' it better be worth hearing because I'm about ready to drag yuh back an feed yer sorry carcass to the firedrake."

"They knew how to kill all of us by killing one man. The Dun soldier was carryin' the pack with the last of our lamp oil." Ged shouted.

"How much oil remains?" Ragnhildr asked calmly

Ged's response bordered on being hysterical, "Only what's left in the two remaining lamps!"

"How long before we run out, and how much longer will it take to get through to the other side?" Korah demanded.

"If we use only one lamp at a time, we'll have light for a few hours, maybe close to a day. Tied together, we can keep from getting separated, but we won't make as good a time yuh understand. But it'd take least two full days, with good light. There are several passages openings I've marked to get through, they're like a maze. I don't have a prayer ah finding 'em in the dark. Without light we're as good as dead don't cha see? Without that pack we've no oil, no light, no chance. We've no choice but go after that pack!"

Chapter Nine

onghus the steward found himself staring a beautiful dilemma in the face. She lay asleep on a cot in the back of his master's house. That morning she came charging across the pastures on one of Korah's old, but still prized mares. The unlikely pair just barely managed to stay ahead of a pack of wolves. Both were physically exhausted. Bane Wolves, as they were now called, were larger and more ruthless than the native species. These recent invaders to the Capall planes, had clearly kept the mare running for much of the night. She was frothing at the mouth and her black coat was glistening from the sweat and foam of her exertions. Cailin was far too old for such a trial and might not survive the ordeal.

The woman who called herself Caoine, was likewise spent. Despite several traits common among the Capall, she clearly wasn't a rider. The way she clung to Cailin's back and mane she clearly possessed no idea how to keep her seat. That she remained in the simple saddle was in a greater part due to the efforts of the gentle mare than her skill as a rider.

She claimed to have been sent by Korah himself. He had ample reason to doubt her story, not the least of which was a complete lack of evidence to support it. She'd said she carried a letter from Korah, but that it'd been lost. Her reason for this? The pack of wolves attacked at night, and she'd just enough time to get on the old mares back and flee; her few possessions, including the letter, regrettably, left behind. Clearly the part about the wolves was true enough. What he knew about his master would also be in keeping with her story, Korah frequently adopted stray animals, dogs, cats, birds fallen from a nest, from the time he was a boy. Recently, he followed the same pattern, adopting a teenage boy. But it was the rest of the story he couldn't be sure about. She said a great captain, as she called him asked her to bring back the mare and then stay, taking charge of the kitchen.

That's when the fat hit the fire so to speak. The sneers from the other serving maids started soon after the woman's arrival. Hair hacked short was a universal symbol of a lady of ill-repute. A night-lady ahead of a pack of jealous wives would certainly need to get away quickly to prevent worse than a bad haircut. But the good steward also very much doubted that this frail woman could possibly succeed in stealing a prized mare from a camp of armed men.

Now that she was resting, and sleep smoothed all the lines of exhaustion and terror from her face, he could see at one time the woman was indeed beautiful. He could also see that while malnourished, even desperate, she somehow seemed to him to have always been a lady of worth. He trusted his instincts. He wouldn't have risen to his position of household steward without strong discernment of quality and character. That she'd experienced a great deal of suffering was evident. That she had endured so much pain, gave clear testimony to her strength.

He also saw one more thing, providing the strongest evidence of the truth of her words; with the stress lines eased from her face while resting, he saw the image of Korah's most recent stray, Riordan.

Korah kept his voice deliberately calm, trying to keep the expedition from total panic, "I watched the worm drag the soldier and the pack down that fire crack. We'll find nothing but certain death down that hole."

"Aye," Caraig growled, his brows knit together in concentration, "I've another idea, might be it'll keep us in light for a few hours longer. Could be risky." The beleaguered crew responded with blank stares only, so after a moment the Dun Captain reluctantly continued, "I've a couple metal fire boxes, to keep coals for fire-starter. If we were to go back to the ledge and lower 'em on a bit of chain, might be we can snag some firestone to light our way for an extra hour or so, till the stuff cools. We could save precious oil until it does."

"Not worth the risk," Korah objected. "When isolated, molten rock cools quickly, but until it cools, a metal box would prove too hot to hold."

"Not if the boxes are attached to chain," Caraig countered. "Far as keeping em from cooling, I was countin' on Sir Bellows-breath to help us out. Anybody who can get wet manure to burn in a down-pour, aught to be able to handle it."

Ragnhildr added another suggestion, "If our archers can remove the heads from some of our arrows, we can dip the shafts in the remaining oil and ignite them with the firestones before they get too cool. Perhaps we can buy enough time to allow the lamps to get us the rest of the way through."

"Arrow shafts make lousy torches cap'n, no offense," growled Ged.

"As we've already pointed out, we now have a giant fire-breathing princeling to keep them burning," Caraig responded. "Let's get moving, knowing that worm is in here with us gives me the creeps, sooner we get out the better."

Going out almost to the end of the narrow ledge, they positioned themselves directly over the lava flow. Using links of chain at the four corners of the metal box, they were able to obtain a load of the firestone with the first draw, "There yuh see, easy as getting water from a well."

Caraig said. "Now, just one more and we can hightail it outta here."

But the second draw did not fare nearly as well. When the box lowered into the molten rock, it seemed to catch on something. Even the combined strength of Caraig and Mereah could not pull it free. Then the rope attached to the chain links burst into flames and turned to ash.

"What happened?" Korah asked, a look of surprise on his normally calm exterior.

"I know not," Mereah replied, dumbfounded, staring at his now empty hands. "Somehow, we were prevented."

"We've other worries to deal with," Caraig almost sounded panicked. "I was counting on those chain links to carry the firebox. No way even Sir Dragon's Breath can carry it in his hands."

"What choice do we have?" Mereah asked calmly. He stepped forward and lifted the already red-hot box. Great beads of sweat formed on his brow, as he clearly fought against the pain. The distinct smell of burning flesh was absent, however. "We must move quickly my friends; I am not certain how long I will manage to endure." As the Rapha` Prince strode away he announced, "I will go to the forefront with our guide. Do not delay in pursuit." With that Merah strode away back to where the rest of the party along with the baggage and horses waited.

"Make way!" Caraig bellowed as the giant strode into the narrow passage. For a moment there was a mad scramble as the quest tried frantically to clear a path. As Mereah almost ran past everyone, Caraig barked another series of orders, with such an air of urgency and authority they were obeyed without hesitation. "Ged, to the front, tell the great oaf where we're headed. The rest of yuh, grab yer gear and an' follow as best yuh can. Run after the light or risk gettin' lost in the dark."

Chapter Ten

Riordan walked behind Korah who led the horses. Ged, Caraig, and Mereah now had point, carrying the fire box. Rather than make torches from arrow shafts, they would occasionally break one up and put it among the firestones. The wood quickly ignited and gave brighter light than the stone's red glow. It also seemed to help Mereah control the heat. They'd been following the dancing orange light and red glow for several hours now.

The captain whispered to his page, "Be on the watch lad, Aella is sensing something new afoot."

"I'm not picking up anything from Sorcha," Riordan confessed discouraged, "Why can you sense what the horses feel but not me?"

"Horse sense is not an idle phrase lad...they often perceive when something is amiss, long before we are aware of it. Pay attention to their behaviors, you'll begin to pick-up subtle clues that reveal much. Watch the tilt of their ears, or flaring of nostrils, those kinds of things can tell a man a lot. What I'm sensing is from my bond with Aella, however. She's picking up smells of creatures she's not familiar with. They're before and behind us, so we're caught in between. I've got the horse's lad, slip back and quietly warn Ragnhildr and the others."

Dropping back, the young rohi whispered to the expedition commander, "Ragnhildr sir, Korah asks that I warn you, an ambush may be coming. We have someone or something ahead as well as behind us."

"How does he know this son?"

Riordan shuffled his feet, answering sheepishly, "Well sir, his um, his horse told him,"

Aislin scoffed, "That's ridiculous..."When once more everything went pitch black.

Ignoring his daughter's skepticism, Ragnhildr projected his voice loud enough to be heard at the front of the formation, "Mereah, Caraig, what happened?"

"My pardon commander, an unexpected wind snuffed out the flame," Mereah replied. "I attempted to preserve the Firestone, but another power resists my efforts."

"Another power?" Ragnhildr asked, "Explain."

"More sorcery," Ged growled in response.

"Did anyone see anything, or anyone?" Ragnhildr inquired.

"Not a thing," Caraig responded. "And I was walking ahead of the flame to keep my eyes adjusted to the dark. My night vision is better'n most, still I couldn't see more than a few feet ahead."

"Nobody saw anything," Korah interjected, "But Aella smells something, not far away. Don't think it wants to be seen. Not too big of a something, maybe several somethings."

"Make sense Korah," snapped a frustrated Ragnhildr, "Can you be more specific? Several small somethings? Are you telling me a pack of rodents extinguished our light?"

"I didn't say rodents. It was a scent Aella has never sensed before. Be at the ready, some mischief usually follows when the lights go out."

"Whatever or whoever they are, they've done their work well," Remarked Mereah, "Caraig and I are unable to ignite anything, including our lamp. Even our flints won't make a spark."

"They've blinded us that's certain," snapped Ged, "So why don't they attack?"

"Simple," Ragnhildr replied calmly, "They're just continuing an earlier assault. Why risk combat when a lack of light will do their work for them. Ged, how much further until we escape these caverns?"

After waiting in silence for a few dark moments, Ragnhildr queried again, more forcefully, "Ged?"

A few seconds later there was a high-pitched squeak, and Mereah's deep voice broke the silence, "Our guide for some mysterious reason decided to sneak away rather than answer your question. Care to explain yourself Mr. Ged?"

An indiscernible muffle was the only response, prompting Ragnhildr to suggest, "Mereah, perhaps if you loosened your grip on the garments surrounding the throat, and lower our guide far enough for his feet to touch the ground."

Riordan whispered to Korah, "How did he know?"

"By the location and sound of the weasel's voice," Korah replied.

"Alright, alright," Ged squeaked. "I don't know!"

"I don't know, what?" Demanded Ragnhildr.

"Where we are!" Screamed Ged. "I've followed the marker's I placed to find our way out, they must ah been removed. Haven't seen anything familiar for more'n couple hours!"

"Are you sure?" Caraig growled.

"Course I'm sure, idjit! Been in caves an' mines most ah me days. Ah read rock like some folks read books. Tain't seen a marker fer better'n hour."

"Then being lost in the dark is the least of our worries," Ragnhildr murmured quietly.

"What are yer talkin..." Ged started to protest, but Jireh cut him off.

"He means, what if the markers we followed were not removed, but *moved* to take us in the wrong direction. Likely placed in such a way as to lead us someplace we don't want to go."

"I also meant," Ragnhildr said coolly. "That perhaps our guide is in league with our foes, and that was his motive for attempting a hasty exit."

Korah spoke in the direction he last heard their guide's voice, "Ged?"

"Fellers, I unerstan' yuh don't trust me, but yer got ta believe me, the lads an I passed through these caves without the least bit ah trouble don't cha see? Ah was sneakin away cause of all the threats. When ah realized I'd got yer all lost, ah figured I'd best make meself scarce."

"Why you treacherous lil..." Caraig sputtered almost too mad to speak, "If it turns out we *were* betrayed, yuh won't have to wonder if my *promise* - not threat, promise - to snuff yuh out will be kept. I also promise to make it slow and painful."

The gravity of their situation seemed magnified by the impenetrable gloom. Riordan focused on locating everyone by the sound of their voices, and the whispers among the soldiers further back in the tunnel. When Korah spoke out in a normal tone, the dark made his voice sound like a shout. "I have an idea," getting only silence in response, he continued. "Aella occasionally picks up scents from outside the caverns. *We* may be blind, she is not. I'll feel my way along just ahead of everybody, probing for pits or side passages, but she may be able to guide me."

Aislin scoffed, "Again, this nonsense about listening to an animal ..."

Ragnhildr cut her off, "Daughter, I have taught you better. He is of the Capall. In days of old, their creation gift was a supernatural bond with their horses. Pray indeed it is restored because this course of action may be our best hope. Korah, please proceed. I recommend we begin by reversing course. Stay connected, remain alert. If we give the appearance of finding our way, I believe our foes, whoever or whatever they may be, will attempt to prevent it."

Again, the only way to measure time in the trek through shadow, was by the measure of nerve-wrecking exhaustion. Even meals were forgotten in their desperation for deliverance from an endless black maze. Distance was measured inch by monotonous inch while seeking to prevent falls into pits or missing alternative side passages. When tunnels opened into larger caverns the pace really slowed as most of the empty space had to be explored by feel.

After what felt like an eternity in Sheol, Korah finally broke the silence, "I know it seems as though we are making no progress, but take heart, the scents and smells Aella are discerning are becoming stronger. Be wary, however, we are not alone. Whatever foe brought the mischief of extinguishing our lights remain behind and before. I believe they intend to prevent our escape."

"The 'orse told yuh all that?" Ged growled.

"That's right," Korah responded dryly, "She also told me that you need a bath. Your stench is interfering with her ability to locate sources of fresh air." Several in the party chuckled softly, and Riordan felt sure the little nicker from Aella was a soft horsey laugh.

Then the attack came. Several of the Dun acting as rearguard started shouting out in dismay, followed by sharp outcries of pain and terror. Weapons were drawn and swung wildly in the dark out of sheer desperation. A battle was taking place but who the attackers were was impossible to determine. Suddenly the sound of a blunt weapon smashing bone was heard, followed by agonizing screams. Then silence descended like a death shroud. Fear and confusion increased ten-fold from the inability to see, and the anticipation of the unknown.

"Riordan, Korah," Ragnhildr whispered, "Stand ready to protect the horses. If they have discerned our method of navigation, I fear they will attack there next."

"Aye," Jireh responded softly, "Lad, draw the Riail dlí let us see if the blade is able to aid the discernment of our foes. Sorcery is at work here, long past time it be unmasked by the light."

Riordan drew the Yara blade forth, and immediately he felt a surge of courage flow from the blade. The pitch-black remained, however, prompting the armor-bearer's question, "Can the blade itself be a light?"

"I'm not sure lad, but the area of dominion for the second-born children of Elohim was light. We can hope the Riail dlí will grant to the sword's bearer those same gifts."

"What should I do?"

"Lad, I hate to confess, I don't rightly know. Perhaps if you focus on revealing our enemies' dark purpose."

Riordan began to focus on bringing the blade into submission to his will. Rather than yielding light however, the harder he focused the more he felt a burning sensation moving through his hands. He felt the anxious waiting of the captains around him, but the pain in his arms forced him to stop for a moment. He then refocused and redoubled his efforts and suddenly a starburst of brilliant white light exploded from the blade. Riordan was so surprised he dropped the sword, and the light went out.

Caraig shouted excitedly, "Bats and badgers!! Anyone else see that? Bring the light back lad, quick."

Riordan picked the blade back up after blindly feeling around for it on the cavern floor. When he tried to regain his focus, memory of the pain he felt moments before made this impossible. His efforts to control the blade had resulted in the most excruciating pain he'd ever experienced. Once burned, he found it impossible to place his hands back into the flame. Even the slightest attempt brought back the burning sensation and the sheer terror of repeating the experience. Finally, he tearfully stammered, "I can't."

"What do yuh mean yuh can't?" Snapped Caraig, "I saw something fleeing from the light, anybody else see it? Bring back the light, quick!"

Korah intervened, "Back up Caraig." Then asked gently, "What's the matter lad?"

"When I focus my will on the Riail dlí, to control it, it burns, it's like my hands are in flame, and the burning spreads up my arms. I can't bear the pain!"

"You got too boy, our lives are depending on it!" Ged growled.

"Maybe not, everybody just calm down!" Jireh ordered. "Caraig, Mereah, take out your flints and see if you can manage a spark."

From somewhere close but several feet above his head a deep voice said, "Aye."

After a moment of rustling sounds from rummaging through packs, they heard the sound of striking flints, and to everyone's relief bright sparks flew. "Well now," Jireh murmured, "There's a sight for sore eyes. Then to everyone's amazement, Mereah captured the tiny glowing embers and kept them suspended in mid-air.

"Caraig my friend, light the lamp before the sparks expire."

In moments the foot lamp was burning again, but now seemed a bright beacon because their eyes were adjusted after so long a time in deep shadow. Ragnhildr, in a composed voice suggested, "Let us go back and see who is injured."

Walking back through the formation Caraig excitedly went on about something he'd seen during the bright flash of light. "I tell yuh, I saw somthin! They were scurrying away from the light, size of rodents, but I'd swear they were on two legs."

Mereah chuckled while suggesting, "Mayhap they *were* rodents. Talented, trained one's mind you, able to run about on two legs."

Caraig drew back his war hammer, "Well I know one great oaf who'll be crawling on all fours yuh big idjut." Korah and Riordan laughed softly at the jest, Jireh and Ragnhildr exchanged knowing glances and said nothing.

Following the lamplight back they found the body of a Dun soldier all sprawled out. With the boot lamp casting enough light to see the fallen warrior, his comrades drew back from the corpse at their captain's approach. Caraig examined the soldier's face in a vain attempt to identify him. A thousand cuts were over all his exposed skin, shredding his face and rendering it unrecognizable. Strangest thing of all, there was not a drop of blood.

Korah looked to Jireh, "Ever see anything like this?"

The Shophetim didn't answer directly, but looking to Caraig he asked, "Could you lift his left arm up and away from his body?" When this was done, a very precise incision, starting near the pit ran down to almost below the ribs was revealed. "If we had the time for closer inspection, I suspect we would find the heart's removed."

"Why go through the man's side?" Riordan murmured.

"To get past the chain mail." Caraig replied. "there's a large opening in the links under the arm." Looking up from the corpse, the Weapon Master recognized his sergeant standing there, "Nahor, what happened here?"

"Wish I could tell yuh cap'n, surely do. Somethin' came at us in the dark. All the lads started gettin' bit, stung, or stabbed below the knees where our hauberks don't reach. Well, we all started swinging low trying to hit something, *anything*. One of us must-ah smashed Nabric here in the knee. He went down. Those things whatever they were, were all over 'im–I guess–cause ah couldn't see cap'n. Then came a flash O' light, an well, I only saw for a fraction, an' they fled from the light yuh see." Nahor stammered for a moment and shuffled his feet, too embarrassed to continue.

Ragnhildr started to get impatient, "No! We do not see! How in the name of El could we as we were not back here? What did you witness that we did not?"

"Well... begging yer master's pardon sir, it looked to be wee little men."

"Little men?"

"Aye, with bright shiny blades."

ed quickly got them back on track once their lamps were restored. Delighted to discover Aella's leading by scent had served them well, their guide hoped they would be free of the caverns within two hours. They were once again following the marks that Ged and his companions had made on an earlier excursion.

"Will we be attacked again?" Riordan asked quietly.

"I don't think so. Our blindness served our attackers well," Korah replied. "However, they may have discovered our ability to detect their presence by scent. Should they hazard another attack, it's likely they'll make the horses their targets, hoping to blind us once more."

"What were they?" Riordan asked.

"I'd only be speculating at this point," a slight grin grew on Korah's face as he replied, "Quite sure they weren't trained intelligent two-legged rodents though."

The proverbial light at the end of the tunnel appeared two hours later. A small pinprick at first, that grew into a beacon, they shielded their eyes while allowing them to adjust after days of low light conditions. Escaping the shadows, they emerged onto a small rock platform on the steep slope of a desert mountain. Two hundred feet below flowed the South Branch of the Saoirse River. A narrow path followed a series of switchbacks through the rocks to reach the riverbank below. Riordan noticed a distinct change in temperature from the coolness of the cave. It was also in sharp contrast when compared to the crisp late autumn air of the western mountain valley they'd passed through several days earlier.

Turning around, Riordan's eyes followed the slope upward to almost dizzying heights. Jireh's deep voice spoke softly from just behind his shoulder, "Aye lad, we've been descending for most of our long journey in the dark. We are a few thousand feet lower in elevation than we were when we entered the caves."

An eavesdropping Ged piped in, "Where we're going is lower yet. Soon you'll learn it's possible to be hot, even in dead O' winter."

"And where's that?" Korah asked.

"Cap'n?"

"Where we're headed. Where is that?"

"Well." Ged drawled, "Roads right in front of yuh cap'n. If folks can get movin' an' adjust their eyes ta bright light whilst they walk, we can reach the next key spot fore nightfall."

"Any more surprises Ged? I'm starting to really dislike your surprises." Ragnhildr warned.

"Aye, any centuries-old dragons wielding magic we should know about?" Caraig growled.

"Now, I didn't know 'bout none O' that, no more than the rest of yer!" Ged protested loudly. "Me lads an I came through a lot quieter, ad nary a lick O' trouble see?"

"But you suspected there might be trouble." Korah said quietly. "You saw fit to warn us about making too much noise."

"Just a pre-caution cap'n, can't be too careful, see?"

"Aye, we do see," Ragnhildr now towered over the Dun adventurer menacingly, "You needlessly endangered the Crown Prince and Shophetim of our people. We almost lost both in the span of a heartbeat. Any more such surprises, and not a member of my command will hesitate to separate your head from your shoulders."

Turning to address the rest of the expedition, he ordered, "Alright lads, grab something to eat quickly and let's get moving. I want to get as far away from this foul cave as possible."

Korah tapped Riordan on the shoulder, "Take along some of the gear lad, and mount up, we'll be scouting ahead. I'm also tired of surprises." Turning to their guide, Korah asked, "Follow this path north downstream through the canyon?"

"Aye cap'n. Follow the path down the mountain an' you'll come to ah shallow place to ford the river. After crossing, keep going north several miles until yuh come to ah break in the wall, a spring flows out of it an' pours inta the Saoirse. Your road 'll take yuh through the crack an along the stream."

Tossing Riordan some jerky, Korah grinned, "Not much time for a break son, you'll need to eat in the saddle. Hopefully, won't have to sleep in it as well."

Ragnhildr approached Korah who was already mounted, "Be wary. That serpent is much too large to use the same exit. So, there may be a bigger crack or lava tube somewhere close by."

Korah acknowledged the cautionary word with a nod, "Whatever attacked us there in the tunnel however won't need much of a hole to get out and cause mischief, we'll all need be on high alert. Not likely they'll try anything without cover of darkness, but..."

"Expect the unexpected," Ragnhildr finished the thought. "We'll be careful. We should have expected blade-wielding rodents, eh?"

Korah grinned in response to the Irial Commander's rare use of humor, then guided Aella down the ancient trail. Riordan looked back and watched as soldiers sorted through packs to prepare a quick meal. No one was sure when they'd eaten last, but everyone's stomach clocks were screaming it'd been quite a while. Then he cast a longing glance towards Aislin, as she listened intently to instructions from her father. With a sigh, he turned his gaze forward and descended the steep path.

Riordan resisted gravity by moving his feet forward around the white stallion's front flanks, while leaning back at about the same angle as the sandy path. As a result, the young page slid along with his blanket saddle up onto his mount's shoulders.

"Doesn't quite seem the right thing to do, but when on a grade like this, I think you'll find it a bit easier if you lean forward and brace against your horse's neck," Korah suggested. "Grip Sorcha's flanks with your knees to keep your backside from flipping over your head."

After they leveled out, Riordan heard shallow water rippling through rocks. The trail rounded a massive boulder, and the Saoirse River came into view. The horses trotted eagerly forward, waded in to about their hocks and drank deeply. Korah and Riordan left the last of their water for the pack animals, so they too dropped into the cold water and drank their fill. The water had the crystal quality only obtained by being filtered through loose sand and gravel.

Riordan studied the canyon while filling water skins. Their road crossed the river and journeyed towards the base of a high plateau. The wall under the table rock rim was a sheer vertical cliff offering little to no surface breaks or cracks. They followed the ancient path across the Saoirse, up through desert sand and thorn until reaching a narrow shelf of rock between the river and cliff. The faint traces of their road followed the wall north and further downstream.

Korah paused to brush his hand along the rock, examining the surface, "Come spring, this path will be submerged by a flood. Tarry too long and we'll need to swim."

They rode in silence for a few hours until coming to a break in the east wall. The path followed a tributary to the Saoirse River that had carved a narrow crack through the mesa. "Now here's a situation lad, this canyon's thirty feet wide at the bottom. Not much more than maybe forty-five across at the rim. All an enemy would need up there is a handful of rocks to take the whole expedition out. We'll need to keep a watchful eye."

Riordan replied, "If we can't get to the top, no one else can either, not a human anyway."

"Maybe," Korah replied thoughtfully, "Maybe not. We don't have any way of knowing the capabilities of unknown enemies such as whatever attacked us back in the caverns. That's why you and I are scouting ahead. I'd really like to avoid any more surprises our friend Ged forgot to mention."

"I'd think he would want to avoid more surprises his self," The rohi speculated. "When you tossed him over the ledge back in the caves, pretty sure he soiled his britches."

Korah chuckled, "It was mostly Jireh's idea, I merely gave Mr. Ged a shove. Well, don't see as we have any choice, our guide says we've got to go through this cut. I'll watch the trail, how about if you focus on the rim above?"

They set off through the canyon. Because it ran in a roughly east-west direction, they hoped to have good light much of the way. The transparent stream was about five feet wide, and it joyfully tumbled over sand and rock as it scrambled to join the river. Korah commented, "The trail has seen hundreds of years use, but not much of late."

Riordan's scan of the canyon rim revealed myriads of red shades. Each layer popped out and glowed from sunlight and while beautiful, it was also blinding. Korah noticed the struggle and commented, "Another reason this cut could be so easily defended. Archers up there would be almost invisible much of the day. Anyone below defending themselves would be shooting hundreds of feet up, while looking straight into the sun. We'll have to hope for the best."

After an hour's ride, the canyon shifted south resulting in a major change in light. With the cut being so narrow, the canyon floor would see direct sunlight for only an hour or so a day.

Riordan appreciated the change. Temps dropped considerably in the canyon wall's shade, and his eyes appreciated a break from the glare. The path they followed climbed slowly, over natural steps cut into the stone. A series of large bathtub-sized pools and small falls gave the stone glen a magical, peaceful feel, despite Korah's concerns of possible danger.

As they climbed, the rim drew closer and was several feet wider, yielding more space to the sky. In a half-hour, the cut shifted direction back to the east, and again filled with light. A small amount of vegetation and stunted trees flashed vivid green against the red stone. Riordan was puzzled, although late fall, the trees were still covered with leaves, with only a few starting to tint gold. Then he realized they were cultivated fruit trees.

A flock of Mountain Bluebirds flitted through the branches and filled the canyon with a symphony. Korah remarked, "These songsters save themselves a long journey by seeking lower elevations rather than flying south for the winter."

Korah froze and whispered softly, "Stand fast son, caught bird-watching; look up the canyon, about a hundred yards. See the stone wall? Too perfect to be a natural formation. If there are sentries, chances are we're already spotted. The trees don't offer much cover, so don't make any sudden aggressive moves. We've no choice but walk right up to the gate and knock at this point. Sorry lad, got careless."

Riordan couldn't see how it could be avoided. If there were a settlement in this canyon it seemed obvious the location had been selected for the very reason that the only approach was up this very narrow and easily defended canyon. Then Riordan thought of one possible way, "The walls are rougher here, and not nearly as high, I could climb," He suggested.

Korah cut him off, "If there is anyone up ahead, they've spotted us already lad. If they have a way to the top as I suspect, they could easily pick you off. No son, we either go back, or walk boldly to the gate. You start climbing, anyone watching might think our intentions are less than friendly."

So, they walked their mounts forward. It became increasingly evident they were approaching a fortification built to blend with native stone. As they drew near, they saw no signs of life, however. A narrow gate stood open, and a crude wooden retractable bridge lay across a shallow moat carved out of sand and rock.

A body lay just past the thick wooden door. Looking deeper into the shadows the captain quietly drew his bronze sword and silently urged the young page to do the same. They dismounted and Korah crept cautiously over the bridge while Riordan stayed with the horses. As the captain crossed the gate threshold the stench of decay assaulted his nostrils. Using his cloak to cover his nose, Korah bent down to examine the body. The squat thick frame indicated the corpse belonged to one of the sons of Dun. All the evidence pointed to a brief struggle. The fact that there seemed to be no attempt to close the gate or retract the bridge seemed to imply the attack came as a complete surprise. The decay of the victim's flesh didn't allow for an examination of the body for wounds or other indicators of a cause of death. Korah did note there wasn't a drop of dried blood anywhere.

He placed his index finger across his lips urging Riordan to remain silent. Korah then stepped out from the shadow of the stone arch and looked up to a narrow catwalk on the wall. No guards or bodies, no indication of a struggle. Puzzled, he peered deeper into the keep. He saw the water for the stream they'd been following flowed from the mouth of a cave about fifty yards deeper in the cut. The cave marked the end of the canyon, but all around the entrance the red stone had been ornately carved into arches and columns, and frescoes of gods and goddesses and many fantastic creatures. The overall effect was that of an entrance into a fantastic ancient temple. Korah also noted a stair carved out of the canyon wall, leading up to the top of the plateau. Looking back, Korah signaled Riordan to bring the horses forward.

Sorcha tried to bolt, not wanting anything to do with the place. Pulling hard on the stallion's lead, Riordan chastised the big baby for having to be dragged past the corpse at the gate. Korah took Aella's lead and they walked closer to the cavern entrance. Riordan stopped when Korah did about twenty yards out, looking anxiously towards his captain, he whispered, "Are we going in?"

"I'm learning to trust Aella's nose," Korah answered quietly. "So, I was letting her search for any inhabitants."

"And?"

"And, if anything living is within, Aella doesn't smell its scent. She can't. The place is filled with an overwhelming stench of death."

Chapter Twelve

Riordan trotted along the plateau rim. Creeping up to peer over the edge, he could see the path they'd followed earlier, and even from this height, he could clearly hear the stream flowing. Korah wanted him to be sure that there weren't any enemies waiting above. The captain remained below, deciding it best to wait for the others before exploring the cave settlement.

Then the young page had an idea. Running along the edge, in about forty minutes he came to the point where he could see the expedition moving through the cut two hundred feet or so, below. Remembering how hard it was to see anything looking up at the rim because of the sun he formulated a plan. An impish grin spread across his face as he gathered a fist full of small pebbles. Ensuring the sun would be right behind him, the miscreant took expert aim, and with a little luck, bounced a pebble off Caraig's shoulder. He was so pleased with himself, he almost forgot to get out of sight.

The narrow cut amplified sound from below, allowing the young page to hear the Weapon Master mutter something about flies. He tossed another stone, again targeting Caraig. This time he couldn't resist remaining close to the edge so he could witness the results of his mischief. The pebble made a soft pinging sound as it bounced off Caraig's iron cap. Much to Riordan's disappointment the Dun Captain said nothing and walked on. So, the page tossed another rock.

"Cut it out yuh great oaf!" Caraig growled at Mereah, much to Riordan's delight. The Rapha` Prince walking directly behind the stout son of Dun, plus a reputation for pranks made him a prime suspect.

Mereah responded with the face of innocence that only the truly innocent can manage, "Cut what out?"

"Yuh know full well. Do it again and I'll take yuh out at the knees."

"Quiet back there!" Ragnhildr hissed.

Riordan tossed another pebble, once again bouncing the small missile off Caraig's cap. The Dun Captain, true to his word tackled the Rapha` Prince. The giant fell laughing, "You're attacking the wrong man! I'm innocent I tell you."

"You clown's need to quit horsing around." Ragnhildr snapped, "We've yet to have a report from Korah and so have no idea as to what may lay ahead."

Disentangling themselves from one another's wrestling holds, Caraig growled, "This time, walk ahead of me, where I can keep both eyes on yuh."

Riordan allowed the party to walk peacefully for several paces, then he tossed another stone, this time bouncing it off Mereah's bronze cap.

With an impressive display of might, the prince spun to grab Caraig's cloak at the throat while lifting the Dun Captain several feet off the ground in one smooth, swift motion. With a grin he spoke softly, "You chose the wrong person for your childish act of revenge my friend."

Caraig *tried* to proclaim his own innocence. His voice, however, was muffled by his cloak being drawn around his mouth. Powerless to respond until his feet touched the ground again, Caraig finally bellowed, "I didn't do nothing yuh big idjit..."

Deciding he'd caused enough mayhem, Riordan pulled back from the edge and trotted back along the rim to rejoin Korah. To avoid suspicion, the miscreant wanted to be back before the rest of the party arrived at the gate. Regaining the top of the stairs, he trotted down to where the Capall Captain waited.

Without so much as a glance at the lad, or taking his focus off the cavern entrance Korah asked, "You were gone a bit long, engaging the enemy I presume?"

Not wanting to reveal what he'd been up to, Riordan's eyes looked up, as though seeking an answer from inside his head. Finally, he replied sheepishly, "It's amazing up there, you can see practically forever. Oh, and um, the others are close by, they'll be here soon." Quickly changing the subject, he asked, "Anything from the cave?"

"No, I fear what we'll find when we go in, but not because I think there is any danger." Nodding towards the corpse of the Dun sentry, "This one's been dead for months. His killer or killers are likely long gone. If anyone from the community was still alive, they would not have left the corpse to decompose at the gate. I will continue to wait here, why don't you go down to meet Ragnhildr and report what we've seen."

Riordan broke into a gentle trot and went back through the gate, following the stream through the canyon. He met the others less than ten minutes later. Ragnhildr greeted him, "Welcome back lad, where's your captain?"

"He's waiting further ahead. The end of the canyon is blocked by a wall and gate. There's a cave opening on the other side."

"Any inhabitants?" Ragnhildr asked.

"So far, none that are alive. We found a sentry, a son of Dun. Korah thinks he's been dead for months. The Cap'n is waiting for us there." Riordan looked like he wanted to say something more, but hesitated.

"What is it lad?" The commander asked.

"He thought there might be a settlement inside the cavern. He's worried they're all dead."

The commander looked back at their quest's guide, "Any information you'd like to share?"

Ged started to stammer in response, "Well, no... err yes, what I mean to say is don't rightly know. There is a settlement It's why I brought you folks along an' that's the truth. Everyone was alive an well last time through. Good folks too, I'd hate to think anything happened to 'em. But the route ta where we're going, the one the lad's an' I took is likely guarded don't cha see? This here way, there's somethin' I'm hopin' is a back door. It's just that, the lads an' I couldn't figure out how ta open it."

Jireh came along-side Ragnhildr to ask Ged, "What made you think this cave is a back door?"

"This small colony of folks ahead, been there over a thousand years. My info came straight from their mouths, I traded with 'em to get the old dagger, asked where they got it... they show'd me what looked like a secret entrance, an ancient door. Their legends say it's a magic door, an it leads to an ancient king's treasure hold, built by same king as forged the dagger. We need tah get moving though cap'n, sounds like the colony up ahead is in trouble, or worse."

"Alright, but no more surprises," Ragnhildr warned. "Lead the way Riordan."

The party found Korah squatting and staring into the cave entrance of the colony. Holding his nose and stepping past the dead sentry, the Irial Commander drew close and whispered, "Any signs of life?"

"Nothing but flies moving inside. Aella only detects rotting flesh, but the stench would act as a perfect screen for the scent of an enemy. We'll need to be careful. I'm betting the sentry never saw who or what killed him."

"Caraig, I'd like you and your Dun soldiers to take point," Ragnhildr ordered. "Be prepared to throw up a quick shield wall and block the passage should there be an attack. I want the archers to follow. Mereah, Jireh, it doesn't appear that the passage was built for persons of your stature. However, if you could remain here and make sure no enemies follow us in? I would hate to become bracketed once inside."

"Agreed," Jireh replied. "Perhaps our young armor-bearer should remain back as well, to look after the horses."

Riordan looked anxious, not sure he liked the idea of being held back. "Good idea," Ragnhildr responded, "Also, I would consider it a favor if my daughter might remain here in your care as well."

"Father!?" Aislin protested, making it clear she felt insulted by being left behind."

Ignoring her protest, Ragnhildr signaled Caraig to get moving, the Dun Weapon Master nodded, drew a wicked-looking war hammer and led his warriors through the entrance. A few yards in, they found two more sentries, the stench of decay almost overwhelming. His face covered with his cloak, Caraig bent down briefly to examine the bodies as best he could in the low light. "No sign of a struggle," he murmured to Nahor. "Another Dun, and what looks like one of the Irial. Neither one knew what hit 'im."

Nahor removed a torch from a bracket on the wall. Once lit, the Dun warriors found several more also in brackets along the passage. A beautiful community was revealed as the darkness receded. It became immediately evident that the central passage where they were standing was carved by water, then enlarged by craftsmen. On either side of the stream, homes and shops had been skillfully carved out of solid rock. Columns and ornate arches graced the entries for many of the rooms. A sophisticated system of conduits and aqueducts supplied water to homes, businesses, and elaborately carved fountains. Incredibly detailed reliefs and sculptures of amazing creatures of myth and legend astonished all but Ged who had seen them before. Some were species that somehow escaped all accounting. One creature's long neck made it so tall that the head reached above the treetops.

"Ever see anything like this before?" Caraig asked Ragnhildr.

"This one, that looks like a walking mountain, I'm not sure if there isn't rumor of such a creature... it disappeared after the cataclysm that brought the first age to an end." Then the Irial Commander called attention to an elaborately carved fountain, the scene depicted a great sea monster attacking a long ship with many sails. "A leviathan I believe. Sailors coming to port at Bethel tell of terrifying, narrow escapes from a creature such as this. Perhaps we will have time for closer examination later, first - we must ensure there is no longer any danger."

Moving from house to house, they found a dozen more corpses, a few were Dun, a couple more could have been Irial, one just a child. No sign of anything living. Ragnhildr motioned for Ged to come join him, "Something puzzles me, there is enough accommodations for a thousand souls at the very least. It's clear by furnishings and food larders, there were far more than the dozen we have found murdered. Where is the rest of the colony?"

"Puzzled me-self Cap'n, an make no mistake, when the lad's 'n I came, hundreds *were* here, mostly Dun, an' folk I took to be Irial."

"Took to be Irial?"

"Yes Cap'n, a few seemed like the Irial, cept'n looked a bit different, sort of like yer darlin' lass, if yuh take my meaning."

The comparison didn't seem to surprise the Irial Commander, although he slipped into thought for a moment, "Take me to this secret gate."

"Aye," Ged replied, "We've but to follow the water passage in a bit further."

"Can Mereah and Jireh negotiate the passage?"

"Aye, though the Rapha` Prince might have ta duck his 'ead a mite."

Ragnhildr motioned for Quillan, "Return to where the others are waiting. Bid them to follow the water passage and join us at our guide's mythical gate."

Riordan, leading the horses, walked beside Aislin just behind Quillan, Jireh and Mereah. The prolonged presence of the Irial Shieldmaiden set his heart racing and made his palms sweat. He felt stupid for not saying anything. Then again, it was the fear of saying something stupid that prevented him from uttering a word. Caught in a downward spiral of inadequacy and self-doubt, he barely noticed the ornate carvings or heard the awestruck comments made by his companions. Aislin noted his awkwardness, and it only served to confirm in her mind Riordan was just a boy.

After about a twenty-minute walk the carved rooms of the colony gave way to the return of a natural cave passage. Moments later they caught up to the others. Ragnhildr was examining a beautiful relief mosaic. The watercourse flowed from under the foot of the mural, but the stream was depicted as continuing in the picture itself. The fresco was in vivid colors. Instead of paint, the artist used precious and semi-precious stones. More startling, the transparent gems glowed from having light from behind or within. The scene depicted a mother of pearl unicorn leaping over a stream that flowed through an orchard or garden. The mythical beast's cerulean horn seemed to tear the morning sky like fabric, revealing a deep cobalt night, with stars, comet, and a sickle moon.

Nahor, the Dun sergeant searched for a tiny crack or a concealed mechanism along the edge of the mosaic. As they approached, they heard Ragnhildr's question for Caraig, "Yes, I understand that, but I do not understand how this was done! We have no instruments or tools remotely capable of such precise cuts. You know as well as I, some of these gems are harder than iron. Look here, the water is formed from a single aquamarine stone. Either it was sliced from a gem the size of a boulder or turned into liquid and poured out like water. Even more bewildering, the unicorn, except for the horn was sliced from a single giant piece of mother-of-pearl."

Caraig only managed an astonished shrug. The beauty of the relief and the skill required to achieve its construction left even the Dun Captain speechless.

Drawing closer, Riordan could see the mosaic's trees were fruit-bearing, yielding ruby and gold fruit. Three trees bore pearl blossoms set against leaves of varied shades of emerald. The unicorn seemed so life-like Riordan held his breath waiting for it to move. Ragnhildr looked over his shoulder and spotted the new arrivals,

"Ah, Jireh, pointless to ask I know, but have you ever seen the like?"

"Here is wealth well beyond the ransom of many kings," Jireh replied. "A wonder our friend Ged restrained himself from breaking it up for booty."

To Riordan's surprise Caraig spoke up to defend the adventurer, "The Dun dearly love beauty formed of stone. The Shophetim of all our people knows this full well. A rare treasure such as this, not even the most calloused of heart among our people would dare to mar it."

"What is your impression Jireh? Think you this is a door of some kind, or a marker?" The commander inquired.

Caraig spoke up, "We've managed to reach underneath where the stream comes through an' tapped with a pole. If a door, it's at least ten feet thick"

"This work is beyond the skill of even the craftsmen of the colony we passed through," Jireh mused. "And its far older, I think. Not a door, at least not in the conventional sense, I seriously doubt you will find a hinge or a latch. Its' purpose, I believe is meant to be discerned from the mural's meaning."

"This was my thought as well, "Ragnhildr spoke up, the lift in the lilt of his voice barely concealing his excitement. "In many ancient legends, unicorns possessed magical powers. See how the horn seems to tear the fabric of one world, revealing another?"

Jireh stood stroking his beard, deep in thought. Then Riordan noticed something, the others missed; the stone that formed the unicorn's horn looked familiar. Walking forward to get a closer look, the young rohi drew the Riail dlí, the translucent blue of the blade and horn were a perfect match. Aislin noticed the young page making the comparison and curiosity drew her close behind. Her hand came to rest on his shoulder, just as Riordan reached up to touch the blue horn. Jireh snapped out of his thoughts and saw what the lad was doing, "Riordan! Wait, don't touch ..."

Too late. Riordan and Aislin vanished.

Chapter Thirteen

Riordan's hand briefly touched the unicorn's blue horn, then pushed forward into absolute blackness. Jireh shouted something, then his voice was cut off leaving only silence. Aislin gasped, pulled her hand from his shoulder and stifled a scream. A fraction of a second later she frantically demanded "What have you done?"

"Nothing!" Riordan shouted as he swung his arms, in front of him, frantically probing the dark trying to find the mosaic once again, "I just wanted to see... Jireh, Korah are you here?" The only answer came from the gentle musical note of water falling softly over a small fall, somewhere ahead.

"Father, can you hear me? Father?" All attempts to reach their companions failed. Aislin fought against the panic rising in her chest when she accused her companion, "Well you must have done something! Think hard, what'd you do?"

"I already told you, I didn't do anything! All I did was try to get a closer look at the unicorn's horn, then everything went black!"

Frustration turning to anger, Aislin demanded, "Well do something now, you got us into this mess, get us out!"

Riordan's own frustration made his voice rise in anger, "Out of where? I don't have a clue as to where we are."

"Well light a torch then!"

"Great idea," Riordan's voice dripped with sarcasm. "Well, would you look at that! I've got one in my pocket already lit. Darn lucky my britches didn't catch fire."

Aislin's hand slugged his shoulder real hard. She only missed his head from swinging blind in the dark. When finally she spoke, her voice sounded cool and measured, "You're right of course, I apologize. Why would I expect a *mere* boy to be prepared for an emergency, so as of right now I'm in charge. So put your torch back in your *britches* and shut up while I think."

Prodded on by pride, all trace of infatuation momentarily forgotten, he chose to ignore her instructions and walked away. Hearing his footsteps Aislin screeched, "Where are you going? Riordan, get back here, we must stay together."

"You don't need a *mere* boy around to muddle your thinking," came the terse reply. "So while you figure a way out of this mess, I'll follow the sound of falling water I hear from somewhere ahead." Then she heard a loud "OW!" followed by a thud, and she realized he had tripped over something walking blind.

In full panic mode, she screamed, "You're going to kill yourself wandering around in the dark you idiot. We need to think this through before we do anything."

"The stream that flowed through the canyon and caverns came from a source somewhere beyond the unicorn mosaic," came the relatively calm reply. "Maybe the stream I'm hearing is the same one. But you shouldn't follow an idiot. Just stay there - I'm confident you'll figure this all out. When you do, you're so smart you'll also know where to find me."

Her furious reaction? Try to find a rock to throw in the direction of his voice. As the sound of his steps started to fade, however, Aislin grew increasingly uncomfortable about being left alone. No ideas of her own came to mind, and she grudgingly had to admit the *boy's* plan had some merit. Then, from even further off she heard him stumble once more, so she furiously commanded, "Stop right there, I'm coming. But only so I won't have to explain to Korah why I let you go off alone and kill yourself."

So, they stumbled off blindly together in the dark. Somewhere ahead, a guardian noted the portal had been triggered and moved to intercept.

~

Riordan and Aislin vanished Before Jireh could finish more than a word of warning. Shocked, Ragnhildr shouted, "What happened? Where did they go?"

Jireh rushed forward and in desperation slapped the mosaic horn of the unicorn. "I don't know!" Growing suspicious, the Shophetim turned and glared at their guide, "Ged?"

"Why are you looking at me? I don't know how this works! Why do you think I brought you folks along!"

Ragnhildr drew a dagger as he grasped their guide by the throat, "Your little surprises almost cost us our nation's Crown Prince and Shophetim. This time Korah's adopted son and *my* daughter… I warned you."

"I don't know what happened, I swear!"

Jireh placed a staying hand on Ragnhildr, "Easy friend, in this our guide is being truthful. I believe the mosaic is a portal. Somehow Riordan triggered it. Did anyone see what he was doing just before the two of them disappeared?"

Korah quickly interjected, "He examined the horn of the unicorn, then touched it."

Caraig shot back, "Jireh just touched it, why didn't he go through?"

Jireh stroked his beard, thoughtfully, "Horn of the unicorn, aye. I believe our young rohi saw something the rest of us missed. The stone used to form the horn in the mosaic, is all one piece, and a different stone than the others. Do you recognize it Korah?"

"Yara stone."

Caraig was still puzzled, "Yara Stone?"

Mereah jumped in excitedly, "Aye. Same stone as used to forge Riordan's blade."

Ragnhildr released his grip on Ged's cloak as he sought to govern his emotions, slightly embarrassed to have lost control, "So are you saying possession of Yara acted as some form of a catalyst?"

"It would explain a great deal. It raises other questions, however. If indeed a back door for one of Bearach's Wards, why use Yara Stone as a key for the portal? It's not likely any of his agents would be in possession of something so precious, or so rare."

"Why not?" Ged asked.

"The foundational elements of Yara aren't mineral, it's law, and truth," Jireh replied. "The very things Bearach, like his father before him rejected out of hand. Strange tools indeed for his servants to use."

Korah murmured, "But if Yara is the Portal's trigger, it means… "

"Riordan is the only one who can open it, a difficulty-yes." Jireh replied. "But it also raises another possibility that may be of some comfort. Ged, are you certain the dagger came from one of Bearach's Wards?"

"That's what the folks of this colony told me."

"What were their exact words?"

"That this door, or *way* they called it, opens to an ancient treasure, and that's where the dagger came from. Yuh saw the inscription on the dagger yerself."

"Aye, but that tells us where the dagger was last located, not from where it originated. Seldom does a blade remain with the smith who forged it. Ragnhildr, I believe this may give us cause for hope. There were powers other than Bearach, son of Atara in the First Age of the World. Not all of the sons of Elohim embraced the choice that led to our world's destruction. The Yara that keys this portal would prevent entrance by means of sorcery, while at the same time ensuring only a true servant of El could gain entry. I know not what awaits Aislin and Riordan on the other side, but be comforted, it is likely they are now in a safer place than we."

Korah mastered his anxiety and asked, "So what do we do?"

"For now, we wait. If a marker for the other side of the portal exists, we must hope they find it and return to us. If not, if this *is* the back door, we need to find the front. Any relics of power or ancient treasure will be there. My hope is Riordan and Aislin will also be there."

Concerns for his daughter's safety eased momentarily, Ragnhildr reassumed the role of Expedition Commander, "Right. I want everyone to fan out, in groups no smaller than four. Search the colony for anything that might prove useful. If nothing else, we need to replenish our food stores. If anyone finds another mosaic marker, or material resembling the stone used to form the unicorn's horn, find Jireh or one of the captains immediately."

While Jireh continued to study the mosaic, the room emptied as every warrior drifted back down the passage to forage as instructed. He searched his memory for any detail that might help interpret the mural. He almost gave up; then he noticed a detail he missed earlier. The starry sky revealed in the arch of the unicorn's horn, had a different pole star. A detail that revealed that the mosaic may have been created at least a few thousand years ago; or that the portal may not only transport to another place, but it may also lead to a completely different time or age. That detail he decided, he shouldn't mention to Ragnhildr or Korah, they had enough on their plate.

He turned and almost tripped over Ged who was still standing there, watching intently, "Nice speech," Ged growled, "All the talk of back door, front door safer place an' all, comfert fer a poor daddy's heart I'm certain. Just remember Jireh, I've been to the front door, or close to it, with me lads. They're all dead. If the boy and the lady don't show up right quick, but instead get tah the front door before us, we best be a move-on, fer their sakes."

Chapter Fourteen

The one seldom heard and that human eyes
cannot see
Some say the ghost of one who died in agony
Francis Duggan

orah and Jireh after scouting ahead stood where the Saoirse River emptied into a small inland sea. "The Marbh," Jireh murmured. "The Saoirse is named for our people's new life of liberty, but here, its waters are trapped in a sea void of life. The Marbh is so low in elevation no water that flows in escapes."

"I have heard of this place," Korah responded in a hushed voice. "Its reputation is rather sinister."

"Fish have not been able to live in the Marbh for thousands of years," Jireh replied, "Nothing exists in the whole barren vale except rock and dead water. Animal life, all varieties, even rodents, and reptiles avoid the region, so, it's not hard to understand how the reputation came about."

Korah looked grim, "I know I haven't lived as long, or seen as much as you Jireh, but even I have heard the hushed whispers and stories concerning this place."

"So, what would you like to hear from me?"

"That the tales I heard were just that, tales-but *taller*."

"Since assurance seems to be what you seek, I hesitate to say this... the stories I've heard about this place were half as frightening as the truth," Jireh replied. "We must be careful. Camping on this end tonight, we'll have plenty of freshwater from the Saoirse. If we leave at dawn, we should get all the way around before sunset tomorrow. We should camp further back though; I have no wish to spend a night on this accursed sea."

Ragnhildr and his captains gathered at the lough's shore later that afternoon, "I do not like this delay, Jireh, I fear for my daughter. I recognize what you said about the portal being a gate to a place other than Bearach's Ward, but unless you somehow *know* what awaits her, a delay of even a few hours is asking me to risk much. There will be light for a few hours more, and a full moon after. I insist we press on."

"Better arrive a bit later, "Jireh drawled, "Then not at all. The Marbh valley is at least as dangerous as the caverns we came through to get this far. It is not wise to journey along these shores at all, let alone at night."

"I will not allow old myths and legends hinder me. Until I know Aislin is safe, finding my daughter is the new core purpose for this quest. As far as I know, perhaps at this very moment, all that stands between her, and deadly danger is an untrained boy with a pretty sword."

Irritated that Ragnhildr showed little concern, or regard for Riordan, Korah replied, "In the future friend, please remember this; that *boy* is my adopted son. Also keep in mind that he stood alone against one of the greatest powers ever to threaten Jeshurun. It was not Aislin, nor even Ragnhildr that challenged and defeated the Anak of Dagon."

Mereah chuckled, "I sought to face that grim sorcerer myself, but with little hope for survival. I ran to the combat only to find Riordan the faster. It may comfort you to know Ragnhildr, he didn't even need the "Pretty" sword. The mighty deed was accomplished with nothing more than a simple rock."

"The lad has great heart Mereah, but such an astounding victory was not won by any strength Riordan possesses," Jireh interjected. "Our hope however for their safety is in the same Power who is our Adonai. May He be a strong shield and tower for them both. However, despite my bold words, I also won't rest easy until I have them both in sight. I pray I do not error, but perhaps our need does outweigh the risk."

Caraig spoke up, using his gruff tone to mask his concern for their two lost sheep, "Well, I tain't sceered of no lake monster, so if we need to go, I'd rather do it than stand here for another hour of gum-flapping."

On the west bank, sheer rock walls plummeted hundreds of feet straight down to the murky water.

Passage along that shore was confined to birds, bats and mountain goats. The east shore wasn't much better. The party was forced to follow a narrow path that only allowed travel in a single file, rarely two abreast. Piercing thorns and razor-edged rocks prevented leaving the trail. Exploration of the narrow strip of land caught between still more unscalable cliffs and increasingly toxic and deadly shores wasn't appealing anyway.

Caraig, trotting along in an effort to match Mereah's long stride, offered his commentary on the landscape, "Whilst not making plans for a sea-side cottage anytime soon, the Marbh isn't *that* bad. Not sure what's got Jireh so spooked."

"We aren't out of this valley yet my friend," Mereah replied, "Whatever it is that's capable of *spooking* the Shophetim of our people, it's likely to be dangerous indeed. Jireh is not frightened easily."

"Aye, grant cha that. Never known 'im ta be sceered of nuttin. Aww, dawg-nabbit, now yuh got me spooked!"

With the sun set behind the mountains an hour ago, the Marbh valley lay cloaked in deep shadow. Mostly concealed by the black waters, from just above the surface, a pair of luminous eyes watched the expedition. The great serpents grow until they die. This meant the leviathan was much too large now to follow Elohim's pitiful children through the lava tube they used to flee. His larger exit was concealed long ago by the slowly rising waters of the Marbh.

Once just a dumb brute, the Watchers gave him intelligence in long ages past. Now he was grown into their image, having learned how to increase his power by extracting life-force from beating hearts and blood. Leviathan knew far more than even Elohim's blood-letting priests, concerning the life of all flesh, being found in its blood. Just before sunset his own servants bearing bright blades emerged from their many holes to make another offering to his bloodlust.

The Marbh Sea served the creature well. Besides concealing the entrance to his stronghold, the murky depths provided necessary cover for the serpent's approach. While lacking wings, he could swim across most of the small sea's width without surfacing. Once his great bulk reached the shallows however, he had no choice but to surface. But by then, it would be too late for the hapless fools on shore.

The one power they possessed that he feared, the ancient Yara blade, he no longer sensed in their midst. It was time they learned that just because they escaped the caverns, by no means were they safe. The attack would come soon, before the moon rose higher than the surrounding mesas.

Ragnhildr, now riding Sorcha took point setting a pace difficult for the soldiers on foot to match. Korah who refused to ride while his cavalrymen walked, noted the short-legged Dun were starting to fall behind. Leaving before dawn and continuing on after dark meant the men had been on their feet for close to twenty-four hours. Their meals consisted of jerky and hard tac, which they munched as they ran. Finally, Korah, concerned about the condition of the soldiers and remaining pack animals, mounted Aella and road hard to the front to catch up.

"Ragnhildr, believe me, I understand and share your concern, but we cannot sustain this pace much longer. The soldiers are nearly dead on their feet. With the loss of pack-animals, several of our guard have been pressed into service carrying baggage. I also fear arriving too late. But if we arrive exhausted and half-dead, we may be in time but of little or no help."

The Irial Commander pulled back on Sorcha's lead, and glanced back in desperation, a wild look in his eye. This was the first time Korah had ever seen the commander not in command of his emotions.

Closing his eyes, Ragnhildr took a deep breath. When they reopened his focus had returned, and his face dispassionate, "Of course. Forgive me, I lost Aislin's mother shortly after her birth, she's all I have left. I'll slow down. And as soon as I see a place to stop that isn't all sharp rock or thorn, I'll call for a halt."

Tension washed from Korah's face as an anticipated confrontation never materialized. With a nod, he turned Aella while snapping a respectful closed fist salute over his heart, "I'll inform the men."

Korah rode back to rejoin the others. All the men, however, were focused on green and red lights shimmering and moving through the dark and murky waters. So intent were they on the phenomenon they hardly noticed his return, "Soon as we come to an adequate place to stop, we'll call a halt for a few hours rest." When no one acknowledged his pronouncement he murmured, "Don't everyone thank me at once."

Dismounting, the Capall Captain joined their vigil, his eyes likewise drawn to the glimmering lights.

The Shophetim turned and looked back at Korah, "We all need rest. It will not be granted. The danger I feared is upon us. Tell the men to keep their weapons at hand and prepare to flee."

Caraig scoffed, "Nuttin but pretty lights. What has got yuh so spoo. . ."

Mereah placed a massive hand over the Dun Captain's mouth and whispered, "SSSShh, the apparitions are changing form, something comes."

On cue, just offshore the phantoms wheeled like a cyclone and rose from the boiling and churning water. The swirling lights slowed their rotations and took an increasingly human form. Many of the men gasped as a beautiful woman with bright red hair, wearing a translucent green dress, hovered over the water. Pale bare arms reached out to the quest as she raised her voice in a keening song,

"Hear the cry of the betrayed ones,
The lament of the captive dead
For a lie our hearts were taken
For a lie promising freedom
Twas truth and freedom slain
Bang the drum slowly,
Keen for my captive heart!
My children are from bondage born
Their only inheritance sorrow and death."

As she sang other female forms rose from the water and joined her keening. Mesmerized by their haunting song, they failed to notice that as the women sang, they also aged. Flaming red hair flowing in a spirit breeze grew lifeless and gray. Firm white flesh turned ashen gray. The green light in their eyes extinguished into lifeless black orbs, even as their song rose in pitch to a screeching wail.

"The ground keens our loss
Appalled by innocent blood's stain
Where is our deliverance from corruption?
Where is the oppressed captive's Champion?

Called to break the stronghold's chains
When will he set the captive spirits free?"

A massive dark form moved through the waters extinguishing the lights and breaking everyone from a trance. Jireh cried out, "Ware, the Water Watcher comes!"

The women sank back into oblivion, leaving only the first who had appeared, and she had aged to the point that her hair became scraggly strands, her skin barely covered her fragile bones. She stretched out her spindly hand, palm up in a warning gesture. Her frantic wail reached a volume that required mortal flesh cover their ears.

"Fly fools, soon t'will be too late!
Fly, fly, Leviathan comes,
Devourer of blood and hearts,
Fly or share our fate!"

A massive serpent exploded through the surface, dispelling the fleshless apparitions back into shadows and bondage. Confident in his awesome prowess, Leviathan abandoned concealment. He wanted his victims to see the death and carnage they had in store. Laughing to himself, he cast a web of fear. The pathetic mortals would wet themselves as they fled like rodents.

He hadn't enjoyed such a hunt since the collapse of the First Age. It relished the anticipation of savoring their life's blood and feeding on their fear.

One of the humans struggled to control a pack animal, oblivious to his danger. One snap of the massive jaws, and only a bloody foot escaped immediate consumption. His purpose was not to merely devour flesh, however. He was a Uafásach, a soul destroyer. While twelve-inch dagger teeth gripped its victims, ancient dark arts extracted the victim's life force, feeding on its power and adding it to his own. Throwing his head back and snapping his jaws once more, the lifeless shell slid down his gullet; the soulless captive joining the other spirits that inhabited the Marbh.

Mereah felt an almost overwhelming sensation of terror, as he, along with everyone else, fled in panic; all except Jireh. The Shophetim held his ground, prepared to purchase with his life the time for the quest to escape. Pulling up short, fighting both fear and shame, the Rapha` Prince remembered Korah's sons experiencing victory through song. He recalled his own conquest over fear and despair in Jeshurun's Key. Once more, Mereah started to sing. As he sang, he recalled his courage.

"Yahweh is my light and my salvation
Whom shall I fear?

El Shaddai is the strength

and power of my life

Of whom should I be afraid?"

The Rapha` Prince, then turned, picked up a torch cast aside by a fleeing soldier and with great strides moved quickly to support Jireh.

Caraig heard the prince's song, and his fear melted into shame. He prided himself for fearing nothing. Yet here he was running away while Jireh, and Mereah stood their ground. As much as it hurt his pride however, he couldn't get his fear under control. Then he heard the prince's voice raised in song, and he felt courage seep back into his soul. Halting his flight, the Dun Weapons Master turned and strode back to join the fray; his voice joining Mereah's.

The Uafásach felt only mildly surprised the centaur resisted. The Irijah are long-lived creatures; their years allowed for the accumulation of both discernment and wisdom. Both are effective counters to a fear spell. While this level of maturity in forms of spirit warfare was rare, Leviathan wasn't concerned. Spiritual resistance played havoc with dark spells only. The Leviathan hadn't come across a creature capable of offering a physical threat since the end of the First Age. He welcomed the challenge. Smiling to himself, the dragon started towards the centaur thrilled the creature lacked the good sense to flee.

Mereah watched as Jireh coolly dropped a large stone into a sling and started his wind-up. As the monster came on, the Shophetim released his deadly missile and smote the creature right between the eyes. With a terrible roar Leviathan reared back on its hind legs shaking its massive head.

Mereah paused to gape at the sheer size of the serpent. Nothing, including facing the tanniyn serpents on the Cnámh plain, prepared the Rapha` Prince for the enormity of the creature. Easily fifty feet from back legs to snapping jaws, he felt a desperate need to strike while the creature had its underbelly exposed. Acting purely out of instinct, exercising dominion over heat and flame, he launched a fireball.

Ever the careful and calculating creature, the Uafásach was rarely caught off guard. For the first time in over a millennium, it found itself experiencing long forgotten sensations of surprise, fear, even pain. That several races of Elohim's children exercised the dominion of their birthright came as a shock. Fear's sensation came when he realized he had grossly underestimated his quarry.

Also, the pain was real. None of the attacks by themselves would prove fatal, but he was taking damage. The sling stone shot pain through his brain rendering him momentarily senseless. The dragon could withstand heat, but the fireball possessed the intensity of ore melted in a forge. Now, still more of Elohim's children joined the fray. A son of Dun overcame his fear and joined the Rapha` in song. A lance-bearing Capall rider came charging in, and now some of the Irial cast off the spell-caster's web of fear and were returning to the fight. Fear became desperation. Leviathan attempted to cast a spell of shadow and darkness to cover its retreat. The spell shattered however against the wall of light from the scion's song.

To retreat in the face of the enemy went against the massive serpent's every instinct. Shock and awe overwhelmed most of the monster's victims, so that it rarely resorted to combat. To be forced to flee with potential prey watching would take away a key advantage.

Reluctantly the Leviathan started backing down to the Marbh's inky depths. In an attempt to recover some of its dignity, the creature suddenly did a one-eighty, swinging its spiny tail in a deadly arc that sent combatants diving for cover. When the party looked up from their hastily selected shelter, Leviathan had already escaped into the cold black waters of the Marbh Sea.

Chapter Fifteen

Home is behind, the world ahead
There are many Paths to tread
Through shadow, to the edge of night
Until the stars are all alight

J.R.R. Tolkien

islin and Riordan trembled in dark shadows. Moments before, with courage fortified by foolhardiness, the young page almost walked over a ledge. The Irial maiden followed conveniently close behind to better berate the foolish boy, (as she called him). When his foot stepped out into thin air, the lady's quick reflexes enabled her to snag the hood of his cloak at the sound of his outcry. Locating a cavern wall, they leaned against it breathing a collective sigh of relief.

Aislin listened to both of their hearts beating rapidly, "Think this through," She reasoned, "Father taught you better than this, think! I must understand not only my circumstances; I must understand the one I share them with. He's just a boy, yes. But he wants to be a man. He believes he should be the one to lead, despite his lack of years or training. I hurt his pride and lost his trust. If I can't get it back... if we *can't* work together, we will die."

When she finally spoke, her whispers echoed as an unwelcome intrusion into the reign of dark silence, "Your father Korah, is a great man. You must be as proud of him as he is of you."

"Korah is my Goel, my father by redemption, and yes, I am proud. Some say he is Capall's greatest warrior."

Remembering the woman, they had rescued from the mob in Joktan, and her striking resemblance to the young page, she asked, "Tell me about your mother, did you ever know her?"

"My mother abandoned me to the care of my father when I was a baby. I have no memory of her. Just an ache, a huge hole in my chest where my heart should be."

"She must have loved you," She said softly, "I am sure there is more to the story than you know. My mother died giving birth to me. I never doubted that she loved me."

Riordan responded with a hard tone, "The woman left me with a man for whom I was an embarrassment. He masqueraded as my uncle because he was too ashamed to name me as a son. I was given a name of shame, then made into a rohi, a sheep herder. Among the Capall, the lowest slave, even a donkey has higher status. I have spent much of my life trying to convince myself she loved me. It's just wishful thinking. I am less than an orphan. An orphan can dream that his mother and father loved and wanted them. Truth has a way of turning such dreams into nightmares."

"And yet, look at you now, anointed as a future leader of your people. No longer orphan, but adopted, redeemed by a great captain, the chieftain of your people. You are blessed."

With a start Riordan realized the longing that drove him to the point of distraction – to somehow speak even a few words to the Irial maiden, were happening. Thrown together by their circumstances, they were having an entire conversation! All his powerful emotions and attractions came flooding back. Then, as sometimes happens, his lips started moving before his brain started thinking, "Your mother must have been very beautiful," He blurted out. The young page hoped Aislin couldn't feel the heat from the blush reddening his cheeks. Realizing the implications of what he just said, he stammered, "I mean, I can see how much your father loves you. He must see your mother's face, in you."

"He does, and I know it brings him painful memories." If Aislin noticed the gushing compliment, she didn't let it show in her voice, "But warm memories as well. My mother was a great lady. Although I sometimes... I try to be the son my father did not have, so I will be less a reminder of pain, and more of a cause for joy."

After a few moments of reflective silence, she refocused on the matters at hand, "Riordan, we are in serious trouble. Without light, we will wander in these caves until we fall to our deaths, perish from thirst, or starve to death." Pausing just long enough to swallow a small bite of her own pride, she asked, "What do you think we should do?"

Sensing a huge change in the maiden's attitude, his heart quickened at the new reality; she just asked for his opinion! She needed him. Finally, a chance to prove his worth! He couldn't let her down.

Reaching with his hand, he drew forth the Riail dlí. Something about its power brought clarity of thought, and peace to his spirit, "When attacked in the other caverns, I was able for just a second, to call forth light. Maybe I can summon enough to establish our direction. I've been trying to follow the sound of water. I've a bit of food in my pack. We'll need water sooner. I think there's more than one source for the sound I'm hearing." After speaking, the rohi realized he had just spouted out a series of short, excited statements, sounding like an eager child. Once more he was glad for the inky blackness that hid his red face.

New hope filled Aislin's heart, "I'd forgotten! Can you manage it again? The light I mean?"

She heard the hesitancy in his voice as he replied, "When I try to control the power of the blade, it burns.

Last time, it felt like my arm was in a boiling cauldron. But I don't see as I've much choice."

The maid could tell by Riordan's voice he was trying to please and help. She had no idea how painful of a sensation that he experienced, so she didn't dare question the effort, "I'm sure you'll do your best, we'll pray it is enough."

Lifting the blade, he focused his concentration. Immediately the burning sensation returned to his hands and in a panic he stopped. Once burned, he had no desire to try and put his hand back on the hot stove. He was about to renew his efforts when he saw something, very faint, a tiny prick of light in the distance. He whispered to Aislin, "Did you see that?"

Wondering if the rohi was stalling, she whispered softly, "See what?"

"I don't know, it was there just a second ago, wait, there it goes again, did you see it?"

"See *what*?"

"That! Looks like a small bouncing blue light."

Frustrated the Irial maiden lost patience again, "Bouncing blue light? We don't have time for games. . . wait, I *do* see something."

Riordan started to get excited, "It's getting brighter, I think it's coming closer." With bated breath, they watched the apparition float, almost dance towards them. A pale blue glowing orb, about the size of a child's fist drifted to within five feet of the pair and then hovered.

"It's beautiful," Riordan remarked in awe.

"I think it is a wisp," Aislin suggested quietly.

"A wisp?"

"My father described them to me, he said they can be seen sometimes at the edge of the Mothar Crann, the great forest."

After hovering for a few moments, the wisp drifted back a few feet in the direction it just came. They would be able to follow by walking along a narrow ledge. It would be almost impossible in total darkness, but only treacherous if they stayed close to the wisp's light. Riordan took a step forward, when once again Aislin grabbed his arm, "Where are you going?" She hissed.

"I think it wants us to follow."

"My father warned me Wisps are creatures of magic. While they are beautiful and rare to see, he also said to never follow them. They appear in the forest and entice people to chase after them. It's said they lure unsuspecting victims to their deaths."

Almost on cue, the wisp floated a few feet further away, stopped, and resumed hovering. Riordan whispered back to his companion, "It does seem to want us to follow, but I don't see that we have much choice. I can't bring up sustainable light. Without it we're dead anyway."

The wisp started moving again and Riordan started to follow when Aislin pulled him back once more, "Perhaps I didn't make myself clear, this creature could be leading us to our deaths."

"No, you were crystal-clear. Perhaps *I was* not clear. Without light, death is a certainty. *Maybe* this is a wisp and *maybe* its' leading us into a trap, and *maybe* if we follow, we'll die. I choose maybe death over certain death, now come on."

And so, they followed the creature of magic, hand in hand, ever deeper into a land of shadow. With every step they discovered how terrifying *maybe* can be when it grows in a person's imagination.

he captains stood on a rim of rock overlooking the Marbh Sea, a thousand feet below. They'd escaped the haunted loch of the damned just before dawn. The rising sun was still hidden by the Irijah mountains, so they remained in the shadow of the peaks. Ragnhildr gazed thoughtfully into the dark valley, as he inquired about the status of the men, "How many died?"

Korah replied for the others, "One of the Capall was consumed by the Leviathan. After the beast was driven off, we found one of the Irial archers, ritually sacrificed in a manner similar to the Dun soldier slain in the caverns. We believe he was attacked while we were distracted in the battle."

"Ged, was this yet *another* one of your surprises?" The commander asked, his voice like ice.

The adventurer stared at his feet shuffling in the dust, "Cap'n, I've told yuh, I've never fear'd nuttin in me life. Last night I ran like a schoolgirl. If I'd a know'd about that serpent, an those spooks, I'd a not gone by that water for all the treasure in the world, that's a fact."

Caraig piped in, "Speaking of spooks, who or what was that glowing lady, ladies I should say? Were they with the dragon?"

"Banshees," Jireh responded. "Dead spirits of the Leviathan's victims. Their keening voices are the cries of the captive dead. Legends say they appear to announce and keen for the next to die. Someone usually does die when they appear, but not from their hand. I believe in this case they came with the intention of issuing a warning."

"I desire to know more about the dragon that attacked last night Jireh," Korah inquired, "Same nightmare as appeared back in the caverns? I'm also concerned about my reaction to the creature. I did something I've never done before; I put my heels hard to Aella's ribs, driving her to flee. Of all the captains–it shames me to say–you alone stood your ground. I'm not sure I'll soon recover from the shame of it."

"The great serpents never stop growing until slain," Jireh replied. "That dragon's age is measured not in years but millenniums. It's possible the creature's intelligence also allowed it to become a Spell-caster. After casting a Web of Fear, none of our reactions were natural."

"Well isn't that lovely?" Caraig quipped dryly. "A super dragon that's a wizard too."

"More than a wizard," Jireh answered. "It has risen in malice and power to the place of the Watchers themselves;

it has learned to extract life energy from blood sacrifice. Leviathan doesn't just consume flesh, he is Uafásach, a Soul Crusher, eater of heart and blood, imprisoner of soul and spirit."

"Does its victims have hope of redemption?" Korah asked.

"Among the Irijah it is said, they will remain captive, until Shiloh comes, and sets them free."

"Shiloh?" Caraig growled. "Shiloh who?"

"A deliverer," Ragnhildr jumped in. "A redeemer to undo Ard Ri (High King) Atara's choice of folly from the First Age. A long story for another time. For now, we need to continue with our quest. A mere hour's rest for the men hardly suffices I realize, but I wish to put more distance between us, and this accursed place."

As Ragnhildr promised, they moved slower and took frequent rest stops. Despite the slow pace they still managed to reach their next waypoint just as the sun set into a blood-red horizon. Before them a white river raged through a tunnel of rock. An ancient road ran along the river's edge, disappearing into the black passage.

"Now I understand our need for haste." Ragnhildr murmured. "Snowmelt in spring would render this road impassable for any but a fish. Ged, does the water rise often or predictably? How long is the passage?"

"I know'd there'd be no foolin' yuh cap'n, and yuh ave guessed right, this is the front door the lads an' I found. I hoped we'd open a back door an' avoid it altogether. It's the only way in, an' then only at certain times of the year. Course if yer a mountain goat type critter, and can go over a four-thousand-foot vertical wall, over the top may be another way."

All the men's eyes followed the cliff wall to dizzying heights. Ragnhildr took command with a simple pronouncement, "We will risk the passage in the morning. Simple meal tonight, no fire. Captains, set up a rotation of one-man watches, changing guard every two hours. We will depart before sun-up tomorrow."

The captains watched as Ragnhildr walked several paces towards the water passage, as though studying their coming dark road. Mereah spoke softly to his friend Caraig, "Concern for his daughter weighs heavy on his heart, and I must confess that while I share his concern for the valiant lady, my own heart would shout for joy to see our young rohi again, safe and sound."

"Aye, and although he doesn't allow it to show, Korah is sick with concern for the lad as well. Nothing wears on a man more than the unknown fate of a loved one." Caraig stared off into the distance, a mournful look on his face. His hand reached up to wipe a suddenly runny nose.

"My friend," the Rapha` Prince said softly, "I know you're named for hard stone, but I do believe your eyes are misty." Forced to jump back in order to avoid the Weapon Master's war hammer, Mereah laughed, "No fear, the secret's safe with me." Then in a much more somber tone, "In this matter I share your heart."

It was the night's last watch, the waning moon hidden behind the mountains. Although a pale rose line was started on the eastern horizon, the heights of the Irijah's prevented any detectable sign of the dawn coming in view for at least another hour. One of the Irial archers had the enviable last watch. Awake and alert, unlike the middle watches, he had an almost uninterrupted night's sleep. The youngest of the Irial on this quest, the sentry Binn was loved by his companions for his quick wit, and lilting voice. He was also known for his sharp eye and skill with a bow. Detecting movement along the watercourse flowing out of the rock passage, Binn carefully notched an arrow to the string, then remained concealed in the shadows. At first, the form seemed to flit from concealment to concealment. But when within twenty yards of the archer's position he stepped into the clear and stood still. Binn drew the arrow back to his cheek, the intruder's face lifted and stared into his eyes. The visage at first seemed dark and featureless, but stepping into better light, much to the sentry's surprise, he was looking at his twin. Slowly he relaxed the tension from the draw of his bow, and while he maintained confused focus on the approach of his perfect match, he failed to see several much smaller forms emerge from the shadows on his flanks. The last thing the young archer saw in this life–his own face leering triumphantly over his prostrate form, quietly laughing at his dazed confusion.

islin and Riordan followed the wisp ever deeper into the cavern. The mythical creature led them through a confusing maze of passages and rooms with multiple exits. They realized with a growing sense of panic; even with a reliable light source they'd never find their way out again without their unknown guide's help.

The young page also realized somewhere in their journey together, the Shieldmaiden had placed her hand in his, and held it tight. So now he felt enchanted by competing spells, the wisp's hypnotic dancing blue light, and the intoxicating touch of the Irial maiden. He walked without uttering a sound, scarcely daring to breathe lest the spell be broken. He failed to realize, however, far from a romantic gesture, the maid took his hand to ensure he didn't run off on another fool's errand.

Then two welcome developments took place. First, the melodic note of flowing water returned. And second, much to their relief, it became clear they were drawing closer to another light source. Reluctantly, Riordan broke the spell of silence to discuss what might lay ahead, "Aislin, I see light. If the wisp is leading us to a trap, I think it best you stay back in the shadows. Whatever it is we are about to face, if it is an enemy, likely our strength is not sufficient. We must trust that the Riail dlí, will prevent any weapon forged against us from succeeding."

"If I thought for a second," Aislin hissed, as she yanked her hand from his, "You were implying you need to protect the helpless little female, I'd shoot an arrow into your backside."

After a moment's reflection, her tone softened, "I'm sorry. I realize you are speaking the truth. Without the sword you wouldn't have possessed the slightest hope of defeating the Anak of Dagon - nor would I. Very well, I will drop back. I'll do my best to provide you cover with my bow."

Nothing could have prepared them for what lay ahead. They walked out of a constricted passage to emerge into a subterranean world, filled with light and life. Somewhere from within the room a light source radiated a soft blue glow, casting the place in perpetual twilight. Hundreds of feet up, stones glittered like sapphire stars. From off in the distance nightingales sang the flute-like notes of an early spring evening. Crystal water flowed from a series of small falls, cascading from a rocky rise about seventy-five yards away. Lush vegetation grew all along the banks of the stream. Much to Riordan and Aislin's dismay twelve fruit trees, were growing on either side of the brook. Some of the trees were in flower, while others were bearing fruit. Vines ran wild through the trees filling their upper branches with violet-black grapes. Wildflowers of every height, color and scent grew profusely covering the cavern floor. Climbing roses covered the red granite and white quartz walls. There was also wildlife, everywhere. Not the usual cave suspects such as bats; but an endless variety of songbirds, honeybees, small mammals, and butterflies.

Aislin nervously whispered into Riordan's ear, "Lush gardens don't grow deep in the earth's bowels. We need be wary. I am certain a strong enchantment rests on this place."

The wisp paused for a moment as though to let them engage the sights, sounds, and smells with all their senses. Then the floating dancing movement resumed as it glided alongside the brook through the fruit trees towards the small waterfall. As they followed the creature, they realized all the light filling the massive chamber emanated from the water source, a large wellspring. Then one more surprise, sitting on a small boulder, beside the spring sat a very small man dressed in vibrant green and yellow. His eyes were closed as though in meditation. Aislin sidled behind Riordan's shoulder, her cautious warnings and plans to stay back in the shadows forgotten. "A Sióg," she whispered, her eyes filled with wonder. "My father told me about them. He thought they all perished at the end of the First Age."

They both were startled when the wisp drew close to the little man and then disappeared inside him. His head lifted, the eyes fluttered open, and he spoke in a musical high-pitched voice, "fáilte a chur roimh ta Croí an Domhan."

Chapter Eighteen

After traveling all day and through most of the night, the light at the end of the tunnel was literally in sight. Debating their next course of action, Korah argued, "The men have been on their feet for over twenty-four hours, with only short breaks. We should rest here and leave this passage under the cover of darkness."

"Korah has a point," Mereah suggested. "If what our guide has suggested is true, and this passage is the only entrance into the valley, it's sure to be watched."

"In which case," Ragnhildr insisted, "It will also be watched at night, and more closely. However, should our presence here be discovered, and should potential enemies possess the means to increase the flow of water, there'd be no need to risk combat; they could simply flush us out of the passage."

Caraig rejoined the captains and their debate after checking on the men, "Pointless to worry about whether there is a watch at the end of the tunnel. Our presence is already known."

Raising a strong hand to silence a chorus of inquiries, Jireh asked the pertinent question, "How do you know this my friend?"

"Hard to say just when it happened, but during our march through the night, one of the Irial disappeared."

"A desertion?" Korah speculated.

"Highly unlikely, "Ragnhildr noted grimly, "To face the horrors of the Marbh valley and the dark, deadly journey back through the caverns alone? For what purpose? Self-preservation? The certain suicide of such an action would outweigh any possible gain."

"If a warrior viewed our continued course as likewise suicidal, desertion might seem a viable option." Murmured Jireh.

"*If* he deserted, mighty big *if* mind you, and down-right peculiar," Declared Caraig. "Since he left all his gear."

Korah paid close attention to Ged's reaction to this bit of news. Something about the way he reacted told the Calvary Captain their guide wasn't at all surprised, so he asked, "How about you Ged? What do you think happened?"

Hanging his head so to avoid eye contact with all present, Ged replied gloomily, "Got nary a clue about anyone missin' cap'n, cept-in that's how it started with me own lads, not long after our making it through this here tunnel. One lad a night, for a couple nights, just disappeared. Then they, or somethin' attacked, I... I ne'r even seen em, the lads droppin' around me. I can't even say how I got out alive."

"Can't or won't" Jireh was thinking but chose to keep his thoughts to himself.

"I believe it is safe to say something or someone has been anticipating your return." Ragnhildr speculated. Jireh watched Ged as he squirmed at the suggestion. "For this reason," the Commander continued, "I will not hide in the shadows longer than necessary. I propose we send Korah and Quillan ahead as scouts. The main party to follow. Korah, is it agreeable to allow Quillan to ride Riordan's stallion? I would like you to return quickly with a report. We must know what to expect when we emerge from the water passage."

The two scouts were ready quickly and the captains watched their departure for as long as the pitch-black just beyond veiled torches allowed. Ragnhildr continued, "Before we proceed, I wish to discuss something of some importance to our mission's success. When attacked by the Leviathan at the Marbh Sea, I wish to know how some of you overcame the creature's magic attacks. Specifically, the web of fear. I have witnessed, during our travels on numerous occasions events I found rather puzzling. Such as Mereah igniting soaked and soggy dung, or Caraig performing feats of almost god-like strength. Most recently, counterattacks I would not have thought possible, except for sorcerers, were used against the serpent. Will someone please explain Mereah hurling fireballs for example? It is highly likely we are headed into still more deadly combat; I must seek any advantage over our opponents that I can make available to all the men."

Mereah hesitated as he glanced at the faces of the captain's, unsure whether he felt comfortable with what he was about to share. "The secret to overcoming fear came at a high price; the Dagon Anak was about to set loose his dragon on the prostrate and helpless forms of Korah's wounded but living sons. Then, the eldest defied unspeakable terror, with a song of redemption. The Anak had no answer. As you may remember once the spell of the Anak's fear was broken, the Dagon were routed the next day."

Jireh then interrupted, "There is more to the story than our prince is telling, he left out quite a bit of the important part that he played, prevented by his giant-sized modesty I expect. As to his transformation into a fire-breathing Rapha`, I expect his story is the same as the others; he is learning mastery of Dominion Gifts."

"Caraig?" Ragnhildr asked quizzically.

"Aye, I'm able to draw strength from the earth and rock beneath my feet. In time I may be able to manipulate the weight and density of stone, even as my people during the First Age."

"Jireh, is all of this due to the restoration of the Riail dlí to one anointed for its use?" Ragnhildr asked.

Jireh hesitated, then answered, "We believe so."

"Then why have none of the Irial experienced these effects?" Ragnhildr asked skeptically. "And why only the captains?"

"Perhaps," Rumbled Jireh's deep voice, "Too many, Riordan is a simple rohi. The captains who know the lad personally, know he is far more. While Dominion Gifts are a reality, they require a certain measure of faith to exercise; not just in the blade, but the one who wields it."

"You ask me to put my faith in a mere boy?" The Irial Commander demanded incredulously.

"I ask you to trust the Spirit of Elohim who in *His* wisdom has placed *an* anointing on a mere boy. Perhaps you assume the hope of victory rests in mortal flesh and strength? You are a mighty warrior Ragnhildr, the greatest of a great people. Still, my friend you do not suffice. A warrior is only as strong as the might that empowers him. Elohim chose the boy, by means of the Riail dlí, not for his great strength but profound weakness; so that the lad will rely on a power far greater than his own."

Quillan emerged from the darkness an hour later to give a brief scouting report, "You were right to be concerned about the capability to flood the passage. There is a dam holding the water back that forms a very large lake. Open the floodgates and all in the passage would be swept away.

Past the dam, a narrow road travels between high mountain cliff walls and the lake. A small force could easily prevent our entering the valley, at any point. There wasn't a sign of occupation of any kind, however, for at least a thousand years."

"Oh, they're there alright, just can't see 'em," Ged muttered.

"Failing to detect the presence of invisible warriors…" Quillan quipped.

"Or intelligent trained sword-bearing rodents," Mereah added.

"Korah and I rode on," the lieutenant continued, cracking a grin. "Within a few miles the canyon opens into a wide valley, sheltered by snow-capped peaks on all sides. Korah remains at the shore of the lake, while I returned to report that the way is clear for the main party to proceed."

"You can laugh if yuh want about me imaginary invisible warriors Cap'n, "Ged growled. "Just don't say I didn't warn yuh. The way is bein' watched see? If'n it weren't, I'd of no need fer yer lads. I'd set meself up as king in that there valley, it's the most beautiful land I'd ever did see."

"Your warning is noted, and I agree; there is a Power that watches the valley. I can already sense it." Ragnhildr responded. "Quillan, I'd like you to catch back up with

Korah and scout further ahead for a defensible site for a base camp."

"Too soon for that cap'n," Ged objected. "This here valley must be over a hunert miles long, maybe fifty-wide. It'll be a thirty-mile hike just along the big lake."

"He's right Commander," Quillan said, "and there's little or no cover for the entire waterside portion of the trek. The good news is the path is so narrow, a few mighty men could hold it against an army."

"Very well, find the best-sheltered site you can along the shore and wait for us there. Does it strike you as possible that another Leviathan could be lurking in the lake?"

"Unlike the Marbh, the water is fresh," Quillan declared, "and as clear as any body of water I've ever seen. Whatever the danger we eventually encounter, I'd be surprised if any foul creature came from the lake."

Korah and Quillan rode along the lake, when the lieutenant pulled up on Sorcha's reigns, and remarked, "I believe I see our deserter."

"Peculiar we didn't see him much earlier," Korah remarked. Urging their mounts into a slight gallop they closed the distance between them quickly. When the archer Binn heard them coming he looked up and attempted to greet them but collapsed just as they drew close.

Quillan jumped from Sorcha's back and snatched a water skin. Lifting the archer's head, the Irial officer was unable to get him to drink. Noting torn clothing and blood on his brow, Quillan tried to get a response by gently shaking the young warrior's shoulder. "Binn, can you hear me? What happened?"

Noting the near disappearance of the sun behind the mountains, Korah commented, "We'll need to stop here, it's not ideal, but conditions are about the same for the whole distance along the lakeshore."

"We're only about half of the way around the lough." Quillan objected.

"I understand that," Korah replied. "But the others won't make it even this far before dark, and they've been on their feet far too long as it is. Your man there won't be able to go anywhere without rest, and until we can speak with him, we won't know what happened."

Quillan did his best to try and make the wounded man comfortable, and spoke without looking up, "You'll need to ride back and warn the commander, I'm able to hold here."

Korah hesitated, "Are you sure? Ragnhildr will be along quick as he can, it's not like he could miss us, this road is the only way unless they decide to swim."

The lieutenant placed a bedroll under Binn's head then replied, "Still, the commander will wish to be informed. Don't be concerned for me, Caraig is not the only expert with a blade, I could hold this narrow road against a small army.

With a nod for acknowledgment, Korah turned Aella and set off at a gentle gallop. Satisfied Binn had suffered no serious injuries or broken bones Quillan rose to take care of Sorcha and unpack his gear. Thinking any danger would come from the east, he stepped forward a few paces beyond Binn's prostrate form. He then scanned as far as he could see across the lake and into the valley. In a few more miles, the mountains fell back from the lakeshore leaving space for green meadows, and occasional massive trees.

As he turned around to check on his patient, Binn was sitting crossed-legged, watching him, a sardonic grin on his face. A chill swept down Quillan's spine as he took a good look at the archer's face. The Binn he knew had bright green eyes. The color of the eyes was gone, pitch-black orbs were in their place. Without using his arms or hands at all, the young archer stood up. The movement from a cross-legged position was so unnatural as to be creepy.

"Why do you doubt your senses? I am *not* the young fool named Binn. Your eyes tell you this."

"Binn was not a fool. Young yes, but a faithful and true companion," replied Quillan, doing his best to remain calm. "What have you done with him?"

"Binn now resides in a better place. Would you like to join him?" The apparition hissed. Then the face slowly transformed from Binn's to Quillan's.

It was a move that Quillan had practiced for over a hundred years, notching an arrow, and loosing the deadly shaft in one quick, fluid motion. At the range of just a few feet, the archer couldn't miss. A dismissive wave of the shape-shifter's hand however threw the missile off course where it shattered against the rock wall.

"You are right to be afraid. In order to completely assume your form, I must steal and imprison your soul. Your blood and heart will be sacrificed to Moloch, my master. Painful, and horrifying for you, delightfully exquisite for me." The mocking smile returned to its face; the creature made a gesture with his right hand that made it appear as a claw. Small forms about ten inches tall appeared to step right out of the rock wall and drew small bright blades. Unspeakable terror invaded Quillan's heart, as an invisible fist gripped his throat strangling his screams.

Chapter Nineteen

"Though my soul may set in darkness, it will rise in
perfect light;
I have loved the stars too fondly to be
fearful of the night."
Sarah Williams, Twilight Hours

he Sióg leapt into the air, then four translucent wings unfolded and slowed his descent back to earth. Drawing a six-inch sword, he crisply swung the tip of his blade to just over his brows in salute. He then threw out his hands wide as he performed a deep graceful bow, "Coinnigh amhrán Bard an' Ard-roghnaithe Ard Ri, coimeádaí an dlí de foirfe dlí." Recognizing the confused look on the young couple's face he spoke again, "Hail Ard Ri's chosen Bard an' Song, Hail wielder of Riail dlí an' keeper of de perfect law." Straightening he continued, "For tree millennia 'ave oi waited fer ye."

Riordan was so enchanted by the lilting musical voice that he felt disarmed. After all, how dangerous could the little feller be? Thus, when the Sióg sheathed his small blade, he did likewise. This irritated Aislin however, and she wasn't nearly as quick to yield her trust. In a gentle, yet firm voice she demanded, "You seem to have us at a disadvantage. You appear to know us, but we do not know who you are, or *where we* are."

Bursting with uncontainable mirth, the man of fairie laughed so hard diamond tears glistened on red cheeks, as he answered, "But oi don't know ye daughter, not at all. Forgive me, oi 'ave waited waat is for even one such as oi, ah long time. If oi tell ye why oi don't fear yer arrival, even de coming of two mighty warriors such as yerselves, will dis sooth yer troubled 'earts?"

Aislin's cool stony stare didn't drop for a second. Not sure if the naming of her and Riordan "as mighty warriors" was meant as a compliment or as a sarcastic slight, the shieldmaiden prepared an angry retort. Riordan cut her off hastily by answering first, "It'd put *both* of our hearts at ease, wouldn't it Aislin?" Ragnhildr's daughter answered with a sweet smile and a secret kick to the Rohi's ankle. The Sióg started his story, watching curiously as Riordan jumped around on one foot.

"Oi am Niamh of de Sióga. Yer arrival means my long wait is over, an' soon oi will be able ta rejoin me family. Oi 'ave nothin' ta fear, for de lad bears ah Yara blade, de rule of law. Sometin' servants of de Nephilim, de Fallen Ones could not long tolerate. Also, only de bearer of Yara is able ta pass troo de portal. Another reason do oi 'ave ta trust ye; Yahweh Elohim is true, as a scion of 'is image, oi 'ave ah gift ta discern lies, an' malice. In ye, oi see neither. My pulse, does my answer suffice?"

Riordan had a little bit of difficulty interpreting Niamh's dialect. Despite the feeling they were often speaking a different tongue, the rohi felt mesmerized by the lyrical quality to the Síog's voice. Aislin however, glared defiantly, her arms crossed, as she demanded, "What is this place?"

This question triggered a few of Riordan's own, but with far more enthusiasm and much less skepticism, "The waters glow... trees grow deep in a cave, stars shine where there isn't a sky, is this place magic?"

The Síóg eyes laughed, "Magic ya say? Aye children, but magic similar ta yer own. Already 'ave ye 'eard dis place is Croí an Domhan, 'eart of de Earth. Croí an Domhan be a seed buried deep at earth's 'eart, it will remain 'idden until death 'as run its full course. Den even de seed must die, in order ta sprout ah whole new world."

Aislin continued to voice her skepticism, "Worlds are not formed from seeds."

"All living things come from a seed Mo chuisle, (my pulse)" Replied the Síóg.

"So, now we're to believe the earth is a living thing?" Aislin scoffed.

"Does Domhan live ye ask? Oi can give ye only ah sad answer, Domhan lives *no more*. Ah choice for death killed 'er. Ah livin' thing once indeed. Although de corpse be laid out, 'er beauty lingers still, but fades a bit more wit each generation."

Sorrow suddenly replaced mirth in Niamh's voice, "So much beauty 'as already died. Mores de pity, but Domhan's children in each generation stick crimson stained knives into 'er body of decay, attempting ta speed up 'er decomposition."

"Is there a reason left to hope?" Riordan asked softly.

"Reason ta 'ope lad? Better ta ask for waat reason do we despair? Elohim be de One who promised; a Mighty Covenant is woven inta 'is name, and 'ee will not cease working until de chaos an' death of our lives be turned ta joy. No offense lad but if 'ope twas in ye, or meself, ta clean up dis world's broken bloody mess, I'd ah despaired long ago.

'Get on wit ye, walk about. 'ere be living tings, not ta be seen again until de world be made new."

Together they walked among the twelve fruit trees. Three trees were in blossom filling the air with an amazing scent. Three others were bearing the fruit of summer. Three more possessed bough's heavy laden with mature fruit, and were vibrant with autumn color, potency and life. The last three bore the orange and yellow foliage of autumn but without fruit.

Answering unasked questions Niamh explained, "In Croí an Domhan length o' days does not mark changin' times or seasons. Be ye hungry children? Take an' eat fruit, not known since de world changed."

Riordan's pallet was severely limited to a few sour crab apples, and berries. Aislin, however, was the daughter of a high chieftain of her people. The Irial sailed great ships from their ancient capital at Bethel, importing many exotic delicacies. Nothing prepared her for what she was about to experience, however. The fruits were not only vibrant in color, but they were also fragrant with life and health. It's impossible to describe the flavors, because there wasn't anything they'd ever tasted before to compare as a frame of reference. Later Aislin could only say, "I wish you could taste and see for yourselves."

In the tasting, however, they experienced more than an amazing explosion of smells, sensations and flavors, there was a rush of health, strength, and energy. "For over tree tousand years 'as such meat sustained me. In all dat time, oi 'ave never known illness nor weakness, nor want." Said Niamh. "If ye thirst, ye may drink freely also, just understand so close to de wellspring, de water be potent."

Dropping into the thick flowers and fern on the stream bank the couple bent down to be greeted by still another world; silver fish with speckled dots in myriads of colors on their underside swam over precious stones resting in gold dust and sand. The biggest shock, a small shimmering silver-haired lady sat on a stone just above the water. Her face was timeless; she could have been five, or five-thousand years old; her laugh liquescent and immortal. She splashed Riordan's face, just before diving and disappearing in the water. "Water Nymph," Niamh explained. "Wonderful fellowship when she's not playin' tricks."

From somewhere deep in the music of the waters, Riordan heard a merry laugh. He bent his face to the water to drink, while Aislin dipped with delicate hand. The stuff of life; refreshment and renewal coursed through their veins as they drank. Filled with new strength, their weariness and fatigue were instantly banished. Riordan looked up from his drink, his eyes met with Aislin's and deep astonishment registered on both their faces. Speechless they climbed to their feet and stood by the bank of the spring.

Niamh spoke quietly, almost reverently. "Drinkin from de well-spring oi aven't aged ah day in tree tousan' years."

Noting that the light emanated from the spring, Riordan walked over and peered into the well. Despite the intensity of the light, he could see clearly into the depths.

"Behold Uisce Beo," Niamh said. "De Living Waters."

They then discovered an enchanted forest meadow deeper in the cavern. Filled with wildflowers, climbing rose, and many scattered trees. Several species Riordan had never seen growing on the prairie. Massive maple, beech, oak, willow and chestnut trees, that had never suffered from disease or blight. Butterflies and songbirds flitted from flower to tree, their wings luminous with a full spectrum of light. Small creatures, beautiful and bizarre greeted them shyly, but unafraid. "Ere at de earth's heart, de Sha'ar sought ta preserve life dat was passing, an soon ta be lost wit de death of de First Age. But in dis finite space, only a tithe of a tithe be preserved.'

"Be ye ready ta trust me? Oi can show ye de rest of de Miqlat, waat ye would call de refuge. Not near so grand a place as de earth's 'eart. De creatures sheltered dere were released wen it became safe. Still it be our road if ye will consent ta walk it wit me for a time."

"Please," Riordan pleaded. "You've yet to answer, how can we see stars though underground? I even recognize many of the same constellations from our night sky."

Niamh seemed pleased the question was raised once again, "Oi never told ye? Now aren't oi de clumsy lout? Dey be blue lóchrann stones. Sapphires dat contain ah touch ah starlight. Legends say dese stones be placed by de hand o' Elohim. Dese stones mark de position ah stars on a day dat once was - or will be. Oi believe de lóchrann stones mark ah day in de future, ah grand day filled wit' cause for sorrow an' rejoicing."

Aislin placed her hand on Riordan's arm, their eyes met, and she asked what appeared to be an agreed-upon question, "Niamh, when Riordan and I came here, we were separated from family, and companions. Can you show us a way to return?"

Niamh became serious and grave, "Yer friends 'ave chosen ah 'ard road lass, yer father 'as abandoned all other quests ta find ye. Don't despair Mo chuisle, dere always be cause ta hope. Ah mighty company, wit strength not measured in numbers be wit yer fathers. Elohim 'iself sent ye 'ere, ye be on a different mission now. When it be completed, yer father's will ye find. When de time comes, ta leave de Croí an Domhan, oi will go wit' ye. Perhaps no more dan dust will oi be lass, but if it be in my power, ah will go wit' ye, if only ta point ye in da right way."

Chapter Twenty

Long ago, the Changeling was an Irial infant, switched from the crib with a still-born creature of dark fairie. Weaned from mother's milk to grow on a diet of hate, his dark gift for assuming the identity of other humanoids was taught and perfected by his adoptive Clan. The familiar spirits had inhabited their host for so long, from so young an age, it would be highly doubtful it ever had a recognizable personality of its own. Easily assuming the identity of its victims, it then injected pure vitriol from controlling demonic spirits to replace their souls. The same spirits that even now sought to break Quillan's resistance, and take his soul captive, thus allowing the Changeling to assume yet another persona. Once resistance was overwhelmed, several of the dark fairie waited with sharp blades and delicate instruments to extract every precious drop of lifeforce from heart and blood, as a sacrifice for their master, the Watcher named Moloch.

Quillan's ability to resist, however, proved greater than any victim the changeling had ever encountered. The Irial Lieutenant controlled his fear and started singing songs of power. Fear was the demon's chief controlling force; despair - the mace used to bludgeon and crush the hope that warded his victim's souls. He could take a life, still a beating heart, but without terror, without despair, he could not take possession.

The Irial warrior had made an important error; attacking the Changeling with a bow in close quarters was an all or nothing proposition. Resistance by singing, however, was an unexpected defense. So, the demon grabbed Quillan by the throat as an attempt to silence his song. If he can manage to inspire enough fear, his efforts for possession might still succeed.

Another power, greater than his own however, aided the Irial's resistance. Starting to fight against his own panic, the changeling realized he must quickly take Quillan's life before losing his own. He doubled his efforts to tighten his cold grip, in a furious attempt to kill the light of life in the lieutenant's eyes. Then something hit his back. Looking down, his last sight was the tip of a lance protruding through Binn's leather armor.

Fighting for air, Quillan started to pass out when the grip of his attacker suddenly relaxed. The changeling's eyes changed once more, revealing lifeless white orbs as the familiar spirit abandoned its host. Unable to relax the death–grip Quillan found himself pulled down to the ground by a grim corpse. Breaking the iron grip at last the lieutenant pulled air into his lungs in great gasps. Hearing Korah's hurried approach he asked, "Thank you Korah, how did you know this creature wasn't Binn? What tipped you off?"

"Besides his going for your throat?"

"Well, yes, I suppose that was a fairly strong clue," Quillan managed a weak smile. "Something must have raised suspicion, however, why else would you have turned back?"

"Binn stank of death. I didn't detect it, Aella did. Warned me something didn't smell right. So, we rode on a bit, then waited to see if anything revealed itself. When the thing attacked, we came fast as we could. I threw the lance from a distance, hoping to strike before the creature became alerted to our presence."

"I owe you my life, thank you." Quillan said quietly.

"Expect you'll have the opportunity before all's done to return the favor," Korah replied. "If it's all the same to you though, I don't think we should separate again. I think we'll just wait here together for the others to catch up.

Ragnhildr, Jireh, and the others left the opening of the water passage and paused to examine the stonework used to construct the massive dam. The torrent that poured from a water gate was at least two hundred feet above where they were standing.

"Well, Quillan did mention a dam, quite the understatement I'd say. Caraig, ever see anything like this stonework before?" Ragnhildr asked.

"Not in my whole life. It's not just the size of the blocks, an' some of 'em weigh a hundred tons or more; it's also the precision of the cuts. They're cut in precise patterns to interlock with one another. It's like instead of granite they were blocks of butter cut with a hot knife."

"I'm also curious about the transport and placement," Mereah interjected. "A hundred of my people working together with ropes and levers would struggle mightily to move such stones, how they were lifted two-hundred feet in the air and placed with such precision would baffle any people."

"My question Caraig is not just how, but why? Smaller blocks would be infinitely easier, and faster." Ragnhildr observed.

"Unless they possessed knowledge or technology we lack," Jireh suggested.

"Only reason I'd use such massive blocks is if I wanted to ensure the structure would survive any amount of violence thrown against it." Caraig speculated. "For that reason, I doubt holding back water is it's primary purpose. If that water passage was the only entrance to this valley, almost any defense right here would prove to be impregnable. An attacking force must pass through a thirty-plus mile bottleneck, with no possible room for cavalry to maneuver, no war equipment beyond a small ram or catapult could even fit to make it through. But can you imagine coming through the water passage, a major part of yer army still twenty miles back, and find yuh gotta tackle this? Over two hunerd foot tall, thirty, forty feet thick, best siege engines ever built wouldn't dent this wall. Even if they could..."

"You're missing the point Caraig, a solid defensive wall doesn't require two-hundred-ton inter-locking blocks," Ragnhildr spoke a little impatiently.

"He's right about one thing, blocks of this size would ensure surviving violence of catastrophic, even apocalyptic proportions. If, as I suspect, this structure was built in the first age, it would suggest they knew the devastation was coming well in advance." Mused Jireh.

"Why do you suggest the First Age Jireh?" Mereah asked, expressing genuine curiosity.

"Little is known about the Drochshaol. The devastation was so complete that almost all evidence of very advanced civilizations were scoured from the earth. Almost nothing was preserved but bits and pieces, a few stories, and incomplete genealogies. But consider, before Atara's fall, all of Elohim's children were being apprenticed in their specific realms of dominion. This means being tutored by an intelligence and power sufficient to speak a universe into being. We are less than infants in understanding compared to our forebearers."

Here Jireh let a deep sigh escape. "Our hearts are not crushed by mourning and sorrow only because we have so little understanding about how much we have lost."

"Much as I would love to investigate further," Ragnhildr replied, "We still have many miles according to our scouts, and it's already a couple of hours past mid-day."

A ramp about ten feet wide had been built along the sheer canyon wall leading to the top of the dam. An engineering marvel in its own right, the ramp used sophisticated columns and arches creating not only aesthetic beauty but a strong structure that needed far less building material. Only Ragnhildr had ever seen such sophisticated construction before. The over-all effect on the quest besides awe, was that the dam and ramp must have been built by supernatural beings using magic. A gatehouse tower warded the top of the ramp, once-massive gates ripped from their hinges by some unknown force. Caraig pointed out the presence of murder holes in the stone arched ceiling as they walked through the tower passage. "If there was any doubt that this was a defensive structure, just look up."

Mereah was slightly confused, "What function do the holes in the top of the arch serve?"

"The reward for attackers gaining and passing through the gate," Ragnhildr replied grimly, "Is to have boiling oil or worse poured on your heads."

The party was greeted on the other side by a road of stone, built to be around five feet above the regulated surface of the lake. Although mostly hidden from view the captains realized the road was every bit of an engineering achievement as the dam. The paving stones were cut and placed with such precision that the surface was flawless, even after thousands of years.

"A handful of kids with slingshots could guard this valley." Caraig murmured."

"That we're being watched is almost certain," Mereah added. "They must have something special planned for us. I don't find that very comforting."

The valley, a long narrow east-west cut through towering snowcapped peaks would have the sun overhead for much of the day, until it set behind the western mountains. Noting how rose-stained summits mirrored the glass lake surface, Mereah remarked to no one in particular, "I could live many times more than the allotted lifespan of my people, and never see a sight or a place to match this. If I died tonight, I think I might be content."

"Such words should not be uttered in places of grave peril, "Ragnhildr scolded. "For myself, I will be relieved when we reach the encampment of our advance party and find them unharmed."

Chapter Twenty-One

iordan and Aislin wandered among the many wonders of the Croí an Domhan for a few moments more at Niamh's urging, "Soon enough will ye 'ave a sore trial, for a few moments more, find rest an nourishment for yer souls. 'Ere is food and drink ye may never taste again – for none can say if yee'll ever return."

After tasting more of the potent fruit and drawing deep from the stream of living waters, they rejoined Niamh where he sat at the shore of the wellspring, "Right, so ye be ready den?"

Hardly noticing their nod, Niamh jumped up and led them past the spring and out of the Croí an Domhan through a separate passage. "After Atara's choice, de Sioga' lost deir power ah flight. Aye, oi know oi ave still me wings, but me folk, be not birds, we fly by harnessin' light, an dat power wuz lost. Owever, de Yara blade ye carry lad stirs something wit in me. Time ta stretch me wings."

With that Niamh took a couple running steps, leaped into the air and flew. An ethereal trail from light refracting into myriads of colors followed in his wake. Of Niamh, almost nothing could be seen any longer. His voice spoke from the light, and they recognized it, but it sounded different, almost as though the speaker wasn't a creature made of flesh and blood any longer, "Behold the glory of creation restored. Niamh oi be, of de Sioga', second-born race of Elohim's children, called ta be bearers of 'is glory an' light. Children of 'is image, follow me."

Speechless, Aislin and Riordan did follow the rainbow light trail down the short passage, stopping at another mural created by a mosaic of precious stones. Once more the tip of a unicorn marked the center of the portal gate. Niamh gently touched down and Aislin stepped forward and asked, "Niamh, is there significance attributed to the unicorn in these murals?"

"O aye lass, but can it be dat dese creatures be forgotten in de new world?"

"No, not forgotten, but they have passed into myth," She replied, "Did they truly exist?"

"Did dey exist? Ah lass, rarest of creatures dey were, even before Atara's choice. Pale blue coats, like a white 'orse forever under starlight. Atara's son Bearach hunted 'em mercilessly. Ta extinction some said, an I fear it be true."

"Who would wish to destroy such a fair creature?" Riordan demanded. "And why?"

"Why indeed?" Niamh answered. "For deir 'orns lad. Unicorns 'ave power over space an' time. De tips of deir 'orns contain Yara, like de lad's blade. Disappear dey could, den reappear someplace else."

"They were teleporters?" Aislin asked excitedly.

"Teleporters? Sure, dey were lass an de tyrant Bearach thought de power come from de 'orn ya see? Also, ee 'ated em like no other. Sure, either it be because Yara tipped de orn truly, or dey were just deadly sharp, nuttin could turn dier 'orns, not even dragon scale. One of de greatest of all worms, did a unicorn slay. It disappeared escaping de creature's breath attack, reappeared again in deadly charge, drove 'is 'orn inta de black creatures 'eart."

"That's why craftsman marked the portals with unicorns." Riordan murmured as he realized the connection.

"So they did lad, an den used Yara Stone as de trigger. Ya passed de portal because ye alone of yer companions possessed it. De lady must ah been touchin' ye when ye touched de 'orn."

Slightly ahead of Riordan, it suddenly dawned on Aislin, "But if Bearach was capturing unicorns and killing them for the Yara in their horns ..."

"Ee killed em in vain lass, Yara stone be anathema ta all 'is servants. De lawless can't tolerate truth or law." Niamh answered. "Now Riordan, if ye'd be so kind an take us through the next portal. Wait till all be touchin ye lad."

"Sure," the young page answered, then he gave a short laugh, "Wait, can't you take us through?"

"Take ye troogh? Lad, I'd 'ave ta possess Yara for dat, an it be precious rare. What ye ave in yer blade be more'n all de nations of de world combined."

"You mean to say..." Aislin asked, shock registering in her voice.

"Aye lass," Niamh smiled, "Oi be waitin' in de Croí an Domhan since de end ah de first age, wit no 'ope of parole till ye arrived. My eyes 'ave waited long ta see yer face, dough it signals me time at last is come ta an end."

Hearing this, Aislin looked at Riordan almost as though seeing him for the first time. With a glance to see if everyone was ready, Riordan reached up and touched the Unicorn's horn and they vanished from the passage.

Chapter Twenty-two

arraig chose to stand first watch alone and allow the others to rest. He remained on watch through much of the night until shoving his fist in his eyes couldn't forestall his own need for sleep any longer.

Waking two dun infantry to stand watch he walked a few feet to where the rest of the camp lay right on the stone-paved road. With all the snoring he wondered if he'd be able to sleep after all. Not bothering to unbuckle the numerous braces of blades, axes, and a trusty hammer, he wrapped his cloak about himself and fell asleep almost before hitting the ground.

It's difficult to say if even a veteran of countless campaigns such as Carraig would have made a difference. He'd trained the two sentries himself, and they both had been around the mountain a few times. Both were alert and looking in the right direction as the Druid Enchantress approached, still they never saw her. Careful to manipulate the light breeze to take even her scent away from the horses, the spell-caster approached boldly, confident in her ability to avoid detection. The pair standing watch were a little puzzled, but not alarmed by the strange mist rising from the lake. Soon they joined their comrades in deep slumber. The mist slowly moved through the rest of the camp ensuring none of the sleeping warriors would awaken and so resist. Then a thin strong wiry plant root snaked its way through the camp, encircling the necks of every man in the party.

The Quest woke from the enchantress's spell in bonds. In addition to hemp bindings that bit their flesh, a thin cable of some kind encircled their throats.

Only cold, gray, predawn light filled the valley. A solitary shapely apparition, bearing a staff, and dressed in form-fitting forest green cloak, stood a few feet away. Beautiful, but cold, her long red hair hung down past her waist, framing a fair face with large green eyes. No one heard her speak but everyone in the quest heard a message in their heads, "A thin line connects you all at the neck. Any act of aggression or attempt to escape will result in a grisly demise, for all. Carefully get on your feet and follow."

Caraig's first thought was of kicking whoever was on sentry duty during the night, then remembered posting the Dun soldiers himself. Their failure would be his as their commander, so now he had to be content with kicking himself.

Korah's first thought was a fervent prayer, he must survive and escape somehow, for Riordan's sake. A quick glance at Ragnhildr confirmed his suspicion that the Irial

Commander's first thoughts were the same, with his chief concern being for his daughter.

Angered by the delay created by the quest's mental processing of their change of fortune, the Enchantress spoke calmly, but with no ambiguity concerning the threat, "Do not lag, you are warded by powers you cannot see. There is no end to their creative means to torment the *unmotivated*."

No one doubted the truth of what the enchantress said, but it just wasn't in Caraig to accept capture without offering resistance. The instant he attempted to burst his bonds however, every member of the quest felt the line at their throat tighten, drawing blood on some, restricting air for all. Everyone went to their knees, unable to reach the wire because the bindings on their wrists were connected to ankle bonds. Their agony continued for a full minute before the tension on the wire relaxed allowing them to breathe, "That was foolish." The Enchantress spoke her voice bloodless and flat. "I am Dalbhach, High Priestess of Moloch, I do not bluff, nor do I show mercy. You will receive no other warning. Test me again and you all shall die. Now get up."

Suddenly they all experienced a burning sensation in their feet, as though being jabbed with red hot knives. Muffled cries of pain could be heard, despite the cable around their throats. They were quickly moved down the ancient road, each man left to his own thoughts. Korah quickly established a connection with Aella and discovered she'd been taken captive with Sorcha, and the pack animals. Jireh concentrated on discerning if the neck line applied by sorcery was merely an illusion. Caraig continued to grow in understanding of his dominion gifts. Even now he could feel strength drawing from the rock at his feet. Confident of his ability to burst his bonds, but not certain he could do so in time to save himself, or his friends. So, he shuffled along battling his temper and trying to keep a cool head.

The rock canyon wall to their right fell away after a few more miles so that the valley grew dramatically wider to the south. The snow-capped mountains drew back from both sides of the lake the further east they traveled, leaving green gently rolling hills in their wake.

At last, the sun broke above the red outline of the eastern mountains, staining the surrounding snow caps pale rose. Korah decided the worst part of their captivity was that this part of the journey needed to be savored rather than endured. The growing light burned away the lake mist and revealed the whole valley. Innumerable waterfalls stained red by the rising sun were like veins of blood flowing through living rock. All the majestic splendor reflected perfectly in the mirrored surface of the loch.

However, within another mile it became clear there was trouble in paradise. The stench of death assaulted their nostrils. Soon they saw the carcass of a massive creature. Great patches of a shaggy coat still hung from the animal's back. A long furry nose stretched out like a great rope between two massive curling tusks, and great chunks of raw red flesh were ripped open and exposed on the creature's side. Then the killers of the great furry beast revealed themselves. A serpent's head covered with gore emerged from just behind the last rib as it poked out from the animal's insides. Another reptile running on hind legs emerged from the tall grass and leaped easily to rest on the great shaggy head. The lizard's snout appeared to be shorter than a crocodile's but still filled with razor teeth. The wicked-looking creature boasted two long slender forearms ending with three razor claws on the appendages. Caraig considered the grim prospect of a sleek, fast crocodile armed with slashing weapons and claws, hunting in packs.

"When my master Moloch made plans to return to this valley, he was offended by the life that he found here," Dalbhach announced cryptically. "The raptors, better suit his purpose, so he resurrected the breed for pets. They are faster than the ostrich and have insatiable appetites. Should you somehow manage to escape, you would not get far, and your deaths would be most unpleasant."

As the sun climbed higher towards mid-day the lake mist burned away revealing all they suspected *and feared* about the valley was true. They were in paradise. Fertile volcanic soil mixed with an abundance of freshwater, and a mild climate, combined to make the valley the greenest, most beautiful place any of them had ever known. Like an incredible work of art however, that was slashed with a jagged blade. Their hearts filled with mourning and grief, as they realized the glen's forests, meadows and creatures were being exploited, raped, and slaughtered.

Some of the creatures remained, so the whole land wasn't all corpses and bones – yet. A small herd of the most magnificent horses Korah had ever seen had survived, along with other creatures' fleet enough to stay ahead of the swift predators. Other less fortunate species had already been exterminated, lost from the world forever.

Starting before first light, the forced march lasted until sunset without a break for food or water. As they drew closer to the east shore of the lake, they could see a massive stone wall standing with its toes in the water.

"You may take a moment to remove food from your packs, "Dalbhach droned. "Any weapons you hoped remained hidden there have been removed. Try anything foolish and you will all die."

Taking advantage of the brief pause, the captains took in their surroundings. A tall gate with crumbling towers reflected perfectly on the glass surface of the lake. The wall ran north and south for about a mile before climbing a distant hill. Vines, shrubs, and a few trees grew up against the battlements, covering the stone in greenery. In the few places where the stone peeked through the vegetation, the foundations appeared to be black obsidian, with white marble above. The walls were at least fifty feet high, with the remains of even higher towers spiraling above that. The city must have been uninhabited for a long time judging from the decay and plant growth. High as the walls were, the most imposing structure was a step pyramid keeping silent vigil from deep within the city.

"The ancient city of Síocháin," Croaked Dalbhach. "The name means peace, something this place has seldom known unless it's the peace of death. The craft of the builders were so skilled, that most of the structures survived even the devastation that ended the First Age. Its builders were called the Sha'ar, the remnant. It delighted my Master Moloch to reclaim their works for his darker designs. I hope it pleases you, this is the last city you will ever see."

islin, Niamh, and Riordan materialized into another cavern. "Draw yer blade lad, da lóchrann stones will light." Riordan drew the Riail dlí forth. Like stars of twilight, slowly the stones on the ceiling started blinking on and glowing with a pale blue light. The chamber proved more massive than any yet seen. The Sióg watched them curiously, appraising their reaction as they passed what appeared to be multiple stalls and cages. Some were small, others extremely large and sturdy. None showed evidence that they'd been used for a very long time. "Welcome ta de Miqlat, de Refuge. 'ere de Sha'ar preserved all dat dey could, lest it be lost wit de Drochshaol, de Age of Sorrow."

Aislin voiced first what was on both of their minds, "Was this a massive stable, or perhaps a zoo?"

"It was waat de name implies, 'ere a remnant of people's, animal an' plant species took refuge from a cataclysm dat scoured de earth clean of de blight 'at withered de promise of Elohim's children. Dis cavern be sealed. Outside de very planet itself stumbled, waves an' storms crashed against its rock, an' it endured."

Riordan asked the question this time because Aislin didn't wish to appear skeptical or foolish, "How did you manage to bring all the animals to this one place, and fit them into this cavern?"

"How did we?" Niamh laughed. "De Sha'ar were a remnant of dose who repented of Atara's choice. Dey were asked only ta obey, all matters of logistics, provision an supply be de concern of deir Adonai. Goin beyond human limits, finite beings experience de infinite an impossible. Understand many of de creatures t'wer mere cubs, eggs, even seeds. An' more den beasties were preserved children, knowledge also. Follow me, oi will show ye." Without waiting for a response, the Sióg took flight leaving the familiar trail of refracted light. He then led them to still another passage across the chamber where he hovered, waiting for them to catch up.

~

Their brief rest over, the captives resumed their journey coming to a fork in the road. The north road led to a narrow causeway that ran between the lake and the city walls. Dalbhach however, led the party straight east entering an old-growth forest. The understory consisted of several varieties of thick shrubs, some of which were evergreen, and a wide variety of berry briars and wild rose tangles. Travel would be impossible if not for the road. Despite all the lush growth of the forest, however, not so much as a blade of grass or dandelion green could establish a toehold between the paving stones.

The walk through the forest continued for several miles before coming to another intersection, this time a four-way. Without hesitation, Dalbhach turned left and started back towards the ancient city. The sun had set behind the western mountains a while ago, and the forest filled with alarming calls and cries of unknown creatures that transformed the fairy-tale forest into creepy haunted wood. In a few minutes, they came to a southern gate. The trees had grown right up to the walls, indicating the city was much older than the ancient grove. So prevalent as to be visible even in low-light, vines and climbing rose thorns scaled and covered much of the fortress and reached around inside the open gate with tendril fingers. The passage through the wall indicated it was over twenty-five feet thick.

Once inside, they were surrounded by giants of varied heights and rounded shapes. In a short time when the giants never moved or made a sound; they realized the giants were buildings and strong towers that lay in ruined heaps and were now largely covered by vegetation.

The line of captives moved silently toward the center of the city, slowly the architecture changed, and became more sinister. The top of the step pyramid came back into view, and it appeared as though some form of a furnace was housed at the top. Garish red light cast dark blood shadows, while faint pleadings for mercy or cries of anguish coming from the small dwelling on the pyramid's top tier whispered of an ominous future.

Dalbhach led them into a large oval-shaped building. They were escorted down a couple of flights of stairs to a pitch-black hall. The Enchantress lit a torch, but the flames were able to only push back some of the gloom; enough to see several heavy stone doors. One of the doors swung open under its own power. Caraig wondered if there was a little invisible jailer. Jireh guessed that the Enchantress was showing off.

"This is your new home," Dalbhach announced sternly. "Attempts to escape from even one of you will result in the death of all of you." Two Dun soldiers who were first in line, hesitated to pass through the open doorway, and the thin cable started to tighten once more around all the party's necks. "Perhaps I didn't communicate my wishes clearly, allow me to clarify, you can enter your new home, *now,* or I will send you to your graves much earlier than intended. Don't make the mistake of thinking I care one way or the other. If any of you die before the solstice, Ged can always be counted on to recruit more victims for sacrifice. Now go. Move to the far back wall and remain there until the door is secured."

Clearly the dungeon had been designed and built to accommodate all races, for Mereah only needed to bow slightly to keep from knocking his head. Once inside the chamber however, he found he could stand upright. The men all filed to the back wall and waited for the door to close and lock. Then the line, slowly unwound itself from their necks and almost slithered across the floor before disappearing through a small crack under the door. The men all stood around allowing their eyes to adjust to the dim light. Ragnhildr was the first to move, walking over to look out the small, barred window of the dungeon door. The druid enchantress had placed the burning torch in a wall bracket in the hall but had apparently left. Satisfied Dalbhach was gone, he turned and nodded to Caraig and Mereah who snatched up Ged by the ankles and wrists, stretching the Dun Adventurer out between them like a rope used for tug of war. Ragnhildr then slowly approached Ged and asked casually, "So tell me, friend, what exactly did our Mistress of Death mean when she said you could be counted on to recruit *more* victims for sacrifice?"

"How should I know?" Ged pleaded, "I'd ne'r seen 'er before today, I swear!" The commander nodded to Mereah and Caraig who used their considerable strength to pull his arms out of their sockets, "Aaaaaahhh,.. I don't know any... aaaaaahhhh, . . alright, alright, I'll talk, I'll talk!"

Ragnhildr placed a restraining hand on Caraig' shoulder, "Let up for a minute lads, but each time a lie escapes his lips pull a limb off."

Caraig flashed a grin, "Since e's told a bunch of lies already, can we take at least a finger er something right *now*?"

"No," The Irial Commander answered. "I think our friend Ged here has realized his luck has been pushed beyond its limits."

"Every thin' I told yuh wer true... aaaaaahhhh," he started screaming as the rack treatment stretched his frame once again. "Wait... Wait, I just din't tell yuh all of it, din't tell all..."

Ragnhildr nodded to his fellow interrogators, and they relaxed the stretch, "Alright Ged, what *were* the little details you neglected to tell us?"

I got the dagger the way I said, an' I came to this valley like I told yuh, only the lads weren't killed yuh see, least not all. Some were captured, an' are being held hostage."

"And what was the price of their ransom?" Korah demanded.

Ged hesitated, and licked his lips, only spitting out his answer when Caraig and Mereah started to pull once more, "Dalbhach said Moloch required persons of power for ritual sacrifice on the coming winter solstice."

"So, you thought to deliver us all for an offering, so yer *lads can go* free?" Ragnhildr asked quietly.

"Now don't go assuming' the wurst cap'n, I didn't plan on the Shophetim, or Crown Prince taggin' along. Besides, what I was 'oping for was ta make it through the backdoor like ah said, so we could come upon these buggers from a way they wouldn't expect. Then it'd be a rescue mission don't cha see? I didn't know the lad an' lassie would go through ah backdoor, leavin' the rest of us behind. Lastly, I hoped some a' Jeshurun's mightiest would find a way ta overcome that Enchantress, then I'd 'ave mah revenge, free me lad's, *an'* lay claim to whatever treasures lay in this place. I t'wer only thinking of what's best fer all concerned."

Ragnhildr's face drew close to Ged's, "The reason why you didn't tell us the truth?"

"Couldn't C'apn, I'd no idea if you knew everythin' that ya'd 'ave agreed to the expedition in the first place. If'n ya didn't come, they'd ah kilt mah lads sure,"

"What I see," Growled Korah, "Is that your *deception* doomed your "lads" *for sure*. Because of what's at stake, I'm certain the king would have sent us on this quest regardless. However, our not knowing what we're up against has almost gotten us killed several times already and may yet succeed."

"Not to mention the insult of thinking we wouldn't make the trip cause we were too skeered," Snarled Caraig. "As it is, since yuh killed us all, I think it be time Mereah an' I start pulling yer limbs off."

Suddenly the root twine that had all their necks in the noose when captured shot out of the dust on the floor and encircled the necks of Caraig and Mereah once more, and started to choke off their air, "Even this one's blood is too precious to be shed in that manner," Dalbhach's icy voice droned from the other side of the prison door. "Soon enough there will be time for violence and blood, sooner than you might like. For now, unhand the Dun groveler."

As Mereah and Caraig grasped at the cords around their throats, they had to let go of Ged, who was unceremoniously dumped into several century's accumulation of dust.

"Ya can't leave me with 'em Dalbhach," Ged protested, as he made circles with his arms and shoulders, trying to get feeling back. "They'll kill me sure, soon as yuh leave again. Sides, this wasn't the deal. Yer promised me the lads would be freed."

"And they shall be fool," Dalbhach promised, "Free from the burdens of this life, and the tyranny of a beating heart. Free to merge their life-force and blood to restore the power of my master, Moloch. Soon they shall know freedom beyond their wildest dreams."

"Or nightmares, "Jireh muttered.

Chapter Twenty-Four

Because the dungeon was in perpetual shadow, there could be almost no accounting for the passage of time. The rancid daily meal, however, along with Caraig's unerringly accurate stomach clock allowed Jireh and Ragnhildr to develop a crude calendar. According to their calculations, imprisonment would be concluded one way or another within a few more days. Based on Dalbhach's dark hints, for good or ill, their captivity would end at winter's solstice.

"Can't come soon enough to suit me," Growled Caraig. "If'n we don't get some air, the stench an' filth of this place alone could kill us all." The Dun Commander looked at the over-flowing buckets placed in a dank corner. "Don't know how we could 'ave made so much stink, they ain't fed us enough to make a respectable fart."

"I would assign friend Ged to latrine duty," remarked Ragnhildr dryly. "Except he'd have no place to empty the buckets, other than the corner as we have already been doing."

Ged was squatting in the opposite corner, his back to the wall, a sour snarl now a permanent fixture on his face.

Caraig growled angrily, "After what he pulled, serve 'im right if we were ta make him eat our slops."

"We don't have time for vengeance," Korah murmured. "Ged, you're the only one of us that has prior dealings with this Enchantress, any idea of what we can expect next?" Their former guide's only response was to sulk, forcing Ragnhildr to be persistent, "Ged?"

Finally looking up and making stormy eye contact with them all, Ged snarled, "We're all ta be slaughtered an' sacrificed to the demon Moloch. Dalbhach may want to make sport with us for a bit, but make no mistake, we're all gunna die."

"It's the way of the Nephilim to burn their sacrifices alive to release their life-force," Jireh said softly. "Unless they consume their victims directly. The more horrifying the process, the more energy they draw from the procedure. The demons also feed on fear. Control your fear then, as we've learned, by meeting it with song."

The all too familiar animated rope slithered under the door once more, only this time rather than looping around everyone's necks indiscriminately, the Dun sergeant Nahor, and three of the remaining warriors were selected, leaving the captains untouched. The sultry voice of Dalbhach spoke through the barred window of the dungeon door, "Those not selected are ordered to move and stand against the far wall. If among the favored few, you must come with me. As always, any attempts to escape, by any one of you, will result in the immediate deaths of all.

The captains stood and watched helplessly as the last remnant of their soldiers filed out the dungeon door. Once satisfied Dalbhach was out of earshot, Ragnhildr snarled in a rare betrayal of the depth and power of his emotions, "We've got to find a way to counter the Druid's spell! I will not be ensnared and led like a sheep to slaughter. Jireh, is it possible that the line that entwines our necks is illusion only?"

The Shophetim gave his response only after several moments of grave thought, "I think it need not be real to be effective, what matters is that we believe it to be real, and so react accordingly."

"Are you saying we would die, even if the cable around our necks isn't real?" Mereah asked, his raised eyebrows betraying his dismay.

"Any lie or illusion believed becomes reality to the deceived," Responded Ragnhildr.

"The noose entwining our throats is quite real, however," Korah countered. "Unless the red marks around our necks are also part of the same illusion?"

"The risk of resistance is great," remarked Quillan. "If we resist and it is not illusion, we all die. And unless we somehow remain unbelievers, the illusion becomes reality, and we still die."

"I'm with Ragnhildr on this," Caraig growled. "I've had just about enough of being led around like sheep for the slaughter. The Enchantress means tah kill us all anyway, might as well die resistin' any way we can."

After a few more moments of brooding silence Ragnhildr came to a decision, "Jireh, you have the most experience of all of us in facing the attacks of magic users, draw on that experience and find a way to counter the attacks of the enemy. In the meantime, none of us should throw away our lives needlessly, we must delay in hope of learning the means of our deliverance."

A few hours later stone slabs were drawn up by a hidden mechanism, causing the captains to shield their eyes from light streaming through a new opening. Dalbhach's icy voice spoke through the barred window of the dungeon door at the opposite wall, "It is permitted for you to witness the fate of your friends. This is a rare act of courtesy from your new master, Moloch."

After their eyes adjusted, they could see the raised slab exposed a long, barred window. Outside, in what appeared to be some type of arena were all that remained of the soldiers that began the quest to recover the Wards of Power, two Dun Infantryman Nahor and Cuan , Marcas, a Capall Cavalryman, and Oran, an Irial archer. They each carried what looked like a great wooden spoon with a three-foot handle, "Your warriors will be engaged in a game of combat." Dalbhach's dead voice droned behind their backs. They shall be pitted against similar opponents to hurl a small ball through the opposing team's hoop goal, using their rackets. The only rules in the game are that the ball must be passed to be advanced and then thrown through the opponents' goal. The first team to score three times, lives for another day, and another contest. The losing team, alive or dead, will be sacrificed to feed Moloch's fires. Pray for your soldiers to whatever god you may serve, as their opponents are very determined veterans. They have survived three such combats already."

Almost on cue, a tall wooden gate opened on the other side of the arena and out walked four sons of Dun, club rackets in hand.

"What madness is this?" Caraig growled.

Ragnhildr muttered under his breath, asking no one in particular, "Will our warriors willingly fight and condemn to death their own people?" Then looking back in the direction of the Enchantress' voice he yelled, "What if our men refuse to participate?"

"That would be unfortunate," Dalbhach opined. "Their opponents do not share that conviction. None from the other teams still live."

"Lads?" Caraig yelled, "This is fer real, an' tain't no game, fight fer yer lives!"

"Do these represent the survivors from Ged's little band?" Ragnhildr murmured. "The ones he meant us to ransom with our lives."

Ged's ears perked up and he went to the large, barred window to investigate, "Those *are* my lads."

"Ged, didn't you ever learn about making deals with devils?" Jireh asked. "Not only did our betrayal fail to free your men, it seems Moloch intends we become the very instruments of their deaths."

"One thing I don't quite understand," Mereah said. "Why have an arena when there are no spectators?" This was in reference to only a few of what appeared to be humans or perhaps Irial scattered through the stands.

"We're the intended audience," Korah murmured.

"I personally have witnessed the efficiency of our enemies' deception," Quillan interjected. "There very well may be more in attendance than we realize. I was attacked by a shapeshifter. In the middle of the fight several of the little men Caraig first saw back in the caves, seemed to step right out of the rocks. When Korah slew the demon, the little people simply disappeared."

"So how long did yuh intend to let folks think I be daft?" Caraig growled as he slugged Quillan's arm. "I told yuh I knew what I saw!" Then the Dun Captain added sheepishly, "Err... exactly what did I *saw*, anyway?"

"The Second-born of Elohim, the Sióga." Jireh responded. "The Sióga chose light for their realm, and over light they once exercised dominion. Such folk would make powerful servants for demonic strongmen like the Watchers, if they could be corrupted."

Caraig interrupted, "Have to continue the history lesson later Jireh, game's about to start."

Sure enough, a horn sounded mournfully, and a small ball was thrown into the middle of the arena. Swiftly, Oran the Irial archer ran to the center and scooped up the black orb, flipping it back to his Capall teammate. Satisfied that the reception was made the fleet Irial warrior turned to sprint closer toward his opponent's goal. As soon as he turned to make his break, however, one of Ged's retainers smashed his knee using his racket as a club. As the archer fell a second blow was delivered to his skull, and he lay unconscious in the dust.

"It's a game lads," Caraig yelled, "But it's to the death! Play accordingly!"

The Capall rider Marcas who received the small sphere from his now unconscious companion dropped it in the dust while the two Dun Infantryman drew along-side their ally to take a defensive position in front of the ball. Their opponents advanced confidently because they had numerical advantage.

"How well trained are your Cavalrymen to fight when not on horseback Korah?" Ragnhildr asked.

"Almost all their training is for mounted combat," Korah replied glumly. "Marcas does have a height and reach advantage, however."

"Won't do 'im a lick ah good," Caraig stated matter-of-factly. "All the Dun are required to train as infantry a couple Months a year, an' much of their training is to turn an opponent's size advantage against him."

Mereah started to make a crack about the difficulty for the Dun to find smaller foes to train against but thought better of it under the present dire circumstances.

Two of Ged's adventurers advanced to engage Nahor and Cuan, while the other two advanced to engage Marcas from the flank. Recognizing the intent of the maneuver Caraig yelled out, "They're tryin' to divide yuh. Stand together."

The warning came too late, once the Dun infantrymen were engaged, they could do little for their outnumbered companion. The Capall soldier swung his racket from around his head in a hard-striking motion at one of his Dun opponents, but his telegraphed strike was easily parried. The second attacker seized on the opening and dove into Marcas' knees, flipping him off his feet where he was likewise clubbed unconscious.

Cuan quickly disarmed his opponent by slipping his racket under his enemy's and flicking it up in the air. Almost instinctively his opponent let his eyes look up and follow his cudgel so that he hardly saw the follow-up blow that felled him.

"That one, I trained meself!" Caraig almost crowed.

"Well done," Mereah exclaimed, "But can your two overcome three of their own people?"

"Clearly they had better training," Ragnhildr said hopefully. "But they're also facing some very tuff, experienced opponents."

The captains could do nothing but watch as the drama unfolded. The attackers divided with one of their party seeking to take advantage of numbers and get behind Cuan. To prevent this the defenders were forced to back towards a wall, but that meant they could no longer defend the ball. When backed far enough two of the attackers suddenly broke off, with one racing towards the goal while the other bolted back for the ball. A moment's hesitation while trying to decide which maneuver to defend against, made it too late to defend either. Here Ged's men revealed their greater experience as they took advantage of numbers and made a relatively easy pass to an open and unguarded man resulting in an easy goal. A horn sounded ending the round.

Dalbhach cryptically announced, "The Champion's have a one goal to none advantage. The next round begins after a five-minute rest period."

"Two of my men may be seriously injured!" Ragnhildr shouted. "What if they cannot continue? May I or one of my captain's be a substitute for an injured man?"

"The game must continue, regardless of physical ability to do so. No substitutions are allowed." The spell caster's icy acidic monotone was becoming maddening. "However, the adventurer Ged is there with you. Should your men not survive the games, I grant you this mercy; the opportunity to express your displeasure to your betrayer."

iamh led the children, (for so they were to him) to a new passage. Emerging from a rough-cut antechamber they moved into another hall, with walls and ceiling of deep purple crystals and amethyst. They stopped before a large elevated reflecting pool. The chamber came alive when they entered, as thousands of crystals in the ceiling flashed myriads of colors that were mirrored perfectly in the still waters.

"Ah children, dis is Bema's Eye. For four tousan' years de crystals an' pool 'av remained dark, but dey are awakened nigh by de presence av Yara law from de Riail dlí.

"Are the water's magic?" Aislin asked?

"Magic? Dey are not lass, but powerful sure. Magic be an attempt to suspend law lass, De Bema acts in accordance wit de laws of its creator. Oi was instructed ta reveal to 'ee who carries de Yara blade de truth of law's creation." Speaking to the pool Niamh forcefully called out, "In de beginnin' Elohim created…" Instantly the cavern went pitch black.

Nahor and Cuan crouched low to receive instructions from Caraig through the low barred opening into the dungeon where the captains remained captive. In minutes it would be time to start the grim tournament's second round, "What's the condition of yer team-mates?" Caraig asked.

"The archer will never rise again," Nahor announced. However, if we can delay the outcome, the Capall rider may be able to assist in another round."

"That's assuming yuh survive the next bout," Caraig added grimly. "Too bad yuh took it so easy on your man Cuan, appears 'e may be up an' around fer the next round."

The soldiers looked across the arena to see their opponents working at reviving the man they'd knocked unconscious, "I was loath to kill one of our own people," Cuan replied dispassionately.

"In this contest, the rider and archer *are* yer people now," Caraig replied in a mild rebuke. "Can't be helped, but listen, this is what I want yuh to do..."

At the start of the second round, the outnumbered Dun soldiers held back allowing Ged's henchmen to take the ball unopposed. Required to advance by passing, the center man scooped up the small leather sphere and waited while his teammates split and ran along the walls. As per instruction, the Jeshurun soldiers didn't move until the first pass was attempted. Immediately after the opponent's direction and tactics became clear, Nahor charged toward Ged's henchman, hurling his racket like a javelin as he ran. When the receiver made the catch, and turned his attention to advancing the ball, the thrown racket hit him right between the eyes and he dropped like a stone. Before the others in Ged's company could respond, Nahor then rushed forward, picked up the fallen man's racket, took two steps and flipped the ball with all his might seventy-five yards through their opponent's unguarded goal.

Korah looked down at Caraig and grinned, "T'was a neat stroke that."

Mereah, located a few feet back from the others where he sat on a very uncomfortable Ged, gave a soft chuckle, "However such a clever stratagem ever came from a head so full of rocks is a great mystery." The Rapha` Prince returned the Dun Captain's scowl with an innocent ear-to-ear grin.

Reminded of the adventurer's presence, Ragnhildr walked back and squatted by Ged's blueish face, "Might take some of your weight off our *guide*, Mereah, wouldn't want him to suffocate *before* we roast him alive."

Laughing good-naturedly, Mereah boomed, "My apologies friend, in my excitement over the coming contest, I forgot ya were down there. If not for your chain mail, you'd make a most comfortable seat."

Echoing none of the prince's humor, Ragnhildr asked menacingly, "Now, tell me again why I shouldn't allow Prince Mereah to squish you into jelly?"

Speaking before regaining his breath, Ged sputtered, "Onlyiest way... ta get me lad's back. Lyin' lady wizard promised..."

"I promised to set them free," Dalbhach's vitriolic voice burned their spirits like acid. "And I shall. They shall be released from their miserable existence very soon. Your seed sown in treachery is rewarded with fruit after its' kind. Does this surprise you?"

The Enchantress's way of suddenly appearing at the small dungeon door window was really starting to give Korah the creeps. Worse still, the vine-like rope came gliding across the stone floor like a viper of malice. Rising like a cobra, the knotted end swayed while its' next victim was selected. All eyes were transfixed when it struck faster than the eye could follow, and before any resistance could be offered it entwined itself around Jireh's neck.

"Stay where you are," Dalbhach's flat voice intoned. "Resist, and the centaur dies before his time." Then as a way of emphasizing her point the rope started to tighten around the Shophetim's throat choking him. All hesitation to obey was hastily abandoned as the captains retreated to the wall with the barred window opening.

"Resist fear and despair..." Jireh managed to gasp before being silenced and led as a sheep to the slaughter.

Chapter Twenty-Six

"In the beginning Elohim created," Niamh spoke, his suddenly deep voice reverberating through the chamber as the room went black. "Domhan was ah black chaotic void, until Elohim gave voice ta 'is covenant an commanded 'Let there be light.'"

The Bema's black pool exploded with light blinding everyone in the chamber. When their eyes adjusted, there were millions of lights swirling in a whirlpool vortex. Then as though they were somehow moving closer to the maelstrom the lights at the edge grew into large balls of flame. Finally stopping at one large burning sphere that had nine smaller spheres swirling around it.

"Children, can ye tell me wat ye witnessed?" Niamh asked, his voice soft with reverence and awe.

Stunned, it took Aislin several moments to answer, "The first day of creation."

"De first day sure, Elohim spoke but ah word, an' stars sang out ah song of light."

Light wasn't the only thing exploding, Riordan's entire worldview was blowing apart. "The stars of night, are great balls of flame?"

"Balls ah flame? Niamh laughed, "Sure lad, but at such ah distance as ta appear as small points ah light."

"But this looks more like the sun than a star."

"An' so it be lad."

"I understand!" Aislin laughed excitedly. "The sun *is* a star, just much closer!"

"But," Riordan objected in his confusion, "If this is our sun, where is Domhan?"

Wordlessly Niamh pointed at a small blue sphere circling the flaming ball. Riordan's brain exploded. Finally, he stammered, "This is impossible, the sun is a lamp, chariots pull across... it's much smaller. "

Aislin laughed, "Riordan don't show your ignorance!" Actually, she was as confused as the young Rohi but was too embarrassed to admit this tiny detail.

"Na chariots lad, all creation's steps be governed by law. De same law dat be de power of de sword ye carry."

"If all creation is ruled by law," Riordan began, "Why does it seem so many live by their own law, or no law at all?"

"Tragically," Niamh winced, "Elohim's children live by deir own law now lad. It be de freedom offered by Atara's choice."

"By their own law?" Aislin asked incredulously, "What does that mean, surely there must be consequences for such a choice?"

"Consequences ye say?" Niamh replied, his voice trembling. "Aye lass, dere be consequences. Unless people reverse deir choice, Domhan will descend back inta chaos an void from which she came. But dat need not be yer choice. Elohim made ah covenant on behalf of all creation, ta work for its highest good. All must choose lass, live by Elohim's covenant law; or walk in yer own way, de way of chaos an darkness.'

"Riordan, yer own life, was it not also ah chaotic mess? It be from people in yer life livin' by deir own law. Nigh, yer life be ordered by Elohim. Yer movin' from chaos back ta light, an' ee's workin in yer life, until all be made right. In de beginnin' Elohim, made a covenant for creation's good ye see, movin' all creation from chaotic emptiness an void, ta light, order, and life."

~

"I'd welcome any suggestions as to how we might counter that rope weapon," Ragnhildr murmured.

"It's sorcery!" Caraig snapped. "The one among us with the best idea of how to fight it was just led helplessly through that accursed door."

"Peace Caraig," Mereah spoke softly. "Dalbhach seeks to divide us that we may be more easily conquered. We dare not let her succeed and battle amongst ourselves."

Ignoring the Rapha` princes call for peace, Korah leaned over and grabbed Ged by the throat of his cloak, "Where did they take Jireh?"

Losing all restraint Ged shouted back in the Captain's face, "How should I know? Spect he's the next main event."

Letting go of the adventurer's cloak, Korah straightened his back and stood pondering the enormity of the suggestion. Is this the way they would all end their lives? Gladiators in a demonic blood sport? Or worse yet, their life's blood drained out to feed the flames of Moloch's altar? And where was Riordan and the shieldmaiden Aislin? Were they safe, or facing similar dangers alone? Once again those he loved faced danger in his absence. The unknown held more power to inspire fear and despair than any foe the captain had ever faced. The unknown stole those most precious to him. While away fighting wars against the Dagon, he lost his beloved wife to the unknown dangers of childbirth. It's doubtful he could have done anything to prevent the tragedy–and yet, somehow, he should have known and prevented the unknowable. Unknown dangers robbed him of his three sons, the last reminders of his beloved's face. The blame, he assigned to himself without mercy or forgiveness. Somehow, he should have known–should have been there. The *unknown* cost him everything.

Korah was pulled from his dark thoughts by the horns announcing the start of the final round of the blood contest. He walked to the barred window looking into the arena. Relieved to see his rider on his feet, but disappointed to see all four of Ged's henchmen also in action.

"Four to three, still not great odds," He remarked offhandedly to Caraig.

"We've faced worse," The Weapons Master remarked dryly. "Also, one of Ged's is still wobbly from that last shot to his skull, our lads might get through this yet."

"What's the strategy this time?" Korah asked. "Another shot to the head?"

"Naw, Ged's lads would be ready for it this time. I told 'em to get the ball an' fort up. Make 'em come and take it."

At the horn Marcas raced forward, using longer legs to cover more ground quickly and thus reaching the prize a couple of strides ahead of the Dun adventurers. He then used his racket to flip the ball to the sidewall. After making the pass the cavalryman followed his own throw and raced to the wall joining his Dun partners right in front of the barred window where the captains were watching.

"What are ya up to Caraig?" Ged demanded.

"Even the odds if I can," The Weapons Master snarled back.

"Yer plannin' on cheating!" Ged accused.

"Ya can't cheat in a game without rules." Was the short response. "Mereah, sit on this dirtbag lest he try to be of any help to his lads."

As Mereah subdued their former guide, Ged cried out in desperate protest, "Yer condemning my lads to ah 'orrible death! They'll burn alive in Molech's furnace!"

"No, you condemned them," Ragnhildr replied forcefully. "By failing to warn us about what lay ahead, at a time when we could have actually done something to prevent it."

Soon as Marcas reached Cuan and Nahor they turned their backs to the wall, with the game ball directly behind them. All the captains could see of their two men from this vantage point were the backs of their legs, for the barred opening was at the arena's ground level. While the captains weren't really in a position to help, at least it gave the warriors the comforting feeling of having strong advocates in their corner. Their opponents on the other hand were forced to contend with nagging doubt, maybe, just maybe, they were the ones outnumbered.

As the four approached cautiously, despite the shelter of the coliseum walls small gusts of wind swirled dust around the attacker's legs. Korah started to ask Ragnhildr what he made of this, but the Irial Commander had his eyes closed, his forehead wrinkled in intense concentration. The Calvary Captain decided the matter could wait.

As anticipated two of Ged's men separated and attempted to engage the battered Marcas, cut him from the herd so to speak, while the other two kept Cuan and Nahor occupied. But efforts to take the flank were thwarted from fear of venturing too close to the low window where the captains kept watch. Marcas had a longer reach with his racket and height advantage over his Dun adversaries, so they couldn't attack without coming well within striking distance. Also, the Cavalryman was no longer under any illusions of a "game" or fair play. This was deadly combat.

The contest seemed to grind into a tense stalemate, neither side able to overcome the other's advantages. Unexpectedly, a strong gust of wind burst against Ged's adventurers, causing a slight loss of balance, and a shifting of their stance to brace against the wind. They also had to turn away slightly from their opponents to prevent sand and dust from getting in their eyes. Marcas and Nahor both seized the opportunity to strike decisively. Swift blows to the head rendered two of Ged's men unconscious.

In an act of desperation, one of the remaining Dun adventurers dove into Marcas's legs and tackled him. But a sharp rap across the attacker's skull from Cuan ended that exchange. Nahor kept the remaining adversary occupied while Marcas disentangled himself from his unconscious opponent, allowing Cuan to sprint as fast as his short Dun legs could carry him toward the opposite goal. All that remained of the contest was to make the pass and then score on a final uncontested shot.

Korah glanced suspiciously over towards Ragnhildr and remarked, "That sudden gust of wind, rather fortuitous wouldn't you say?"

Oblivious to Korah's meaning Caraig laughed, "Luckiest thing I've ever witnessed! Did yuh see how it affected Ged's men and not our own?"

Mereah, still sitting on a gaged Ged replied, "Methinks the good captain implied the gust was more than just luck Caraig. What do you think Ragnhildr?"

Finally catching on, Caraig joined the others as all eyes turned towards the Irial Commander. "No need to be coy my friends, our survival requires honesty amongst one another. When this quest was launched, I told you of my hope to regain the powers of dominion, endowed by our creator. The temple libraries in Bethel contain records concerning these gifts, legends of the scepter of Adon as well. Did you not realize I would try to learn all I could concerning these powers before even setting out on this quest? So, why does it surprise you I have begun to manifest creation gifts, those of *my* people. Without weapons or a militarized force, gifts of dominion may be our only hope for escaping from this prison."

Turning his attention back to Ged, Ragnhildr's voice became stern, but still offered some hope, "I understand the why of what you did, but still it proved a treacherous betrayal of our trust; if you had told us the truth – all of it – we may have found a way to avoid capture... perhaps a way to rescue your men. Even now, I would not willingly abandon them; if able to devise a plan for our escape I pledge to do all I can for your companions. *But* I would have your unquestioned obedience to my commands, *and* undivided loyalty to your king and his captains. Or I swear, after the quest ends, you shall be dragged before the king for swift justice."

Ged nodded, but that wasn't good enough for the Irial Commander, "I would hear you say it."

Ged stood up so that he could respond standing on his feet and with as much dignity as he could command, "Alright Cap'n, ah'll pledge me loyalty, an do all I can to aid our escape... the success of our quest, an what's more... if you'll help rescue me lad's, I'll be forever in yer debt. I'll never ferget it."

Ragnhildr held out his hand and after spitting in his, Ged took it. Caraig growled his disapproval, but Korah looked back from the barred windows just as a horn sounded and called out, "Somethings about to happen."

Sure enough, one of the gates opened and Jireh stepped into the arena. Waiting for him were the stone hammers he used as weapons. Moments later, a second gate split wide, and calls of approval sounded from the arena's few spectators. "What is it? What's comin' out?" Caraig wondered.

"Not sure," Korah breathed, "Nothings appeared yet."

Then a massive three-clawed foot did step out. The weight of the creature so great its footfall sent out tremors from the impact. This was followed by a challenge scream unlike anything the captains had ever heard.

"King of Heaven," Ragnhildr whispered cryptically.

Chapter Twenty-Seven

Reflections in the Bema pool changed and magnified the third planet in orbit causing it to grow before them, "Elohim appointed de sun ta rule day, an' de moon ta rule de night, an' dere was a second dawn, an' Elohim saw dat it was good.

After a slight pause, Niamh asked, "Now wat do ye see children?"

Riordan couldn't answer, he was still trying to wrap his head around the idea the world wasn't flat, and that the sun and moon weren't drawn across the sky by chariots. Aislin looked on with wonder and suddenly exclaimed, "I see, Riordan don't you see? Domhan spins, and as it turns different parts are exposed to the sun, creating day and night!"

"Aye lass, but 'ere be much more ta see." A thin line like a pole appeared, going through the planet at two white patches, making it appear as though Domhan tilted sometimes toward or away from the sun. "By Elohim's law, days, months, seasons, years, even centuries an' millennia are al' established. Dis is possible because Elohim also be Yahweh, master ov law."

"Jireh taught me the seasons, the movements of the stars, were all part of a great celestial dance." Riordan interjected quietly.

"Did 'e nigh?" Niamh asked gently laughing. "Did yer man nigh? an' yer man Jireh spoke true lad, Tebel, an de sun, an' all de stars do indeed move troogh de 'eavens as part ov a great dance wit guided steps." Then suddenly, discerning perhaps the real cause of the young Rohi's distress, he added, "Ye can still trust waat yer teacher taught ye lad, 'is words be true. Ee spoke symbolically ov a time far past, a remnant ov knowledge long lost. Before de world's devastation, children ov Elohim knew much dat is nigh forgotten. Learning an' science was poured inta symbol an' story, so not all would be lost after de world was broken.'

"Sum dance steps be quick, such as those dat govern night an day, or seasons. Watch nigh, as troogh de power ov de bema, centuries pass in moments, pay particular attention to Domhan's axis."

Riordan caught on first, "The world wobbles."

"Well done boy-O." Niamh picked up a small top and set it spinning on the smooth cavern floor. "See 'ow while de top spins dere also be a slight quiver? Domhan does also, but so slow, more dan twenty tousan' years be required ta complete wan rotation. In dis way, de stars not only reveal de time av night, an seasons, but also ta dose who can read de signs, a new age."

"With the change being so gradual, and over such a long period of time, how was this ever discovered?" Aislin asked incredulously.

"Life endured long before de firstborn embraced sorrow, child. Even so, Elohim's creation be babes, while de Watchers existed for many millennia before de offspring were born. Twelve Watchers rise ta Domhan's stewardship wit de changin' ov de new era. Dis will continue 'til de maturation av Elohim's scions be made complete. As each age passed, on de spring equinox, a different watcher claimed stewardship for dat epoch."

"There is a stone monument in the Irial city of Bethel," Aislin responded. "My father said the granite blocks were set to mark the equinox. He thought this was for the purpose of marking the time for planting."

"Such monuments an' structures exist all o'er Domhan lass. It's quite possible many be now used for agriculture. Dat isn't deir original purpose. Mighty stones deemed ta endure were chosen because dey marked de changing ov ah new age, an' de rising ov a new Watcher as Creation's Steward. No more important event be known ta exist an' only 'appened every two tousand years or so."

"Which of the Watchers moved into power during the Drachshaol?" Riordan asked.

Niamh looked at Riordan with eyes of wonder, "Well were ye chosen lad, dat question goes straight ta de 'eart ov de matter. When de constellation Draco set in de rising sun of spring's first day, de Watcher Nathair became de custodian an' steward. Mighty in works an knowledge of Elohim twas de Serpent Prince – but crafty. It seemed 'ard ta 'im dat 'ee be asked ta tutor 'is eventual replacements. 'e it twas 'at planted da seeds of Elohim's children ta rebel. Gifts of dominion were lost. Also lost, deir greatest treasure, de persons dey were called ta become. 'igher den de Messengers an' even de Watchers were de children destined ta be. 'ow far 'ave da mighty fallen. Created ta soar wit' eagles, Nathair taught us ta crawl in mud wit' worms. Such bondage did ee call freedom. Naught but faint memory remains ov who we were called ta be."

~

"Jireh," Ragnhildr hissed loud as he dared. "See how the monster sniffs the air? I believe him to be almost blind, hunting by sense of smell. Remain still while I make you invisible using air movement to carry away your scent."

"Send Caraig's odiferous perfume the monster's way," Mereah suggested. "Or would that be too cruel?"

A distinct whaaap sound attracted the massive tanniyn's attention and it resulted in a rapid series of impact tremors as the monster lowered its head and charged the barred dungeon window. Korah and Ragnhildr jumped away just as the massive head slammed into the wall, knocking Mereah back and Caraig down. While the creature stood there shaking its head, trying to clear cobwebs from its skull, the entire party got a close-up of the massive, muscled jaw and rows of ten to twelve-inch dagger teeth. Screaming a deafening roar of frustration, the party realized the creature's bark to be almost as bad as its bite. Besides the horrific smell accompanied by dragon slobber blowing their hair back, the sheer decibel level seemed sufficient to split eardrums.

Huddled up, hunched over, their hands over their ears, none of the warriors in the dungeon noticed Jireh choosing to take advantage of the tanniyn's distraction by shooting in and slamming the head of his great stone hammer into the creature's eye.

Unbelievably, the decibel level increased as the creature stood almost upright and threw its head back screaming in rage and torment. Jireh barely escaped being swatted by the stone-crushing tail as the creature thrashed about in agony. The Shophetim's respite was very brief as the dragon quickly forgot its pain to seek revenge. Heavily muscled legs suddenly propelled the beast forward in enraged pursuit.

Ragnhildr flashed Caraig and Mereah a withering scowl, "Fools, that is Jeshurun's Shophetim in the arena, do you find that an occasion to joke?" Jumping up he raced to the barred window shouting, "Jireh, I shall attempt to confuse the monster's ability to track you, you must put some distance between yourself and the creature if you can!"

Running full tilt required far too much energy for a "What do you think I'm doing?" verbal response. All Jireh could manage was to dig deep for an additional burst of speed that gained the great centaur a few more yards of safety. Strong breezes sprang up suddenly forming small dust devils swirling across the arena. Hoping he had managed to blind the tanniyn's right eye, Jireh swerved right to see if this would break from the great carnivore's line of sight. Confused, the predator did slow to a walk, moving its head side to side attempting to regain its prey's scent. Jireh, in the meantime, tried to maintain a position behind and to the right, out of sight and hopefully out of mind.

"Jireh," Ragnhildr cried, "Another power strives against me, seeking to control the direction of the wind, I may not be able to conceal your scent much longer."

No sooner were the words spoken than the creature's body repositioned allowing the great head to snap around and fix its good eye directly on Jireh. After a great sniffing sound, confirming the Shophetim's location, the creature once again roared and charged. Jireh wheeled and fled. The length of the monster's strides, however, allowed it to close the gap quickly while it took Jireh precious seconds to reach top speed. Impact tremors filled the centaur's ears, causing a mad panic. The resulting surge meant the creature's great jaws snapped shut just short of the centaur's rump, missing flesh and muscle, but giving it a vice-like grip on the horsetail.

Shaking its great head, like a large dog playing tug-of-war with a cat's tail, Jireh found himself being slung around. Fighting frantically to keep his footing, he also suffered the agony of much of his tail being ripped out by the root. Surging forward once more, Jireh barely escaped a second attempt to clamp great jaws on his back and sever his spine. Fleeing around the arena, breaths coming in frantic ragged gasps, an eternity passed before the dragon started to tire and slow down.

"The tanniyn is an ambush predator my friend, not used to long pursuits," Ragnhildr called out. "I will attempt to conceal your scent once more. I may only be able to give you just a few seconds, you must strike a decisive blow in that moment – it is all I can give."

Jireh turned and faced the creature. All of fifty-feet in length, it stood momentarily still in order to pull in massive gasps of air. The tanniyn stood upright placing the deadly rows of dagger teeth a good ten feet higher than the top of Jireh's head.

The Shophetim felt a sudden change in the direction of the wind. A strong breeze blowing directly in his face was more than refreshing, it proved to be a signal for the centaur's desperate final attack. Breaking quickly once more to the monster's blinded right eye, Jireh prayed the change in the wind would carry away his scent making him all but invisible. The great maw started to turn as the predator tried to relocate its prey but did so without any sense of urgency. In this the monster's greatest weakness was revealed – a far greater detriment than poor eyesight – its appalling lack of intelligence. It just didn't occur to the minuscule brain that losing sight of what it hoped to make its next meal, would be an indication of danger. Not until excruciatingly sharp pain shot up from its kneecap and ankle. Attempting to respond to this new threat by pivoting, the creature failed to comprehend the non-responsiveness from its leg, until it buckled. A great dust cloud shot into the air from the resulting fall so that the dragon's undamaged eye barely perceived the heavy stone hammer's arching trajectory towards its thick skull.

Satisfied the dragon wouldn't be able to rise again, Jireh paused a moment to wipe perspiration from his brow. He almost felt relaxed, when blaring horns jarred the entire arena back into a state of readiness.

Archers suddenly appeared at the top of the arena walls, with arrows on string. At the same time the tall gate that admitted the massive tanniyn cranked slowly open, this time admitting several warriors brandishing spears and moving quickly to surround the Shophetim of Jeshurun.

The alarm and distress of the captains over this new development erased all the elation they felt over the centaur's victory. Their agitation turned to panic as the stone block that allowed a view into the arena slowly, agonizingly ground along its stone track back into place. The last sight they had of Jireh was of him dropping his great stone hammers and raising his hands in surrender.

"The horn blasts signified the match as a disqualification," the sultry voice belonged to the Enchantress Dalbhach. "Outside interference of the contests is not permitted. The Irial commander's treachery by using even rudimentary sorcery was not wise."

"The interference was my doing, not the centaur's," Ragnhildr objected. "Any punishment should fall on the head of the offender."

The all too familiar deadly vine shot under the door and wrapped around the expedition commander's neck, tightening enough to make breathing almost impossible, "I agree. Therefore, at solstice's dawning you shall be the first sent to face Moloch my master. As for the rest of you, do not attempt to intervene. I will be forced to kill your leader immediately, and one of you would then be selected to take his place. The crown prince perhaps? Oh yes, I know the great buffoon's identity."

"Korah," Ragnhildr rasped, "You are the new commander, rescue Aisli..." Before the Irial Captain could finish his request, the line around his throat tightened cutting off the rest of his air. Ragnhildr collapsed to his knees and the captains started to rush to his aid.

"Stop!" Barked Dalbhach, "or you'll kill him rather than aid his cause."

The dungeon door swung open as though under its own power, and Jireh similarly bound passed through the door. Ragnhildr was then forced to his feet and all-but dragged into the outer hall. The door slammed shut emphasizing the finality of the moment.

Chapter Twenty-Eight

If you want to make sure of keeping it intact, you must give your heart to no one… avoid all entanglements; lock it up safe in the casket or coffin of your selfishness. But in that casket — safe, dark, motionless, airless — it will change. It will not be broken; it will become unbreakable, impenetrable, irredeemable.

C.S. Lewis

he Bema Pool was alive with images of all manner of lovely and fantastic creatures. "Above all dese beasties, Elohim crowned 'is creation wit 'is greatest work, children of 'is image."

Once again, the crystals in the cavern ceiling glowed myriads of colors, and images of the seven races emerged as reflections on the glass surface of the water.

"An' Elohim saw it be very good," Niamh completed the thought. "Do ya understan' waat dat means? t'be sure ya don't. Elohim's image be a treasure-never realized. It be lost nigh, for several tousan' years. Over time, even de 'ope of it be forgotten. Nigh only a longing, fer ye know not waat remains as ah memory buried deep in an empty place in yer souls."

Korah sat collapsed against the dungeon wall, hanging his head. Jireh sensed his struggle, and so stood close by, waiting for the Capall Captain to speak when ready, "Ragnhildr chose a poor rescuer for Aislin," he murmured. "I once was husband and father to a beautiful wife and three strong, proud sons. I have lost them all. I could save none of them, and now, I fear even Riordan is lost... I do not suffice."

Sensing the captain needed to voice his pain more than he needed words of comfort or advice, Jireh remained silent. In a few moments, Korah continued, "Yahweh Elohim asks much of me, my friend. He has taken all that I considered precious. We sit here, each one waiting his turn to be sacrificed to a monster, and so I deem Moloch cruel. Yet, in my heart I cannot stop asking the question if our El is not *also* cruel? He has given so much, but the love and joy... strength of heart I received, love of wife and family, pride in my sons; it all took root so that when taken away... it didn't just leave a hole in my heart, it ripped it out. Without cause to hope, I will soon despair. My death certainly comes soon. If I am never to see the goodness of our Adonai, while in the land of the living... how can I... how can I surmise my wife and sons are resting in El's mercy? I don't see evidence of mercy. My only experience in *this* life is brokenness, pain, and meaningless death."

"El did not take your wife, or your sons."

"But when the Anak was torturing my sons to death, couldn't a mighty power such as our El stop him?"

"Elohim is sovereign, how could we be in His image if His gift did not include our own sovereignty, the gift of free will?" Jireh replied. "Without choice, we would be manikin-puppets. But the consequences of this gift are both wonderful, and terrible. Human goodness is truly good, because of choice. Love, goodness, these are meaningless without the ability to choose, even that which is evil. Do not blame El, or even yourself for the evil choices of others. It is a powerful but terrible truth, that no one is exempt in these matters, for good or ill."

"Even Elohim?" Korah asked sadly.

"Especially Elohim. Or did you think that somehow El could escape the inevitable consequences of His own gift? Your heart is broken; that is the surest sign your heart is becoming like His."

"Then the price of freedom is too high." Korah lamented. "An unfeeling puppet or golem would be free of pain."

"Also free from life and joy. Nothing more than animated dust and clay." Jireh countered.

Mereah, no longer content to just listen, added softly, "My friend. I know I spoke of this before, far too briefly, but I watched your youngest sons give their lives as a sacrifice that our people might live. Without their service our nation would have been lost. In your pain do not discount their choice, they did not spend their lives in vain. The secrets of my own victory over despair, I learned from your scions, who met the enemy's spite with song. This was a power that dismayed even the Dagon's Anak. I will meet this enchantress's use of despair and fear to break our spirits in like manner."

Mereah then stood and in a deep baritone started singing an ancient song of power.

> O Yahweh, when, fallen, You lifted me up,
> Broken, I cried out and You restored me.
> Dead, You rescued me from the grave;
> Alive–out of the pit of my despair.
> Let the restored sing songs of thanksgiving,
> His anger is for a moment,
> His lovingkindness lasts for eternity.
> Weeping and sorrow may endure for a night,
> Darkness and despair seem to last forever
> Certain as the dawn, joy comes in the morning.

Then Jireh joined in, followed by Caraig. After a moment, Korah rose to his feet, dusted himself off, and joined the song.

> You hid Your face, and I was terrified.
> I cried out to You, O my Adonai;
> my mourning turned into dancing;
> My sackcloth removed,
> I wear joy as a cloak,
> O Yahweh once more–hear my cry,

Be my all-sufficient strength.
Yet again, be my comfort and mighty help!

Rohi's Songbook

As they sang, the song's crescendo grew in potency and the dungeon flamed with light and power. Joy flooded the dank corridors, filling even the most remote crevices with light of truth. The halls of Moloch's Shadow found no answer. Terrified, the jailers knew the inmates were the ones holding the keys.

Chapter Twenty-Nine

There are no ordinary people. You have never talked
to a mere mortal.

C.S. Lewis

aat if I was ta tell ye dat oi was planning on giving ye, a gold coin fer every star in de universe, would ye be 'appy?"

Both Aislin and Riordan nodded silently, not sure where this new line of questioning was going. Was this a trick question?

"Sure, an' why wouldn't ye, but de gift be far greater den ye know; de stars yer can see number in de tousan's, but look now in the Bema," and here Niamh barked a verbal command, Nocht."

Gazing now at the Bema pool, points of white light flew past as though traveling at high speed in a snowstorm.

"Each point of light yer see be ah cluster of stars, an yer might not even know dis number, but already billions of points of light 'as been revealed."

"Each point of light is a star?" Riordan asked with awe in his voice, and starlight gleaming in his eyes.

"Stars lad?" Niamh asked with a laugh. "Nay, oi said each point of light ye see are clusters ov stars; each cluster containing billions ov stars all der own. If oi gave ye a coin for every star ye could *see* in de night sky, ye'd 'ave enough ta fill a large room wit' gold. A handsome gift. But waat oi promised wasn't a coin fer every star ye could see, but a coin for every star. Yer understandin' ov the gift be limited by waat ye see. Yer sight 'as blinded ye ta all but a tiny fraction ov de gift's reality an true worth."

"The gift is far greater than our understanding?" Aislin offered.

"An' ow could it not be? Elohim's gift be 'is own image. Ta understan' de true nature ov de gift, requires comprehension ov de infinite, ov eternity. Understan' dis, de image be not tangible, nor in-erited children, it be *learned*, in face-ta-face relationship. Such a gift takes time, Ye don't grow inta Elohim's image in a night, or a year, or even a millennia. Wen yer fathers learned 'ow long de growth process wuld take, dey exercised deir sovereignty, by seekin' ah short cut, an easier way.'

"Nathair, knowin' Elohim's children would one day replace de Watchers as stewards, sought ta supplant 'em. Nathair provided ah easy way, one 'e 'imself 'ad once chosen. 'E convinced 'em dey would never complete deir maturation while in servitude; dat dey would surpass Elohim - if dey wud throw off 'deir yoke."

"Gettin' dem ta abort de process necessary for perfection, Nathair made certain dey would ne'er come inta der own. Children, yer enemy is powerful, but 'is greatest power, be lies an' deceit. 'E directs all 'is power ta wun purpose, keepin' ye from de truth, ov who ye truly are."

~

Ragnhildr kept assuring himself it was just a nightmare. But when he opened his eyes once more and beheld the same horror, he realized he was wide awake in grim reality. He was bound fast in a stone chamber that perched on the top tier of the step pyramid that rose above the ancient city. Four large openings were oriented perfectly to the four compass points. The Irial Captain, back to the north, faced the profile of a large bronze idol that had the body of a man, and the head of a bull. Placed in the center of the room to face the coming dawn, the minotaur statue was in fact a great furnace. Filled with burning coals the metal glowed orange, while the eye openings and nostrils blazed with red flame.

Through the opening to the east, Ragnhildr recognized the constellation of the bull aligned perfectly on the horizon so that the rising sun would be housed in the center of the star cluster.

The icy voice of Dalbhach confirmed what the Irial Commander suspected, "You are indeed privileged to witness a momentous event. A new Watcher is coming to power. Nathair the Serpent is not being replaced. The great dragon will never relinquish power. However, others among the Watcher's have joined the Serpent's rebellion; soon Moloch will be released in this world-on this, the shortest, darkest day of the year. Because of your treachery, you will soon be sent to meet him."

Dalbhach turned to the south opening and beckoned with her hand. Quickly the sound of an infant's wailing could be heard, faint at first but steadily growing louder. Soon a troop of Sióga came through the south opening carrying a male infant over their heads. Observing the shock registering in Ragnhildr's eyes, Dalbhach droned on, "You remember the Sióga I see. They are not a source of hope for you, they are children of light no longer. They are corrupted. Worshiping shadows, so that in shadow they can be perfectly concealed making them Nathair's and now Moloch's useful servants and thieves."

Snatching the boy child by his ankles Dalbhach lifted it high chanting in some dark tongue. Then just as the first rays of dawn pierced the temple, the infant was laid in the upturned hands of the idol. Immediately flames roared up from the bowels of the minitour consuming the child leaving only the stench of burnt flesh. Several more innocents were sacrificed in this manner without Dalbhach betraying even a hint of remorse.

Her gruesome business complete, the Enchantress drew close to Ragnhildr, embraced him seductively and whispered into his ear, "It's a pity that your turn to die is coming so soon."

Before he could respond the hemp line around Ragnhildr's throat tightened restricting his air. She released the rest of his bonds and then compelled him to follow. "The sacrifice of croí will secure Moloch's avatar to be released into this dimension. More must be extracted however, for his strength to zenith. Lifeforce extracted directly results in a greater surge of power. For this reason, you are being sent to meet Moloch face to face."

Dalbhach led Ragnhildr through the pyramid's north opening and partway down the steep steps. "As the sun rises higher in the sky, precise placement of stone blocks will cast shadows creating the image of an uncoiling serpent along the east side of the north stair. As you can see, the process is already begun. In moments the shadows will reach the serpent's head at ground level. When this happens, a passage will open to Moloch's chambers. You will pass through to face him. Refusal is to invite the immediate death of all your companions," and here Dalbhach fixed Ragnhildr with a steely gaze, "Including your daughter."

Ragnhildr lunged for the Enchantress's throat, but the hemp cable around his neck instantly tightened cutting off his air. "Yes, I know about your beloved, the portal she entered with the fool boy brought her straight to me. You will be sent to meet Moloch unbound, and unfettered. Perhaps with newly awakened gifts of dominion, you will be able to resist. That is the only hope that either of you shall have. Will you be so foolish as to throw even this faint hope away? Look at me now and nod your assent, lest I use your life to feed the furnace, with your daughter Aislin sent to face Moloch in your stead."

Ragnhildr stopped fighting the line around his neck and it relaxed the tension enough for a nod in response, "Wise choice. Proceed down the pyramid steps, a gateway will open before you reach the bottom step. Proceed through the opening, Moloch will be waiting for you deep in the valley of shadow. Understand this, my master requires victims, to add their life force to his. I instructed Ged to find men of power in vain hope–perhaps–that they might succeed in defying his might. This is the reason for your selection, you are mighty among the Irial; you have begun to manifest dominion gifts that will be of greater aide than swords. I risk much, but I offer this small aid, remember, all that takes place in the heavens falls in your sphere of dominion. Now go."

Ragnhildr started down the steps. Shadows created by the rays of dawn formed zig-zag shadow patterns of a slithering serpent moving down the stairs. He reached the final step just as the sun rose high enough to connect serpentine shadows to the head of a striking stone viper at the pyramid's base. The sound of grating stone drew his eye to a small knoll, that seemed to be the focus of the shadow serpent's gaze. There at an angle to the pyramid courtyard, a slab of stone slid open revealing a stairway that descended into the depths.

Dalbhach spoke from behind Ragnhildr's shoulder. "This whole structure was first used by Nathair four millennia ago, now it is to be Moloch."

Suppressing rising bile in his throat, caused by an almost absolute certainty of a horrible impending death, Ragnhildr began his descent into Gehenna's shadows.

Chapter Thirty

We never know how high we are
Till we are called to rise;
And then, if we are true to plan,
Our statures touch the skies —

Emily Dickison

e Bema, also looks inta de future." The Bema Pool reflections revealed a star so bright it made the many stars around it all but disappear as it lit up the countryside below. The Sióg paused and looked at Riordan, with a mysterious gleam in his eye, "Waat do ye see?"

Riordan looked at the crest on the tunic that his grandfather had given him, prominent in the upper right corner was the symbol of a star. Comparing the two gave him pause, he started to stammer a response, but in the end said nothing.

Finally, Aislin asked, "Is that a comet?"

"A comet? Ah good guess lass, but nay, it's a conjunction, of two 'eavenly bodies, each herald de birth of kings. Wun ah king of 'eaven, another ah king of men. Dey be drawn together so close, as ta appear as one. Rare are dey so joined in de celestial dance. Such ah conjunction would herald de comin of an earthly king, an a 'eavenly one, joined as wun."

Aislin suddenly realized Niamh stared at the coat of arms on Riordan's tunic, and it was her turn to become puzzled.

The reflections in the Bema changed once more, this time revealing the midday sun going black plunging the land into darkness. This in turn revealed a blood-stained moon in the failing light. Niamh remarked, "Dis one, be disturbin' an ah don't know all it implies; do yer see 'ere below? Dere's ah man under ah black mountain, bein' crushed by enormous weight, 'is blood pourin' out. My 'eart quails, waat dark day would be accompanied by such dire signs? An' more puzzlin' still, de man be from among de Capall, but 'e wears Atara the Irial king's crown."

The Sióg said no more but gazed at Riordan with a mournful eye, and a tear glistened and rolled down his cheek. Slightly alarmed Riordan whispered, "What is it? Do you also have the gift of sight? Do you see something?"

"Waat do oi see? Too much. Pain lad, yer pain be far from ended, an' will pursue ye long past yer grave, ta yer children's children." Niamh turned away to conceal the sorrow written on his face, "Ah don't know where de heaviest stroke will fall, oi suspect it be on yer son. Ah know it isn't much comfort, just remember wen ever it be darkest, yer never alone. Adonai 'e be yer shield, de 'ammer will fall 'ardest on 'im."

Aislin looked over at Riordan in wonder. He'd never seemed anything more than just a boy. An extremely ordinary one at that. Yet Niamh seemed to see something in his future that had eluded her completely.

~

When Ragnhildr reached the bottom of the steps a long passage led straight into impenetrable gloom. A lone torch cast enough light to see only a few feet ahead. Just enough to see a few extra torches alongside the wall. Now the first of many choices presented itself. Use a torch, and he might as well blow trumpets to announce his arrival. Any creature with eyes would see the light long before he would see enemies lurking in the shadows. Did he dare risk it?

On the other hand, there may be deep pits or shafts in the floor, or side passages needing to be explored; In the end, the danger of missing these outweighed the danger of alerting enemies to his presence. Most likely any waiting enemies knew he would be coming regardless. Still, he found it very hard to explain the courtesy of a lit torch. He very much doubted it was out of the kindness of Dalbhach's, or even Moloch's heart.

Fear. It suddenly occurred to Ragnhildr that whoever, or whatever waited for him ahead, wanted *him* to see what was coming. As in so many warped, broken, distorted creatures he had previously encountered, Moloch fed on fear. Well, so be it. He must control his emotions regardless, if he was to have any hope of rescuing his daughter. Retrieving a few extra torches, he walked deeper into the gloom.

Within fifty feet he came to a significant change in the chamber. He had three choices, side passages to the right and left, or straight for a few more feet before coming to a wall and another hall going left. A maze then. He remembered the great furnace idol back in the pyramid, a man, with the head of a bull. He didn't need to search long in his memory for legends concerning a great minotaur feeding on human flesh and blood, his lair somewhere deep in a maze. Those who entered the monster's domain never returned, or so the whispered stories always said.

That's why the torch, Ragnhildr reasoned. He was the quarry and Dalbhach wanted him to have at least the illusion of a sporting chance. How thoughtful.

Before starting down any passage, he looked around for a rock, something to scratch the stone wall and mark his passage. The corridors were filled with years of dust and cobwebs, but nothing hard enough to make a mark on the granite. Then he had an idea that inspired him to pat himself on the back. He shuffled his feet to easily see his own tracks in the dust. Whenever he saw a cobweb, he ripped it down. In this way, he could at least see where he'd been, just in case the maze got him going in circles.

Mindful of the limits of his torch he moved quickly. Three times he chose passages that led to dead ends. The fourth time he discovered he could sense closed passages leading nowhere by the complete lack of movement in the air. Twice he ventured down passages that led him back to his original starting point. Selecting a new corridor without evidence of prior travel, Ragnhildr quickly realized he was on the right track; the air whispered of a faint scent of death. In about two hundred paces with no turns left or right he drew close to the source, a mummified corpse. No maggots or signs of scavenger molestation of any kind were seen, giving a clear indication that nothing living wandered the maze. Examining the victim closer, it appeared the person simply refused to participate further in his trial and chose to just lay down and die. Despair, aided by fear, froze him to the spot that became his final resting place.

Further careful examination, however, disclosed several very strategic cuts in the skin, revealing whoever the person was, his blood was drained and harvested.

The cloak worn by the victim was tattered material woven from plants but in a pattern of greens that would make the wearer almost invisible in woodlands. Ragnhildr considered thoughtfully the great forest Mothar Crann. None dared to enter the dark wood as it was long said to be haunted. Unseen spirits that inhabited the trees slew any that dared enter. Ragnhildr however knew of at least one of the Irial who dared enter the dark grove and lived to tell the tale. He doubted he'd live long enough to have another opportunity. But the thought stirred a fond memory of a woodland lady, who succeeded in enchanting his heart.

Moving on, he considered further the evidence gleaned from the mummified victim. The multiple cuts were from a small fine blade or blades-not a suicide certainly. No, Ragnhildr felt certain the victim was sacrificed, and that indicated that perhaps, despite appearances, the Irial Commander was not alone in the maze. Chuckling just a little, despite his circumstances, he remembered Caraig insisting on little men being behind some of the attacks in the passages beneath the Irijah mountains. He'd allowed the good-natured ribbing, all the while knowing it was close to the truth. He knew enough about these "Lil Men" that if encountered alone and unarmed, the "lil men" could very well become the instruments of his own death.

~

The dark, dank musty dungeon was transformed so that it now fairly crackled with life, energy, and power. While the other captains continued to sing a song of power, Caraig walked over to the heavy door, lovingly caressing the stone with his hands. "Dalbhach needs to learn a prison of stone is not an adequate hold for a son of Dun."

Korah out of curiosity walked over to see what Caraig was about, "Do you see something my friend?"

"I feel something," Caraig whispered, trying not to break his concentration. "This door is several inches thick, carved from solid granite," the Weapons Master paused as he continued his probe of the door. "The hinge, however, is brittle iron, and the pins attached to the hinge, over the centuries are losing their bite," Caraig changed focus from probing the door to drawing strength from the rock beneath his feet. "The weakness of the hinge should allow me to..." The Dun placed both hands on the door surface, with feet firmly planted he uttered a word of power, "*scaoileadh*" and with a mighty heave threw the door against the opposite wall of the hall. The little light they had went out leaving them in darkness.

Korah laid his hand gently on Caraig's shoulder, "Every negative word I uttered about your cooking I take back my friend."

"Is our escape prevented?" Mereah asked in a giant's whisper, which is still much too loud for stealth.

"If it wasn't before, it is now with all your bellowing," Caraig growled.

In an even more exaggerated whisper Mereah asked, "What happened to our light?"

"The reason our diminutive friend is so grouchy," Korah replied, is that he doesn't want to tell you, that he snuffed the hall torch accidently when he threw the prison door against the wall."

When the prince started to laugh Caraig stomped on his foot. "An none of *that* nonsense neither," He hissed. "Guards that can't see will still find us with all yer bellowing."

Wiping suppressed tears of laughter from his eyes, Mereah loudly whispered again, "Perhaps I can help," as he pushed the man of Dun aside and stepped out into the passage. "Our wardens are coming down the hall quickly, several of Caraig's tiny men."

"How can you see anything?" Korah was so puzzled he forgot to whisper.

"I can't," Mereah replied. "But during my travels through the caverns, I began to see heat, that emanates from living things. The blood of whatever comes down this passage burns hot, such as what pumps in our own hearts, but far closer to the ground. I think they might make even you feel like a giant Caraig. It would be better if you allowed me to meet this threat."

Without waiting for a response, the Rapha Prince stepped forward to meet the swift-moving prison guards charging down the hall. Blades drawn, relying on the absence of light for concealment, the little "men" prepared to slice and dice as high above Mereah's ankle as they could reach; and then drain and harvest his blood. So it was that just as they were about to start their attack, they were caught completely off guard when a swift kick sent several of their brethren flying fifty feet back down the hall where they tumbled and rolled and lay still.

"Yes, tiny friends, I *can* see you. *Our* blindness is no longer a shield for you. I have no wish to cause harm, but as I have just demonstrated, you do not want me for an enemy."

Caraig muttered, "Be afraid, very afraid, his singing alone can kill."

Then in emphasis of his warning, Mereah stomped savagely mere inches from several heat signatures; then a big grin crossed his face as he watched the faint red glow emanating from dozens of beating hearts scurry back down the hall. All except one.

Korah's curiosity got the better of him, so he asked, "Are they gone? Are they Caraig's tiny men?"

"We be the Sióga," a small high-pitched voice piped in. "You would do well not to underestimate my people or judge them by their stature. "

Caraig couldn't contain his laughter until a hot searing sensation of being stabbed in the foot changed his guffaw to a howl. No one could really see, but since the howling sounds were moving up and down everyone guessed the Dun Captain was jumping up and down on one leg while holding an injured foot.

"I am named Ciar among the Sióga. We don't have much time, *my* people will be back. They will come as a swarm and attack with overwhelming numbers. Each Sióg carries a potent sting. I can aide your escape but require that I and my family be allowed to depart with you."

"Ciar of the Sióga," Jireh piped in, "Why should we trust you?"

"No time for that now. You only have time to choose. This only can I tell you; my people's service is compelled by Moloch and his Druid Shaman Dalbhach. I am not alone from among my people in seeking to escape servitude from their dominion."

"We need light," Korah suggested hopefully, "And our weapons, if you know where they are kept."

As if in answer, the captains heard a striking noise and Ciar held a small torch as high as he could. Its small flame shone like a beacon in the pitch-black. "Light I can manage, but your weapons are in a small armory further down this hall. That is also the direction from which the pursuit will come. You cannot go that way."

"We won't get far without the means to defend ourselves," Caraig argued. "We have no other choice."

"I agree," Korah joined in. "And I must find Aella, I'll not leave her here to be sacrificed or slaughtered. She's close, I can sense it."

"Too long *already* have we delayed," Ciar moaned. "Behold even now are the hounds of hell unleashed."

The Sióg's small torch cast enough light to reflect off from several sets of eyes bobbing and weaving while moving down the hall towards them.

"Wolves?" Caraig speculated.

"Worse, I think," Jireh murmured. "Remember the sleek crocodiles that ran like the ostrich when we first were brought into the valley? Dalbhach called them her special pets."

"Whatever they be they're closing fast," Ged remarked with just a hint of panic in his voice. Ciar didn't give his panic a voice, he just dropped his small torch and ran. The flame went out, as did the reflections of the eyes moving towards them. Once more the captains stood alone, facing yet another foe in the dark.

"Get behind me friends, though their blood burns not as hot, I can still see them. I alone have the sight to face this enemy." Mereah strode forward over the protests of his companions, his ability to see heat did allow him to see the foremost creature leap from several yards away. What he couldn't see was that at the forefront of the creature's assault it was all razor-sharp teeth, claws, and great hooked spur-like scimitars. Weapons designed to slash and expose the vitals of prey much larger than itself. Even a giant.

Chapter Thirty-One

iordan was in a somber mood while reflecting on the revelations Niamh had shown him. He had hoped the pain that threatened to wither his soul had come to an end. There were strong reasons to believe this. Korah, his redeemer had proven a patient, gentle, man. Firm in his discipline, the Capall Captain sought to teach and correct rather than punish. "Judgment is an act of love meant to restore relationship, and to redeem from error." Korah explained when applying discipline.

This stood in stark contrast to the correction brought by Brannan. His "uncle" only knew how to punish, while displaying an almost felt need to torment. A need seemingly fed by years of resentment and shame. The contrast between Riordan's life then and now was indeed stark, night and day, black and white, potent joy versus crippling depression.

Also, he had friendships such as he never knew before. In Jireh, Caraig, and Mereah, Riordan experienced the joy of having companions that he knew wouldn't hesitate to lay down their lives for him. Nor would he hesitate to do the same for them. Is there a greater love than that?

However, Niamh hinted that the Bema revealed signs that the pain and sorrow of his childhood would continue throughout his life. Were his friends in danger now? Would he lose them so soon after finding them?

Almost as though the Sióg read the concerns of his heart, Niamh suggested, "Our time tagether must draw ta ah close, yer friends 'ave need of ye. Oi 'ave a few more tings to show ye, but time presses, an' we must leave de Bema."

Walking halfway around the edge of the still pool they entered another hall. The long narrow passage was filled with carved statues and mosaics on the wall.

"Dis be de 'all of 'eroes. De devastation dat ended de first age threatened ta wipe away all memory of mighty deeds. 'ere dey be preserved until all Elohim's children 'ave deir courage revealed."

He stopped before a mosaic detailing a tale of one of the Irijah, battling alone through a host of fierce foes; men riding great tanniyn with massive jaws and daggers for teeth running on two heavily muscled legs. The great dragons counter-balanced by a massive tail ran with their heads parallel to the ground. Still, they towered over the centaur they sought to devour. "Time would fail me ta tell Benaiah's tale. Few dere be in any age who could match it. By 'is efforts, much 'at was fair be preserved. Bearach, Atara's son sent armies ta destroy 'is works an' take 'is life. Faithful service often comes at a great price, Benaiah didn't see the cost as bein' too much ta pay."

Niamh then stopped before a mosaic of one of the Capall, riding with the morning sun to his back, driving a great lance through the heart of a huge winged tanniyn. In front of the mural, a great lance was displayed. Fifteen feet long, the lance was still stained with dried blood. "Dis be de lance of Aonghus, a young son of Capall. Many of 'is people followed King Atara in 'is folly. An so, de Capall lost deir bond wit deir 'orses an' took ta ridin' strange beasts of great power. Ciaran, de black was one as followed de evil king, an 'e rode a mighty dragon, wit scales so strong, be it blade or lance, dey all broke on its steely 'ide. De Sha'ar were driven ah day 'n night afore the beastie, when Aonghus rode out ta meet 'im with morning light on 'is brow, an' ah song in 'is 'eart. Do ye recognize waat 'e used ta tip 'is lance lad?"

Their eyes followed the length of the lance to see just a hint of a translucent blue at the point. Aislin's eyes went wide, "Is that ..."

"Aye lass, Yara, same as the lad's blade. Na much more'n a grain ah sand, but enough ta pierce da dragon's scales 'owever. In da same way our enemy's lies are powerless ta stop ah single grain of truth. Take de lance lad, twas preserved 'ere knowin' it'd be needed again. Mayhap ye know ah mighty cap'n as would know 'ow ta use it."

Just past the lance placed horizontally on a small wooden rack lay a wooden whistle, ornately carved for most of the two feet of its length. When Niamh gazed upon it, his eyes got misty and looked up the way people do when accessing a fond, long-ago memory. "Why is this instrument preserved here?" Aislin asked. "Does it have some virtue or power?"

It took Niamh a moment to emerge from a cherished place in his thoughts, but at last he replied, "Does it 'ave power? Aye lass, twas lovingly crafted takin' 'five hundred years ta complete, by a folk who considered so much time on ah instrument time well spent. Benaiah kept it here ta preserve de memory of a lady, whose spirit remained untainted by Atara's folly an' malice. Oi 'ope Benaiah would approve, oi think ye should take it, lass. It does indeed possess a power, even if only ta give de lady as played it, ah voice once again. Take it lass, ye will find it preserves a small touch of a time now lost. It also carries a melody of 'ope dat such music will be 'eard again." Aislin lifted the instrument off its stand carefully, and gave Niamh a graceful bow of respect, demonstrating her understanding of the value of such a gift.

Then she turned briefly towards her companion and asked politely, "Riordan, would you mind walking ahead and viewing some of the other exhibits, there's something personal I'd like to discuss with Niamh."

The rohi shrugged his shoulders and walked ahead pausing to look at the carvings and mosaics along the way. When far enough so as to not hear hushed voices, Aislin turned to Niamh and asked, "Why do you fill the boy's head with grandiose ideas about his importance? Some of Moriah's Captains do the same, but they are only setting him up for huge disappointment."

"Why do I fill 'is 'ead?" Niamh asked confused. "Let me ask ye lass, I've waited for over tree millennia for de one promised ta come through de portal. 'E be de one dat possesses de Yara Blade, an is de one who arrived as promised. Do ye think 'is comin' be ah mistake?"

"He's just a boy."

"Ah, my pulse, at's where yer wrong. E carries a significant burden of pain, dat 'as matured 'im beyond 'is years. 'e was ner' a boy, ner' given dat precious gift. All 'is life 'e will long for wat 'e knows not. Denied de opportunity ta be a child, 'e will remain childlike, but with ah maturity tempered by pain."

"I've suffered loss as well, it never affected me!"

"Never lass? Some of de anger ye sometimes express be denial of an attraction ye feel. Shared pain draws people tagether like a magnet. Nigh don't frown at me. Be careful of it, if pain is de core of loves bond; wit out healing, dat which binds, also rips 'earts apart."

"You didn't hear what I said, he's just a boy. A stubborn, clumsy, *stupid* boy at that."

"Stupid? Lass, oi know ye can't 'ear me now, but yer being thrown together is not an accident anymor'n yer coming through de portal together. In a few years, oi pray you'll remember waat oi said."

When they caught up to Riordan, he stood transfixed by a mosaic image of a white tree, with leaves of deep crimson. On a small altar in front of the tree, a gold chalice lay on its side as though tipped over. The spilled contents looked like blood.

"De Baryith lad," Niamh volunteered an answer to an unspoken question. "Tree of life an' symbol of Elohim's covenant. Its blood was spilt when de covenant was violated, an de Scepter of Adon usurped."

At the talisman's mention, Riordan's heart skipped a beat, "Is the scepter here? The Quest that sent me here searches for it."

"Do dey nigh? Do dey know de scepter's misuse ended de first age with devastation?"

"Yes." Aislin and Riordan answered together.

"Still dey seek it? De scepter be warded, children, until Shiloh comes, 'e be de one who will restore its purpose. We must go now, yer friends are in danger, an oi fear comin' too late. At de end of dis hall is de last portal lad, take us through it, an' we'll be close to where yer friends be captive. Hurry now."

Ragnhildr started making considerable progress. Reasoning Moloch's chambers would be furthest from the entrance and fresh air, he chose passages where the atmosphere reeked of death and decay. This required unspeakable courage. All his natural sense of self-preservation had to be silenced.

Also, the deeper into the maze he went, the more keenly he discerned a spirit of malignant, lingering, malice. He moved deeper into a spiritual stronghold with each step. The power that reigned here was a principality, a demonic strongman. The ignorant called beings like Moloch a god. Maybe not *the* God, but in all of creation few wielded more power. He felt about as confident in this combat as a field mouse attacking a lion. The terror of what he was about to attempt threatened to completely cripple his heart. Only his love for his friends and his daughter could propel him forward, despite the horror and dread that grew with every step.

With nowhere else to go, Ragnhildr turned to the lone power, that he knew to be greater than the one he faced, "Yahweh Elohim, I regret that I have waited until now to call on you. Were I in your place, I'm not certain how I'd respond to a person that comes only because his life is in peril. In a small way, my only defense is that my life is my least concern. My folly has brought not just myself to this place, but several of Moriah's finest... and even my own daughter.'

"Perhaps my greatest folly, believing my first loyalty belongs to the king. I think Jireh would tell me that it's not the belief that is faulty, it is the confusion as to who is my king. It's not Ruac, or even the young man wielding the Yara Blade; you are my king. Forgive me for taking so long to acknowledge this truth.'

"That I am walking to my death is all but certain. Perhaps if I had walked with you through the centuries, learned your ways, I'd have at least a hope to survive. My survival is nothing. I seek the strength not to save my life, but to remove the threat to my daughter and those who have followed me to this place."

At first it seemed his prayer went no higher than the cobwebbed ceiling. The thought that he was on his own made fear rush to his throat like acidic bile, causing him to choke. He knew his enemy was even now feeding on that fear. The knowledge of this did nothing to help control his growing terror.

Looking ahead, down the long corridor, he detected a faint, but growing red glow. So, he'd managed to find his way through the maze, a new thrill of fear leaped to his throat and quickened his pulse. The temptation to turn back was incredible. The time of his death at hand, Ragnhildr chose to meet his fear with a song. The only song he could think of was one the boy Riordan sang back in the kings Great Hall,

"Adonai is my Rohi, I shall not want."

Chapter Thirty-Two

The Heroism we recite
Would be a daily thing,
Did not ourselves the Cubits warp
For fear to be a King

Emily Dickinson

ereah could tell by the change in height of the creature's heat signature it had pounced and was flying through the air straight at his chest. He used the only weapon he had, a mighty fist to strike where the red glow was brightest, hoping that was its beating heart. His blow struck true, even though it passed through raking razor claws. He heard bones snap, then the force of the blow threw the attacker back through the rest of the charging pack. The strike took several raptors off their feet, throwing the others into momentary confusion.

Then to all the captain's dismay, from the snapping and snarling noises, they realized the penalty for the creature's failure was to be devoured by the remaining predators. This savagery purchased a momentary reprieve, albeit while listening to a living creature be ripped to shreds and consumed. The clear message -

you're next, and your attackers are incapable of mercy or remorse.

"Flee my friends," Mereah commanded, "Our new companion Ciar was right, I may block these creatures' passage for a few moments. It will purchase the time for you to escape the same direction he chose."

"Stop wasting yer breath yuh big idjite," Caraig growled.

"We don't sacrifice friends' to save our own skins." Jireh responded.

"Friends!" Merah cried, unable to conceal the panic in his voice. "There isn't time to waste on posturing and false bravado. My father sent you on this errand, I could not bear his folly being the cause of your deaths."

In the confusion, no one noticed as Ged slipped quietly down the corridor.

A second creature suddenly lunged forward, attempting to speed past Mereah's flank to attack Korah. The Rapha Prince thrust out a mighty arm and managed to snag the creature by its long skinny forearm. Rather than try to stop the raptor, he pulled it off its feet and swung it around, throwing it back at its pack once again. But not before the lizard managed to sink several razor teeth in Mereah's forearm.

The failure of the second attack seemed to again purchase a moment's respite when instead of a direct attack they heard a series of clicks, guttural barks, and whistles.

"Jireh," Korah asked. "Are these creatures plotting a stratagem?"

"They do display traits, similar to wolves," Jireh responded, anxiously. "Much more savage, however."

"I'm afraid our circumstances grow even more dire my friends," Mereah murmured. "I can see by their heat, Caraig's little men, our wardens are returning."

"Here to harvest our blood no doubt," Jireh grumbled.

"Something else coming from further down the hall," Korah noted. "Some kind of pale light."

At that moment, the raptors attacked once more. Two charged suddenly close to the wall on either side of Mereah, making it very difficult to prevent both of them from streaking past. Mereah swung a powerful kick to his left that slammed one of the lizards hard into the wall, but his effort to snag the other failed as it deftly ducked under his grasp. Then while he was stretched out and focused on stopping the streaking carnivores, a third pounced, claws and teeth forward, searching to find their way to his vitals. Teeth and claws attached themselves to Mereah's shoulder and arms, while the wicked six-inch spurs slashed and opened his lower abdomen. The Rapha Prince managed to peel the creature off only by shredding his own flesh. With mighty hands around it's slender neck he slammed the raptor hard into the paving stones, crushing its ribs and snapping its neck. He looked over to his right and saw the creature that had eluded him, its body broken. Caraig used the door from their cell like a swatter. The other that he had kicked against the wall Jireh had finished off.

"How?" Mereah asked weakly.

"Their claws click on stone," Caraig responded.

"Are you hurt?" Jireh asked, not liking the sudden weakness he heard in the giant's voice.

The Rapha Prince went to one knee because a lengthy verbal response required too much effort, "I wish you had fled when given the chance." He whispered, pain filling every syllable.

The remaining raptors now hung back, knowing the giant would soon lose enough blood to end all resistance. Now all their attention was on the light that floated almost into their midst. The refracted colors cast just enough light to see that two other figures had also arrived and stood just behind. The distinct sound of a sword being drawn made a faint echo in the hall.

Caraig announced, "I Found the little man's torch, anybody got a light?"

In answer, a brilliant white light exploded in the hall startling and confusing the lizard pack. Everything hidden in the hall was revealed, including Riordan with the Riail dlí drawn. Two of the swift-moving raptors were already dead at his feet. A third creature was dead with an arrow through its throat.

Startled by the light, and new arrivals, the serpents demonstrated at least some sense of self-preservation as they scurried back down the hall. A troop of little men, upon seeing the hasty retreat also turned tail and scurried off in search of shadows in which to hide.

The bright light that startled and blinded the raptors started to fade but returning shadows could not conceal Mereah collapsed on the floor. He laid on his back, holding deep slashes to his stomach in a feeble attempt to stem the bleeding and to keep his innards from spilling out.

Caraig was at the prince's side immediately and his combat experience took over. Looking up, he saw Ged returning and with him was the sióg Ciar carrying another small lit torch. Irritated that in all the excitement he didn't notice Ged leave, he threw his tiny torch at the Dun Adventurer barking, "Light this, I need flame and heat to cauterize the wounds."

Jireh went down to his equestrian knees and gently lifted Mereah to cradle him in his arms, "I don't think searing the most serious wounds here across the abdomen will help Caraig, some of his intestines have been cut and torn. *Cauterization* might stop the bleeding, but it won't heal the internal damage."

Frustrated, Caraig lashed out, "Well we gotta do something, we can't let him die!"

"*We* can't help him," Jireh replied calmly. "But I think Riordan can."

"Me?" Riordan replied confused, "How can I help?"

"The Riail dlí lad, remember when I first brought the blade to you, what happens when it is used on the innocent?"

Even as the effects of Niamh's light casting faded away, the light of comprehension filled Riordan's eyes, "But if he's not innocent, I could kill him."

"Mereah can't travel lad," Jireh responded. "And unless we stop the hemorrhaging of his most serious wounds he will bleed to death in mere minutes."

"What can Riordan do to help?" Caraig almost shouted.

"I don't know about Riordan but taking your foot off my hand would be a nice start," Mereah mumbled weakly.

Caraig grimaced apologetically, "Sorry, thought I..."

Jireh jumped in anxiously, "Caraig, if you're finished adding to Mereah's injuries, you can find and light a real torch, not little people matchsticks. I need more light to assess the rest of our friend's grievous wounds." As Caraig ran off excitedly Jireh added, "And something suitable for bandages!"

Hearing Jireh's Instructions Ciar volunteered, "I can help the Dun find what you need," as he turned and ran after Caraig.

Jireh looked up at Niamh and asked, "My friend could you manage another burst of light and sustain it for a few minutes longer?"

"In order ta cast light, oi require ah light source greater dan dis wee torch," Niamh replied. "De light burst used ta surprise the beasties oi prepared from outside, while under de sun. Perhaps dis will 'elp."

Niamh sat and the wisp form emerged providing a small amount of pale blue light. As Riordan looked on anxiously Aislin slipped in beside him and took his hand. For just a second the thrill of her touch made him forget his concern for his friend.

Jireh was applying pressure with both hands on Mereah's abdomen. The added light confirmed his fears. His hands were like a child's finger in a crumbling dike, he was doing little to stem the prince's blood outpouring.

"We don't have time to wait for light or bandages, in mere moments it will be too late. Riordan, draw the Riail dlí and do what I tell you. Quickly. Take the point of the blade and place it here in the wound, we don't have time to question. Run him through deep and then pass the blade out through the side of his body."

"Jireh!" Riordan protested, "I'll kill him."

"Disobedience will kill him, *delay* will kill him, do it *now!*"

Riordan plunged the Yara blade in the slashes the raptor made in the abdomen. Everyone watching gasped in wonder, instead of almost cutting Mereah in half, the original wound was gone, not even a scar remained. "Now here," Jireh pointed to a second-deep hemorrhaging wound. The Yara Blade passed through Mereah, once again sealing the wound without leaving a scratch. Only the clothing the sword passed through remained torn.

Caraig came charging up carrying a lit torch and several garments and cloaks to tear up for bandages. Watching the Riail dlí's second pass and the result he couldn't help but exclaim, "What in El's name just happened?"

"Maybe Riordan can explain it to you," Jireh suggested calmly.

"The Riail dlí is a two-edged sword," Riordan murmured. "It cuts, it also heals, but only when used on the innocent. Jireh, how did you know it wouldn't kill him?"

"I didn't. There simply weren't any other options. But remember, I watched from the heights when the Anak attempted to use the Riail dlí against you, the blade didn't leave so much as a scratch. The irony is if he had used his own sword, he'd be alive, and you'd be dead."

"But the blade only heals the innocent. By all rights, I *should* be dead."

"Riail dlí, the Rule of Law," Jireh answered. "From the beginning Yahweh's highest law was love. Even his judgments are an act of love. Mercy, grace, healing, these also are outworking's of El's law."

"Jireh," Aislin broke into the conversation, anxiety coloring the tone of her voice. "Where's my father?"

Suddenly the urgency of Ragnhildr's rescue snapped back in first place of urgency, Korah responded by taking charge, "Your father is in grave danger, we were on our way to attempt his rescue when attacked. Mereah shielded us all, but his sacrifice is what left him sorely wounded. Jireh, how does our prince fare?"

"Some nasty cuts and bites remain; my biggest concern is his loss of blood. He's not out of danger yet."

Niamh's wisp form returned to his body. He then flew up and floated down slowly landing lightly on Mereah's chest, "After gifts ov dominion were lost, in Elo'im's mercy gifts of Ruach, wer given, 'ealing be one of 'ese."

The Sióg hovered just over Mereah's forehead and removed a tiny vial from his clothing. Placing a drop of clear liquid on his finger, he anointed the giant's head and laid a tiny hand on the great brow.

Korah looked down at Mereah's prostrate form, he had fallen into a deep sleep. "Rest is often ah gift from de healin balm," Niamh assured them. "Nigh, we wait,"

Korah anxiously interrupted, "Jireh, my heart warns me that Ragnhildr's need is urgent..."

"Absolutely right, I'll stay with our prince, go to his rescue."

"Ciar, where are yuh?" Caraig asked, looking around. "We require our weapons, so lead the way" agnhildr could see a high archway where the hall ended. Deep within the opening, a flame was burning and cast a small amount of light on a huge human torso. He had completed the maze, all that was left now - walk in and face whatever fate awaited him. He could turn back, but the thought of his daughter being sent in his stead was a threat more potent than his fear. Peering into a large, dimly lit chamber, a giant, three times taller than even Mereah, stood on the far side. At first, he thought it wore a helmet, then it stepped forward into better light; the demonic visage of a raging bull glared back. A hot flame burned within as revealed by glowing red-hot eyes. The thick neck gave way to a man's hairy, heavily muscled chest, protected by breastplate. A human torso gave way to the thick rear legs, tail, and hooves of a bull. In his left hand, he held a cat-o-nine tails, each whip strap ending with cruel hooks. In his right, he held a skull scepter crowned with cruel metal spikes; the empty eyes and nose flickered with supernatural flame.

"Never has my maze been solved so quickly. Therefore, I name you rat, and dung eater. That is as much honor as you shall receive from me vermin." Moloch didn't speak. Every syllable dripping with vitriol, forced it's way into his thoughts. "Submit, and I will devour your heart quickly, ending your physical torment. I'd rather you resist. I relish increasing your agony.

Ragnhildr felt his stomach twist, and his best efforts, were required to keep his knees from knocking. Moloch received his answer when the Irial Captain started singing,

> "Though I travel through the door
> of death and shadow, I will not fear,
> evil cannot touch my heart... "

The song infuriated Moloch, and a ball of flame formed above the scepter head, and the great minotaur launched a massive fireball that detonated in the same spot Ragnhildr occupied a second before.

~

Concern for Mereah had overshadowed the surprise reunion until Caraig looked up at Riordan and quipped, "Welcome back kid, where'd you get the firefly?"

"No time for that now!" Aislin insisted, "Where is my father?"

Jireh reacted quickly, and asked Ciar, "Where would Dalbhach have taken a victim for a solstice sacrifice?"

The sióg looked as though at first he was afraid to answer, but after a deep gulp replied, "The step pyramid.

There is an altar and furnace shaped as a minotaur at the top. But you must flee, Moloch will soon be released, and none can oppose him."

Ignoring the cryptic pronouncement, Caraig snarled, "We'll see about that. Lead me to my weapons."

"You cannot oppose Moloch, none can, I won't be a part of it!" Ciar cried, his voice dripping with panic.

Slowly the hovering blue light lowered to merge with Niamh, he opened his eyes and stood up, "Do na shame our people. 'Ow-ever long ye 'ave served Moloch or 'is servants, it ends taday. Too long ave ye 'uddled in fear an' shadow. Be strong an' courageous, yer aide be required."

Ciar nodded in resignation and started moving down the hall, only to pull up short after just a few steps. Blocking their way was a century of Sióga with bright blades drawn. Niamh drew up and flew forward hovering protectively. "Oi be Niamh, last living Sióg of de First Age, appointed as Guardian of de Miqlat, by de Sha'ar, Elohim's remnant. Well Nigh on tree tousand years 'ave oi waited ta rejoin me people. Oi can't begin ta tell ye me shame at finding my own blood serving de same darkness as destroyed de world. Ye can redeem yerselves an' join us, or choose to side wit evil, but ye cannot 'inder dese persons, dey be under me protection."

Caraig whispered to Korah, "We're protected by a firebug with a toothpick?"

"Careful," Jireh hissed. "That *firebug* could dispatch every one of us is in only a few heartbeats *if* he so chose."

Niamh continued only slightly annoyed, "Oi 'ave no wish ta battle me own, but oi will. We go ta make war wit' yer master, join us, step aside, or ye can cross blades wit me an' the lad 'ere. 'E bears the Riail dlí, ah Yara Blade, an talisman of unequaled power. Choose quickly, we be in dire need ah haste."

Ragnhildr rolled across the floor to put out the flames racing across his cloak. Even his eyebrows were singed from the Fireball. Now Moloch walked slowly, menacingly forward. Another fireball launched, with very little velocity. A direct hit would be fatal, but there was plenty of time, Ragnhildr got out of the way easily. The ponderous speed had the effect of creating anticipation and suspense, it was the size of the detonation however, that caught him by surprise. The blast knocked him off his feet, and set his clothes on fire, *again*. Rolling to put the flames out, when he jumped to his feet Moloch was there, looming over him. The cat-o-nine tails snaked down and wrapped around him like the tentacles of a giant squid. The end hooks dug in so that when the whip was pulled away Ragnhildr was sent spinning with pieces of fabric and bloody flesh still attached to the barbs.

Less than thirty seconds into the fight Ragnhildr's clothes were in tatters, his flesh burned, battered, and bloody. He knew that he was already in a major crisis. He must find a way to counterattack or die in mere seconds. He had lasted this long only because he was being toyed with. Lacking even the simplest weapons, he didn't see many options. About the only possibility in terms of physical attacks was to bite the minotaur's ankle. While sure ankle-biting would be an attack Moloch wouldn't expect, he didn't think the tactic would prove very effective.

A little slow getting up, Ragnhildr realized if his enemy had wanted to finish him off, he could have easily just trampled him. Instead, the Minotaur stood back, like a chivalrous knight waiting for him to rise. For many years he'd studied the dominion gifts of the Irial. Dalbhach had confirmed what he knew, the gifts of his people were dominion over the heavenly realms, including the atmosphere. Sometimes, when trying to make things happen the very act of effort and over-thinking ensures failure. And sometimes when a person is at the end of their rope, they jump into action and let things happen. It was at that kind of moment that Ragnhildr simply reacted, he clapped his hands together and cried out an ancient word of power, *tintreach*. Immediately a bolt of blue lightning shot from his hands and slammed into Moloch. For the first time in untold millennia, the Watcher was struck by a successful attack. Never had his veneer of imperviousness been even remotely challenged. He also knew full-well, that while the Watchers were immortal, his avatar, the physical mortal form of the giant minotaur could be killed. The lightning blast almost took Moloch off his feet, and the mortal bull's flesh was severely burned. While the minotaur did its best to control his bellowed outcry, the smell of burnt flesh spoke to Its vulnerability.

More astonishing, the lightning bolt wasn't the result of a magic spell. The Irial chieftain was exercising dominion over creation-a power lost to El's children several millennia ago. The use of Creation Gifts presented clear evidence of the sons of El reaching a higher level of maturity, preparing them to take their proper place; something the Watchers worked tirelessly to prevent. The cat needed to end the mouse game *now*. Moloch raised his scepter to strike a crushing, fatal blow. The Irial warrior was no longer where he had fallen, having already fled across the chamber. But his flight was not for the purpose of escape–far from it, he needed a moment's time and distance to prepare another attack. Even now, he rose from the chamber floor, carried in the vortex of a small cyclone. Already hurricane-force winds were blowing objects around the chamber, turning small pebbles into deadly missiles. The wisdom of this assault was evident. A launched fireball could easily be extinguished or worse, it could be returned to sender. Lowering his horns, the Minotaur employed brute strength to push through gale-force winds and close the distance to his adversary. Leaning into the wind, Moloch managed to gain several yards before getting struck by lightning once more.

The stench of burnt flesh and singed hair, and the agonizingly new sensation of pain, spoke to the effectiveness of the Irial warrior's attacks. Bellowing with rage the demon chose to fight fire with fire, and a bolt of lightning shot out from the end of his scepter.

Ragnhildr was too focused to celebrate his success. If he could have taken the time to think about it, however, no one would have been more shocked about the effectiveness of his attacks than he. Twice the great Minotaur was rocked by his assaults, the physical damage evident. After the initial strike, it took a while for a fresh charge of electrical energy to be gathered. The windstorm surprisingly aided the formation of conditions conducive to the creation of lightning. His heart started swelling with something he hadn't felt in a few days – hope. Somehow, he was going to win this combat, he would rescue his daughter, perhaps, even recover the Scepter of Adon. All his hope was crushed however as several thousand volts of electricity surged through his person, burning his flesh, blasting him against the far wall, and breaking his body. Getting knocked unconscious would have been a mercy. Mercy eluded him. Lying helpless on the cold stone, Ragnhildr could see the demon Moloch approaching, fiendish cruelty and malice in its eyes. Knowledge of his failure to slay the Minotaur filled Ragnhildr's final thoughts, crushing hope's brief moment with despair.

Ragnhildr was pulled back into consciousness, a drowning man drawn out of dark waters to a still darker shore. A great bull's hoof pinned his right arm, grinding flesh into stone while crushing bone. A voice forced its way into his mind, burning inside his head as if acid was poured through and behind the eye sockets, "Elohim's dominion gifts made you mighty. Not mighty enough. Only now do you learn the truth; the Holy God is no longer the El of *this* world. Your service is a waste, Elohim cannot – worse – *will not* save you. Remember this in your torment, realize Elohim is your abandoner, you may choose to curse Him er you die. I pledge to listen to your pleadings for mercy, but like your prayers to Elohim, they will fall on deaf ears. No pleas? Dalbhach chose well, you do not disappoint. You should know, however, you did well to fight. The promise of a swift death was a lie. I do that."

Shifting more weight onto the pinned arm, Moloch lowered his scepter, blue-white flame poured from the skull's eyes consuming flesh and bone in a controlled burn. When the flames stopped, Ragnhildr's right leg was burned away and consumed, the wound, perfectly cauterized to preserve his life and extend his suffering and screams.

iamh started up the dark hall only to draw up when he realized his kindred still blocked the way. Flying forward he drew his blade, "Waat will it be lad's? Is it a scrap yer after? Time presses, will ye move aside, or even join us? Tell me quick."

Slowly they parted and opened a path through their midst, allowing the captains to proceed, with Ciar leading the way. After the last of the hero's strode past, the Sióga closed ranks and fell in behind.

In moments they came to an intersection where they could only turn left or right, "The storeroom, where your weapons are stored are this way," Ciar spoke softly, still worried about the consequences of his aid. "To the right is an exit that will lead to Moloch's Altar at the top of the step pyramid. That is where Dalbhach would have taken your leader. I suspect however that your captain's fate will be to negotiate Molech's Maze. The entrance can be found past the pyramid's north side."

Upon hearing this news, Aislin sped down the right hall and Riordan ran after her. "Riordan!" Caraig yelled, "Hold on, while we gather our weapons!"

Riordan paused just a moment, removed a lance that stretched through loops on his pack and threw it crossways to Korah. In response to the questions on his redeemer's face, the lad called out as he ran, "I'll explain later."

With the pair already out of sight in the dim light, Niamh chimed in, "Retrieve yer weapons an' come quick as ye may, oi will ward de children." The Sióg then flew down the hall without waiting for a response.

"And who's going to watch over you?" Caraig raged in frustration. "That's just great, Riordan is going to face a demon and a Druid Enchantress protected by a firefly."

"Can't be helped," Korah urged as he pulled Caraig in the opposite direction. "Let's retrieve our weapons, we're useless until we do." Hoping he wouldn't regret the split-second decision, Korah charged headlong down the left hall.

Niamh, Aislin, and Riordan remained hidden in their perch on top of the pyramid, the serpent shadow still visible as it slithered down the stone steps. The effect, however, would soon disappear as the sun climbed higher into the sky. The engineering and stone craft, required to achieve this illusion every solstice was lost on Aislin and Riordan, but not on Niamh. "Sure," Niamh whispered.

"An follow de shadow ta de dragons 'ed, 'e points ta an openin' just beyond."

"That's where my father will be!" Aislin started to shout before being shushed by their guardian.

"Aye lass, but de way be guarded." Niamh directed their attention to the presence of Dalbhach keeping watch over the entrance of Molech's maze.

"There's only one woman," Aislin whispered urgently. "Surely we are capable of overwhelming her. Especially if we have the element of surprise." As she spoke, the shieldmaiden was already notching an arrow to string.

"Lass," Niamh cautioned. "Oi don't question the courage of yer 'eart. But dere be a black power 'at wards de lady, an takin 'er unawares may be 'arder dan ye tink. If engaged, combat will take time, an' speed be waat's needed now. Oi will create a distraction, be ready ta move quietly, but quickly wen oi tell ye."

A moment later the forms of Caraig, Mereah, Jireh and company walked around the base of the pyramid. At the sight of Dalbhach, they turned and fled back into the ancient city. Riordan started to shout to his companions when Niamh silenced him, and indicated it was time to move quickly. Dalbhach meanwhile used a small instrument of some kind to emit a shrill whistle, most certainly an alarm of some type. In moments, reptilian hunters appeared and tore off in pursuit of Caraig and company; Dalbhach close behind.

Again, Riordan reacted before thinking, "We have to..."

"Dey be not yer friend's lad," Niamh had to refrain from shouting. "Dey be de distraction I promised. "Nigh, move quickly, it'll be mere moments before de Druid Lady realizes she be fooled."

In fact, it took two minutes to confirm what Dalbhach suspected all along. One of the raptors made a leap attack that flew right into the back of the Rapha' Prince; the result was its claws grasped nothing but air, followed by all the images disappearing. The druid almost smiled. Almost. Turning she watched three forms, one a flying sióg slip through the maze entrance.

Moloch, her Master would be well pleased with this day's sport. The Watcher was able to elicit a much greater share of life force from a sacrifice able to resist. The greater an opponent, the greater the reward of extracted power. The boy and maiden would give little yield, but a Sióg of the First Age could potentially provide the richest yield of croí.

Only a few feet into the entrance, a frantic Aislin screamed her frustration, "We have three options, we must split up! Riordan, you take the passage to the left and I'll. . ."

"Lass, oi know yer love an concern for yer da' but cool 'eads must prevail. Ah misstep could get us killed, an' den oo'll 'elp yer father? Waat we must discern is wiich passage yer father chose last. Ya see 'ow ee shuffled 'is feet in dust ta mark 'is passage? 'E wanted to know where 'eed been so as not ta go in circles."

"We don't have time to follow where he's already been, we still . ... "Aslin started protesting again frantically, until Niamh interrupted, almost losing patience himself.

"Lass, we don't need ta go tree ways oi'm tellin' ye. Look, passages ta left an center show signs yer father went dat way, an also back. De right, marks in de dust only travel one way. Dat's de way we be needin ta go."

Without a word Aislin charged down the hall to the right, followed by Riordan. Shaking his head, Niamh hurried to overtake his young wards.

After retrieving their weapons Ged split off from the others hoping to find his men and release them from their cells. Once again fully armed Korah, Quillan, and Caraig, escorted by a few score of Sióga climbed the steep steps and peered cautiously down the north slope of the pyramid. Their eyes came to rest on Dalbhach standing guard over an entrance to a dark passage.

"Can't say I'm disappointed to see the wizard lady here," Caraig said in a low snarl. "Payback is long overdue. Let's go."

Korah was about to advise caution when the druid's eyes lifted and even at the distance of at least a hundred yards their eyes made contact. Dalbhach's hand snatched up making a clicking sound, and in seconds a half dozen "pets" charged up the steps of the pyramid.

Almost immediately from just behind Korah a bowstring hummed twice in rapid succession, two raptors collapsed in a heap thrashing wildly while spewing dark blood. A third arrow also flew towards its intended target when suddenly it stopped in mid-flight, reversed course, and sped straight back at a shocked Quillan. The Irial Lieutenant watched wide-eyed as the missile hurtled with deadly velocity towards his heart. A slap from Korah's buckler at the last fraction of a second knocked the missile off course so that it tore a deep gash in the archer's cheek. The wound spewed blood in an arc across the small temple as Quillan spun and fell to the paving stones.

Korah and Caraig had just enough time to block the opening to the chamber as the raptors raced up the north steps. The creatures, while capable of inspiring terror also demonstrated their capability to exercise prudence and cunning. They pulled up short when it became clear that they couldn't get through the small opening which would allow the hunters to surround the defenders.

Two of the raptors kept Korah's and Caraig's attention while the other two trotted over to the edge of the steps and dropped out of sight. "Now where do yuh think they're going?" Caraig queried.

"I think we both have a pretty good idea," Korah replied dryly. "Question is can they jump from the lower tier to come in through the side, or will they go all the way around to the south stair?"

"Don't think they'd have any trouble making the jump," Caraig surmised. "Quillan, if yer not kilt we could use yuh."

"I'm trying to staunch the bleeding," Quillan huffed. "Head wounds are the worst."

"Just a scratch!" Caraig scoffed. "But you'll have some serious wounds *real* quick if yuh don't find a way to prevent two more lizards from comin' in the opening to the east."

The Irial lieutenant trotted in the direction Caraig indicated, went behind the still hot furnace and peeked over the edge. His vision filled instantly with claws and snapping teeth. Quillan jumped back into the minotaur idol, his cloak preventing nasty burns. Hoping he didn't soil himself, he watched as gravity pulled the reptile back to the lower tier. Then the second raptor made its leap as the gaping jaws and razor claws from its forearms came through the opening trying to find purchase on the smooth paving stones of the chamber floor. Reacting quickly, Quillan kicked the lizard in the snout causing it to lose its hold and fall. Drawing a bright blade, the lieutenant called to his companions, "Two nasty creatures trying to join us, I can prevent them from this side. Don't know what I'll do if they attempt the south stair. It will occur to them to try in a few moments."

Korah looked at Caraig and suggested, "I think it best we take these two now before we have another two at our backs."

Caraig looked over and grinned, "Yuh make me proud horse master. I'll take the one on the right." As the warriors stepped out however, the cable vine shot out and managed to get purchase around Korah's neck. What was different this time was that the men were armed so that as the noose tightened Caraig cut the vine with his ax.

The distraction was all the raptors needed, however, they leaped to the attack and Caraig and Korah were driven down to the stone steps in a blur of tails, claws and snapping teeth.

"Oi be sure dis be de way now lass, de marks be made by ah man who knows where 'e goes. E no longer stops ta look at side routes anymore."

Their excitement of being sure of their path was interrupted by an outcry of absolute anguish. "Children dese 'alls make ah channel for sound, we be closer, but nah close enough. 'Elp must reach yer father soon, only oi can reach 'im in time... "

"Go!" Shrieked Aislin, "Save my father!"

"Follow yer fathers tracks in de dust. Riordan, ye must ward the lass now, dere may be more dangers dan Moloch in dis maze."

On a mission of urgency, Niamh was suddenly gone. A light trail down the hall lingered for a moment and then it too was gone.

Despite the impossibility of keeping pace, Aislin was determined to try. Breaking into a full sprint she left Riordan, who was slightly slower to react, several paces behind. This proved disastrous. An ill-wind, where no wind should be, put out the light of their torches. A hidden door opened under Riordan's feet spilling him down a ramp into a completely different hall and a whole new level of labyrinth. In the pitch-black the young armor-bearer never saw the ramp move soundlessly back into place in the ceiling.

"Aislin?" He called the maiden's name, soft at first, then more frantically when hearing no response. Regaining his feet, he stumbled on, hoping his companion must be further down the hall.

Aislin on the other hand, ran on blindly until she stumbled over something in the dark. Her nose told her the *something* was something very dead. Picking herself up, she was at last alerted to Riordan's absence. She called his name but instinctively knew the young man wasn't there, so she wasn't surprised when there wasn't a response. She was about to feel a bit uneasy about being alone in the dark with an unknown corpse when she heard more anguished screams from her father. Without light to guide her, she followed the cries of torment deeper into the heart of Moloch's Maze.

Ragnhildr found himself being forced once more, back into consciousness. Moloch was in a half squat, bent at the waist and looking right into the Irial Commander's eyes. Ragnhildr had known a few persons who were able to look into his soul. His beloved wife, Aislin's mother could, but that was a welcome intrusion bearing the joy of unconditional love and acceptance. Moloch's encroachment into the soul was more akin to a kicked in door. Once past the outer defenses, the eyes bit like savage fangs in the unprotected soft underbelly of the spirit. The bite did more than tear and rend, vitriolic poison was injected into the wounded spirit. Caustic acid seared and burned with toxic shame withering all hope, extinguishing the light of life.

Satisfied Ragnhildr was conscious, the great Minotaur reached down with his scepter. Positioning the golden skull's eyes just above the commander's remaining leg, flames shot forth and consumed it up to the hip, then cauterized the wound as before. The intent was clear. Moloch meant to consume Ragnhildr's croí, by making him a burnt offering, one agonizing limb at a time.

Reveling in the surge of power, the minotaur lowered his scepter and consumed an arm. So engrossed was Moloch in his harvest of torment that he didn't note the spectral light flash in his peripheral vision, then he couldn't see at all as something bright and sharp attacked his eyes.

Thus, began one of history's strangest combats, as a tiny and ancient creature of fairie was unleased as a light fury, against the great minotaur avatar of the demonic Watcher Moloch.

araig cast the reptile's carcass aside, withdrawing his long-knife from the creature's throat and brain as he did so. His armor had kept him in good stead, he had barely gotten a scratch. Jumping to his feet he appraised Korah's circumstances and realized the cavalry officer was in trouble. The captain was using both hands to prevent the raptor's jaws from snapping shut on his throat, but this meant he couldn't reach for his blade. Nor could he prevent the creature's great frontal claws from shredding his belly. The curved spurs at present were caught in Korah's woven mail shirt, but the bronze weave would be shredded in moments. Almost casually, the Dun Weapon master's battle ax swung a one-armed backhand, removing the predator's head, and spilling hot blood all over. Without even checking to be sure Korah was uninjured, Caraig charged back up and over the steps to the small temple on top of the pyramid to check on Quillan. Charging through the opening, in his haste, the Dun Captain almost ran the Irial Lieutenant over.

"SSSht, stand still," Quillan hissed. Standing about twenty feet away, heads swaying slowly from side to side, eyes locked on target were the two remaining raptors.

"Why don't they charge?" Caraig whispered.

"They have learned to fear my bow." Quillan replied. "So, they bait me, hoping I'll shoot and miss and so be on me before I can get another arrow on string. Do you have a blade at the ready?"

"You're kidding right?" Caraig replied with a low growl.

"Then I'll chance a shot and so end the stalemate. Be at the ready, hit or miss, at least one will be coming. They strike with the speed of the falcon."

Quillan let fly. The archer's skills were such that most creatures would have been killed instantly, but as it were, the shot hit nothing but air. It took less than a half-second for the raptors to close and strike. Quillan barely had time to drop his bow, he tried to draw a long knife but knew he'd never make it in time to save his own life. What he didn't expect however is to be yanked down and out of harm's way. Now occupying the same space was Korah wielding a lance. Unable to correct course mid-air from its leap attack the raptor skewered itself on the horse master's spear.

The second reptilian hunter was doing its best to shred Caraig's armor with the scimitar-like leg spurs. Dun crafted armor has no equal, however, so all efforts to tear, maim or rend were futile. The creature on the other hand possessed no armor save a scaly hide. Nothing capable of turning a cold iron blade.

As Korah removed his lance from the raptor, he pulled Quillan to his feet, "No time to rest or even celebrate, our troubles aren't over."

"More lizards?" Caraig scoffed. "Not much of a match against armored men, let 'em come."

"More of Dalbhach's sorcery I'm afraid," Korah replied. "Hurry, You'll need to see for yourself."

Curious now, Caraig and Quillan moved to the temple opening and looked down the north stair. Moving up towards them was a great wooden man. Twenty feet tall, with limbs made from oak logs. The featureless face and jerky ungainly movements were reminiscent of a poorly made marionette puppet.

"I hope you brought an ax," Korah quipped.

"A battle-ax horse master, not one for choppin' wood," Was the surly reply.

"A wood-chopping ax might have been a better choice," Quillan observed.

"You mean you're carrying around forty plus blades on all those braces and not one will work for fighting a stickman?" Korah asked incredulously. I'm leaving you home next time."

"Our friend's behavior does betray an alarming lack of preparation." Quillan continued.

Caraig on the other hand responded simply by pulling a mace with a stout oak handle and throwing it as a missile; choosing violent action and a savage snarl as the best response to his critics. The flying mace struck the wooden golem square in the middle of its featureless face and bounced off. Stickman's head snapped back violently. Bits of bark were sent flying, maybe some splinters, but the head itself slowly bent back into position. The golem's pace up the steps, however, didn't even slow. It would be on them in a moment.

"That would have killed a hill giant," Quillan observed, his voice filled with awe. "What now?"

"I'm open to suggestions," Caraig stated flatly.

"The real fight here is not against the creation, but against its creator," Korah called out.

"Make sense horse master," Caraig snapped. "We're runnin' out of time."

"This creature is lifeless animation," Korah cried, as he moved around to a flanking position. "Dalbhach is pulling the puppet's strings, we won't defeat the creature unless we first defeat her."

"I'll keep stickman busy," Caraig shouted, "You and Quillan are going to have to deal with the sorceress."

"Already on my way," Korah yelled as he raced past the golem.

Quillan on cue, sprinted to the creature's other flank. Confused as to which opponent to engage first, the wooden giant veered one way, then another. Caraig took advantage and rushed in with a battle ax hacking at a leg, careful not to bury the blade in the thick wood.

"Better hurry horse master," Caraig shouted while avoiding the golem's attempt to swat him. He knew, after imprisonment, in his present condition he'd eventually tire. He doubted a creature of magic ever would. "I'll be choppin' on this tree all day without making more'n a few scratches."

Korah didn't take time to respond. Once satisfied Caraig was keeping the animated creature occupied he turned his focus back on Dalbhach standing at the bottom of the stairs.

Then new threats arrived, in answer to another summons; first to appear, a great cat with fangs hanging down several inches from its upper jaw. Worse yet, a great bear even while running on all fours, the top of the beast's shoulders were over six feet high.

Korah heard the thrum of Quillan's bowstring and watched the arrow's flight toward the bear's chest. The missile, however, once more stopped in mid-flight, reversed course and sped back at the Irial Archer at blinding speed. Quillan, while prepared, still barely dropped to the steps in time to avoid being killed by his own arrow.

"Caraig?" Korah called out. "How's the fight with stickman? We've more company."

Caraig was in the middle of an evasive maneuver that took him between the golem's legs followed up by planting an ax in the back of the knee joint. Such a blow on a living creature would have severed tendons and crippled it. Stickman, however, didn't have tendons or nerves to cripple. When the golem spun in response to the attack Caraig couldn't extract his ax in time, so he lost the weapon, forcing him to run and retrieve the great iron mace. Once more, he had to dive to escape a long wooden arm swinging like a cudgel. "More'n welcome to take over for me here horse master if yuh think yuh can do better. Keep up the pressure on Dalbhach however, this-thing slows whenever the lady's attention is drawn away."

Quillan and Korah heard the suggestion but couldn't respond as they were already engaged. Both the great cat and the massive bear demonstrated alarming speed as they sped up the pyramid steps; the great cat veered off for Quillan while the bear selected Korah as its target. The bear stopped about ten feet from the Calvary officer and rose up on its hind legs to roar as an intimidation tactic. It didn't really work. Korah had faced death so many times before he was able to keep his head and saw the bear's rising to stand as an opportunity since its vulnerable under-belly was now exposed. Taking up the ancient lance delivered to him by Riordan, he made a mighty throw that buried the lance up to the handguard in the beast's chest. The surprising result of this however was that the bear dropped back to all fours and resumed its charge. Korah was able to take one swipe with his sword at the raging beast before it overwhelmed him. Out of the corner of his eyes he saw Quillan go down under the weight of the large, fanged cat. Then the horse master was locked in the great bears crushing embrace.

Riordan continued to call Aislin's name as he stumbled forward in the dark. He drew forth the Riail dlí, the talisman always felt reassuring in his hand. Reasoning the Irial Maiden couldn't be far away, he surmised she might be hurt and unable to answer. Speaking into the dark, attempting to conceal his fear he expressed what he hoped was a credible threat, "The sword that I carry is a Yara blade, against it, darkness is a poor defense."

Almost as if in response, a light appeared, faint at first, but clearly moving his way. The waiting for the torchbearer to draw near seemed an eternity of anxious moments, but in fact in just a few seconds the light revealed the identity of the approaching figure–it was Aislin. Holding up the light she remarked, "There you are, I feared for your safety after our separation. Are you well?" She asked in a voice that almost purred.

"Where'd you go?" Riordan demanded, feeling both puzzled and relieved at the same time.

"Silly-boy, something put out our light, it took the longest time to find the means to re-light it."

The young armor-bearer was now puzzled, just moments ago the maiden was frantic to rejoin her father and lend him their aid. Now, all sense of urgency was absent, in its place, the tone of her voice almost seemed like she was flirting, "Is this the way Niamh flew when he went to aid your father?" Riordan asked, barely able to conceal his bewilderment.

"You can sheath your sword, can't you see it's me?" Aislin said this with a light-hearted laugh. The young page, however, kept the Riail dlí at hand. "You wandered into a different passage while in the dark silly, it's such a stroke of luck that I am with you since you seem to always lose your way. You should take the lead since you have a mighty blade to protect us."

Riordan walked past the Irial maid and started down the hall. Despite the assurances that the maiden had his back, the hairs on the back of his neck started to stand up.

Chapter Thirty-Six

While though the tempest loudly roars
I hear the truth, it liveth
And though the darkness 'round me close
Songs in the night it giveth

Nick & Roma Ryan, Enya

islin held her hands out in front of her as she ran head-long in the dark. She didn't know what extinguished the light of her torch. It didn't matter if Riordan was or wasn't behind her. All she knew was that her father was in danger, somewhere up ahead, Niamh had sped off in this direction and she had only to follow the sounds of combat and the sound of her father's torment. As she ran headlong, a faint red glow in her peripheral vision alerted her to an opening passage to her left, so she pulled back just before running into a stone wall. Turning toward the glow and growing sounds of conflict her path forward became clear. As she sped down a new passage fear for her father's well-being lit a fire to her feet. If Riordan had in fact been behind her, he would have been hard-pressed to keep up. Somewhere in the back of her mind she wondered why she didn't detect any sounds indicating the Rohi was following. Truth is, fear for her father drowned out all other voices of concern. As the fiery light grew, illuminating the passage with every step, she ran ever faster without looking back. Staying far enough back so as to be undetected, one of Moloch's special servants followed noiselessly behind. His purpose, ensure the girl reaches Moloch's chamber before her father's demise. The Watcher would extract greater energy from the girl's father when he realized his daughter would soon share his fate. In turn, Moloch would likewise draw more energy from the daughter experiencing the terror and horror of her father's gruesome end. A demonic win-win.

Niamh wedged himself deep enough in the great minotaur's ear that a probing finger couldn't reach far enough to drive him out. Currently, he survived Moloch slamming an iron gauntlet against its head several times. While the concussions were certainly severe, they didn't prevent the Sióg from carving up the tender insides of the minotaur's auricle with his bright blade. When the slapping stopped, the miniature warrior realized his opponent was about to switch tactics, so he flew out just before Moloch raised his scepter and shot flame into its own lobe.

Niamh was tiring. The first difficulty was that his blade was only five inches, but his opponent well over thirty feet tall! The great minotaur wore plate armor in places, had the super thick hide of a bull everywhere else. How does a man of fairie fell an opponent when wielding a sword capable of inflicting only pin-prick wounds? Worse, the beast was possessed by a demon of ancient cunning. Moloch would know that in time, away from a replenishing energy source, Niamh would lose his greatest advantage, lightning-fast speed. Such speed requires massive amounts of energy. Without the means to recharge, he would soon be forced to slow, to conserve energy. As soon as Niamh started slowing down, however, he'd be dead.

Roaring from the agony of self-inflicted wounds, Moloch switched from pouring flame into his own body to casting a whole wall of flame from his scepter. The Sióg' managed to just escape below the flames before the Minotaur cast another deadly spell. A vortex formed and the swirling winds threatened to suck Niamh in. Because of the diminutive warrior's size and lightweight, he proved particularly susceptible to this form of attack and was forced to expend a tremendous amount of energy to resist the powerful winds. Light from sun, moon or stars, all served to provide Niamh with energy. The light from the flames of Moloch's scepter however, caused an energy drain, it was sucking the life right out of him. Niamh came to a stunned realization, the energy used to resist the Minotaur's spells was causing the demon to grow stronger, while rapidly diminishing his own precious energy reserves. A decisive blow must be struck–and quickly, or this combat would be over.

For his part Moloch relished the fight. This Sióg' was not one of Dalbhach's minions, but one of the Sióga from the world before it was broken. What's more, the man of fairie had been preserved by some lore of such incredible power and potency that its eventual consumption would yield a life-force that was ten-fold of the Irial Warrior's.

Eventually this old world Sióg' would realize the fix he was in, that the more he resisted the faster he would hasten his own demise. Inwardly laughing, Moloch relished feeding further on the diminutive warrior's coming panic and despair when the tiny gnat realized the full extent of his plight.

His servants had promised the greatest harvest of life-force since the dark age. Indeed, with this much energy, and more victims arriving soon, Moloch would soon have the power to escape his banishment from the life-less realm.

~

Dalbhach hovered over the body of the great cave bear that had answered her druidic summons. She admired the gallantry of the Cavalry Officer pinned by the great beast's bulk. The man had somehow managed to bury a lance and a long blade into the great beast before being overwhelmed. Even now the bruin's breathing was shallow, its heartbeat all but at a stand-still. The warrior had managed to kill a savage foe many times his own size. The irony, however, was that now he was being suffocated while pinned underneath the creature. She had in her possession a dart, tipped with a poison capable of bringing instant death, but why administer such mercy? With a low, amused laugh the Druid looked further up the pyramid slope where the Dun warrior was still valiantly battling the wooden golem. Again, she could end the combat mercifully, but why? The golem would never tire, never relent. Weapons meant for piercing flesh, no matter how skillfully applied, would never do more than scratch the thick oak limbs. The Dun will eventually tire, make a mistake, and the combat will end. She laughed softly at the stout warrior's desperation as he already realized the inevitable outcome.

She started to turn her attention to the Irial Archer when the last thing she expected to happen - did. The Rapha' Prince stepped out of the confines of the small temple on top of the pyramid, and drawing flame from the idol furnace, threw a raging inferno at the wooden golem. So, not just the Irial Commander was rediscovering Dominion Gifts.

Instantly the wooden giant kindled into a roaring blaze, so hot even her druidic arts would prove inadequate to stem the blaze. Next, the great centaur, the one named Jireh also emerged from the pyramid temple. Already a large sling-stone was loading into the leather pouch. Unlike wooden arrows, her druidic spells didn't give her power to deflect or redirect stone. The summons that brought the great cave bear and long-toothed cat had already been utilized; a second wooden golem would take far too much time to muster, and it would be pointless regardless. Running out of options, Dalbhach decided discretion was the better part of valor. Besides, it will only mean more participants for Moloch's maze. So, she threw up a lush hedge of vegetation to cover her exit and disappeared.

Niamh picked himself up off the stone floor very slowly. Cyclone winds had hurled the Sióg' across the large chamber. To resist the spell would have sacrificed his rapidly diminishing energy reserves. Worse still, he realized that the more he resisted, the stronger Moloch became. The great minotaur's scepter functioned as a sacrificial altar, absorbing his croi' even as he battled the Watcher's spells. Now he was battling fear as well. Strong negative passions also fed the flames of the scepter and empowered Moloch.

Then, after thinking it can't get any worse, Aislin charged into the chamber. Riordan wasn't with her. The Yara Blade was the only weapon Moloch would have reason to fear. The presence of the young maiden, however, was the greatest danger to Niamh yet. His only advantage was incredible speed, crucial to the evasive, hit-and-run tactics that were his only chance for victory. The arrival of the young lass changed all that. Aislin in effect acted as an anchor, forcing him to switch tactics, from that of rapid hit and run strikes to providing a defensive barrier. He would soon be crushed like a bug.

Oblivious of her danger, the Irial Shieldmaiden showed her valor by letting an arrow fly. Moloch made no effort to evade or block the missile, choosing instead to allow it to bounce harmlessly off his impenetrable hide.

An eerie laugh started in low, then grew into a crescendo as it filled the chamber. Soon the sound level would be deafening. Moloch casually reached down with his scepter and burned off Ragnhildr's remaining arm. The commander's agonized screams could be heard even over the insane laughter. As anticipated, the maiden became enraged and charged across the chamber.

Ragnhildr blocked out his anguish long enough to frantically scream, "Aislin, for my heart's sake, flee! Flee this place!"

Moloch strode forward a few paces and positioned himself between father and daughter. When she attempted to run between the minotaur's legs, the flaming scepter dropped down to block her path. Enjoying the game, no threatening moves were made, the demon was feeding off the girl's fear and frustration.

Then Niamh flew slowly and came between the Watcher and the maiden, "Oi know yer black 'eart feeds off despair. Sure, an' aren't ye ah brave one, makin' ah young wee lass fear for 'er Da. Oi also know ye don't fear me. 'Owever, oi know dere be one ye do fear; 'im do oi serve. Aye, sure enough do oi know me 'eart will soon stop beatin'. Oi never planned on gettin' out ah dis scrap alive, so long as yerself didn't make it either. In de name of 'im I serve, 'im as ye do fear, oi declare de lass will not be touched. Not long as breath wit-in me remains. Nigh, let us dance tagether, ye an' oi, one last time."

Then Niamh answered the demon's laughter with mirth of his own, full of joy, and courage. Across the chamber, the brutalized, and tortured remains of Ragnhildr used the last of his strength, weakly at first, to start singing;

Yahweh, you have created me
You call me by name, I am yours
Though I walk through the fire,
I will not be scorched, nor burned,
The flames can never kindle upon my soul

Isaiah the Seer

Enraged Moloch turned his back on Niamh and moved toward Ragnhildr to silence him. The Sióg however for the first time in the conflict no longer felt his power draining away. His people were empowered by the light of their dominion. But there exists more than one kind of light. The power of El's light and presence inhabits the prayers and praise of his servants. A strange grin lit Niamh's face as he experienced a surge of renewed power. Refracted light shot across the chamber as the Sióg attacked with the fury of a light storm.

iordan, I am exhausted, I can't continue without rest." Aislin was lagging, barely able to lift her feet.

"What about your father? He is in torment and danger, with only Niamh to aid him." The Rohi was puzzled by his companion's loss of focus. Just moments before she was running head-long through the pitch dark, heedless of the danger to attempt her father's rescue.

"Neither of us will be able to do my father any good without rest," the maiden replied. "But I don't wish to tarry exposed here in this hall. Here is a side chamber, perhaps we would be safe there for a moment."

Aislin pushed the heavy wooden door open and started to move inside. Riordan pulled her back protectively and frowned, "Better let me check it out first, let me have the torch."

When the maid stepped out of his way she paused, when her face was inches from his, she murmured seductively, "I hope we won't need an escort, not after all this time alone together."

The thrill that raced to Riordan's heart was quickly replaced by bewilderment; really? Not once she shone even the tiniest fraction of romantic interest, but now when on their way to her father's rescue she wants to flirt? He pushed abruptly past and held the torch high. The room was small, like a holding cell, rather nice for a dungeon, with fresh straw on the floor. When the armor-bearer turned to tell the maiden it was safe to come forward, he saw the lady was already in the room, and the door was closed behind her. On her face was a look of complete innocence, but her eyes smoldered with a peculiar look of lust.

Moloch could only hope he could somehow stop the latest ingenious attack by the Sióg warrior. While the Watcher's Avatar sought to crush the remaining life from Ragnhildr, the bothersome insect Niamh flew straight up the minotaur's nose. The great bullish head was now roaring uncontrollably, exhaling in great snorts trying to blow the little maggot out. Every attempt to exhale forcibly and remove the pest only resulted in the Sióg digging into the nasal passage with his blade and holding on. The outcome was that rather than expel the Sióg, the minotaur snorted out globs of its own blood.

The cursed girl, her doomed father, everything else was forgotten. If the misbegotten fool Niamh gained the sinuses, he could cut all the way to the great bull's brain, ending the avatar's life, banishing Moloch back to the abyss.

Now, the Watcher's problems were further multiplied. A mighty centaur, Rapha' Prince, and a Dun Warrior rushed into the chamber. The Dun was barely higher than the minotaur's ankles, the Centaur and Rapha' were just higher than its knees, but the demon could discern their true power. These were not sacrifices sent by Dalbhach– they were hero's here to end his reign before it could start. Acting quickly–ruthlessly–and he could still absorb all their life force. First order of business, however, terminate his Sióg tormentor. He changed tactics, instead of trying to blow Niamh out of his nose, he lifted the scepter and deeply inhaled sacrificial flames.

"Why did you do that?" Riordan tried frantically to pull the door back open but it was locked. How this was accomplished without a key was puzzling, unless somehow Aislin had a key? He turned to ask if she had locked the door and watched as she dropped a skeleton key down in the cleavage of her bosom.

Smiling wickedly, she said, "Ooops. I dropped the key, want to help me find it?"

Then Aislin slowly transformed. Still beautiful, but the kind of beauty that inspired lust, and fear. Her skin was so devoid of color as to be ice-cold, with not an ounce of red blood in her veins. The nails on her fingers slowly grew long into claws, while the eyes turned into empty black sockets. A wicked smile revealed two long canines, like the fangs of a venomous snake, and when she spoke the voice was devoid of human blood or warmth - the voice of insatiable appetite, "The other tasty morsels have I sent to Moloch. One small portion have I saved for myself. For centuries have I hungered, centuries have I known thirst, you shall prove worth the wait I think."

Grasping clawed fingers reached out for Riordan's throat. The Riail dlí swung up without thought, out of pure reflex, but still came close to cutting the lamia in half in her eagerness to feed. But with supernatural quickness, she was away in a blur to rage at him from across the chamber. Then she started to chant unintelligible words. The incantation burned his spirit like acid. An overwhelming sense of panic and fear withered the armor-bearer's heart and courage. Then the light of the torch was extinguished, and everything went black. Very feminine whispering voices filled the room, making it impossible to pinpoint the source. Soft words, spoken sweetly, yet still icy cold, promised a horrible death; slow, painful, a complete violation of his soul and spirit. Besides having an incredibly unnerving effect, it would be impossible to hear even a heavy-footed approach. The Rohi would never know when or from where the attack would come. The whisperings continued and echoed throughout the chamber. Leaving Riordan almost helpless to fight the bile rising in his throat.

Chapter Thirty-Eight

Moloch exhaled with a great snort, shooting out a remnant of flame and it felt as though perhaps the charred remains of his tiny nemesis. He hoped some life remained because the demon intended the sióg pay dearly for the trouble he'd caused. Just as the Minotaur turned to focus on his new opponents, however, he was slammed by an incredible fireball from the small giant. The detonation knocked the Watcher's Avatar back several steps. Then another lightning bolt! The Irial Commander, despite all the physical damage, was still capable of mounting an attack. He'd forgotten gifts of dominion did not require physical strength, so toying with the man of Irial could prove to be a bad mistake. Staggering, Moloch attempted to raise a vortex to force his enemies back but struggled to bring the black arts into focus. In addition to singing songs of power, the centaur was praying in a language of Elohim's realm. Grimly Moloch realized warfare was also being waged according to spiritual realities.

Something slammed into the Minotaur's ankle. Excruciatingly painful, he felt the bone crack. Impossible one of the Dun could strike so hard unless the weapons master was also exercising powers of dominion. In retaliation, the Watcher attempted to stomp the warrior, then consume him with flame from the scepter.

Caraig dived and rolled to avoid being crushed and burned as he called out to the others, "A little help if yuh don't mind!"

Jireh had already launched two ten-pound sling stones. Mere bits of gravel to the Minotaur–with this exception, however; Mereah had superheated the stones. They hit with sufficient velocity to penetrate the Avatar's hide, and they burned flesh from their place under the skin.

Irritated the Minotaur turned his attention to Jireh and swung the great scepter like a flaming mace. Not as fortunate as Caraig the scepter slammed into the Shophetim's shoulder and girth sending the centaur sprawling. Mereah intervened by hurling yet another fireball.

Responding with a trick used by the Irial of the First Age, Moloch withdrew the oxygen from the room. While only able to be sustained for a moment, this extinguished the fireball and left his mortal assailants gasping for breath. Seconds later, the scepter was used to deliver a crushing blow to the Rapha' Prince. Now only the Dun warrior remained capable of offering resistance.

The Dun Weapon Master, singed and bruised, remained defiant. The fool knew the Minotaur's physical prowess far exceeded its own, it just didn't care. Perhaps it had never been taught properly the meaning of fear.

Riordan sank to the floor sitting cross-legged. Suddenly, he realized the room stank of excrement and dried blood. So, the Lamia's masquerade wasn't the only illusion. The whisperings continued. The bile in his throat, caused by the stench grew into nausea, he felt like he would throw up at any moment. The retching would leave him vulnerable, most likely dead. The rohi couldn't think of more wretched circumstances in which to die.

He couldn't see his enemy. He knew he'd never hear her coming. Instinctively he also knew he'd be dead–or worse–soon as she chose to strike. Why didn't the attack come? Why doesn't she just get it over with? He tried to pray again, he started by simply whispering a name–Yahweh. The name means truth, incapable of deception. He spoke the name again, louder.

The demon in his cell screamed and raged. But unlike before, he knew exactly where the ravings were coming from. Truth cut through deception. His fear revealed as just another lie, his powerlessness, just another deceit. As Riordan spoke the name of truth, he began to discern the enemy's presence. The lamia panicked and raged as the webs of fear and deceit were shredded, so she charged with her claws grasping for the Rohi's throat. Her webs of fear and deceit collapsing, the rohi heard her coming and she impaled herself on the Riail dlí. Contact with the Yara blade was the first real pain the creature had felt for centuries. Truth can be excruciating. The truth of who she once was, who she is now, who she could have been; the web of deceit woven within the cables of her own choices were all ripped away. She screamed her agony, stormed at her self-deceit, as the death she embraced eons ago reached out and at last claimed her.

Sitting in the now quiet stillness of the cell, it was several moments before Riordan realized he was hearing something, very faint, but powerful. The power grew, and after a moment he realized he heard singing. The voice was Ragnhildr's. The voice had the power of one purified by flame. Following the voice, he found the dungeon door in the dark. The locks, like the lies, were no match for the Yara Blade and he passed them easily. He moved through the black halls guided by the light of a song.

Riordan emerged from a small side door into a large chamber where his friends battled Moloch. His eyes took everything in quickly. Aislin cradled her father - what was left of him - in her arms. She wept softly while Ragnhildr continued singing ancient songs of power, although his voice now grew increasingly faint. Mereah appeared to be unconscious. Jireh was also down, his legs positioned awkwardly alongside his horse body. The

Shophetim seemed to be praying in a language the rohi didn't understand, but the armor-bearer could sense power in the words. Caraig was standing firm, Moloch hit him with a series of wizard blasts that shredded the rock all around, except for under his feet. Power and strength flowed from bedrock into the Dun, and at the same time he became rooted to the stone floor. Undaunted, Moloch made a gesture with his fist and lifted the whole floor for several feet around the Dun; then threw the entire mass effortlessly against the back wall.

Then Korah arrived riding Aella. After the Druid Enchantress fled, Mereah and Jireh removed the carcass of the dead bear and checked on a sorely wounded Quillan. With Ragnhildr's need so urgent, the others entered the maze chamber, while he freed the horses.

Aella's hoof-beats echoing in the passage, unfortunately, had the effect of telegraphing where and when they would enter Moloch's chamber. A fireball detonated at the entry just as they came into view, blasting the pair back out into the hall.

Chapter Thirty-Nine

When tyrants tremble in their fear

And hear their death knell ringing

When friends rejoice both far and near

How can I keep from singing?

Enya, Nicky & Roma Ryan

iamh barely escaped being crushed by the rubble when Moloch uprooted Caraig and threw him against the back wall. Badly singed, energy reserves exhausted, he was laying on the floor recuperating while the others took up the fight, but then the dun warrior and all the rubble flew his way. He doubted that he had the energy for more than one more assault on the great minotaur, so he would have to make it count. He crawled over to check on the great Centaur Jireh. Despite absorbing an incredible blow from Moloch's scepter, he still lived, although his body was contorted. Niamh guessed he must have been in tremendous pain, but he didn't show it. Instead, he lay on his side, calmly praying in a heavenly language. "We've not much time," Niamh whispered. "Can oi help ye in sum way?"

"My front leg, shoulder and horseback is broken and shattered," Jireh replied grimly. "At least a few ribs as well. I won't be leaving this place under my own power. You might check on Mereah. He may have been just knocked unconscious. You'd better hurry, Moloch has run out of opponents. I think he's about to start harvesting souls."

Jireh's observation was spot on, Moloch was already walking over to where Ragnhildr lay, his head cradled in Aislin's lap. Niamh realized he would need strong allies if he was going to finish this fight and save the shieldmaiden's father. He moved quickly to where Mereah lay prostrate. A slight jolt of energy from his hand stirred the young Rapha Prince so that he sat up suddenly. Then to his amazement, the rubble where Caraig was buried, shifted. Bruised and bloody hands started pushing away rock and debris. Both the Rapha' Prince and the Dun Chieftain would be strong allies, improving his chances. Then, beyond all hope, he felt the sudden presence of another power enter the chamber. He turned to confirm what he already knew, Riordan had arrived, the Riail dlí unsheathed. Now, perhaps, they would teach even Moloch the meaning of fear.

A cold fury possessed the young rohi, he'd just observed his redemptive father and mentor Korah blasted with a fireball. He also noted that all the friends he had in the world appeared to be down for the count. Aislin hovered by her father. Clearly, the screams they'd heard were because the Irial Commander had endured the cruelest of all possible torture. Consumed with righteous anger, it didn't even occur to his young heart to be afraid. Swinging the Riail dlí in a high arc, the blade passed easily through the minotaur's lower leg, severing the Achilles Tendon, and partially passing through bone, just above the ankle. A definite crippling injury, and in fact the giant's leg buckled, bringing Moloch to one knee. Moving to cripple the other leg, Riordan intended to fell the minotaur like a great tree, bringing his vitals within reach of the Riail dlí. Moloch looked down at the young page and sensed the danger the rohi represented.

Then Korah riding Aella re-emerged from the maze passage, the sharp echo of hooves on stone announcing their return. Riordan's heart jumped with both excitement and relief. Then he made a typical young warrior's mistake, he stopped his assault to celebrate. Power went out from Moloch, the gash on the wounded leg closed, and the Minotaur stood back up.

"I know you." The words were not spoken audibly, instead, they were projected telepathically, and burned like acid in the mind of the armor-bearer. Riordan looked up just in time to see the scepter swinging like a great mace, slamming with incredible force into his body - launching him across the large chamber to collide hard into the far wall. Such a blow would easily have destroyed a thick castle wall. It should have easily crushed every bone in the Rohi's body.

Riordan didn't feel the impact however, nor was even a hair singed by the flames from Moloch's scepter. Power surged from the Riail dlí that enclosed the Rohi in a kind of protective bubble. While the giant's attack didn't break bone, it did launch him spinning through the air until the wall ended his flight, and without ceremony dumped his unconscious body to the floor.

Korah was having a difficult time avoiding the great Minotaur's magic attacks. His only effective range weapon was the Yara-tipped lance, but the captain was reluctant to chance a throw; not daring to hazard the consequences of a miss. Having barely escaped a lightning strike, and still another fireball, he and Aella were getting both battered and singed. More dangerous still, they were growing weary. A howling twister now filled the chamber and threatened to have the strength to lift and capture the weight of horse and rider into the vortex. Korah had no other choice than to turn and ride in the same direction as the wind.

Riordan, returned to consciousness, not knowing where he was at first. Niamh's face was peering over his chest. The Sióg was trying to be heard over the gale-force winds. "Laddie, Oi know ye must be 'urtin, but ye 'ave little time ta save yer friends. De Riail dlí is yer ticket, wen de blade passed trough de demon 'is powers went 'aywire. 'is magic be based on lies lad. Yer blade's forged wit truth. But ye will 'ave ta drive de sword in 'igher up, near 'eart or brain, and keep the blade inside de monster. Drive truth 'ome ta 'is very 'eart."

Out of the corner of his eye, Korah saw that Riordan was on his feet and it appeared that something was being cooked up between Caraig, Mereah, and Jireh. Korah set his face as hard as iron, his redeemed son would have his chance. Chin down, leaning forward, he lowered his lance and charged once more.

Moloch sensed the danger the horseman presented. His lance was tipped with Yara. In defense, the Minotaur stomped and sent a massive shockwave through the chamber floor. This opened a trench shooting out from just in front of the demon's hoof. Weary from neglect; malnourishment, and all her frenzied exertions, Aella stumbled into the opened gap in the stone floor. As her head and shoulders dropped forward, Korah flew over

Aella's ears. With Herculean effort, the captain hurled the Yara-tipped lance.

Moloch sensed the Sióg hurtling in for a final assault, so he threw up a defensive wall of flame to ward against the man of fairie. As he put the firewall in place, he felt a sharp pain in his thigh, just above the knee. Almost immediately his ability to cast spells went haywire, the wall of fire started to collapse. Moloch knew instantly the horseman had cast his lance. The weapon had pierced his tough hide and was embedded in his leg.

Doubling his efforts to sustain the wall of flame, (with some small measure of success) Moloch intended to keep Niamh at bay. The demon could count on a hand the number of times he'd been surprised in his long existence - he was surprised now. A figure did come flying through the firewall, bearing a talisman of incredible power. Not the Sióg Warrior, nor some other great captain, it was the boy. The boy he had crushed earlier. Dropping the flame wall, the Minotaur attempted a Wizard Blast to throw the young armor-bearer back. Horrified he realized his works of sorcery were crashing down around him. Instead of a blast, all he managed was a gentle poof. The tiny amount of Yara buried in his leg wreaked havoc on his ability to cast spells. Moloch attempted to swing the scepter and slap the little runt away. Too late. Using the momentum of flight, the boy buried his blade, to the hilt – through the iron breastplate, straight into the center of the minotaur's chest.

All strength fled from the demon's limbs. Then visions of light started to intrude into the dark prison of his mind. He saw his schemes for dominion over all creation crumbling. His self-deceptions were split like a heavy veil - there is only one El, one Power in the universe. He wasn't it. He saw all the weak, pathetic children of Elohim come to their maturity and perfection. They were glorious beyond his imagining, and were coming as an army, for *him*. Led by one of the Capall riding a great white horse, the man's eyes glowed a blue that perfectly matched the hue of Yara Stone. Truth Incarnate was coming, and Moloch watched all his kingdom of lies crumble before his eyes. Then the demon noted a massive chain, with manacles of Yara Blue... As the Minotaur's heart stopped beating, Moloch was sent screaming, back into exile and abyss.

Chapter Forty

Riordan didn't dare let go of the Riail dlí. With the blade buried in the Minotaur's chest, he was close to thirty feet above the chamber floor. The sword's handle was all he had to hold on to. He knew he'd struck a decisive blow because even the flailing of the giant's arms felt feeble. All attempts to use sorcery ceased. The great bull head dropped to it's chest splattering him with spittle. Then, the heartbeat inside the creature's massive chest, stopped. The body started to sway. Riordan realized with a start, that if the Minotaur fell face-first, he would be crushed. Then the knees buckled causing the Minotaur to fall backward. Breathing a sigh of relief, the young page held on for dear life and rode the falling tree until it crashed onto the chamber floor.

The impact knocked the breath out of the rohi. Although he landed on top of the Minotaur, the demon's armor provided no cushion for the fall. After a moment for recovery, he withdrew the Yara Blade (there wasn't a drop of blood on the sword) and rolled off Moloch's carcass only to have a surprisingly high drop to the floor. He would have liked to have a few seconds more to catch his breath, but as soon as he got his feet back under him Caraig embraced him in a big bear hug; squeezing the little air left in his lungs back out again. "Way tah go kid, I knew yuh could do it!"

After Caraig released his vise-like embrace, Mereah hoisted the rohi off the ground and squeezed some more until Riordan thought he would pop. "Of course, he did it, how could he not? He was executing *my* brilliant plan!"

"*Your* plan yuh great oaf? I was the one that said ta toss 'im! Didn't I Lad? Besides, without my help the best you would ah managed would have been ta bounce the kid off the giant's toe. Ain't that right kid? I said ain't that right? Riordan?"

Riordan was already across the chamber, standing beside Aislin, who was cradling what was left of Ragnhildr in her lap. For both the Dun Weapon's Master and the crown prince, the celebration was short-lived as they were quickly reminded of the steep price paid for victory.

"Riordan, son, I thank you for keeping my daughter safe... while separated," Ragnhildr spoke haltingly, with pauses while he drifted in and out of consciousness. Riordan was thankful Aislin didn't protest the comment about keeping *her* safe. "I have one more charge... for you to keep. I have not a wife... or other family. Will you and Korah watch over Aislin... ward her until El ..."

"Father, I..." Aislin protested.

"Ssshh, daughter," Ragnhildr interrupted. "Time is much... to short. If the captain's will agree to carry me...

to rest beside your mother. Farewell friends. Greater victory.. never .. achieved. Aislin ... so much like your... mother.. so beautiful, so proud."

The Irial Commander lacked the strength to utter another word, his final communications were for his daughter, spoken by his eyes. His heart stopped moments later. Aislin silently weeping, closed his eyes and whispered, "goodbye father."

Riordan felt a great hot teardrop land on top of his head. Looking up he saw Mereah standing just behind, and looking down into the page's face, "We may be facing more losses my friend. Jireh was struck a mighty blow and needs our care. We are at a loss as how to help, but perhaps the Riail dlí?"

Riordan left Aislin and Ragnhildr to rush to Jireh's aid. Niamh was already there examining the Shophetim's injuries. Instantly concern for his old mentor became almost overwhelming; one leg was splayed out and bits of bone pushed through bloody skin. An arm also, hung from his shoulder like it was a dead thing. Most alarming, blood came down from the corner of Jireh's mouth staining the white beard. The great centaur's agony was plain, though he courageously did his best to conceal this.

"Oi don't know waat ye can do lad. De break in de leg, isn't clean, but shattered, shoulder as well. Oi am most concerned about 'is coughing blood. Broken ribs 'ave pierced 'is lungs. Even now, dey fill wit blood."

Re-enforcing the diagnosis, Jireh broke into a fit of coughing and spewed blood, just before passing out.

"We have to do something, tell me what to do." Riordan protested.

"Oi don't know waat ye can do lad, de wounds be not cuts or slashes ta pass de yara blade trough. Still, der be 'ope. Oi can, an will do somethin', let yer 'eart be at rest."

Without another word Niamh drew close to Jireh's broken leg. Laying his small hand on the break, the Sióg sang a song in an unknown tongue. In moments a faint blue glow surrounded the break. Then slowly the leg straightened, and the bone receded back into the leg, as the wound closed. As Riordan and the captain's looked on astounded, they heard a little snap. Looking down, they realized the bone in Niamh's leg, was broken in the same place, and the bone was in sharp shards pushing through the skin. Hovering now, Niamh resumed his song while he laid his hands on Jireh's shoulder. Then suddenly, Niamh flinched as though struck, and now his arm hung uselessly at his side.

"Niamh!" Riordan cried out, "Healing Jireh is killing you!"

"True 'ealing always 'as a blood-price lad." Niamh replied quietly. "Umanity's 'ealing will 'ave a terrible cost far beyond waat oi can pay. But oi can elp dis one."

Niamh's flight and song brought him to hover over Jireh's ribcage as he laid a hand on the centaur's side. The blue glow began again and covered most of Jireh's flank. This time Niamh was struck so severely that it knocked him to the ground. Riordan dropped to his hands and knees to check on him and noticed immediately blood coming from the corner of his mouth. A harsh cough also discharged blood.

"Yer Shophetim will be able ta travel in just ah few moments, but lad, oi will need ta be carried. Oi 'aven't much time. Me exertions 'ave 'astened me end." Niamh was interrupted by a coughing fit that spat out blood. "One more ting oi need tah show ye. Oi expect yer captains will want tah see as well. Soon as de centaur wakens an feels ready, we'll depart."

Jireh did come around in a few moments but had no idea about what happened or how his wounds were healed. When he saw a badly wounded Niamh picked up and cradled in the bend of Korah's arm however, a knowing look came into his eye. The captain then took charge. "Mereah, if you would carry Ragnhildr's body, we must leave this place."

When the Rapha Prince went to bear up the Irial Commander's remains, Aislin wouldn't yield her embrace. In the end, the giant gently lifted and bore them both.

Following tracks made in centuries worth of dust made their exit much easier, taking only a hour or so to find the entrance. Sorcha was there, and Quillan as well.

"Yuh left the poor man here Horse Master?" Caraig scoffed. "Surprised he isn't munched by leaping lizards or crushed by giant stick-men."

"Not about to take a wounded man into combat," Korah offered in his own defense. "I retrieved the two horses, and left Quillan in about as defensible a position for an archer as I'd likely find. Now help me get him up on Sorcha unless you want to carry him around."

Riordan noted that Quillan had deep puncture wounds in his shoulder, in addition to a few nasty-looking cuts on the face. His left arm and leg also, looked shredded.

"Before I protest being described as a burden, carried around like a sack," Quillan objected. "Can somebody please tell me what happened?"

Then Quillan noticed Mereah standing behind the others, cradling a weeping Aislin, and the broken body of Ragnhildr. Suddenly the archer wasn't sure he wanted an answer.

The captains stared at one another uncomfortably, not sure how they should respond. Finally, Korah replied "A giant Minotaur, inhabited by an arch-demon named

Moloch was defeated when Riordan buried his blade in the monster's heart. Victory, however, came at great cost."

Then Niamh softly reminded Korah time was pressing for the completion of a final task. "Right," Korah replied. "Quillan, I promise to tell you as much as I know about your captain's death as soon as we finish our last business."

So Korah and Caraig helped the Irial Lieutenant onto Sorcha's back and they proceeded to follow Niamh's directions. They had first entered Síochán at night, and so they were seeing it really for the first time. As they moved through the city, evidence existed everywhere a great cataclysm had taken place. Few of the spires, towers, arches, magnificent domes, waterworks, and fountains, escaped destruction. Still, many hints of the city's former glory remained. Finally, Caraig asked Niamh the question which was on everyone's mind, "By what magic was Bearach able to construct this place?

Niamh quietly replied, "Bearach did not build dis city. 'e only sent an army ta destroy it. Dis city be de last refuge for de Sha'ar, de Remnant. But it be only a shadow of de skill an' knowledge of de children of Elohim. De devastation of de Drochshaol blasted away almost all trace of de world dat once was. Ye do not yet understan' waat be lost. Ah broken world be all ye ave ever known."

They continued past increasing wonders, buildings with windows that had survived the first world's end. Riordan approached one of these and in shock realized the panes were made from transparent gems; rubies, sapphires, emeralds, even diamonds were formed into flat panels, surviving destruction because they retained their native strength.

After several miles, they approached the east wall, and came to one of the first utilitarian buildings they'd yet seen. The significance of the chimney's presence through the sloped stone roof was lost on everyone but Caraig.

"ere be de armory an' forge. From waat Riordan 'as said, oi tought ye would want tah see it."

"Ye *tought* right!" Caraig chortled excitedly. The Dun Warrior approached the ancient wooden doors. At one time they were solid oak with elaborate iron hinges. The first initial shove proved the door was barred and bolted from within. A few hard hits from the Dun's iron mace shattered the rotted wood creating an opening. Lighting a torch to see inside the chamber, Caraig's eyes got huge, and he emitted a low whistle, "King of heaven, will yuh look at this?"

What he saw was more than just the forge that he hoped for; there were piles of unrecognized ore; also racks of weapons and swords undiminished or rusted despite centuries of neglect. Chainmail that shone brightly, crafted from an unknown alloy. Even a quick glance revealed a level of knowledge and craftsmanship far beyond the weapon-master's level of expertise.

"Be dis one of de places ye seek?" Niamh asked.

"Aye." Caraig replied, obvious awe in his voice.

"We can't linger," Niamh said softly. "Oi won't ask ye ta pass up such obvious treasure ta yer 'eart. But waat oi need ta show Riordan is down de road."

"You go ahead," Caraig said without taking his eye off the prize. "I'll catch up."

Niamh led the rest of the party out through a massive gate on the east side of the ancient city.

Chapter Forty-One

aoine stood staring east across the Capall Plain. She had completed her household duties and now she did what had become her normal routine-watch and pray for her son's return. It had been nearly two months since the morning she left the company of noble captains that were now her son's companions.

She did her best to soothe her motherly worries and concerns. After all, if Riordan wasn't safe with that mighty company, where would he be safe?

Still, it was the days ending of winter's solstice, and if the quest had stayed west of the Irijah Mountains, surely, they would have returned by now. If they had crossed over the mountains somehow, she decided sadly that he would be unable to return before spring.

Her thoughts drifted to the events that took place after departing from the company's camp. She made it to a ravine with a stream crossing the first night. Scouting along the bank she found a ford and after crossing made camp. Korah had placed a flint and steel in her bag of provisions, along with a bit of dry kindling to help start a fire. She managed to get a small blaze going and was just beginning to get comfortable when she heard a wolf howl out across the prairie.

The eerie cry made the old mare Cailin uneasy. After days of heavy rains, she hoped that the wolves wouldn't want to cross the still swollen stream. Looking back at the meager chip fire she realized, the blaze wouldn't offer much protection. After the sun retracted the last of its light, her fire served to illuminate the eyes of a growing number of predators. Then the glowing orbs started down the bank and into the rushing torrent. She had to flee, no time to gather her meager belongings, barely enough time to scramble on the old mare's back and ride.

Within minutes of riding out of camp, she heard the yowls that announced to the pack their quarry had fled. Quickly twenty of the predators settled into their efficient loping run they used to run their prey to death.

Cailin proved to be game enough. After a long day's ride, without much time to rest, she ran three more hours before starting to tire. But tire she did. Even in the pitch-black flecks of white foam became visible on the mare's flanks and neck. Her labored breathing, a sure sign she was about to collapse. The wolves sensed it too and started sprinting in closer to nip at Cailin's heels.

Then, a light of hope. Somewhere up ahead someone had lit a fire. Without any direction from Caoine, the old mare altered course slightly to run to the light. The lady prayed she wasn't bringing a pack of trouble bearing down on someone else.

The outline of a tall, cloaked man stood dark against the light cast by a considerable blaze. As Cailin stumbled into his camp, the man drew a long blade and with little effort dispatched the first three wolves who came within his long arm's reach. The rest of the pack put on the brakes and pulled up short. The predators then paced nervously while they assessed this new threat.

"Hounds of hell, you know me," the cloaked man spoke, his words incarnated might and authority. "Proceed at your peril. Nothing but death awaits you here."

Astonished, Caoine watched as the wolves did indeed stop and consider the man's words, just before they fled. Then she noticed the sword the man bore, the blade didn't appear to be metal, more like a light blue gemstone. None of the slain wolves' blood clung to the blade. Crimson gems were encircled at the ends of the cross-guards, with a blue gem similar in color to the blade, set in the end of the pommel.

"Wolves native to Jeshurun, occasionally go after live-stock, never humans," the man explained. "These Bane Wolves, however, are a cruel hybrid, sent by the enemy to harass and kill the horse herds of the Capall." The stranger then turned his attention to Korah's mare, "Your horse is spent." He stated this as a simple observation. His gentle touch immediately quieted

Cailin and when he whispered "SSSShhhh, daughter, rest now." The mare lowered herself to her knees and went to sleep. "I will brush her while you rest. You left your camp in a hurry, are you hungry?"

"How did you know that?" Caoine stammered. "That I left my camp in a hurry?" She corrected herself.

The man chuckled softly as he knelt to dish up some food unto a wooden trencher, "That's not a great feat, you have no supplies, not even a saddle blanket. That tells me, you left somewhere in a big hurry, Bane Wolves would explain this. Another explanation would be that you are a thief. I don't believe you to be a thief. The cut of your hair offers another explanation still. I reject that accusation as well."

For the first time the man looked Caoine in the eyes. His eyes matched the blue of his sword blade perfectly. In an instant she felt as though this stranger knew all her secrets, knew all her self-accusations. He handed her a plate laden with a savory stew and invited her to sit on a small boulder by the fire.

"Sir," she whispered, almost reverently, "What is your name?"

"I have many names," came the quiet reply. "My names reveal my heart and so are not spoken lightly. The first travelers to this land knew me as Shiloh."

"The first travelers?" Caoine asked astonished. "The people of Moriah came to this land fifteen hundred years ago."

"The people of Moriah were not the first to visit this land," Came the short response.

Caoine gave the stranger a puzzled look. Is this man insane? Not even the Irijah, live much longer than a thousand years. And here this man is implying he's older still. She looked into the man's face, as much as she could see, once again the hood of his cloak covered his eyes. His jaw could have been chiseled out of granite. His short-cropped beard however was snow-white, and the tanned face seemed timeless. He could be in his twenties, or much, much older. She asked again, "What is your name?"

As if reading her thoughts, he replied, "I am Ancient of Days." Then after a brief pause, he said, "You, however, may call me Omen." Caoine recognized the name as the personalization of the word omaine, or trustworthy and true in a much older dialect. Again, she wondered, "Is he reading my thoughts?

"Some sayings are hard to hear," Omen said. "Hear this word and be at peace, the accusations that echo in your mind and heart, are not the voice of truth. Rest now, know that fear is cast out, along with your accusers."

Caoine remembered waking up the next day, and Omen was gone. She had been covered by a blanket; it was even tucked underneath to keep away the coolness of the earth. Only coals remained of last night's campfire, a couple of small fish were roasting over the glowing embers. Like the stew from the night before, the fish, was deliciously seasoned. What herbs or spices were used she had no idea. Cailin, freshly brushed, was already having her breakfast of excellent Capall grasses. The lady remembered feeling renewed and refreshed for most of the rest of the journey.

When the Bane Wolves renewed their assault on the last morning, she felt abandoned once again. After she had a few days to reflect, however, she realized the wolves pursuing her right to the farm gates made her story of the lost letter from Korah more believable.

She hadn't told anyone about the man named Omen. Her credibility was already hanging by a thread. Korah's steward, however, was a just man, and he seemed to recognize her abilities. Whether she had the title of head of the household or not, more and more she was relied upon to fill that very role. She could afford to be patient; the captain's wishes would be made clear upon his return. What she still didn't realize, was that the steward had strong evidence every day of the truth of her words, staring him right in the face; the uncanny resemblance to Korah's young ward, Riordan.

Chapter Forty-Two

And some folks thought t'was a dream they dreamed
Of sailin that beautiful sea . .

Eugene Field

The massive granite slabs that were once the East Gates lay flat on the ground, wrenched from alloy hinges by some great act of violence. Positioned on the inside of the walls, attackers would have to pass through a twenty-foot tunnel in order to reach the gates. Again, the presence of murder holes in the gate archway gave additional evidence that although a beautiful city, it was still a fortress, and built for a time of war.

As in the dam, and other city gates, a lack of seams indicated the base blocks were massive, cut, and placed with absolute precision.

Passing through the gates the broad street narrowed to a path of paving stones. The path started to ascend and narrowed after a few miles, as it drew closer to the eastern peaks. After a steep climb, they paused to look at their back trail. The East Wall of the city connected the high sheer cliffs of both the southern and northern summits.

"I find myself a bit curious as to why the city's builders felt a need for such a defensive wall to the east," Korah speculated. "Looking forward to the high range and peaks ahead of us, I can't imagine an army of any size being able to traverse such heights."

"Aye," Niamh replied weakly. "An army would need wings ta get over such summits."

The eastern peaks were indeed impressive. Great white monoliths, like jagged teeth, sprung out of blue glaciers, all the scene now stained pale rose by the descending sun. A rushing series of cataracts and cascades filled the treeless vale with water song that had a melancholy melody.

The paved road became a narrow path that scrambled steeply through a ravine, then passed a waterfall stained red by the sunset. After a short hike further, they found the source of the stream, a deep mountain lake. With most of the sunlight gone, the still surface was almost black. The faint image of stars was reflecting over the surface.

Before them was an ancient dock, where a long vessel with a high, gilded bow, was moored. The entire craft appeared to be formed from one incandescent pearl. A dragon's head at the top of the prow flowed into a delicately arched neck, while the body and wings formed the bulk of the ship. Sapphire eyes guided the vessel ever forward. In the front of the vessel, in between the wings, a lantern hung from a small wooden arm, focusing a small beam of light over a podium with a rolled-up scroll.

"Behold de loch Scáthán na bhFlaitheas, or in de common tongue Eaven's Mirror. Our journey ends at de opposite shore." Niamh said. "We must take ship."

The dock wasn't much longer than the boat with the water immediately deep right from shore. They found an old gangplank secured to the dock that allowed everyone to board. There was plenty of room, evidence the ship was designed to accommodate a small party of all the races, even Rapha' and Centaurs. What they couldn't find were a rudder, sail, or oars. Nor any other means to propel the craft. Also puzzling, no moorings secured the vessel to the dock, and yet no sign it ever drifted away.

After a few frustrating moments with no idea how the small ship navigated, Korah finally asked Niamh, "Do some of us need to get out and push, or perhaps paddle with our hands?"

"Oi wasn't ah part of dis craft's construction," Niamh answered softly. "But de loch is mighty in spirit an' law. Conventional propulsion would not be effective."

Ignoring this advice, Mereah got out of the boat and found a log lying in the turf and climbed back on board. Reaching in with his makeshift oar he tried first to push off from shore to no effect. Then he tried to paddle and again the ship remained firmly in place. It was almost as though the craft was locked in ice. But as he continued the attempt to paddle, suddenly the log pulled out of his hands and sank.

"What happened," Korah asked surprised.

"I didn't mean to let go," Mereah explained. "But the longer the wood remained in contact with the water, the heavier it got. Finally, I couldn't hold on to it any longer."

"Moloch must have hit you harder than we thought," Korah scoffed with a grin. "Here, let me try."

Rather than trying to find another pole, the Calvary Captain snapped a plank of wood off a bench seat near the back of the boat. "I'll replace it later, but a flat surface will make a better paddle."

Korah likewise tried to paddle the boat forward, to no avail. After a minute or so suddenly he struggled to keep the board in his grip until it too slipped into the dark water.

The captains argued for a few minutes about how to proceed, and several crazy solutions were offered. One included Mereah getting out with a line and towing the ship while swimming. Jireh quickly shot down that idea, "And what happens if the same sinking effect that pulled our makeshift paddles to the bottom, also drags Mereah to the depths."

"Excellent point," Mereah offered, slightly relieved.

"I was joking," Korah explained. Then with a grin said, "Mostly."

"I may have a solution that doesn't involve drowning a Crown Prince," Jireh offered. "It occurs to me that the Sha'ar desired to prevent passage by any means available to their enemies. What power would they choose that the enemy would refuse?"

Niamh's eyes started to shine, with the recognition that Jireh might be on the right track.

With that Riordan walked to the back of the small ship and placed the blade of the Riail dlí in the blue waters. To everyone's disappointment, the ship didn't budge.

"That was a smart guess lad," Jireh said. "Yara however is not the only expression of law."

Then the centaur looked to the front of the craft, and the lantern caught his attention. Moving forward, carved just above the lamp was an inscription in a tongue only Jireh, and perhaps Niamh recognized. Jireh read out loud,

A law of love
Taught the stars to dance.

Brows knotted in thought, Jireh unrolled the ancient scroll and started to read, "In the beginning, Elohim …"

As Jireh read the words the boat lurched forward causing several to momentarily lose their balance. "Friends, I believe we have found our solution."

Jireh continued to read, "In the beginning, Elohim created the heavens and the earth. The universe was a chaotic void, and Elohim spoke words of covenant law and established the rule of law over cosmic chaos."

As Jireh continued to read, the craft moved forward at a gentle cruising speed even as the last light from the sun failed. A crescent moon and an expanse of stars were now mirrored in the meres surface. With stars above, and below, the boat seemed to glide through the heavens. What was startling, however, was the number of stars reflected in the water far exceeded those in the sky. Riordan recognized swirling galaxies from images in the Bema but had no words to describe or name other beauties such as nebula or quasars. In awe he asked Niamh, "There are far more stars reflected in the waters than are visible in the sky, is this heaven?"

"De mirror reflects reality, waat is, not waat de eye can see, or de mind ken." Niamh replied. "De loch allows ah glimpse from 'is eyes . . as ah reminder, waat we see be ah fraction ov waat is."

In stunned silence, they journeyed across the surface until guided to another dock on the far bank of the lough. A landing was carved out of the rock and ice, and a short way up on the bank they saw what was becoming an almost familiar sight; a mosaic of precious stones, the transparent gems that formed the images had a light of their own and radiated with a soft glow. As before, in the center, formed from what looked like a sheet of mother-of-pearl, was a blue-horned unicorn.

Chapter Forty-Three

The water's pure
The well so deep
The only treasure that a man can keep.

Kerry Livgren

iamh," Korah looked at the Sióg cradled on his forearm. "What is your purpose in bringing us to this place?"

"Capall's Son, oi only brout Riordan ta dis place. Before de lad be a door only 'e may pass."

"I've already lost three sons. Riordan is my adopted son a similar portal has already separated us once. I cannot allow this to happen again. Also, I have been appointed as the boy's protector and mentor. What's more, he has been assigned as a page and armor bearer to serve in my command. For all of these reasons and more, where Riordan goes, I must follow."

"Oi understan' yer connections ta de lad, an believe me, oi share 'em. While oi do not know as much about de boy's past, oi 'ave seen powerful signs of 'is future. De appointment of dis door be assigned from de first age, waat yer people now name sorrow. Dis be ah guide for 'is understandin. ."

"Jireh," Korah continued to protest, "You must agree with me, we can't allow this."

Jireh's beard and chin were resting on his powerful chest. All eyes were now turned towards him to pronounce judgment. After a long pause he replied, "If this door was warded by any other power Korah, I'd agree with you." Here the Shophetim raised his hand palm outward to hold back Korah's protest; "But I'm inclined to believe by allowing Riordan to pass through the portal, we will be placing him in the hands of El, and in His protection."

"I have no wish to hinder," Korah continued; "I merely intend to accompany the lad and so keep both eyes on him."

Niamh offered a compromise suggestion, "Let de will of Elohim decide, touch de lad on 'is shoulder when 'e touches de 'orn, if it be El's will, de 'orse master will cross wit de lad.'

Now, oi must needs speak wit de Shophetim of yer people, look back now at de lough behind ye. What do ye see?"

Jireh stared at the surface for several minutes, before responding, "The tarn reflects the night sky perfectly, but not the sky overhead."

"Aye. More dan any other people, de centaur's know de celestial dance. De waters of Dlí Biotáille be seeped wit de power of Yara Law. As such, de waters are a guide ta those who can read waat dey reveal. Learn dese maps, an' teach Riordan. De 'eavens be maps dat can be followed. Signs ov de future can dey also reveal, as part of de ordained steps of Elo'im's dance.

Riordan looked at the water and realized with a start, although a crescent moon was overhead, there wasn't a reflection of the moon in the lake. It was also a different sky than what was reflected in the trip across the waters

"Riordan lad," Niamh called softly, then coughed up more blood. "It's time ta say goodbye." Riordan walked slowly to where the Sióg was still cradled on Korah's forearm. A gentle tug on Mereah's cloak came from Aislin who wanted to be placed back on the ground so she also could go to their guide.

"Now children, don't grieve. Me fate 'ad been sealed when oi left de 'eart of de earth. Oi be six tousan' years old, kept alive by de earth's nurture, an far beyon' me fallen span. My life preserved only until ye found yer way ta me. Now, oi go ta a well-earned rest."

Riordan started to protest but Niamh cut him off, "Wen Benaiah sealed me in Croí an Domhan tree tousand years ago, oi said good-bye ta... here a fit of coughing cut off the end of his sentence. "No tears, I'll be wit dem soon.

Lad, ne'er forget, who ye are. De enemies greatest lie . . 'ides who ye are, an' who ye are meant ta be."

Aislin touched the soldier of fairie gently, "Thank you, for all you taught us, and for fighting to save my father."

"And I wish to thank you for your sacrifice on my behalf," Jireh murmured.

"By takin' yer wounds inta meself, oi 'astened my own end," Niamh replied, "But my life. . soon ta be ended. Ye would 'ave far longer ta see ta de lad's trainin'.

"Out a respect fer de Irial Commander, oi will tell ye one thing more; de stars in de lough ... under dose stars will ye find one of Bearach's wards. If de Scepter of Adon be dere, oi can't say, it be a place ta start. Oi know not de wisdom of dis search, but such courage, should not be in vain."

With that, Niamh breathed his last, the light of peace in his eyes. Riordan cried out in pain and turned quickly towards the mosaic. Korah was just able to lay Niamh down gently and rush over placing his hand on his son's shoulder-just before the young page slapped the unicorn's horn.

Riordan disappeared, leaving Korah grasping air while shouting in dismay. The Riail dlí however fell and clattered on the stones at his feet.

The End

The King's Bard Chronicles continues in book
three Dragon's Sacrifice.

About the Author:

Riordan's story in many ways grew out of my own. The sixth of seven kids born into an Irish Catholic family, the wounds of dysfunction were deep, personal and historical. I say historical because a wounded spirit seems to be an almost universal Irish trait. Or as Yeats would say, "Being Irish, he had an abiding sense of tragedy, which sustained him through temporary periods of joy."

Everyone knows the Irish drink, (go ahead and throw in Highland Scots while you're at it) but even a brief look at their history will go a long way in explaining why. I forgave my father's dysfunction because his drinking flowed from his own wounds. I wanted to give the character of Riordan a real soul, so I gave him much of mine. The King's Bard series has a Celtic flair because of my heritage, but also because the Celtic Heart is one that is wounded. A wounded heart, and the hope for healing, is a point of connection for the whole world.

Will McDonald

Contact Will with questions or comments at thekingsbard@gmail.com He is also available to speak to your group about overcoming ptsd stemming from abuse and domestic violence.

Made in the USA
Las Vegas, NV
31 August 2023